THE FALL OF HADES

THE FALL OF HADES

JEFFREY THOMAS

Publishing History:
The Fall of Hades was first published by Dark Regions Press, 2010; *The Lost Family* first appeared in the electronic anthology *Vivisepulture*, Anarchy Books, 2011; *Beloved Succubus* is original to this collection.

ISBN: 978-1-957121-70-3

Revised Text © 2023 by Jeffrey Thomas
Cover and interior art © 2023 by Frank Walls
Editor and Publisher, Joe Morey
Interior and cover design by Cyrus Wraith Walker

Weird House Press
Central Point, OR 97502
www.weirdhousepress.com

CONTENTS

A Note From the Author:

The short pieces *The Lost Family* and *Beloved Succubus*—despite having been written after *The Fall of Hades*—are not sequels, in that their action takes place chronologically between chapters 31 and 32 of the novel. For this expanded edition of *The Fall of Hades*, I even considered splicing the two stories in that spot, but in the end decided against it. For your part, you can read them at that point in the narrative or afterwards, as you wish. They function as extended side quests, so to speak, as Vee and Jay ascend through the Construct on their fantastical journey.

Dedication

I'd like to express my gratitude to the sadly departed David G. Barnett for having inspired me to write Letters From Hades, *and to Joe Morey for inviting me to write* The Fall of Hades *(and* Beloved Succubus, *as well). Also, I am grateful indeed for the gorgeous artwork Frank Walls has provided for this expanded Hades trilogy. You all have my infernal thanks.*

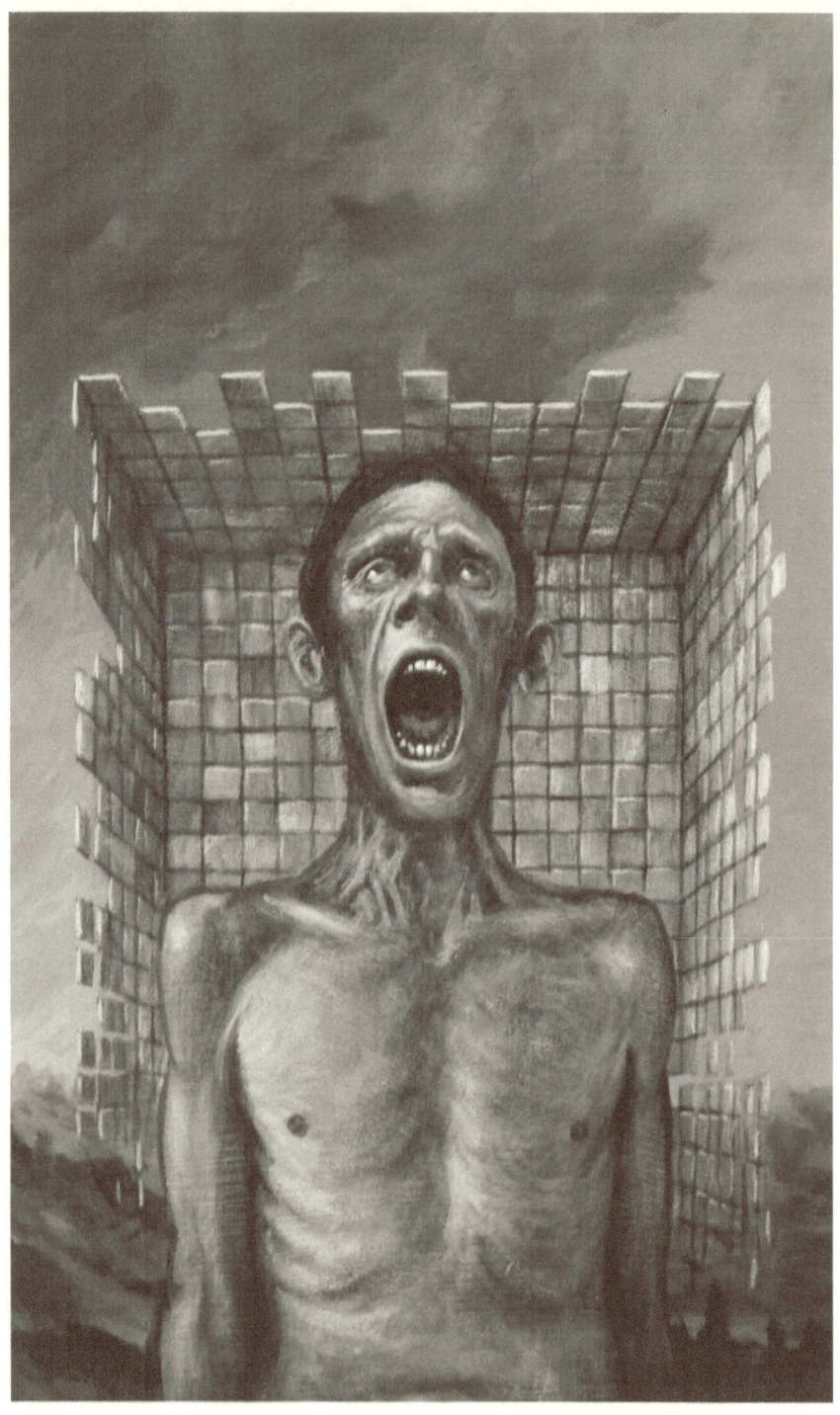

THE FALL OF HADES

1: The Reborn

She believed she saw the drop of water that shattered her prison
– the very drop. As the bead of water formed at the fracture in
the ceiling, bulged with readiness, extended teasingly and finally
let go, she seemed to have an inner certainty that this drop was unlike
the ones gone before; more significant, more potent. The decisive drop
of water, heavy with power, as filled with import as an atom bomb
dropped on a city, or the microscopic splitting of the very first cell. She
had the presentiment that this drop was the demolishing bullet, the
key that would unlock her prison. Or was it actually that she was exerting pressure against the stone unconsciously, that it was her own force
that imbued the magic drop, which would have been just another of an
endless string of drips had she not extended the influence of her will?

She had long ago stopped noticing when she was pushing against
the stone that encased her body like a fossil. Though of course there
were long stretches of time when she lay absolutely inert, as if sleeping,
or in a coma, or dead; stretches during which she just lay within her
womb without applying any force against the stone at all – stretches of
maybe years, decades, centuries.

She had once tried counting the drops of water to keep track of
time, each drop approximately thirty seconds apart. She had steadily,
consciously counted the drops for what her inner arithmetic told her

1

was two months (approximately 172,800 drips of water, falling too far from her parched lips to do anything but taunt her or provide her this exercise, this distraction) before she taught herself to count the drops unconsciously instead, so as to free up other parts of her mind to wander, to dream, or to simply shut off. She had managed this for what she figured was three years (approximately 3,075,840 drops, and was that enough to feed a rain forest, to fill a lake, to drown a world?) before she ultimately lost the cadence somehow, through some mental hiccup, and staggered, faltered, the trick of subconsciously counting off the drips eluding her.

Maybe the hiccup was the increased splitting of the rock around her. She had occasionally heard gentle, whispering crackles, almost subliminal. At times, she had heard this in answer to pressure she exerted. Sometimes she had even heard the distant clatter of a fallen pebble – and more distant, as much a vibration as a sound, the occasional muffled thud of a large piece of stone as it dropped heavily somewhere beyond.

Only her head was free of the encasing cement. She recalled that her captors had wanted her to see what they were doing to someone else in the room beyond, but there was a metal door on tracks that shut up the little chamber in which her block-like sarcophagus rested, and it was now closed, after all these years caked in rust that had streaked down the cement wall. A cage of scabrous metal bars surrounded her head where it protruded from the stone coffin that had been poured, shaped, and squared off around her body. She vaguely remembered, untold ages ago, figures standing around the coffin poking her face through the bars of the cage, with either heated or sharp implements or both. There was a socket in the ceiling with wires hanging out of it now where this apparatus with long, jointed arms tipped with glowing heat or glittering razors had once been suspended, but it had been removed for repair or salvage at some time she could no longer recall, just as she could no longer remember much about the shadowy figures who had operated the apparatus. She supposed that had as much to do with her not wanting to remember as with the long passage of time.

But with her head being free to this extent, she was able to watch the

2

water that dripped down from a crack in the low ceiling like a fissure in a skull, a seam from which this leak pattered every thirty seconds on the flat top of her coffin. Through the years, she had watched the cement discolor, darken, erode into a shallow concavity. Eventually cracks had appeared and spread with the slowness of mountains eroding to deserts. But the process continued, the cracks widening and deepening. Sometimes she watched avidly, sometimes with eyes open but sleeping, glazed like those of a dead person. But wait – she *was* a dead person, wasn't she? She seemed to recall *that* much, at least.

Today – if one could still speak of days, as if speaking of *this molecule of water* in the river of infinity – the final drop fell. It was not the final drop, of course; there would be more. But none that she would remain to watch. Water did not collect in the concavity, but because it was lopsided trickled off down the left side of the sarcophagus. It was on the unseen left flank that she heard a sudden loud crack, a crack like lightning splitting the sky (a surprising image belonging to some previous life). This initial dramatic noise was followed by a slow crumbling sound and the increasing patter of pebbles across the floor – then a great shuddering crash as a whole corner of stone dropped away to the floor of her tomb.

She felt air on her naked left side, from her arm down along her leg. The air was not fresh, was humid and warm, for she had been recycling her own moist breath through the countless years, but it was open air nevertheless. She tried to reach out her left arm, no longer encased, into this air but her muscles had all but petrified, the joints crackling with the effort. She sucked in an anguished sound. There had been many years with constant discomfort but it had been consistent and ultimately something she'd been able to distance herself from. This pain was new, fresh, immediate. She waited, panted until she could get her breathing under control again. She tried shifting her leg, but more carefully, minutely this time. Then, back to a tiny shift of her arm. The leg again, and back and forth, in a process that might have taken hours or days of terrestrial time. Finally she was able to lower her leg out of the space that had become a mold around it, a mold reproducing the creases of her body, the smoothness of her

3

skin, a reversed image of herself. It was now like a chrysalis that she freed herself from gradually, as a butterfly will patiently wait for its delicate wings to dry and unfold.

More rock fell away with solid thunks. At last she managed to rest her bare foot against the floor, and bracing herself this way – with teeth gritted against the torment – gripped the rough edge of the wound in the coffin with her free hand and angled her body out sideways, further and further. She had to wriggle and squirm out of the molded contours of her own form, like a snake from its old skin. She groaned as she drew in her head and squeezed it through the narrow channel her neck had made, scraping and gouging her cheeks and forehead and nearly wedging her skull stuck, but luckily more cement cracked away to permit its passage. At last her upper body dropped out to the floor and she let loose a wail as the fragments of stone there dug into her side and upper arm. Her right leg was still wedged into its mold, but she crawled away from the sarcophagus a little until she could drag it out after her. It fell heavily to the floor as if dead and useless, and she moaned with a fresh stab of pain. She rolled onto her back and stared up at the ceiling until she began to feel the life returning to her right leg as well. Life, in a manner of speaking. Life, with the consideration that – despite the agony that stole the air from her lungs – she was not alive. And she was not really feeding air into her lungs because she didn't truly need air to live. But this phantasmal flesh believed its own lies, its mock sensations and imitation needs, still experienced excruciating pain, however illusory. So she lay, and lay, testing her limbs only gingerly and in movements as slow as the spreading of the cracks over the long years she had begun to count too late and stopped counting too soon. But then what should time matter to the immortal?

Yes, she remembered she was dead. Yes, she remembered how to walk, reborn creature though she may be, once she was recovered enough to attempt it. (And she could afford to be patient; she knew patience if she knew nothing else.)

But if only she could remember her *name*.

2: *The Captive*

She found the sliding door rusted into its track, planted her bare feet in a wider stance and put so much force into pulling on it that the scaly corrosion of the handle sliced into her palms. She winced, but already the lacerations and scrapes on her head and body from squeezing out of her mold were fading. She recalled that her flesh reconstituted itself swiftly, even after serious wounding. How else had she regrown flesh plucked from her face by the arms of the torture apparatus in the ceiling, regenerated lips sliced away, teeth wrenched out, both eyes teased slowly from their sockets? She tried not to recollect those things, but whereas her body would always grow smooth again, she felt as though her mind was so thick with scar tissue that she would never again think clearly.

Her name. Again, had she simply forgotten it because of the passing of too many years in which no one had used it, years in which she was so much a prisoner that her identity was eradicated along with her freedom – decades (centuries? *millennia?*) of obliterating insanity born of ceaseless pain – or had she through her own effort of will stopped knowing herself at some long ago point in order to distance herself from the tortures? Had she protected her true self by hiding it away just as she was hidden in this vault, replacing it with this suffering clay, this sacrificial doppelganger for the torturers to play with? If so, then where was that other self now, and again...again...could she ever call it back, ever know its name?

She strained, grunted, ignoring the hurt in her hands as best she could by bearing in mind their later regeneration. Sweat ran down her ribs; oh this clever ectoplasm! With a grating squeal, at last the door slid open a few inches. She tugged, tugged, pushed the door shut again and then hauled on it afresh in violent jerks. It gave another few inches. She persisted, as always for an unknown amount of time, until there was enough of a gap for her to squeeze though without too much abrading of her unclad skin.

The chamber beyond was more sizable than her humble little sepulcher. What struck her first about it, after so long a time staring

5

up at her own low ceiling, was that this chamber's ceiling was so high up it was lost in darkness, as if this were the inside of a tower or, given its industrial feel, some old shaft or chimney. Also, the air circulated more freely here, was still humid but at least new air was being drawn in. When she stepped further into the chamber and could look more squarely up the shaft, she saw a silhouetted fan at the top of it, spinning lazily and then stopping, twirling a few times again; its motor shot, or at least turned off, though errant gusts of air still stirred it.

Motes were being blown down the shaft, swam in the air around her. She brushed a few of the little white flakes from her shoulder. Not snow. Ash, she supposed.

Through these swirling motes, she gazed at the chamber's sole occupant.

There was a net suspended just above her head, spanning the entire room, anchored to iron rings in its walls. At first she had taken it for something meant to catch debris falling from above (indeed, a few sections of plaster had come away from the walls of the shaft and lay in the net) but at last the truth had dawned on her. The strands of the net were a glistening, vivid red. They were formed of human tissue, gristle and sinew, tendons and nerves. The stuff of the human anatomy unwoven and then woven anew into these taut cables, crisscrossing the room in an immense web.

Where she could see it, the floor was stained black from countless little drips of blood, but much of the floor was obscured by a layer of pale orange husks like an accumulation of autumn leaves. She stooped and picked up one of these husks delicately. It was the dried, dead body of a tiny crab.

She looked up at the net and discerned movement along the strands here and there. Living versions of the dead crabs her bare feet had shuffled through, their shells more brightly orange in life, crawled along or were poised in the web. They appeared to be nibbling at the red vines, picking at them with their pincers. She saw a few drops of fresh blood fall from gnawed veins that partially made up the fabric of the living ropes.

From the very center of the net hung a ball-like pendulum, swaying very slightly in the occasional gusts of humid air that blew down the shaft. The woman moved toward the hanging ball, sliding her feet through the shells rather than walking upon them. That strange white ash or whatever it was drifted around her like pollen.

She stopped a few paces from the ball, level with her face and hanging on a braid of raw muscle and exposed nerves. Now it was obvious that it was an inverted human head, though initially she had been confused by the fact that some molten metal, like bronze, had been poured over it, or else the head had been dipped into a vat of the stuff. In any case, the metal had hardened into a helmet long turned green with verdigris. Somehow, only the area around the mouth was open, the eyes, nostrils and ears being sealed over. She raised a tentative arm, slowly reached out toward the encased head, meaning to feel for breath emitted through its slack, slick mouth.

A shell crunched under her foot, and the head's teeth snapped wildly at her fingers. She withdrew her hand and backed off a few steps, now unmindful of the sharp-edged shells. The head's tongue lashed madly, and spittle sprayed toward her. Then, the head began to talk. How it could draw air with no apparent lungs, the woman did not question, since again, the process of breathing was spurious in this realm anyway.

"Who's there? Who is that?" the head rasped. The voice was only remotely human, more eerie than even the head's appearance. It then began to jabber, as if speaking in tongues: "The Lord is my shepherd I shall not want He maketh me to lie down in green pastures He leadeth me beside the still waters He restoreth my soul He leadeth me in the paths of righteousness for his name's sake yea though I walk through the valley of the shadow of death I will fear no evil for thou art with me thy rod and thy staff they comfort me..."

"Listen," she said, trying to calm the head.

It babbled on: "Thou preparest a table before me in the presence of mine enemies thou anointest my head with oil my cup runneth over surely goodness and mercy shall follow me all the days of my life and I will dwell in the house of the Lord for ever amen amen amen amen amen fuck fuck nooo don't hurt me again you fucks you fucking

THE FALL OF HADES

Demons where have you been huh? Where did you go? You made me think you were gone!" The head began to sob wretchedly. "You made me think you were *gooone*." As if such a teasing absence were the worst torture of all.

Demons. The word resonated in the woman's mind, and she shuddered. It was a word she'd made herself forget, and associated images she'd worked so hard to efface came flickering into her mind's eye. The shadowy figures who had operated the torture apparatus in the ceiling took on a degree of lost detail. Black form-fitting suits of tight leather or rubber. Faces so white they might have been painted that way, as dispassionate as they were beautiful. And she remembered *wings...*

"I'm not a Demon," she told the head. Suddenly she squinted as if to make out some shape on the horizon as more memories flitted just out of reach. No, she was not a Demon, and neither was this man. They had both been victims of the Demons; hostages, or prisoners. And this man was...

"Father?" she said, still squinting, but this time at the dangling, upside-down head – in its bronze shell looking like the clapper of some giant church bell. Church bell...church...

"Demon!" the head whispered. "Trickster...*trickster!* You can't deceive me! You can't break me! Do you hear? We're not all as weak as you think. My faith is stronger than my flesh, and this flesh is not real! You can't touch my soul, you fucks, you fucking *fucks!*" The teeth snapped blindly at the air again with a horrible clacking sound, and somehow there was enough strength in the braid of muscle for the head to sway more widely.

"Are you my father?" the naked woman asked more firmly, ignoring the tirade.

"Our Father who art in heaven hallowed be thy name," the head ranted, "thy kingdom come thy will be done on earth as it is in heaven..."

Well, she didn't need him to confirm it; it was a certainty now. But whatever emotion that name might once have inspired in her had long been burnt away or locked behind protective barriers. She had only the

8

mistiest impressions of sobbing, howling helplessly, as she witnessed his suffering through the open metal door between their respective torture chambers. Could recall nothing of whatever encouragement they might have called to each other or conversations they might have attempted when their tormenters had withdrawn.

The head chanted, "...give us this day our daily bread and forgive us our trespasses as we forgive those who trespass against us and lead us not into temptation but deliver us from evil from evil from evil from evil..."

She wanted to cry, if only to feel that she was alive again; but she wasn't, never could be, correct? How much had she loved this man in life? She tried to picture him as his body had appeared in its mortal form. Strangely, from life she conjured a mental picture of him as seen on a glowing screen. Television was the word she wanted. Father immaculately dressed, tall and proud, gesturing widely, and addressing a flock both seated before him and seated afar in his radiant cathode aura. He seemed removed from her that way, a father she knew as much from watching him on TV as from her personal relationship with him.

"...for thine is the kingdom and the power and the glory for ever and ever amen amen amen amen amen fuck fuck nooo don't hurt me again you fucks you fucking Demons where have you been huh? Where did you go? You made me think you were gone! You made me think you were *gooone*."

She salvaged another vision of him, but more tenuous. This time he was equally charismatic, but a sort of military figure, a general, addressing his many white-robed followers – an army – stoking them up for some holy war. She had an impression of herself standing at his side like a good daughter, loyal to his convictions or at least to him. Wasn't there a mother beside them, too, and a younger brother? Had they escaped this fate, or become captured as well? And if so, were they held nearby? Shouldn't she search for them? But she found no emotional urgency in that thought, either. Numb to her core, she experienced only the barest instinctual concern for the blighted creature before her, as she might feel for any stranger. It was the best she could awaken in herself.

She looked up at the rings in the walls. If she cut him down from them, would his attenuated body at last be able to regenerate properly, reassume its mortal shape? She was convinced that would not be sufficient, that the artisans themselves would have to undo their handiwork somehow. So, shouldn't she go forth in search of them, too? Surely she couldn't appeal to their mercy, but was there any way she could force at least one of them to do her bidding?

The head had lapsed into quiet weeping. She addressed him again. "What is my name?" she asked him. "Father...what is my name?"

He only continued to lament, unmindful of her, as if she were not there. She supposed whatever awareness of a daughter he had once possessed had been burnt out of him, as well, leaving only his appeals of love to some celestial being she wasn't so sure was even listening.

3: *The Ravenous*

A service ladder of rusted metal was bolted into the side of the great shaft, but it was above the level of the suspended net of her father's raw anatomy. She looked around herself, scuffing further through the husks of dead crabs. Uncounted generations of them. At least these creatures could achieve the peace, the release, of death.

There was another, taller metal door on the opposite wall of the room, and she went to it. It had a small glass window at face level, but the room beyond was in utter darkness. By way of consolation, the window afforded her a look at her reflection. Her face didn't surprise her so she hadn't forgotten that, at least. Stringy reddish hair framed the pale face of young woman whose age, alive, she might guess as late twenties. A longish pointed nose she might have liked to see more dainty, a small mouth with thin lips she would have preferred to see fuller, and her own eyes however familiar disturbed her, looking both hollow and intense at once. They were a striking shade of blue, like gas fire.

She tugged on the door's handle, but it wouldn't give. She could probably break the window but it was too small to squeeze through. She worked at the handle for a long time, until her palms were half flayed, until she had to concede that the door was heavily barred on the other side. She squatted down with her back against the wall, waiting for her hands to mend enough that she might use them again. A living crab emerged from the layer of its dead brethren as if it had sniffed her out and wanted a taste, its pincers held high. The woman leaned forward and smashed it against the floor with the heel of her fist.

She returned her attention to the ladder running up the interior of the shaft. After regarding the situation a while, until her hands were sufficiently healed, she stood up and acted on the only conclusion that had occurred to her. She walked to another spot along the wall, equidistant between two of the iron rings, where there was more slack in the net. She crouched low, then sprang up and seized hold of the slick web, fought against the immediate revulsion the touch of it engendered. Then, bracing her bare feet against the wall, she struggled to pull her body up between the wall and the outer edge of the net. Finally she was able to crawl up onto the net and stand, dancing across its bowing surface to keep her balance like a trapeze performer who had fallen in mid performance.

"Hey!" the head protested, dangling like a long rotten nut inside its bronze shell.

The woman walked bouncily over to where the ladder extended past the opening of the shaft. Just below it, she again hunched down, again sprang, the web giving her more springiness. She grasped the bottom rung, her legs kicking at the air until, with a grunt, she was able to lunge upward for the second rung. Soon, she had hoisted herself up, and poised on the ladder, looked below her at the grid-like body of her father. She wanted to call down to reassure him that she would be back for him, but she couldn't say for sure that she would. Ultimately, she said nothing, turned her face upward and began to climb into the murk above. She heard the head's muttering diminish beneath her.

As she hoisted herself up the ladder one of the rungs started to come out of its socket, its left end crumbling into brittle flakes of rust that spun away below, but she quickly switched to the next rung up.

Those white spores swam about her like plankton, so thick the higher she climbed that she breathed through her nose to keep from ingesting them. She blinked flakes off her lashes, snorted them away from her nostrils.

As she drew closer to the fan behind its metal grille, she took note of a number of strange life forms that adhered to the sides of the shaft and even the rungs of the ladder like barnacles, and they did in fact resemble some kind of primitive sea plant or animal. They were white clam-like growths standing vertically from a sticky base, and the halves of the clams opened and closed rhythmically, revealing accordion-like insides that seemed to breathe in and out like a bellows.

While she paused to observe the nearest of these curious life forms, she noted that white flakes occasionally alighted on the rungs and appeared to stick or take hold there, and then noticed several tiny bud-like growths sprouting along the rungs. She realized these were immature versions of the barnacle-things. She intuited, then, that the spores were airborne seeds or the like that were giving birth to these creatures.

As she poked one of the budding organisms with a finger, a clicking sort of rustling sound from below caused the woman to gaze downward. She felt a start inside to see that a good number of those orange crabs were slowly but persistently working their way up the ladder after her. Had they homed in on her fresh meat at last, or were they even making an attempt to prevent her escape?

Escape. Despite her thoughts of finding some mother whose face she couldn't recall, some brother whose name eluded her, or finding some assistance for a father she remembered more as a remote, two-dimensional image than a man, she had to admit to herself that the real reason she was attempting to leave this chamber and go forth was simply the primal instinct to find a more hospitable environment. To remove herself from a place of pain. Yes, she was trying to *escape*.

Wherever one might be able to escape *to*.

She hastened upward again, to distance herself from the ravenous, pursuing crustaceans. Just above her now the shaft dead-ended at the grille, behind which the fan turned in occasional languid spins. She reached up and curled her fingers in the slats, then put more of her weight into it, but the grate wouldn't budge from its frame. She glanced down to check on the progress of the crabs, now saw the lowermost rungs were turned orange with their massing bodies. She switched her attention to the sides of the shaft again, with a mounting sense of urgency.

There: a small service hatch of some kind, and it was slightly ajar. She leaned out from the ladder and caught the edge of it, pulled. It resisted a bit, screeched in protest, but opened wide enough to permit entrance. The woman looked downward dubiously, but there was nothing else to do but take the plunge and hope her father's body would break her fall if she didn't make it. Well, a fall wouldn't kill her, anyway. The crabs couldn't kill her. But nobody likes pain, not even the dead.

She threw herself off the ladder, caught the lower edge of the opening with both hands, braced her feet against the wall as she fought to hoist herself up and in. Grimacing with the effort, she dragged herself through, crawled on her belly using her elbows until she was fully inside. It was a horizontal chute that barely permitted her to rise in a crouch, the walls and ceiling bearing thin metal pipes and rubber-sheathed cables stapled there in bundles. There was light at the far end of the chute, and she was about to crawl toward it when she heard a ghastly, warbling cry from below. Thinking it was her father, she turned around and poked her head out the hatch to have a look downward.

Not her father. She saw that some crabs were even finding purchase on the pocked walls of the vertical shaft itself, and were biting into the strange white barnacles. Their bellows-like bodies were pumping more rapidly, and it appeared that the shrill, ululating cries – more of them now, as more barnacles growing on the walls and the rungs of the ladder were attacked – came from the barnacles themselves. The woman felt a vague pity for the creatures, whatever they were, but a relief that more and more of the crabs were being diverted toward them in their hunger. She withdrew into the service duct again, this time hauled the hatch shut after her. Moments later, she heard the tiny scraping of the first crab to reach it. She doubted that even in numbers they could maneuver the hatch open, but she didn't remain to find out. On her haunches, she made her way toward that distant light.

4: The Remains

There was a more spacious chamber at the far end of the service chute, and the woman had no sooner crawled out into it and risen to her feet when she saw the three skeletons that occupied the room.

The room itself was like the interior of some very complex giant organ, an industrial womb. Thick pipes hung down from the low ceiling, upheld with brackets, intertwined with thinner, flexible pipes that snaked down the walls, even across the floor in places. It was like a riot of tree roots grown through the roof of a sepulcher. And the inhabitants of that sepulcher were the three skeletons.

One was propped in a sitting position against the far wall. One sprawled on the floor. The third slumped in a seat in front of a computer terminal, or at least that was what the woman took it to be. It looked like a computer as imagined in the 19th Century, with its thick oval glass for a screen, its riveted iron casing, the brass wheels on its side and levers and toggles jutting up from a keyboard like that of an ancient manual typewriter. The keys themselves were ivory – or was that bone? More cables than seemed necessary, or logical, ran into the top and back of the bulky thing, some as thick as her wrist. One rubber hose had leaked fluid, its dried residue crusted around the breach. The crystal screen emitted a pale, ghostly light like a fading afterglow that wouldn't entirely fade. There was the faintest suggestion of hissing static, if she bent her head over the keys.

There was another computer station near the first, but the computer here had been removed, apparently; the rear cables lay on the desk disconnected, the severed rubber hose having dribbled its contents down the side of the desk to pool and dry.

The skeletons were dressed in identical rubbery black jumpsuits with zippered closures and pockets, the elbows and knees padded more thickly; there was also some ribbed padding across the chest. The back of each suit was open, however, to accommodate the wings these

14

beings had possessed in life. The bare struts that were all that remained of these structures spread out from the bodies like elongated fingers of bone.

The trio had not passed away peacefully. The one sitting on the floor had ragged holes blasted in its chest despite its suit's padding. The one lying on the floor had apparently been shot in the back while trying to flee this nest of pipes and cables. The one in the chair had been struck a terrific blow with an edged weapon – an axe or sword? – that had cloven its skull, long colorless hair hanging down to obscure its bisected face. This being had been a female, tall and slender and long-limbed like the naked woman herself, and hers was the only uniform that had not been torn open. The naked woman was not squeamish; she took the scarecrow-light body under the arms, eased it to the floor (the split head dropping back alarmingly but remaining attached to its neck), and began unzipping its black rubber garb.

The woman had trouble tugging the snug material onto her own body, which was slick with the mock sweat it shed, so with her palms she gathered chalky dust that had collected on the computer table and smudged it over her arms, legs and sides like powder. It made the donning of the second skin a little bit easier. Once it was on, it clung to her like a scuba suit but didn't squeeze uncomfortably; she found it easy to flex her limbs and draw breath however much it looked to constrict her waist. Even the calve-high black boots with their thick treads fit her perfectly. She might have imagined that the dead woman was some future incarnation of herself, except that her own reddish hair was shorter, falling just to her shoulders, and for the fact that her shoulder blades – left exposed by the uniform's back, open almost down to the cleft of her buttocks like some daring evening gown – did not sprout huge bat-like wings.

Demons. And someone had killed them, long ago. Yes, they had been killed...Demons could die...she remembered that now. Demons did not have immortal souls, such as she and her father possessed: their bodies *were* their souls, in representation. They regenerated the most grievous wounding; the Demons did not. Demons were essentially machines, manufactured things, mass produced golems or homunculi.

All right, then, but who had killed them, and why? The only thing she knew for sure was that these beings had been her captors, her shadowy torturers. No wonder those tortures had ceased long ago. But if someone had come to rescue the Demons' captives, they had overlooked the woman and her father.

She took in the computer again. Had these Demons been able to inflict some of their tortures remotely at the touch of its keys? She stepped closer, looked at the worn symbols on the circular keys and was rather surprised to see that they pretty much agreed with those of a computer with which she would be accustomed, aside from a few that bore odd symbols. The alphabet dominated, and when she spread her fingers over the home keys she found they did indeed conform to the arrangement she remembered from a life that she had otherwise mostly forgotten.

Randomly, she depressed the *A* key, and it made a clacking noise, but what startled her was the oval screen coming to life with an image: a grainy stationary camera shot of a small room, apparently a cell. No one was inside it, but it seemed to contain some elaborate torture device poised over a surgical table like a giant scorpion, with pincered limbs and barbed tail. The woman searched out and pressed the *B* key. The screen changed again, but this time showed only the feeble blank glow it had started with. *C* and *D* were also dead, but *E* revealed a view of another cell deserted except for more torture equipment. She went through the alphabet, finding that most of the cameras in these cells were out, but the few that were still functioning showed only vacant chambers. It wasn't until she reached *U* that she found an occupant: a human body in extremis, teased out into a web, its dangling head encased in bronze gone a corrupted green with age. Her father.

He was *U*. And so...

She hit the *V* key, and a camera that she had never noticed within her own cell showed that cell with its broken remnants of her stone coffin. From here the Demons could have monitored her lonely suffering, though no one had peeked at her in this way for a long, long time.

"So I'm *V*," she said aloud. She smiled sourly. It was as good a name as any. Besides – she wasn't so sure she even wanted, or needed, to learn her true name anymore.

Keys *W* through *Z* were blanks; dead air. But there were those keys with unfamiliar symbols, most of them gathered off to the right. One of these appeared to show the outline of a pistol. She pressed this key, and at once heard a gasp very close to her...followed by a long, low moan like that of a sleeper roused from a bad dream.

5: *The Gun*

The woman, who henceforth thought of herself as Vee, lurched back from the keyboard, crouched for action, looking this way and that. She expected to find one of the skeletal Demons risen and confronting her, not so dead after all, but this wasn't the case. It was only a moment before she espied the true source of the moaning. She had spotted the gun before – a two-handled thing like a short rifle, but little more than a long rectangle in shape – hanging in a bracket on the wall just above the computer station, and she had meant to take it with her if it still functioned. But she hadn't noticed, before, that a cable ran from the gun into a port in the left side of the computer. And she hadn't noticed that a living eye with a red iris stared out of the side of the gun, because until now that eye had been closed.

An eye also stared now from the computer screen, entirely filling it. She saw that the eye on the screen moved just as the one in the gun's flank did. The same red iris. Both eyes blinked.

"Why did you wake me?" said a rusty-sounding voice, croaking from disuse.

Vee hesitated, then stepped a little closer to the mounted gun. When it had spoken to her, she had noticed for the first time the lips in the side of the weapon – a vivid pink against the gun's glossy white body – as they moved. The eye and the pink mouth, situated a little below the eye, were recessed in circles cut in the gun's material, which Vee now understood was shaped or grown from bone, not really white but ivory-hued like the computer keys. There were even squiggly sutures here and there like those demarcating the plates of a skull.

"Sorry," Vee said, at a loss. But then, "Who are you?"

"I am the weapon you are viewing. I have a serial number: J611821."

"All right – but what are you? Are you...someone like me, in there?"

If she wasn't remembering her life, at least some shards of her afterlife were reassembling themselves, her memory in this case sparked by this surprising encounter. And the reason she asked if the speaker might be a soul like herself was because of the images that were coming back to her now. She recollected that prisoners of the Demons were sometimes tortured by having a portion of their body removed (the rest of it destroyed in some way that it couldn't regenerate from, the body always tending toward regeneration from its largest fragment, favoring the head), this fraction integrated into some object from which it couldn't escape until these torturers reversed their surgical artistry. A street might be paved with flagstones stretched with skinned and cognizant (if mute) human faces. (And she had a mental picture of insects like huge crimson millipedes appearing from gutter grates to swarm over the faces, in and out of mouths, nibbling at nostrils from the inside and out.) A troop of Demons might wear boots made out of "living" skin, the tortured subjects not only humiliated in this way but feeling the grinding tramp of each foot fall, a human eye centered atop each boot like a decorative bauble. She recalled that an eye seemed to feature in most of these hideous artworks, as if that were a prerequisite for binding a soul in this manner.

But the gun replied to her question, "No. I am a Demon."

"A Demon? What did you do to be imprisoned in this form?"

"I am not imprisoned; this is the form in which I obtained consciousness. I am a living instrument." The gun didn't have to qualify this statement to stress that it meant "living" in the sense that any consciousness could be thought of as alive in the afterlife. "You have been isolated here a long time, haven't you? I recognize you. Did someone release you?"

"I freed myself. But my memory is mostly gone. I don't know my name, or even my father's, in cell *U*. Do you know our names?"

"I do not, offhand, but I do know that your father was hidden away here because he was greatly hated by the Demons who utilized me. He was an evangelist in life, do you recall that?"

"Vaguely." Those murky visions of her father on television. Later, Vee standing at his side, with other white-robed followers.

"Yes, in life an evangelist, his sermons transmitted across his land. Because of this, in Paradise he was a high-ranking Angel, and he came here to Hades leading an army of other Angels like himself who volunteered to take part in the Great Conflict, and subdue the rebellious Damned and Demons alike."

Angels. Damned. These designations resurfaced dimly in her mind. "So then, am I Damned or an Angel?"

"You are an Angel. You fought at your father's side, a captain in his army."

"Me?" Vee couldn't reconcile this information with her current psyche. Was she capable of such zeal? Apparently so, but she didn't feel any yearning to reclaim her former position, or the fervency that had engendered it. Leading people, belonging to a group unified by an ideal? Maybe it was the ages of isolation she had experienced, and the erasure – purification? – of her mind that made the notion actually seem repugnant to her now. In any case, she asked the gun, "What's this Great Conflict?"

"You have indeed forgotten a lot. And in a sense, slept through much besides."

"So you were one of those who captured me and my father and held us here. We couldn't die because we were already dead, but we could be contained and punished."

If the gun felt any nervousness or defensiveness, its uninflected voice did not betray it as it replied, "Yes, but I am only a tool, designed and created as such. I am not trying to exonerate myself, only to inform you of simple facts."

"Don't worry, I don't plan on taking revenge on you. It looks like someone already killed my captors, though when they came through here they either missed my father and me or else they just didn't care about freeing us. Do you know what happened then?"

"I do not, at least in my personal memory. I was engaged in the Mesh at that time. I can withdraw into the Mesh again and try to access that information if it's there somewhere."

"The Mesh?"

"It is a system of information recording and exchange, that can be accessed through machines like the one you summoned me with, or directly entered by entities like myself who have been designed, or have been adapted, to do so."

"It's the Internet, then."

"That was the model. Damned humans helped allied Demons in developing it. It had been begun at the time of your capture but has been refined since. My function was twofold; I was created as a weapon, but also as a portable information source for the Demonic soldiers who carried me and my kind. There are abundant access ports throughout the Construct through which the Mesh can be entered."

"The Construct?"

"Ah, so much you have missed. Or are missing. I could answer your questions for the remainder of eternity, it seems."

"Please help me. I know you were an instrument of my enemies, but I mean you no harm. And I'm sorry I pulled you out of the Mesh. I didn't realize."

"It's all right, madam. I have been lost in the Mesh a long time, but it is a pleasant place to be lost, like sleep filled with dreams, though the dreams are more like the dreams of others that I am privy to. When you are through with me, if you kindly return me to the Mesh I will be grateful, but it will be...interesting to encounter this more tangible world face-to-face again."

Vee didn't want to remind the gun that it had no face. She said, "So you are willing to help me for a time? As a weapon, too, until I can find a weapon that isn't sentient?"

"Very well. I am a tool and have no personal politics. Anyway, the lines of the Great Conflict, never less than complex to begin with, broke down more and more over the span of time it covered until there were no longer armies, only tribes. But I think it would help to educate you on the basics of how mortals entered into Hades – what is was like before the Construct. For that is the name we know Hades by now."

"Why?"

"First, the basics, if you will. I know this will not enlighten you on your own entrance into the afterlife, because you were one of the Creator's blessed followers and thus became an Angel upon your earthly demise, but it will still be educational, I think. It is a recording I encountered in the Mesh and stored in a file because...well, because I found it interesting. I relive it and other interesting recordings I have plucked out of the Mesh, when I want to be entertained by dreams as my consciousness floats adrift there. They are like bright fish in an ocean that sustains me. You do recall oceans?"

"Yes, but not in association with any personal memories."

"Ahh...if only I could say I had known oceans. But that is what the Mesh provides me – the opportunity to experience, as if they were my own memories, things I never could otherwise. Such as mortality. Or having a body like yours. When I move throughout the Mesh, I often use an avatar form of my own creation, and that is an albino dolphin. It is a creature that intrigues me. No limbs and simple in form, like me, but free to move of its own will."

"It sounds like a blessing and a curse, being what you are. Do you ever resent the form you're in?"

"It is the only form I know. Mostly I feel fortunate, because of my access to the Mesh, though even in the generally placid Mesh there are sometimes frightening and dangerous entities roving about, minds that can overpower other minds."

"So what is this recording you think might educate me?"

"Educate you in part. I will go on further from there. It is a recording of the memories of a Damned man. A mixture of memories from his childhood, his mortal adulthood, and his advent into Hades."

"How or why was this recorded?"

"That I can't say. High-ranking Demons with the ability to scan his mind with their own might have captured him and done so, or connected him directly to the Mesh and plumbed his mind that way. Or, he may well have connected to the Mesh himself somehow. I'm not sure at what point the recording was introduced to the Mesh, only that it represents a time period long ago, before the Construct, and when the Great Conflict was still very new."

"All right, then, how will you show me this? Will I have to enter the Mesh with you?"

"You are not adapted to do that, and there is no equipment here of the type to adapt you, so I will show you on this terminal's screen all that the man saw for the duration of the recording, and you will hear all he heard. His thoughts, however, I can experience but you can not. I can only relate them to you verbally, during and after the recording, to share with you anything you might miss."

"Okay. Thank you, truly." Vee seated herself in the chair from which she had removed the Demon whose clothing she had donned. "What should I call you, by the way? Do you have a name?"

"Only my number, J611821."

"Um, that won't do," Vee said. "I'll call you Jay."

"As you wish," said the gun with its impassive equanimity, and then its magnified eye vanished from the computer's oval screen and was replaced with images from a distant past.

6: The End Of The Line

The end of the world overtaxed even the resources of Hell. Heaven, Adam couldn't speak for, as he had never seen it. Never would.

Portals were interspersed throughout Hades, through which the Damned would arrive. Typically these consisted of a smallish chamber lined with white ceramic tiles, into which the Damned would materialize in the mock physical form they would inhabit for the remainder of eternity. These chambers usually only delivered one soul to the netherworld at a time. There would be a metal hatch with a wheel in the center, and this valve would turn and the hatch open and a Demon or Demons would take hold of the newly deposited soul and drag him or her out into a new reality that fortunately turned a good number of them instantly insane.

After this, the Damned would line up in long queues, at the head of which sat a number of administrative Demons with black, mantis-like bodies but huge bulbous heads like that of an octopus, and yellow-glowing eyes that drilled into the very core of each person brought before them. Maybe they were census takers or record keepers, or perhaps they judged the dead, for after their scrutiny each prisoner was branded on the forehead with a letter that indicated the principal crime for which they had been damned. Then, carrying a new black uniform they had been given, the Damned were herded off into trains that would transport them to an institution at which they would be schooled in the ways of Hades, and instructed in self-disgust, self-recrimination. After graduating from this infernal education, these lost souls would be turned loose to wander the limitless landscape of Hades, seemingly free, but only free to experience this region of sorrows rather than that.

When the world was destroyed, however, too many souls poured into Hades to be processed in such a leisurely fashion.

At first, Adam could make little sense of what they had done to enlarge this portal so as to better accommodate the influx. He could make little sense of anything at all, other than the pain that filled his body. "Pain" was too slight a word to convey what he felt, "agony" insufficient; there had been no word in his mortal life to express it. When they materialized within a portal, the Damned took the form they had been in at the moment of their death. Thus, the logjam of newly Damned now squeezing through this floodgate to Hell bore the wounds of debris thrown from nuclear blasts, or burns from radiant heat, varying in severity depending on how far they had been from the epicenter of the explosions. Many had been vaporized entirely. They manifested as little more than a spot of jelly, primal cells that rapidly divided until the mass gradually took a human shape – seemingly an accelerated birth – though the process felt like an eternity to these individuals, as every one of their nerves was alight with fire, and the other souls trampled upon them as they were nudged out of the mouth of the portal by the masses of more and more new souls appearing behind them.

Adam might have toppled to the ground and writhed there, had the bodies of his fellow sufferers not borne him up and along in a living current. He was blind at first, but his eyes regenerated swiftly – which was not a merciful thing, as it allowed him to see the condition of his body. Not that he needed eyes to tell he was a walking cinder, with red cracks at his joints as if his core were molten. He wanted to shriek his anguish, but his vocal cords were charred. The air was full enough with screams already, a deafening wailing – like the single howl of one vast, burnt and bloody caterpillar-like beast – so when he was finally able to add his own voice to the cacophony he couldn't even be sure his throat was emitting anything.

In the beginning, those who bore him up did so mainly by accident, with the press of their bodies, oblivious to him in their own pain. But as the wide column crowded forward, some of those who had been less injured – killed by radiation poisoning, for instance – consciously helped their more afflicted comrades along. Alternating between staggering, shuffling and stumbling, his naked flesh still scorched but his joints at least now flexible, Adam felt his arm being taken and turned his head a little (an excruciating mistake, as he heard his crisped flesh crackle) to see that an Asian man was lending him support. The man's face was too grave to offer a reassuring smile, however, and he had a bullet wound to the temple that had already healed to a mere depression. Self-inflicted, of course.

"Why?" cried a young Black woman pressed to the other side of Adam, too absorbed in her own distress to lend him similar aid. "Why? *Why?*"

Adam didn't know why he might have been damned to Hades, either. He had never committed any notable sins. Trifling theft as a child. The usual extent of lies. He had never raped or killed, beaten a woman or child or animal. But he would learn that only the very devout, of a single particular religion, would be permitted entry into Paradise. And thus, the gates to Paradise, though also necessitating expansion, were far less numerous and far less choked than these that gave entrance to Hell.

At first, he thought they were survivors of the apocalypse, evacuating town in mass exodus. But when he could see again, he saw that the sky was capped impossibly with a ceiling of molten lava. He saw distant mountains, glassy and black as obsidian, and volcanos disgorging billows of yellow fumes, and on the horizon, an immense and towering city, its uppermost spires even piercing and disappearing into the glowing ceiling of magma. And then there were the creatures, the *beings*, that flanked and herded the wide and seemingly endless river of naked, sobbing humans. These beings were a little shorter than Adam, like giant albino locusts with folded wings, walking on their hindmost pair of legs, while their upper limbs carried black iron spears or a variety of clubs that they used to prod and threaten the people along. The insect entities had two small horns atop their heads, with blank bony masks for faces, and soulless eyes like pink glass spheres that glowed dully from within.

No, Adam understood, especially when he saw the Demons. They were not survivors. But they were not really dead, either.

Like most Americans, Adam watched the beginning of doomsday on television.

They weren't sure precisely who had set off the explosions simultaneously in Washington, New York, Chicago, and Los Angeles, but it went without saying that it was terrorists, probably using nuclear weapons concealed in car trunks, or even suitcases or backpacks. Apparently there had been more bombs set off in other countries, as well; after it began, it was hard to keep track of who was doing what. It appeared, though, that once things were well underway, and there was no going back, nothing more to lose, anyone who had missiles to deploy unloaded them on the enemy they had always most longed to attack. Pakistan launched everything they had at India, for instance, but not before India ensured that Pakistan would disappear from the Earth. It went from politics and religion to mere spite in the end. A desperation not to go down alone. A drowning man, Adam had heard it said, loves company.

(15th Century Qur'an commentator Al-Suyuti had written that in Paradise, "The penis of the Elected never softens...Each chosen one will marry seventy *houris*, besides the women he married on earth, and all will have appetizing vaginas." But soon the terrorist martyrs would be standing in queues in Hades alongside their victims, looking around in dismay as if to say, "Hey – where are the appetizing vaginas?" Only to have a Demon's iron pike poke them in a most unmanly fashion.)

As he watched a growing number of TV stations turn to static, outside Adam heard a few distant but unmistakable bursts of gunfire. Now that there was nothing left to lose, long-simmering hostility was no doubt being vented on a more domestic level. Neighbors shooting longtime annoying neighbors. Wives shooting longtime abusive husbands.

Adam had called his sister. They had talked and cried together. He had told her he would call again, but he wondered if that would be possible, or even if he could find the strength to do so. He had called his mother. She had cried in a softer, more fatalistic manner – her voice washed out and weak, as if she had already been consumed and it was her ghost he was speaking with. As they spoke, he recalled vividly – like a flash of memory in a dying mind – standing beside her rocking chair as a young child, and twisting a strand of her hair around and around his finger while she watched TV. Her hair had been long and dark then. Years later his wife would be fond of his habit of absentmindedly twisting a strand of her long dark hair around his finger, too. That is, back when she had still felt any kind of fondness for him.

At least his mother would be with Adam's younger brother at the end. He talked with his brother briefly, too. They made their voices sound brave, calm, but Adam heard his brother's voice crack when he said he'd try calling back later. Like his sister, he knew this was their goodbye.

The Boston TV channels went out. Adam lived in Eastborough, Massachusetts. He pulled back a window shade to look out at the late afternoon sky. Was the sunset unnaturally red and tattered behind the town's silhouetted church steeples?

Adam felt a numbness that he supposed was akin to his mother's weary acceptance. After all, hadn't the past couple of years been one drawn-out, personal Armageddon for him? Two years ago, his wife had asked for a divorce. They had always argued, but the primary reason she gave was that she wanted children (they had found that Adam was infertile). Adam had suspected that she was having an affair with a coworker, however, and so one night he had gone through the motions of heading off to his graveyard shift job but had sat in his car down the street watching the house. After seeing the suspected party admitted into his home, Adam had waited a bit and then let himself in, to find his wife favoring her coworker with a sexual act that did not involve her appetizing vagina and would surely not result in the production of children.

He had wanted to keep the house, so he had refinanced and taken out an additional fifty thousand dollars so as to pay his wife for her share of the equity. But later, he had found it hard to support mortgage payments of almost two thousand dollars a month, and after a year of this had decided that he must throw in the towel. With the house market as poor as it was, the best solution seemed to be a "short sale," letting a realtor step in and negotiate with the lender to take over the house, so that Adam might walk away free of his debt (if free of any profit), rather than let things go into foreclosure. Adam had moved into a studio apartment in town, and rented a storage unit for most of his belongings. He had thought the process would take a month or two at best, yet here it was already nine months, and the short sale people hadn't managed to attract an offer that would satisfy the lender. And during all this time, Adam had moved only a fraction of his belongings from the house to his storage unit. Tomorrow he would deal with it. He'd devote next week to it. And yet the house still sat there only partly emptied, as if he still lived in it. His life felt fragmented between the house, his apartment, and the padlocked box.

Worse, he and his wife had a dog, a beautiful white Akita with a black mask. She was generally a sweet, loving animal, but she *was* an Akita, and one time his wife's new boyfriend had teased the dog by trying to snatch away a grape it was nosing around and the dog had bitten him, the wound requiring stitches. The boyfriend wouldn't permit Adam's wife to take the dog, so Adam had kept it for as long as he had hung onto the house. He couldn't have it with him in his studio apartment, however, nor could he find any affordable apartment in the area that would allow a large dog. So for all these nine months, the dog had continued to live alone in the abandoned house while Adam sent e-mails and made phone calls, trying to find a place – a kennel, a shelter for unwanted animals, some organization – that would take the dog in, help find it a new home. But with her history of violent behavior, no one wanted to take such a risk. So twice a day, in the morning and night, Adam walked over to his house and took the dog out to do her business. He might stay long enough to wash some clothes, refill her food and water bowls, then he'd leave her alone again, with a radio on for company. She would often snatch up one of her ragged toys as he left, and play with it by herself, still hyped up by his visit. But he wondered how long that enthusiasm lasted as the lonely hours dragged on until his next brief visit.

As he gazed out the window Adam thought of his dog alone in the house, maybe with the radio channel no longer playing. Outside, distantly, he heard people gathered in the center of town singing. Right now they were singing John Lennon's *Imagine*. He wanted to laugh at that.

The utilities were still on in the old house – if unpaid. He told himself he hadn't wanted the pipes to freeze, and he needed electricity to wash his clothes, but the truth was he worried about his dog. She needed to be warm. Needed to hear that radio.

There were still some cans of food over at the house, but Adam packed his car with much of the contents of his fridge and cupboards. He took a last look around his studio apartment, gathered up a scrapbook of family photographs but took nothing more. He shut off the lights, expecting never to return to the studio apartment again.

It was a short drive; just a few streets away. He soon came in view of a shopping plaza that could be seen from both his apartment and his house, built within the past two years. It had proved an overambitious project; a building containing luxury condos anchored one end of it, and only two or three of these had been occupied. The plaza was laid out in imitation of a quaint little village, and was very pretty, if very desolate – only a third or fourth of its store space had been rented. It was like a microcosm of his country, a broken-down ghost town already fallen to economic apocalypse before the bombs had even started flying.

At night, when he walked his dog, he would hear a group of three teenagers loitering around in the plaza. They skateboarded in warm weather, or just seemed to drift aimlessly in winter weather, never varying their outfit of black hooded sweatshirts no matter how cold it was. One of these boys frequently made a loud whooping sound like that of a police car siren coming to life. Adam swore he heard this call every night that he walked his dog. The cry, the boys, unsettled him. He supposed he should feel sorry for these lost souls; their home life must not be all that inviting. But in this age of the Internet and endless wonderful video games, it just didn't seem ...natural to Adam that they shouldn't want to remain indoors.

Within only months of the glorified strip mall having opened, he had noticed a giant white penis spraypainted on the back of one of the buildings. It was a masterpiece of cubist art; just as Picasso's people even in profile exhibited two eyes on one side of their face, like a flounder, so did this penis in profile have two testicles on one side. The further one even looked larger than the nearer one. Adam was certain one of the feral boys had rendered this graffiti. His ultimate achievement as a human being, no doubt, but in the end was it any less meaningful than anything else that would burn to ash?

The Akita was excited to see him, snatching up her toy. He stroked her head and spoke baby talk to her, her face turned up to him adoringly, as if he were her God. But he felt like a God who had let her down. Her small brown eyes shone lovingly in her black mask, her love unlike anything most human beings – or even celestial beings – seemed able to muster. The Creator of the universe wore a mysterious black mask, too, Adam thought, but His eyes could not be discerned through it.

He brought in all his supplies. He supposed they could go down into the basement together, for all that was worth. The radio hadn't gone off, and it soon played John Lennon's *Imagine*.

When he was finished, he took his dog out for a walk. It was close to dusk now, and he wanted them inside before it got dark. As if those teenagers would turn into radioactive zombies, in search of tasty prey.

He heard that characteristic whooping call. But more than that,

29

when Adam walked his dog into the enclosure of the mall village – only a few cars, maybe deserted, in its lot – he saw that dozens of giant white penises had been sprayed across the brick walls of the condo structure, the stores, even across the store windows. And all of the penises pointed in the same direction. All of them arrows pointing to Hell.

֍

Funny how you could adapt to just about anything, even the pain of having your decimated body remade. But as the line progressed, the wails of the Damned became less banshee-like, subdued into whimpers and moans of existential despair more so than physical anguish.

Adam couldn't see what lay at the end of the ponderous queue, but he would twist around occasionally and look back to see how far removed he was from the portal he had come through. He was surprised that it was still not that far behind. Then again, the expanded entry point was huge, as long as the proverbial football field. A kind of metal frame had stretched the portal wide, resembling nothing so much as a gigantic, overly baroque, Industrial Age surgical retractor holding open a gaping incision. There were hooks that seemed to clamp right into the air itself, and the portal truly was like an immense wound, in that vivid red blood streamed and twined down the hooks and arms of the frame as if some unseen membrane were bleeding. A torn veil between the worlds of the living and undead. Though now there might not be any living left on the other side of it.

Intense white light filled the mouth of the portal, the masses of fresh souls it disgorged mere silhouettes, maimed and grotesque, shambling through its glowing haze.

When he'd been closer to the frame, Adam had noticed a point in the left side of the structure where two vertical struts joined at right angles, forming a long corner. Blood had been trickling down this corner for some time now, so that it had begun to coagulate into a scabrous mass over which fresh blood still dribbled to soak into the barren ground. Weirdly, this had made Adam think of something from his childhood. Well, he had been in Junior High then, but just as introverted and miserable as he had been since his first year of school. He would often gaze out through the window of the science room, and stare at a projection of the school where rain water unintentionally channeled down its corner had caused a broad green stain of moss or lichen – maybe his science teacher could have enlightened him if he'd asked – against the red bricks. Adam would lose himself in his imagination, wondering what infinitesimal life might be thriving, might even have evolved, in that vertical green line. He even daydreamed that he was some microscopic entity himself, living within what would seem a verdant Paradise at such a minuscule scale, whatever occurred beyond its borders of no importance to him.

Green line. Red line. Like a border between life and death.

A line to be crossed.

Adam and his dog waited in the basement, listening to sometimes frantic news reports on the radio, but these channels became fewer and fewer in a sea of static until he switched the radio off and played CDs instead (though not John Lennon's *Imagine*). They left their shelter often to go upstairs so he could use the toilet or get something else out of the fridge. He peeked around the curtains at the night but it seemed so still that he might have thought the news reports were something of the order of Orson Welles' *War of the Worlds* broadcast.

He knew better than that, though. Out there, Tokyo might have been flattened like Hiroshima. The Eiffel Tower a mound of steaming metal, the faces scrubbed from Mount Rushmore in a return to raw virgin stone. Everything returned to its original elements. But he didn't mourn these lost wonders, these pinnacles of human achievement. Wasn't every stone of the picturesque Great Pyramids stained with the blood of the men who had hoisted them in place? No, it was the tiny, overlooked details of existence that he mourned, things that only he would have known or cared about – often bittersweet but all the more poignant for that. Twisting a strand of his mother's hair around his finger. The adoring eyes of his dog in their black mask. The green line of moss that perhaps no one had ever consciously seen, except himself, though it lay right outside that window every day and might even be there still, even more wide and vividly green. In first grade, his mother had frequently dressed him in a little red sweater, and he recalled plucking bits of fluff from it and releasing them to float to the classroom floor, a masochistic ritual in that he wanted to cry watching them drift away, bits of himself that he didn't want to remain there; he wanted himself in his entirety to be home, home with his mother. If all matter was never destroyed, only transformed, where were those bits of fluff now? What would his own matter soon become?

No one would ever remember about those floating red dandelion spores of fluff. He had never told anyone. Of course, unless he had written about such things to share with others, they would never have been remembered even had there not come an apocalypse, would have been lost with his death in any case. But there would have been *new* people, with their *own* memories.

He was glad he had been incapable of having children, now. Was glad it was only a dog beside him, waiting to be turned to ash with him when the very air caught fire around the globe.

But would his concrete storage box survive the firestorms? Would his boxes of books, sketch pads of drawings, photo albums and record collections become a nest for hardy, adaptable insects...mutant insects? A breeding ground for a whole new evolution of creatures (like his mossy green line)? He would like that. Wouldn't that be a better legacy than leaving these collections to human survivors?

A rumbling vibration through the cement basement floor, like a train rushing past the house. But what trains would be running now? Trying to outrun the bombs as more and more were launched, all that could be launched, falling even toward obscure little towns?

Adam crouched down and called to the Akita. He hugged her against him and she loved it, lapping his face. Lapping the tears off his cheeks. Making him laugh and swipe his arm across his face and wonder where – if there were an afterlife – the souls of animals went to. In a fair and just universe, his dog would walk beside him in Heaven, for eternity.

৯৩

His dog's soul had simply ceased to be. Animals were lucky that way.

The soul of the young Black woman pressed shoulder-to-shoulder with him had fully reconstituted now, so that she appeared as she had in life. Adam saw that she was very attractive. He hoped he hadn't reconstituted enough to become visibly and embarrassingly aroused by her. They didn't realize that formerly the Damned would be issued black uniforms upon their arrival at the head of their queue; these new souls would go forth as nude as infants. To expedite matters, the Damned were no longer being branded on the forehead, either, or shipped off to educational facilities such as Avernus University. The only part of the ritual that was being maintained was that every soul had to undergo a moment or two of intense scrutiny from those bubble-headed officials with their gleaming black exoskeletons. Where normally only a few would wait at the head of the line, here there was a whole regiment of them to process the Damned.

Adam said to the grim-faced Asian man on his right, "I know there's no day and night here, but I'd say a couple of days have passed already."

To his left, the attractive young woman said, "And I know we're dead and all, but I'm thirsty and hungry. I'm so hungry I could eat one of those giant termites."

Adam didn't want to admit that he was hungry, too, from the scent of cooked human meat.

The Black woman had told him she was from the city of Worcester, a few towns over from Eastborough, and the Asian man had lived in Boston's Chinatown, so this group was from the same general region. Thus, Adam often craned his neck in search of his mother, brother or sister but saw no familiar faces even now that most of the faces around him had reformed.

The young woman said, "Hey, so what's your name?" Her voice was shaky as it tried to sound casual. Still, she had calmed a lot from her initial hysteria. "I'm Ciara."

"Adam," he told her.

"Huh. A-damn," Ciara joked.

He looked at her blankly for a few beats until he got it. "Yeah," he snorted. "*Adamn.*"

❧

Some of the drone Demons carried compact black submachine guns. These might have been identical to an earthly model, but Adam wasn't gun savvy enough to know. Not all the Demons carried them, though; were they that troublesome to produce? Occasionally as they patrolled the outer edges of the line – and Adam was not far in from the right side – the insect-beings would strike the Damned with the wire butts of these guns, either to keep them from lagging, or for carrying on too loudly, or for no apparent reason at all other than that they were Demons. Sometimes, some of the Damned would try to bolt from the line, make a run for it, out of sheer mindless panic more so than from design, and this was when the Demons would open fire. Adam cringed every time, expecting to be strafed along with whoever the Demons were targeting. Several times, though, he saw the guns jam, and the blank-faced Demons worked at the weapons to try to clear them. The Damned didn't get far, though, as other guns soon cut them down, after which they would be dragged back to the line and roughly hoisted to their feet, their wounds soon to begin healing but the pain excruciating until it was done.

Maybe the guns were not only hard to come by, but substandard. And Adam had the impression that was not the only thing amiss here.

On one occasion when a Demon sprayed a Damned making an attempt at escape, the creature accidentally struck one of its own kind in the line of fire. The insect's white body was broken into chunks, dry and tattered, with no apparent blood or organs inside, white dust even puffing into the air – as if it were a figure made of papier-mâché. Other Demons came to regard it emotionlessly for a moment or two, and then – the perpetrator among them – carried the remains off to the side and laid them down, maybe to be properly disposed of later, or maybe

34

left to decompose. For as the line inched along, slow as a glacier, Adam saw that this being did not regain its feet and begin to regenerate as the Damned did. It didn't so much as twitch with reanimation.

Others noticed this, too. Ciara whispered to him, "You see that? That thing isn't getting back up again. They aren't like us...see?"

"They can be killed," Adam muttered, as much to himself as to her. "We're already dead – we're immortal. But they're not."

And these Demons seemed substandard to him, like the malfunctioning guns. He sensed it, without even knowing that this was one of the new infernal breeds created to replace the more human-like races, which had increasingly come to sympathize with the Damned, to the point where many of them had even thrown in their lot with the Damned in widespread rebellion. This insect race was like a rushed or indifferent sketch by a Creator distracted by other things. Without knowing the particulars yet, Adam intuited that Hades was in a kind of crisis, or decline.

So, he thought, it wasn't just the United States that had gradually gone all to hell.

Once in a while one of the administrative Demons would walk alongside the queue, with or against its flow, maybe as the team at the head of the line rotated its duties. Adam saw them for the first time this way, since he had not as yet sighted the end of the line where these entities sat at their ranked desks. The queue had still advanced so little that he could see the portal behind him even now, however distant. Could still make out that vertical red line in a corner of the frame that pinned it open, the long streak of blood both crusted dry and fresh-flowing. Noticing it once more, he had an odd thought: that maybe in the future he would recall gazing at that red line, as his mind had sought to distance itself from his suffering, just as when he would gaze out the window of the science classroom at the stained green line of moss. Was he even now accruing new poignant memories, that would hold some importance to him later on? That would haunt but bolster him somehow – define him even, if only to himself – in the eternity that he faced?

Eternity, he thought. Eternity...*here*. Mortals had wished to live forever, fought and feared death, since the first mortal had drawn breath. But there had been a better reason to fear death than the cessation of life. They should have feared the *continuance* of life, in the state of immortality.

Adam turned to watch one of the passing officials as if it might enlighten him on cosmic justice, but none of the Demons seemed able or wont to speak English; this was another development meant to keep Demons from sympathizing with humans. These towering officials with their black cephalopod heads and arthropod-like skeletal bodies were an updated, less anthropomorphic replacement of their predecessors.

This one swept Adam with its scorching gaze. Yellow eyes with goat-like pupils that glared at him with contempt, with loathing. That judged and condemned him. Damned him, as if the wrathful, vengeful Creator Himself gazed out through those inhuman eyes. But Adam didn't feel humbled, didn't feel ashamed. That accusing glare, however brief, only stirred his outrage, and after the Demon had passed he shook his head and muttered, "No...no."

Ciara turned to him. "What?"

"Whatever I did, I don't deserve this. I don't. What did you do, Ciara? Did you mug and beat to death somebody's granny? Did you strangle a baby? This isn't right. It isn't fair."

"I know that. It isn't fair."

"Okay, so I didn't go to church. Does that in itself make me an unworthy person, who has to suffer until the end of time?"

"I stopped going to church when I was a kid. Now I wish I kept going!"

"No, Ciara, fuck that shit. It isn't right!"

The Asian man on his other side said, "I'm a Buddhist. Maybe that's why I'm here."

Adam faced him. "And are you sorry you're a Buddhist?"

The man hesitated, as if afraid his punishment could become even worse.

"No," Adam said, "don't be sorry. We aren't wrong. *This* is wrong. *This*."

He wagged his head again, as if it were harder to believe in the rationale behind the punishment they had been sentenced to than to believe in the reality of Hades itself.

Listening in on their conversation, which wasn't easy to avoid, packed as they were in the line, a man behind Adam said, "Didn't we suffer enough in life? I always thought *that* was Hell, and after life we'd at least be able to rest. If not go to Heaven, at least just disappear."

"My wife left me for another man," Adam said. "I couldn't keep my house. I couldn't even keep my dog. And I burned to death in a nuclear war, knowing that my mom and my brother and sister and every innocent child and animal on the face of the Earth was dying horribly at the same time. No...no way." Wagging his head more violently. "This is enough. I've had enough. I didn't go through all that just to end up like this. No. No, I don't think so. I don't think so."

And with that, Adam began to press past the Asian man to his right, began to squeeze his way out toward the far right edge of the queue.

"Adam!" Ciara hissed. "What are you doing?"

"They'll shoot you," said the Asian man.

"Let them," Adam said. "I'm already dead."

The others blocking his way, seeing what he intended, did not try to stop him, perhaps curious to see how far he would take this. They moved aside as much as they could to permit him to pass. And in fact, when Adam reached the edge at last, one young man said, "Fuck it, I'm going with him!"

When Ciara saw others were beginning to follow Adam and the young man, she started insinuating her way toward the edge of the line, too. A current began to become diverted from the main current. A mumbling of voices arose.

Of course, it wasn't long before the Demons took notice. The two nearest drones came scurrying, one with a metal spear in its four sets of pincers and the other with a submachine gun. Seeing the gun, a couple of the mumbling rebels lost their nerve and bolted away from the mass.

The Demon with the gun was confused about whether to spray the bolting individuals or the main body of rebels, but decided on the latter and opened up on them, sweeping the gun's muzzle back and forth. At the same time, the one with the spear jabbed at those ahead of the rebels, who were looking back at the commotion in surprise, lest they break formation, too.

Screams, blood, chaos. Adam felt bullets smash his shoulder and jaw. His mouth filled with blood, which he swallowed and choked on, and though he knew he couldn't die he instinctively went into a physical panic. The others behind him bore him up and along, though. He couldn't see behind him, but he could tell the new current was swelling. It felt like so many bodies were crowding behind him that the entire queue would be diverted in this new direction, away from the high-ranking Demons who waited to appraise their souls.

The Demon's gun ran out of bullets, and that was when a few of the people broke from the line and charged it, tackled it and brought it down. Buoyed up in his agony, his left arm hanging useless and his chest painted in blood, Adam saw that one of these attackers was the Asian man, and he rose with the submachine gun in his fists. Someone else had taken a pouch from the Demon, and found fresh magazines for the gun inside it. He helped load one of them into the Asian man's submachine gun.

After that, everything changed quickly.

One of the official Demons came running with more drones, but it was a mistake for creatures who were themselves mortal. Adam saw the official go down under a volley of bullets, its bony armor cracked and punctured. As it lay kicking and thrashing, Ciara came up beside it, somehow with one of the metal spears – which she thrust through its sack-like head, pinning it to the ground. The creature's death throes were an electrified frenzy. "Ack, ack, ack-ack!" Ciara said. "Yeah, I seen you motherfuckers in *Mars Attacks*."

More guns, spears, bludgeons were appropriated. More people flowed into the new line. People from ahead, in the former line, started turning back to join it as well. And outnumbered as they were, more Demons fell, not to get back up again as the Damned did.

Adam lost track of Ciara and the Asian man, but others held him up as they moved ahead. For lack of any particular direction, they marched toward that city looming on the horizon, perhaps because it was at least somewhat terrestrial in appearance. From this remove, at least.

They did not know that this was a city called Tartarus, any more than they knew that the sky above Hades had up until recently been covered over with a curtain of gray clouds, but that these clouds had burned away to reveal the inverted molten sea behind them, as Hades underwent changes that not even the Demons comprehended. The Damned had no idea that this city of Tartarus was one of the principal centers for the mass production of Hell's Demons. Though, preoccupied as it was with exterminating and reprocessing the older races of Demons, and spawning new ones, Tartarus was just as oblivious to this encroaching army as they were to it. For now, their destination didn't matter, even if the terrain ahead and the things that dwelt there were terrible. At least, it was the direction *they* chose.

Soon, the bleeding lessened so that Adam no longer felt suffocated, and the pain diminished to something bearable. His arm could move again. No longer needing to be upheld, he had fallen back a little. No longer the leader of the new line, just another cell in its growing body, but that was okay. It was okay if most of them didn't even know he was the one who had begun this. He was just glad to have his legs moving under him of his own free will.

Somewhere behind him, Adam heard a familiar, loud whooping sound like that of a police car siren coming to life. Though that sound had always irritated, even unnerved him, he found himself grinning now – his first smile in Hades. Because he knew that for good or ill, there would soon be giant white penises painted on the walls of Hell.

7: The Construct

There was a door in the control room, but Vee found it locked when she attempted to open it. She had disconnected Jay from the computer now and carried the gun in her hands. The weapon said, "Ah, there's a button on the keyboard to unlock this door."

Vee turned back to the keyboard, and punched the key that Jay indicated. It was labeled ESC, for "Escape."

Shouldering a pouch of crudely stitched skin she had taken from one of the skeletons and filled with magazines of ammunition for Jay – each bullet grown from bone – Vee said, "One escape down...who knows how many more to go."

"And just where is it you want to go?" Jay asked her as they set out through a series of twisty, cramped corridors, their low ceilings and close walls lined with conduits thick and thin like the control room they had left behind.

Was it still an objective to find someone to free her father, or was he too irretrievably lost in madness? She decided not to think about it right now. He had waited this long in his delirium, hadn't he?

"I just want to – see what there is to see," Vee said.

And so they continued on through the seemingly interminable maze of corridors, some so narrow she had to stoop and squeeze through them, others now so open and large they felt like subway tunnels. Lights were set into the curved ceilings or even the walls or floor at intervals, though some of them were flickering weakly or had even gone out. And as they traveled, the woman and the weapon kept up a steady conversation.

"You saw a taste of the widespread rebellion that was already sweeping Hades then," said Jay about the stolen memories he had shared with Vee. "There had been rebellion stirring among the Damned for some time, but there was a certain incident that seemed to set off a chain reaction among the Demons as well. A Damned man who called himself Dan Alighieri rescued a female Demon known as Chara, whom he found tortured by Damned rebels and crucified to a tree. The man and Demon fell in love. Soon, other Demons of Chara's type fought alongside the lovers against formerly human Angels like yourself, and a breed of Celestial beings that entered Hades to help quell the uprisings. As a result of all this, it was decided to totally eliminate that particular race of Demons, though soon enough the order was given to destroy *any* race of Demon – and there were many – that bore predominately human characteristics. New Demons were created to replace them, at such places as the great factory city, Tartarus. Tartarus was the city you saw in the recording, that the Damned started marching toward."

"Oh! So they didn't know they were going from the frying pan into the fire."

"There was indeed fierce fighting in that Demonic city. It was never to be entirely taken by the Damned and their allied Demons, though they were never ousted either. But before I tell you the fate of Tartarus, I must tell you the fate – as much as we can know of it – of the Creator."

In a shocking transition from claustrophobic tunnel to vast open space, they had passed through a threshold onto a metal ramp that spanned a dark gulf, not only its floor but its ceiling lost in gloom, the huge shaft also seeming to vanish into infinity to left and right. As they crossed the gradually inclining ramp, Vee heard a rhythmic metallic clanging far below them. Some machine still diligently toiling, though perhaps now to no known purpose.

"The Creator was apparently distraught over the rebellion, seeing the long-standing order of Hades thrown into such chaos. He had a crisis, it is told, and questioned His own views of His disfavored children, the Damned and the Demons, even as they questioned their own positions. The Creator's essence withdrew in contemplation for a time, and then without warning – He immolated."

"Immolated?"

"Apparently, He self-destructed. Committed suicide. I suppose it had been a long time coming, perhaps even before the start of the Great Conflict. Of course, the destruction of Earth and all its life must have understandably contributed a lot to His state of mind. It may even have been the final straw."

"My God," Vee whispered, and then realized what she had said.

"His essence must have been scattered throughout all of Creation, for you will see particles of His being floating about the Construct even unto this time, dispersed through its ventilation systems."

"Are you talking about that white ash stuff?"

"Yes, so you've seen it. Dwellers here call it Essential Matter."

"I've seen primitive life forms that seem to have spontaneously evolved from it!"

"Really? That I didn't know. I hope you can show me this. How intriguing."

At the other end of the long ramp, they stepped through a tall arched doorway and found themselves in a gallery of similarly boundless dimensions, its floor and walls of polished marble – black veined with red – its ceiling and either end again disappearing into blackness. Lining the right side of the great hall were more arched doorways like the one they had just passed through. Some were dark, while light bled in through others. From one doorway came a whistling icy wind, which blew the tattered remains of what must have once been curtains drawn across it. Lining the left side were tall, narrow windows with arched peaks, but each seemed to have been walled up with cement beyond their thick glass panes.

"Do you have a blueprint of this Construct?" Vee asked.

"There are blueprints of sections of it, accessible in the Mesh, but I greatly doubt all of it has even been mapped. Since you have no particular destination in mind, I suppose one direction is as good as another."

"But you don't know where we are now, basically?"

"The Construct has been expanded upon and reconfigured even since I have been adrift in the Mesh. All I know for sure is that you were imprisoned in the basement. We are now at what once would have been ground level."

"Once?" Vee asked. Without consciously choosing, she turned right into the massive hallway. The hard footfalls of her boots made watery, receding echoes.

"With the Creator's destruction, the conditions in Hades deteriorated further. The creatures of Hades do not need to eat or breathe to survive, but conditions here imitate those of the mortal realm. Thus, the sensations of creatures in Hades imitate those of mortals. One who does not eat hungers but will never starve, one who is prevented from breathing will gasp for air but never suffocate. So one will naturally seek a comfortable environment. But the decline of Hades steadily threatened those conditions. The air grew increasingly thin, and the ceiling of magma became turbulent and unstable. Soon, frequent rains of lava fell, finally becoming a continuous, unrelenting deluge. Demons could be killed by this, and countless were. The Damned could regenerate if they found shelter, but those who could not reach sufficient shelter were buried under the lava – and that might be the majority of them, for all I know. The lava would cool to volcanic rock, but the continuous downpour kept increasing the level of the rock. Those entombed within it are no doubt still conscious even now, but trapped in that state forever. Ultimately, the level of volcanic rock reached the uppermost heights of Hades, until all of Hades was buried – a fossil."

Now Vee understood the row of windows on her left, blocked with solid pumice. "If Hades was buried, then where are we now?"

"I told you, there were shelters. I don't know what other, lesser shelters might have survived out there, but I know the only sizable shelter became the factory city of Tartarus, where great numbers of Demons were once grown and trained. The city you saw in the recording. The city that we are in now. Damned, Demons, and even the Angels and Celestials trapped in Hades by the deluge began to adapt the city's gigantic structures to preserve favorable living conditions. Teams of workers, though not always working in harmony with other factions, enlarged and connected the massive buildings – utilizing the city's own technology and resources, often even the mock organic materials once used for the creation of new Demons – until after many years they were all thoroughly interlinked, their boundaries lost, essentially becoming one immense structure that we now know as the Construct."

"But what about Heaven? Did it decline after the Creator's destruction, too, or...?"

"We don't know, and may never find out."

"Could the boundary between Heaven and Hell have been lost, too? If we followed the Construct to its uppermost level, what would we find?"

"What do you think, the ground floor of Paradise?" The gun's neutral voice almost hinted at amusement. "No, madam, you would find only more rock. Nothing exists beyond here – at least, that we will ever reach."

8: *The Natives*

They had been traveling along the hallway for some time, with its end still not apparent in the darkness ahead, when Vee thought she heard movement behind her, the faintest slap of a bare foot against the glossy stone. Whirling around, gun leveled from the waist, Vee caught just a flashing glimpse of a small dark body ducking into an arched doorway. A naked child?

"Who's there?" she called. Her voice echoed away, like a stone dropped down a deep well.

"I suggest we simply keep walking," Jay told her. "You know you are not alone in the Construct."

"Yeah. I'm surprised we haven't seen anyone before this. Do you have any estimate at all how many people made it into this place for protection?"

"I couldn't say, but I can tell you that before the deluge, the number of those dwelling in Tartarus – that is, Demon overseers, Damned laborers, and those Demons who had been birthed and were awaiting training and deployment – must have been about four million."

"Jeez! That's like...like Los Angeles." She remembered that place now. Had she even visited it once?

"Now, I would venture to say perhaps eight million."

"God – and that's comparable to New York City!"

"It could even be a million or two more than that."

"So where is everyone?"

"It's a big place. Bigger, I'd say, than your Los Angeles and New York combined."

Vee had turned to resume walking, but glanced over her shoulder every now and then. "Ten million inhabitants. But after all this time since Tartarus became the Construct, shouldn't all you Demons have gradually died off? You're mortal in your way, right? Whereas the Damned and Angels have the advantage of immortality over you."

"We don't die of old age, but yes, of course, many have been killed in continuing skirmishes or even simply accidents. But don't forget, many Demons aligned themselves with the Damned. And don't forget,

44

this was an enormous factory complex to manufacture Demons. In some regions, that practice has continued, though on a much smaller scale."

Just a short distance ahead, that same small brown-skinned being – or was it another? – stepped halfway out from another of the arched doorways, gazed at Vee for several moments, then darted back into the shadows. This time she had a better look. A small, wiry man with a dome of black hair, his face painted red – with blood? – and various piercing through his face, including a long iron bolt through his nostrils. In his hands he had been carrying a metal rod; as a club, or a blowgun? Vee knew he must have been from some Amazonian tribe. Of course, not having subscribed to the one favored faith, he and all his ilk would have been condemned to the netherworld.

"I hope he's just curious," Vee muttered, slowing her pace warily, "and not baiting us." Maybe his whole tribe lurked in these doorways, waiting for the right time to ambush her.

But no more of the Indian's kind manifested, and Vee finally reached the end of the hallway without confrontation. After the length and grandeur of the great hall, she was surprised to see the doorway was of modest size, with a thick metal hatch that stood open, looking scorched as if some weapon or explosion had forced it. From a distance, it appeared that sparse white flakes of snow blew out from the doorway, and had whitened the black marble floor, but Vee recognized this as Essential Matter. Nevertheless, for some time now the air had grown steadily colder, and now it came through that portal as an icy wind, adding to the illusion of snow.

"Look," Vee said, stopping and angling Jay so that his one eye could see what she was indicating: clusters of tiny white mushroom-like growths had sprouted up from the layer of Essential Matter that carpeted the floor in front of the open doorway.

"Fascinating!" he hissed.

"I'm not sure I want to go in there," Vee said, shivering as she peeked into the room beyond. It looked like a great chamber, taller than it was wide, filled with bulky industrial machinery, all of it lost in a combination of sparkling frost and more Essential Matter – flakes of which alighted on her lashes and upon her lips, like crumbs of a sacramental wafer. "Well," she said, "we're not going to freeze to death, are we?"

"I suppose not," Jay said unenthusiastically.

Vee stepped through the portal, the frozen crust of Essential Matter crackling beneath her boots. She saw the flakes were blowing in through a huge whirring fan up near the chamber's high ceiling, the source of that arctic blast. She picked her way between the hulking, sugar-frosted machines leerily, trying to minimize the sound of her footfalls and watching for any tracks on the floor, bare feet or otherwise. She reached the far wall, composed of metal streaming rust from its bolts and seams. A ladder was fixed to the wall. Vee took hold of a rung, winced at the cold, pulled her hand away with some resistance as the frost tried to adhere to her flesh. But steeling herself, she placed a foot on the lowermost rung and began to climb, after first snapping the flap of the ammunition pouch over Jay to hold him in place, lengthwise.

As she climbed, she again threw looks over her shoulder, expecting a pack of Indians to burst into the room firing metal darts and arrows up into her back, but no one appeared in the doorway. At the top of the ladder she hoisted herself up to a smaller hatch, and pushed it open. A corridor beyond, through which warmer air circulated. Ahh! Vee stepped through it gratefully. And so they continued on...to no known destination.

9: The Mass Produced

They had been mounting an iron staircase bolted to the concrete interior of a titanic smoke stack or silo. The mesh steps were rusted, and the concrete cracked and stained with dampness and grease. The staircase – distressingly narrow and with no handrail – had already taken Vee so high that below her the floor was engulfed in darkness, so that she could not see the mouth of the corridor that had delivered her into this gigantic silo. The staircase spiraled around and around it like the coiled skeleton of a monstrous serpent.

Once, weary, she stopped to rest, perching her bottom on one of the steps and wrapping her arms around her knees. She slept that way for an indeterminate time, her dreams a dissolving and reforming collage of images and associated, dislocated sound, the tatters of a former life. She woke with a start, and a vertiginous look into the spiraling vortex that gaped hungrily for her to fall. She rose unsteadily, resumed climbing. With no sense of destination, *up* seemed the only viable direction – up, and up. Her only impulse, her only instinct, for *ascension*.

She even passed huge stenciled numbers painted in white on the curving wall. 3...4...5...6. It had to be an indication of the level she had reached. Or was it the current circle of Hell?

There were other things painted beside or overlapping these numbers, in red paint. At Level 6, there was the quote: *"Then the Lord rained upon Sodom and upon Gomorrah brimstone and fire from the Lord out of heaven; And he overthrew those cities, and all the plain, and all the inhabitants of the cities, and that which grew upon the ground."* Not only that, but the giant number 6 had a slash through it, and over it in red was painted: 666. There were misspellings, besides, as there were in the quote that appeared at Level 7 when she reached it: *"Upon the wicked he shall rain snares, fire and brimstone, and an horrible tempest: this shall be the portion of their cup."*

The winding staircase terminated at this, the 7th level. Another metal hatchway, and Vee opened it on squealing hinges, stepped over its threshold.

It was another stupendous room, a factory floor, murkily lit; only occasional lights spaced here and there inadequately. Not far from the door were several padded cradle-like chairs, like something astronauts might recline in, with an intricate control panel between them, a few bejeweled lights still twinkling upon it. Bullet holes punctured both chairs and Vee thought she saw ancient blood stains. Beyond the chairs loomed a number of massive steel vats that took up most of the room, but lining one entire wall was a row of vertical glass cylinders. Some of these were broken, shattered by bullets. A few still contained a vile-looking greenish solution, with scum that almost looked like bits of macerated flesh collected at the bottom. She moved down this aisle, and came upon a couple of tubes in which a body floated in the greenish fluid, reminding her of the deformed fetuses carnival sideshows called "pickled punks." But these had obviously been Demons in the making, looking close to completed. Dead now, however. They were a little like the insect Demons she had seen in the recorded memory Jay had played for her, but these appeared more like ticks than locusts, bipedal, with pale greenish exoskeletons. Their forelimbs resembled those of a praying mantis, but bladed, and lesser pairs of limbs ended in a variety of surgical-looking implements of torture.

One of the cylinders was punctured by bullets; the fluid had long since all run out, and the insect Demon was slumped at the container's bottom with half its head shot away. Painted in red words across this cylinder was the quote: *"And these signs shall follow them that believe; In my name shall they cast out devils."*

Having reached the end of the aisle, Vee turned and saw an odd obstacle between this and the next factory chamber beyond.

It was a row of human heads, maybe thirty or so, hanging from the ceiling via long chains affixed to metal rings screwed into the top of their skulls. The dangling chains were like the strands of a beaded curtain demarcating the border between this room and the next – and the heads suspended from the chains were alive. Vee saw eyes blink, mouths move soundlessly for want of vocal cords. But shouldn't even severed heads regenerate into full bodies again? As Vee warily neared the heads, though, she saw why this hadn't occurred. The neck stumps had all been capped over with a metal covering, bolted through the flesh into the bone perhaps, that prevented the bodies from regrowing. From Jay's ongoing tutelage, Vee could tell by the brands on some of the foreheads that these were Damned humans, though by the time of the recording he had shown her the practice of branding the Damned had been forsaken, so the heads that weren't branded were also members of the Damned as opposed to being Angels like herself.

The heads swayed ever so slightly on their chains, like pendulums, stirred by a faint vented breeze. Vee stepped closer still, and saw the eyes follow her. Some seemed to blink their lids as if to convey a message to her in morse code. Other heads appeared to widen their eyes meaningfully, and a number of them stretched their mouths in silent screams or else mouthed words mutely.

Too late, Vee realized the disembodied heads were trying to warn her.

10: The Welcoming Committee

The crack of a gunshot *(from a high angle, to the right)*, and a projectile whined off the floor a foot ahead of Vee's feet. A voice amplified as if by a megaphone, also from on high but from another angle, began to call down, *"Demon! What are you doing at our bord–"*

But Vee didn't remain inactive to hear the rest of it. As if another, more experienced soul took over at her body's controls, she swept the Demonic gun up in an arc, letting loose a chattering burst of molded bone bullets in the general direction from which the sniper shot had come. At the same time, she threw herself into a roll, tucking in her head and minimizing the shock to her body by keeping it fast, coming up on her feet and bolting into the chamber beyond the heads. Automatic fire stitched the ground where she had been and tried to follow her, but she found cover behind the imposing column of a steam pipe that skewered up through the floor and sprouted numerous twisting boughs high above before it faded into gloom. Bullets punched into its far side but didn't penetrate, though Vee heard the hiss of liberated steam. Its billowing vapor helped mask her – but obscured her view of what lay ahead, too.

She glanced behind her to see if any other assailants were sneaking up on her from that direction, and saw one of the suspended heads twirling, everything shot off below the nose but the eyes still unhappily active.

"Demon!" came that electronic-sounding voice again. *"You are messing with the wrong fucking Angels!"*

"I'm not a Demon, asshole!" she shouted. "And I'm not messing with anyone!"

"The fuck you aren't, and the fuck you aren't!"

"We should turn around!" Jay whispered. "They must have a settlement beyond this point!"

49

"You heard him – they're Angels. I am, too. They –"

"To your left!" Jay blurted.

It was a good thing his single eye was on his left side; otherwise, the Demonic instrument wouldn't have seen the stealthy figure darting from behind one mechanical hulk to another. Vee whirled and triggered the gun, sending an automatic stream of bullets that way. She heard them clang and scream off a metallic bulk, not hitting the figure but at least letting them know she was aware of them, and pinning them down so they couldn't for the moment advance further.

"What are you trying to prove, Demon? You have a chance to get your ass out of here!" that voice drawled again.

"I told you," she called out, "I'm not a Demon! I'm an Angel, like you!"

"You think we're stupid, lady? You got a Demon gun and a Demon uniform – though I have to admit you look mighty fine in it, Mrs. Peel!"

"I just took these clothes and this weapon off some dead Demons, damn it! Look at me! Do I look like a Demon to you other than that?"

"They come in all shapes and sizes, sweetheart!"

A boom off to her right, and several large holes popped open in the pipe beside her. A jet of steam scalded her neck, but worse, one of the balls of buckshot had taken off most of her left ear. With a cry more of surprise than pain, Vee dropped into a crouch and fired Jay before the shotgun-wielder could launch another blast. She saw a figure in a white uniform, wearing a goggle-eyed helmet with a perforated snout like a gas mask, start to duck back down behind a droning ventilation box of some kind. He wasn't fast enough; the chunks of bone hit him in the face before he could complete the move. One of the goggle eyes was punched in and the top of the helmet split open, as did the skull within it. The exhaust from the ventilation machine sent a poof of misted blood curling gracefully into the air before it dispersed.

The man's amplified screaming from behind the machine incensed the person who had been calling to her. *"So you're an Angel, huh, bitch?"*

Trying to ignore her own blood as it wound down her neck and below her high collar, Vee bellowed hoarsely, "You shot me first, fucker! Okay, if you don't believe I'm an Angel, I'll go!"

"Too late for that now, lady – you shot one of our boys!"

"Fuck your good ole boys, you redneck fuck!"

A few moments of silence, apart from the wailing curses of the wounded man, before the voice finally came back again. *"If you're not a Demon, then stay where you are and put your weapon down. We'll move in and talk to you."*

"Oh yeah, right...and why should I believe you don't mean me harm now?"

"Because now I think I believe you, lady."

"Why now?"

"Because a Demon wouldn't say 'good ole boys' and 'redneck,' I figure."

Vee digested that, and thought it was probably a good thing these expressions had come back to her so readily from her forgotten life. Still doubtful, though, she yelled, "You can come, and we can talk, but I don't feel comfortable putting down my gun, sorry!"

"Too late for that," said a voice close behind her.

Vee spun and on instinct fired Jay as she did so. Her semicircle of bullets, like the swing of a scythe, knocked down two of the four white-uniformed, helmeted figures that were rushing her. Their torsos were thick with body armor, however, and a half-second later all four were firing their own weapons in unison. Assault rifles sprayed her in zigzags, and a shotgun blast sent her crashing back into the tree-like pipe. She slid down it, ragged and pumping blood from over a dozen holes, her nose caved in and blood flooding down the back of her throat. Jay clattered beside her as her arms went limp.

Before Vee lost consciousness, she tilted her head up groggily to blink at the lead figure as he stood over her.

"You sure were pretty," he drawled. *"Well, you will be again. But for now –"* and he extended a handgun, put a bullet into her forehead *"– that's for shooting poor Earl in the head, bitch."*

11: The Holding Tanks

She opened her eyes to see lazy tendrils of blood swirling before her eyes. In the next instant, Vee's body was in an instinctive panic, her eyes bulging and legs thrashing, even though there was no way she could actually drown.

She floated in some nearly gelatinous solution, contained within a large glass cylinder, the inner surface of which she began to thump with her palms. Through the glass she could see that hers was one in a row of such containers. Most of them appeared empty, but in the cylinder to her immediate left floated what was undoubtedly some species of Demon. The naked flesh of its body was eggplant purple, its head devoid not only of hair but of any facial features apart from its metallic golden eyes, which stared back at Vee inscrutably. More acclimated to its prison than she, it hung in its fluid calmly, or at least fatalistically, very slowing fanning wings with a translucent patagium stretched across long, finger-like bone struts. The utterly alien entity was both terrifying and beautiful.

Vee broke eye contact to look up at the hinged cover to the tank, and she started beating at this next. As if in response to her efforts, the level of amniotic fluid began to drop, and Vee pressed her face up into the gap that resulted, gulping desperately for air. The level continued dropping, until she could tread water and keep her head and shoulders above the surface. She looked down and saw that a drain in the floor of the cylinder had opened, letting out the thick solution. She also saw that she still wore her rubbery black uniform, her white skin showing through the chains of holes torn in the material by automatic fire, though her flesh itself had since healed, the only evidence remaining of her injuries being her blood threaded through the clear liquid.

Finally, the contents of the tank diminished to the point where she could stand on its floor. As the last of the fluid gurgled down the drain, Vee heard the hatch in the top of the cylinder open and looked up to see two figures poised above her on a catwalk, staring down at her. One carried an assault rifle, and both of them wore white uniforms and white ballistic vests, though they didn't sport those goggle-eyed helmets. Both men had shaved heads, one of them with a goatee.

"You're looking a little better after your bath," said the goateed man. Even without his voice being distorted through amplification she recognized it; the man with whom she had shared a shouted conversation.

"You're the guy who shot me in the head," she panted, lungs burning. Before the liquor amnii had finished draining away, Vee had vomited up all that had filled her.

"Well, you can't say I didn't warn you," he drawled. "I'm Charles Roper, commander of security for this settlement. But let's talk about you, lady, and your claim that you weren't grown in one of these vats, here."

"What do you mean?"

"I mean your claim that you aren't a Demon."

"That's right, I'm not. I'm an Angel. I was held prisoner, for I don't know how long. I have no memory of who I am, but the Demonic gun I took with me told me that my father was an important figure in Heaven. I couldn't free him; he's still held prisoner back there, down in the basement level."

"Wait a minute, here, hold on...let me take all this in a second. You claim you don't know who you are, but you were a prisoner. Whose prisoner?"

Vee hacked a little more, then continued, "I don't know – some Demons who were killed a long time ago. I guess my father and I were overlooked by whoever shot them."

"You don't know your father's name, either, I suppose?"

"No, but the gun told me in life he was a televangelist. He volunteered to come to Hell to help fight in the Great Conflict; he was like an important general or something. And I was a captain in his army, as I understand it, though I don't –"

"Jesus Savior!" the security commander exclaimed. "Are you talking about Pastor Karl Phelps?"

"I don't know...Karl Phelps?"

"Wait a minute, you just hang on – I know a guy who can help us with this, I think. I'm going to go bring him back here."

"I don't suppose you could let me out of here in the meantime?"

"Just be patient a little bit." Roper turned to the man with the gun. "Earl, I'm going to go find Tim Wade. Give the lady those new clothes, for now."

She heard Roper's boots clang away along the catwalk, leaving Earl to grin down at Vee. He set his assault rifle to one side and produced a neatly folded bundle of white clothing. "You can get out of those wet rags of yours, honey – I got a new outfit for you. Just toss those old things up here and I'll toss these down."

"Not on your afterlife, hick. I'm not stripping for you."

"Hey, bitch, the changing rooms are all full. Come on, or are you trying to hide some Demonic mark or something?"

"Sorry, Earl, but you'll have to go back to watching your sister striptease for you. By the way, I see your brain has almost grown back." There was still a hollow depression in the man's shaved head. "Or did you always look like that?"

Earl's grin seemed to gurgle down a drain as well. "You better hope you're an Angel, bitch, or I'm gonna shoot your eyes out and skull fuck you twice."

"I think I saw that sentiment on a Hallmark card once."

Earl snorted, and pulled back out of view.

12: The Boyfriend

Roper had returned, and accompanying him was another man in a white uniform and shaved head, also with a dark goatee, though he was thinner and younger than the security chief. This man knelt at the rim of the tank and cracked a huge grin. "Oh dear God...my Lord Almighty, I can't believe it! You were right, sir, it's her!"

"Earl," Roper said immediately, "get a couple gaffs and help me pull this lady out of there."

"Is she an Angel, sir?"

"She sure is," said the new man.

Earl mumbled something, sounding disappointed, as he moved off.

The new man leaned over the rim again and said, "Rebecca! Rebecca, honey, do you know who I am? Commander Roper said you didn't know your own name, but I hope you can still recognize your old boyfriend!"

Boyfriend? Vee thought. Had she really changed so much through her amnesia and the long, cleansing years? Because she couldn't see herself ever finding a white man with a shaved head attractive, even though he had wisely gone for an Edward Norton look by compensating for a weak chin with the goatee. Well, maybe he had had hair when they had been involved – assuming this wasn't all some kind of trick.

"I don't recognize you, no," she said.

"You don't? Come on, Rebecca, try now. It's Tim, Tim Wade... that name doesn't ring a bell?"

"I'm afraid it doesn't, Tim. My own name doesn't ring a bell, either. You say I'm Rebecca?"

"Rebecca Phelps, yes! God, when I was just a kid I saw you on TV a couple times at your daddy's side – you were just little yourself. And then we met up here in Hades; I was a volunteer with your father's army, and you were my captain. I served under you!"

"Yeah, Tim, and I bet she served under you, too," Roper joked, nudging him.

Tim chuckled. "Be good, sir." To Vee he continued, "None of this is coming back to you? God, what those Demon fuckers must have done to you." He wagged his head. "We were going to be married, Rebecca, in Heaven once the Conflict was over. But we got trapped down here, of course. Made it into Tartarus before the floods could catch us. Created our colony, here, taking control of Levels 7 and 8. And when the settlement was still new, and we were still fighting to secure its borders and wipe out any local pockets of Demons, you and your father and a group of other soldiers went out one day and none of you ever came back again. We searched and searched and never found you. We figured you'd been taken prisoner by some Demons or other, but we couldn't tell where they'd stashed you, no matter how many of them we caught and tortured. We knew you couldn't be dead. I searched for you myself, Rebecca, I can't tell you how many times. But God, after a while I figured I'd never, ever see you again, honey! This is a dream come true – a miracle, I swear it!"

Earl had returned, and passed Roper one of two hooked poles. They lowered them into the cylinder, and Roper said, "Hook these in your clothes, pretty lady; watch your skin, now."

Watch your skin, Vee thought; this from the guy who had put a bullet in her brain (which might still be in there now). She hooked the loops of several straps in her uniform, while Tim continued to gush. "I'm a mechanic, now, as you can see," he gestured at the grease stains on his uniform, "but I'm still in the militia, too, under Commander Roper here."

"Ready to make Swiss cheese out of anybody who comes knocking, huh?"

Roper and Earl began hoisting her up, while the security commander grunted, "Okay, I'm sorry about all that back there, but we worked hard to win this territory, Miss Phelps. Speaking of Swiss cheese, don't you worry – we got some highly skilled surgical Demons we keep around, who can dig out whatever bullets are still in you."

"Thanks a lot," she said, at last alighting on the grated catwalk beside the three male Angels. She found she was a little taller than the man who claimed to be her former boyfriend. He went to put his arms around her but she stepped back, held out a palm. "Take it easy, okay? I still can't connect to anything you're telling me."

"You believe what that Demonic gun told you," said Earl, "but not us?"

"Shut it, Earl," Roper said.

"Where is my gun, anyway? I hope you didn't destroy it."

"We've got it put away," Roper said.

"Good, because I want it back again. It was very useful to me."

"So I noticed," Earl said, rubbing his head meaningfully.

"You shouldn't trust that thing, ma'am," Roper advised. "If it's a gun you want, well we got plenty of good weapons we brought here in the Conflict, and new ones we've made ourselves since."

"If you can trust your Demon surgeons, I can trust my Demon gun."

"Okay, okay, we'll discuss this later. Right now, let's get you situated in an available living space, and I'll go give our leader a report on all this. I'm sure he's going to be as happy as Tim here is. You don't recall him either, I guess – Pastor Jacob Johnston?"

"Um...no."

"Well, he and your father were great friends. They helped found this place together."

"So what do you call this colony of yours?"

"L.A., of course," Tim said. "Los Angeles! Welcome home, Rebecca." He spread his arm toward a metal hatch at the end of the catwalk. "Come on...let me be your guide."

13: The City Of Angels

Over a great span of time the citizens of Los Angeles had removed much of the floor that separated Levels 7 and 8, and the walls that divided vast factory chambers, opening up one enormous space to contain its countless dwellings. The majority of these were simple box-like affairs made from sheets of tarnished metal or glossy bone, wedged into any available gap in Cyclopean machinery, or stacked in great giddy tiers toward a ceiling of girders and pipes – a solid sky made insubstantial through distance and smoky haze, so high up that it gave Vee vertigo just tilting her head back to gaze at it. Narrow elevated walkways crisscrossed between the towering stacks of boxes, along with laundry lines, electrical cables, and water pipes. Numerous structures were not made from removed sections of floor and walls, though, but assembled from cannibalized machine parts. Not only that, but an abundance of dwellings or places of business (for there were many of these, mostly at ground level, advertised by electrical signs) existed *within* gargantuan machinery that had been hollowed out or otherwise adapted for that purpose. The city, makeshift as it was, was of such size that it extended beyond the limits of her vision.

Tim pointed out, "And see, there's been a lot of use of bone; we have a great bone-producing plant here in L.A.. We use the materials that were once used to manufacture Demons. If it wasn't for that kind of technology, we wouldn't have been able to adapt Tartarus into the Construct fast enough to deal with the deluge. See, we here in L.A. really did more than our part in creating the Construct, while so many of the Damned and the Demons, too, were just finding some little corner to cover their own head with. We had a bigger picture in mind. People like me broke our backs reworking ventilation systems and whatnot to provide proper life support to the Construct that not only benefits our colony, but so much of the rest of it. Though damn, sometimes I think we should try to cut off the life support to any other region outside of L.A.. We've done them too many favors. And they still try raids on our borders once in a while!"

"Who do?" Vee asked.

"The Damned. Demons. Who else?"

They walked on through narrow streets packed with milling bodies, and she was relieved to see that not all the men shaved their heads, though it was a prevalent look. All of the citizens around them wore white garments of one kind or another so that the streets looked to be teeming with termites. Women tended toward an ethereal or at least a more feminine look, in dresses or flowing robes with hoods. Some men wore cloaks or robes, too, and anyone who covered their head did so with either a peaked cowl or even a conical headdress.

She was surprised at the number of women; had so many volunteered to fight in the Great Conflict like herself? There were, of course, almost no children. But Vee did see some, and asked Tim about it.

"Oh, those were Damned children, condemned to Hades for not being baptized Christians, but some people take pity and convert them so they can be adopted. We assemble parties sometimes that go out into other levels looking for them, catching candidates that look like they might appeal to the citizens who put in the proper request for a child. A worthy cause, huh? It's a dangerous one, though, because so many times there are adult Damned around that will try to stop these kiddie posses, as we call them."

Vee changed the subject. "How did you die, Tim?"

"In the Big Bang that ended it all. Do you know about that?"

"Yes, the gun showed me. And me and my father?"

"The same. Your mom is still in Heaven."

"Are you sure there is still a Heaven, after what happened with God?"

Tim stopped dead in his tracks and looked into Vee's eyes with some intensity. "Of course there's still a Heaven. Don't even question that. And what do you mean, what happened to the Creator?"

"Well, you know, when he went supernova – self-destructed. The Essential Matter..."

Tim stepped closer to her, and dropped his voice to a harsh whisper. "Where'd you hear that crap from?"

"The gun."

"And you believed that lying Demon? Do *not* blaspheme like that, Rebecca. I know you don't know any better, but don't let anybody else in L.A. hear you spouting that kind of sacrilege. The Creator did not self-destruct. And this stuff you call Essential Matter, it's just Demonic matter, which this factory city used to be full of and still is. Okay? We clear on that?"

"I hear you, Tim," Vee said warily, giving him a thin smile.

He didn't look entirely convinced, but turned to continue the tour.

They passed what appeared to Vee to be a restaurant, from the interior of which came the scent of grilled meat. It made her stomach roll over and she audibly groaned. Up until now, she had been able to largely tune out the emptiness that ever seemed to yawn inside her. "Oh my God," she said, lingering to savor the aroma. "Is that for real?"

"Nothing's for real, for real," Tim said, drawing too close to her shoulder, "but yeah, that's chow. If you like that, wait until I get you to my apartment, soon enough. I'll have a feast fit for a beast put together for you."

"But where does the meat come from?"

"Come on," he said, his good cheer returning.

They came to a sizable building of riveted metal plates, rust streaking down from the seam of its flat roof (upon which a smaller structure rode piggyback). Tim spoke to someone seated at a desk in a little office off the anteroom that Vee waited in. Smiling, Tim soon returned and took Vee's hand. "Great, I got us permission to have a look at the livestock."

They passed along a few short corridors, but in one of them Vee stopped and cocked her head. She could hear an odd muffled sound, high-pitched and wavering but consistent, that at first she had taken for machinery, but someone opened and closed a door somewhere and in that instant she realized it was a continuous screaming of panic and pain. "What's that?"

"The livestock being butchered. But come on, don't be squeamish, honey – this is the afterlife, right? Only Demons can die, and these aren't Demons."

They turned down another corridor, passing a worker along the way. He looked Vee up and down, obviously confused by her bullet-tattered, form-fitting black uniform. She looked him up and down in his butcher's apron caked thick with blood. Tim and Vee continued on to a door, and Tim hauled it open, pulling Vee by the hand into a large chamber.

Armed guards patrolled around the outside of a single huge cage, filled with dozens of naked human beings. They were all small, brown-skinned, and reminded Vee instantly of the furtive primitives she had encountered below this level. Some of them huddled in little family-like groups, while others hooked their fingers in the mesh and stared out at her forlornly. Some were sobbing, but most were silent, vacant-eyed husks.

"Who are they?" she managed to get out.

"Don't ask me why, but apparently a lot of these Damned who originated from the Amazon made it into the Construct before the floods. They're called Bora Indians. We've caught most of them, though there are still some out there that have slipped past our hunting parties."

As Vee watched, a hatch in the ceiling above the cage slid open and a half dozen decapitated heads tumbled down to thump and bounce on the floor below. A woman dragged one of them, eyes and tongue rolling, into her lap and rocked as she cradled it mutely. Now, stepping closer despite her horror, Vee saw a man with a normal-sized head but a weirdly small, skeletal-looking body dragging himself along the floor, not yet regenerated enough to stand and support himself, and other such figures either more or less reconstituted.

"You eat these people," she breathed.

"Yeah, I know it's kind of *Soylent Green*, but hey, we aren't killing them, right? We harvest them for meat and then seed them again."

Vee was trembling. "How many times a day do you 'harvest' them? This little group feeds the whole city?"

"Oh no, not just them; this is a big plant, here. They've got a cage for a bunch of Zulus who got killed by the Brits back in 1879 – if you like dark meat, heh – and we got some honest to God Aztecs, even, if you like South of the border style. And other sorts of primitive people, too. They're happier if they're with their own kind, so we do that for them. But yeah, we do have to harvest the people a lot every day to meet the city's needs." He shrugged. "We got a lot of hungry citizens here."

Vee turned to him, her teeth fairly grinding, but did her best to control her outrage. She was, after all, a lone visitor in the City of Angels. "You can't convert these people like you do the Damned children you round up? Well, but then what would you eat? Not that we Angels *need* to eat to survive, right?"

"Hey, Rebecca, we still have the craving to eat – you must have felt that. And anyway, we have converted some of the Boras and the others. Come on, I'll show you that, now, too. If you think I don't see them as people, you're in for a big surprise."

Vee didn't think she could handle any more surprises, but she went along, though she made sure Tim no longer took her hand. She walked in silence for a time, followed him up a series of narrow metal staircases like fire escapes that zigzagged up one of the alarmingly tall and uneven stacks of domiciles. Halfway to what turned out to be his own living space she asked, "Tim, did I use to eat those Indians, too?"

"Of course," he said. "You loved Bora steak as much as anybody. I don't know if I'd have shown you, otherwise."

14: The Wives

"Danielle? Miranda?" Tim called out as he let himself into his own metal box, Vee on his heels, "I've got a very special guest with me!"

Danielle was the first to appear, from what had to be a kitchen, her sleeves rolled up and a damp apron around her waist. She was young and pretty, though her hair was in frizzy disarray, her eyes in dark pouches and the line of her mouth hard. She blinked at Vee without emotion.

"Danielle, this is Rebecca Phelps – daughter of the missing general, Pastor Karl Phelps!" He gave her a much-abbreviated rundown on Vee's having by great fortune blundered into their midst. "She and I were engaged, honey, remember I told you that?" At last he turned to Vee. "Rebecca, this is my wife Danielle. She was a Damned who was gathered up in one of our pussy posses – excuse the expression." He gave an apologetic shrug and a boyishly mischievous smile. "We didn't have enough women in our own ranks; so many wives and girlfriends stayed behind in Heaven, you know. So anyway, Danielle was reformed – she used to be a prostitute – and accepted Christ as her Savior. And me as her husband." He winked at Danielle and chuckled, but then made his face serious again. "Of course, all of this was long, long after your disappearance, Rebecca, believe me."

"Congratulations," Vee said to the woman.

"Yeah," Danielle said, her empty demeanor unchanging.

"So, where is my little pet Miranda?" Tim asked.

"Napping," Danielle said.

"Well, I'm afraid nap time is over." Tim gestured for Vee to follow him into a dark bedroom just off the central living room. "Hey, cutie, you hiding in here?"

He switched on a light consisting of a bulb inside what appeared to be a shade stitched from human skin. A small nude girl curled in a nest of blankets lifted her head groggily, long black hair hanging in tangles about her face. She was brown-skinned, with pointed bumps for breasts, her full-lipped face sullenly beautiful.

"We baptized her with the name Miranda," Tim explained, ruffling her hair. "Huh, sleepy head."

"You two adopted her as your child?"

"Child? No – Miranda's my other wife. Isn't she gorgeous? Right out of a Gauguin painting, huh? I mean, wrong part of the world, but she could be, huh?"

"She looks all of fourteen, Tim."

He turned to Vee and said, "Well, Rebecca, she died thousands of years ago, right? So she's a pretty old soul if you look at it that way, isn't she?"

Studying the black pools of the Bora girl's large, heavy-lidded eyes again, Vee could at least agree that she did look like an ancient soul.

"So...we can eat some of the infernal plant life we grow in our hydroponics facilities, if you want to go vegan tonight, Rebecca. Like I say, please don't be squeamish about the other. We only eat cannibals, right?" He laughed, nudged her. "Well, the Bora aren't really cannibals, but the Aztecs were, I guess. Myself, I can only bring myself to eat meat from the females. Funny, huh? Somehow it just seems, I don't know, gay to me to eat the males."

Lord forbid, gay, Vee thought – though she had a suspicion that her former fiancé might even find eating female flesh to be an erotic experience.

She said, "If you can convert Miranda, why not all of them?"

"A lot of these pagan folk refuse to accept Christ. Then again, I'm sure it's hard for them to grasp it all due to the language barrier. I've worked hard to teach Miranda English, but she's shy, aren't you, baby?" He blew her a kiss. "Anyway, salad for you tonight, right? And I'll have Danielle fix up the sofa for you until I can convert my little office back there into another bedroom. I made sure Danielle and Miranda had separate bedrooms, so they could have their own space – not that we don't all cuddle together some nights."

Vee stepped out of the bedroom, feeling suffocated by its humid aroma of sex. "Ah, thanks for your hospitality, Tim, but I was under the impression that my own apartment was going to be provided for me."

His face fell. "Well, yeah, that could be done if you *wanted*. But until then..."

"We'll see what Roper says. When was he going to have me meet this leader of yours?"

"I'm not sure if that's going to happen today. It'll be night, soon. Of course, there is no night or day in Hell, really, but we divide it up that way for our benefit anyway, to make things feel more like home. We dim the sidewalk lights at night, and everybody rests, spends time with their families – you know. Come on, anyway, you have to eat something." Tim turned to call out, "Danielle! Get some supper going, okay? No meat!" Miranda appeared from her bedroom, apparently to help with the meal, and Tim gave her a swat on her bare bottom. "That's right, you run along and help before I give you another spanking, lazybones!"

15: The Church Machine

Roper himself escorted Vee the next morning (that is, morning as portioned out in this city), after she had ended up giving in and spending the night at Tim's apartment after all, lying on his couch and listening to his muffled grunts and sighs from Miranda's room. The girl herself had remained stoically silent.

"If I'm going to stay in L.A.," Vee told Roper as they made their way to the colossal, imposing-looking machine in which Pastor Jacob Johnston had made his offices and living space, "I'm going to need a place of my own – soon."

The security commander had a handgun strapped to his side, another on his belt, and signs of rank on his white uniform that made him stand out somewhat in the white-garbed crowds. As when she had walked with Tim, Vee in her unconventional attire received many strange looks, though a lot of men appeared to be sizing her up. *Fresh meat,* she thought.

"*If* you stay in L.A.?" he said, turning his head. "And why wouldn't you stay here? You got a better place to go?"

"I didn't say that," Vee said, keeping her eyes ahead.

After a few minutes more of walking, Roper said, "You know, I didn't recognize you at first, but I remember you now...shit, it's been so long. I never talked with you before, but I saw you a lot from a distance beside your dad. I was just a captain in one of Pastor Johnston's regiments back then. I was in the Marines in life," he explained with some pride. "Fucking car bomb, Haqlaniyah, Iraq."

"So you rose up in rank, huh?" Vee asked without interest.

"Well, see, after we set up our base here on Level 7 we gradually restructured ourselves into less of a military force and more of a colony – we, being the two divisions led by your father and Pastor Johnston. Anyway, later on smaller Angel units found their way to Level 7 to expand our numbers and fortify our position. Over time, we claimed and opened up Level 8, too. That's a lot of border to keep secure, and then there's the militia to keep on its toes. So, yeah, our colony needed a commander of security, and we went through a number of them until those guys got burnt out on it and retired. Then Johnston gave it to me, even over some of the higher ranking officers in the colony. There were some hard feelings, but then again like I say a lot of these guys just wanted to mellow out and settle down after a time, too. This was back when the Pastor had more confidence in me. Or anyway, when I had more confidence in him."

Vee looked at the man's profile and from the set of his goateed jaw had the sense that he had said a little more than he had intended. She didn't pursue it, but he did say as sort of an afterthought, "Your father was – *is* – a great man, lady, a true man of God who would never compromise his beliefs, and I'm personally going to lead the expedition to free him."

"So there's going to be an expedition to free him."

He looked at her. "Hell yeah, there is. You think we're going to just leave him there? You're going to show us where he is, of course."

"Of course...yeah. Of course."

At last they reached the mammoth machine, and outside its entrance were posted four guards, two to a side, standing as still and unblinking as statues. Besides carrying terrestrial-patterned assault rifles, the white-robed guards each had a sword with a long straight blade sheathed on their belts. But what was remarkable about them was their identical appearance: androgynous, with white-blond hair and eyes even more vividly blue than Vee's. Their flesh was so eerily white it faintly glowed. It was obvious they weren't human beings.

When Vee and Roper had passed inside uncontested, she stopped to look back at the things through the threshold. "What?" Roper said. "You don't remember Celestials, either?"

"I remember Jay...um, my Demon gun said something about them."

"They're beings that were created to serve us Angels in Heaven, but they're the equivalent of Demons in that they don't have souls. Therefore, they're not immortal. Gazillions of them were sent into Hades to fight in the Great Conflict, and they can fight like a bastard, but the ones that made it into Tartarus haven't fared well over time because like I say, they can be killed, and they were at a disadvantage here in the devils' playground even though the Demons can be killed, too. So their numbers have decreased a lot over time. Still, we got a barracks of them here, and Johnston uses them as his personal bodyguard. They're pretty much just robots, so I guess he likes that they never question his policies."

Once again Vee had the impression that Roper was betraying some personal bitterness, but he left it at that and led her further into the machine.

Vee soon realized its ground floor served as a place of worship. Before following her guide to the stairs that would take them up to the colony's administrative offices – Johnston's in particular – she glanced into a great chamber in which long metal benches had been bolted to the floor as pews, the walls and high ceiling still bulky with servos, pistons, hydraulic and pneumatic mechanisms. A huge cross, sans body, formed of two riveted girders hung suspended from chains above the altar. Vee didn't want to guess at the source of the many burning candles, but couldn't help but suspect human tallow.

Two more Celestials flanked the Pastor's office door. They stared straight ahead as if they didn't even see Roper, but he gave them a polite nod before knocking on the gleaming metal door.

A voice on the other side invited them to enter.

16: The Pastor

Pastor Jacob Johnston rose from behind a desk of black iron, on which perched a baroque computer resting on little wheels, that he had pushed out of his way for the time being. As opposed to so many of his male citizens, Johnston had a full head of hair, neatly cut and brushed back from a broad forehead, as white as his grin of strong teeth. He spread his arms, and in his white smock with its cowl hanging down his back he looked like he was encompassing his flock for a sermon, but Vee realized he meant to embrace her. She decided it was best not to resist the gesture. Fortunately, it was a brief one. Holding her away from him by the elbows, in a resonant voice the Pastor said, "Oh Rebecca, tell me it's not true you don't remember who I am."

"They tell me you were friends with my father," she said blandly.

Johnston shook his head sadly, let go of her arms and said to Roper, "Thank you, Charles; if you would wait outside."

Vee looked back at her escort, and had the impression that he was unhappy about being so dismissed. Roper left Johnston's office with a brief glance at the only other person present in the room – a tall man with bright red hair styled like Johnston's, with the same broad forehead but a decidedly more solemn expression. This man wore a gun on the belt that cinched his cloak. With the door now closed behind Roper, Johnston gestured to the red-haired man and said, "You must not remember my son Fred, then."

"Sorry, no. Nice to meet you, Fred."

Fred only nodded, and remained standing by one wall as Johnston reseated himself.

"Fred commands my personal unit of Celestial bodyguards," Johnston explained. "Please." He indicated for her to take a seat opposite his desk, which she did. "Something to drink? Are you hungry?"

"Not hungry, thanks. I'm fine."

The Pastor knotted his hands atop his desk as if to offer an opening prayer. "Rebecca, Rebecca," he sighed. He took her in – the limp hair framing her pallid face, those intense blue eyes – and said, "I hate to say it, but you look like you've been through Hell."

"Hardy-har," she said.

"Sorry, I know that your reception here was less than pleasant, and I know indignity is harder to forget than pain, but I hope you'll forgive Charles and his men. There are many, many hostile people out there we must keep at bay."

"I understand."

Johnston's creased smile deepened. "You may have forgotten

much, Rebecca, but it looks to me like you're the same scrappy girl I remember. I'm told you gave Charles quite a fight. You were pretty formidable in your father's army, I'll tell you that. A lot of us called you the 'Demon Hunter.' When we were still settling in here on Level 7, you and your father either separately or together would lead excursions into the levels above and below, to hunt and exterminate as many Demons as you could, to make our position more secure. You don't recall any of that?"

"No."

Finally the man's smile receded as his face's creases shifted to his brow in concern. "And how do you account for your memory loss?"

"I don't know," she said in her subdued tone. "Too much time alone with myself? Too much self-disgust?"

"Self-disgust? Why would you be disgusted with yourself?"

"Well, logic dictates that I should keep my opinions to myself, but I have to admit I'm not thrilled with a lot of what I'm seeing around here in your town."

"Such as?"

"Pussy posses?"

Johnston's smile returned faintly. "And who called them that?"

"My ex, Tim Wade."

"Ah. Well, an unfortunate expression to describe a very serious and important endeavor to find the men of our colony mates, and to redeem Damned souls. Forgive Tim – he remembers you as you were, a young woman with a spark in her eyes, a sense of fun, who might not have objected to some of the things that bother you in your state of forgetfulness. So what else here troubles you?"

"Your livestock. Living in their pens like that. How many times have those same individuals been eaten, again and again? I wonder if Tim ate his wife Miranda a couple hundred times before he married her."

"You're not jealous, are you?" Johnston teased.

Vee made an ugly sound, something like a laugh. "Hardly."

"Well, yes, our meat source..."

"Does it make it easier to eat them if they're primitive? Or did I miss the cage of atheists?"

Johnston sighed and leaned forward over his hands. "Rebecca, let me tell you a few things about myself. When I volunteered to lead my own division of Angelic troops into Hades, to help battle the rebellious Demons and Damned, I had a furnace for righteous bloodshed burning in my guts. But our situation, being trapped here, required a redirection of our energies; made us have to slow down, take deep breaths, and look to creating as comfortable a future for ourselves as we could manage here – in the hopes that someday, somehow, our Creator will liberate us from this trial. The long years – and God only knows how many they've truly been, but we estimate over two thousand – have not, *can* not age me, of course, and yet I feel I have evolved with time, grown wiser. There are always going to be critics in any society, large or small, and my critics have interpreted this as becoming too mellow, too weak..."

Johnston was interrupted by an odd event. There were massive clockwork gears set into the walls of his office, and suddenly these began to turn. A green fluid that looked to Vee like antifreeze gushed through a thick, transparent plastic pipe that ran across the ceiling. Then, the building reverberated with a deep gong that sent vibrations through Vee's body. Another gong followed, and another...

"What's that?" she asked.

"Is it noon already?" Johnston said. "We made the church into one big cuckoo clock – our attempt to keep track of the time, or at least to organize our days. And as I say, there are those who would call me the cuckoo who lives in it. You see, as time went on here in Los Angeles and our men pined for their women, we saw the advent of homosexuality, and I realized we were living like prisoners, becoming perverted and dispirited. That was when I decided to allow the Damned to be pardoned and converted through baptism into our church, and many men took Damned for their wives. It was a great boost to morale, and our city flourished as a result. But there were still many who rejected this idea and saw it as a dangerous compromise. They refuse to take the Damned for their wives, or accept them as converted, their position being that the Creator Damned them and thus they are irredeemable. But am I not a man of God; does He not act through me?"

The gong sound had stopped, as had the movement of the gears, though Vee still felt the echoes of the vibrations in her chest. She had indeed counted twelve of them. She continued to listen patiently to the Pastor as if he were counseling a troubled soul.

"Despite my reforms, for countless years I resisted the temptation to take a Damned wife myself, because my dear wife Abigail was left behind waiting for me in Heaven. But...finally I did so, not all that long ago. And I tell you, Rebecca, it was like I entered a whole new phase of my evolution; I felt my soul soar to a place it hadn't been for a long, long time. My Elizabeth is a wonderful, compassionate soul, despite the misdirection that caused her damnation, and she has taught me to be a more compassionate soul, as well. I have been trying to open up my parish to more new ideas, to take us out of stagnation into a more enlightened future of greater opportunities. Which takes us back to your question about our eating habits."

Vee grunted to encourage him to continue.

In a lower, confidential tone the Pastor aid, "Rebecca, my wife has helped me to see the wrongness of consuming this source of meat, too, and I no longer do so. I have tried putting greater effort into our farming projects, but I tell you, our people crave flesh, and so it has been discouraging for me. In a former Damned city like Oblivion, before the Great Conflict, I understand that the citizens would sell their own bodies as meat for money. But the citizens here will not subject themselves to that pain and humiliation, when there are what they feel to be lesser beings for consumption."

"You said money. In Hell?"

"Oh yes, and we have our own currency here in Los Angeles, too. Religion and money are the sturdiest foundations of society, Rebecca."

Vee didn't know if Johnston were speaking ironically, or with conviction.

He continued. "In search of a solution to this issue of cannibalism, I even had a number of Demons of various species captured, with the thought of harvesting their meat instead, but the citizens overwhelmingly refused to try Demonic flesh. The same goes for my efforts to have palatable raw matter composed by some of the equipment that was

70

once used to mass produce Demons, hoping that without having to see a Demonic body in their mind's eye the people would be willing to try it, but again my idea was met with almost unanimous rejection. These attempts to turn our people away from eating these poor Damned souls have only increased the criticism I suffer, and so to remain an effective leader I've had to give in to the will of the people on this issue." Johnston spread his hands open in a gesture of helplessness.

Vee conceded begrudgingly, "Well, at least you've tried. But you shouldn't stop trying."

Johnston cocked his head and narrowed his eyes at the woman opposite him, obviously taking another measure of her. "You might still be a scrapper, but you're far from the girl I remember, after all. You were once as fervent as the strongest of my critics – as fervent as your father, who was against the idea of exonerating the Damned. Poor Karl would never have approved of my taking a Damned woman for a wife. No, that would be unthinkable to him."

"But you two were great friends, I hear."

"Yes, of course, but we did have our areas of disagreement, to be sure."

Vee pointed to the computer on the Pastor's sizable desk. "Do you access the Mesh?"

Johnston looked to the device, smiled, and said, "Yes, I do, Rebecca. In fact..." He rose enough from his chair to turn around and part the neat line of hair at the base of his neck, revealing a small orifice lined with a black rubber collar. Sitting back down again, he said, "I've had myself jacked, so I can interface with the Mesh directly. We have some very talented Demon surgeons in captivity, here, and some of us have begun entrusting them to jack us into the Mesh. Again, something that has brought its objections, but we must look to the future, as I say. We must not be content with our safe little life here on Levels 7 and 8 when there is a whole gigantic Construct above and below us still filled with resources we could use, and more importantly, more souls we could save. Do you know there are some Angelic enclaves that have thus far preferred to remain autonomous? Schisms, I suppose you could think of them, some almost hostile to us while others are little

71

more than rumors to us. But I feel we should not stop reaching out to them! And then there are the Damned in their settlements, too."

Vee nodded, her eyes still on the computer. More cables than seemed necessary, or logical, ran into the top and back of the bulky thing, some as thick as her wrist. From the back anyway it looked identical to the machine that she had inadvertently used to awaken Jay, and to unlock the door to escape from her prison.

"For instance, we are aware of one large colony on Level 42, a group who call themselves the Enmeshed..."

"Just how many levels are there in the Construct?" Vee interrupted.

"Oh, we don't know for sure; maybe two hundred or more. Some say three hundred. That's another thing we should address, but which has been met with fearful resistance – more ambitious exploration. Anyway, from what we've gleaned from the Mesh ourselves, the Enmeshed are primarily a group of Damned, but with Demonic members and even a small number of Angels included, who prefer to exist within the Mesh itself."

"Really?" Vee said, interested. It reminded her of what Jay had said, about his own preference for existence, contentedly swimming as his albino dolphin avatar.

"It seems that at any given time, about seventy-five percent of the Enmeshed remain within the Mesh, while the rest see to their protection and other needs of the colony, and apparently they rotate positions – guard duty, as it were – every so many time periods. Anyway, I'm using the Mesh as a tool to reach out to these and other people who have access to the system. Of course, if the Enmeshed were to join forces with us they would have to eject the Demons amongst them, but otherwise I myself would welcome them with open arms."

"Have you had any favorable response from them yet?"

"Well, no," Johnston admitted, "but we are aware they've probed us via the Mesh, so I pray that at least some of them are considering us as a means of winning the salvation of their souls. At the very least, I would hope the Angels among them would come down here to us...or help see us safely up there."

Vee nodded again, again conceded, "Well, I see you are thinking in some pretty new directions. But how do you think my father will react to all this if we can free him and bring him back here?"

Johnston smiled and lowered his eyes to his blotter, toying with a writing instrument. "Well, to be honest I don't think he'll be pleased by a lot of what he sees – we'll certainly have some animated discussions, to say the least. Your father is a man of steadfast beliefs, which can be both a positive and a limiting quality...but, what can we do, Rebecca? Now that so many people have already heard he's been discovered, through your arrival here, there's great excitement."

"I guess after all these years stuck here, anything would be exciting."

"Life is always a challenging balance between change and stability, Rebecca."

"So it would seem. Well, having been a televangelist, I hope my father will at least appreciate your efforts with the Mesh to some extent."

"Yes, one can only hope." Johnston spread his arms again. "So, you will want to lead our team to where Karl is being held, then, naturally."

"Yes. I guess that's what a good daughter would do."

"Mm. Well, Charles wants to lead the expedition, and from what you told him about the way Karl's body has been refashioned, we'll send a pair of Demon surgeons along to help extricate him. Fred, here, will also go along to protect you, and protect your father on the return journey."

Vee glanced at Johnston's son with something like surprise; he had remained so silent that she had almost forgotten his presence.

"Thanks, Fred," she told him.

Fred only nodded again in return.

Johnston asked, "Do you feel up to taking our team to your father now, or..."

"I guess now's as good a time as any," she told him.

"Well, you and Fred had best be going, then; Charles is waiting to take you."

Vee rose from her chair and started for the door, which Fred had opened for her, but Johnston called her back. "Rebecca, you told Charles your father wasn't in a very good mental state."

Lingering in the doorway, Vee said, "That's right. I'd say he's gone insane. Good luck to your Demon surgeons in extricating him from *that*."

"Well, perhaps he'll recover and recall himself. And I think you may recall yourself in time, too, Rebecca. What do you think?"

"I sure hope not," she said, and then turned and was on her way.

17: *The Demon Wranglers*

Vee was surprised when Roper brought her back to the holding tanks where she had been briefly held, like a specimen pickled in formaldehyde, to find Tim Wade among the team gathered to accompany them. He had an assault rifle cradled in his arms and a big grin on his face, though he hadn't as yet noticed her approach. She was not surprised to see that two purple, winged Demons – one of them probably the same creature she had seen in the neighboring tank when she'd been interred – accompanied the group, knowing these were the surgeons (torturers, actually, Roper had explained) that would help free her father from the form he'd been rendered into. She was, however, shocked to see that one of the Demons had been forced onto hands and knees while Earl, whom she had briefly killed before, in one hand held a chain attached to the tight iron collar the entity wore, while in the other he gripped a pistol that he kept trained on the Demon. A third man, whom she didn't recognize, knelt down behind the Demon, holding onto its folded wings, his pants lowered to reveal white, stubbly buttocks that pulsed as he roughly copulated with the creature, though Vee couldn't be sure if he had entered a vagina, anus, or some other orifice. Without a mouth, the creature made no protest. Even if it had, the sound might have been drowned out by the encouraging shouts from Tim and Earl. The second Demon stood off to one side motionless, the end of its chain secured to the catwalk railing. Both Demons wore cuffs around their wrists, these attached to their collars by another length of chain.

Tim's grin turned to dismay when he saw that the others had arrived – Vee, Roper, Fred Johnston, and two impassive Celestials. Vee didn't know if it was her presence, or that of Roper or Fred, that caused the grin to go out of him. He nudged Earl, who looked over and smiled like a boy caught teasing the family cat. "Johnny," he said to the man violating the Demon, "hey, that's enough, man!"

The young man he addressed looked up, gave a boyish grin of his own, and slipped out of their captive. As he rose and tugged up his white pants, Vee saw the pink indentations on his knees from kneeling on the grated catwalk, and his bobbing erection smeared with a thick white fluid.

Fred Johnston snapped, "You disgraceful, Demon-fornicating morons!"

"Hey, only Johnny was fornicating with the Demon, sir," Earl explained. "You got to forgive him; he was raised on a farm."

Fred hardly looked amused, but Roper couldn't resist a laugh. "Johnny, in life every sheep in Tennessee must have trembled at your name." To Vee, the security commander explained, "Johnny here died back in the Civil War, the Battle of Bull's Gap, 1864. A good ole Confederate boy. And you sure do love those bulls' gaps, don't you, Johnny you sick pup?"

"Sir?" the former rebel soldier said, confused at the pun..

Earl gave the Demon's chain a tug and it moved a little unsteadily as it rose and went to stand by its partner. Vee admired the being's composure, but then the two Demons were not immortal as the Angels were and no doubt wary of being killed.

"I'm going to mention this incident to my father, Charles," Fred said. "I think you should train your men to conduct themselves with a little more dignity, and is this the best team you could assemble to come with us on a mission like this?"

"Well, Fred, Johnny here is one of our best Demon wranglers, and he's also one of my best snipers. Tim is Rebecca's former fiancé, as you no doubt know. And Earl was a tunnel rat in Nam; used to go down there with just a flashlight and a .45. These men might be bad boys, but they're definitely bad asses."

"Yeah, I know, Earl's so good that he got himself killed in one of those tunnels," Fred remarked.

"Hey, sir," Earl spoke up in his own defense, "do you know what the survival rate was for us tunnel rats?"

"No need to get your daddy worked up over this, Fred," Roper said. "Like Earl says, for Johnny we've got to make an exception – this poor inbred rebel doesn't know any better."

"And these other men who were encouraging him?"

"We just couldn't believe he was doing it, sir," Tim said meekly.

Vee had noticed the blatant bulge in the front of Earl's pants. Tim carried his assault rifle low, maybe to hide one of his own. *Fiancé?* she thought. *What was I thinking?*

Johnny retrieved his helmet from where he had set it down and lowered it onto his head. Up close now, Vee noted that the helmets were fashioned from sutured plates of bone, like a second skull. Across the front of his, above the eye holes, Johnny had painted a crude Confederate flag. Earl donned his own, across the front of which he had simply painted REBORN TO KILL.

"We got to let Johnny get out his gay tendencies, anyway," Earl joked, his voice distorted, as he adjusted his helmet's fit.

"Hey," Johnny protested in his own muffled voice, "that thing ain't a man! I don't see no pecker on it."

"Don't see no pussy on it, either."

Vee looked back to the Demon, saw rivulets of white fluid slowly winding down its legs and realized Johnny had created his own orifice with the combat knife he wore on his belt. Both tall Demons were covered in old scars that looked like nicks and gouges, these having healed bright white against their glossy dark skin. The torturers given a taste of their own medicine, she supposed.

"Raping a female Demon would be okay," Vee mumbled, "but let's not rape a male Demon – what a sin."

"It's bestiality, and much worse," Fred fumed. "And we need these things healthy, anyway, so they can help us, not cut up by you lunatics."

"Won't happen again, Fred." Roper slapped him on the arm as he moved past to collect his own gear.

Fred said, "Can we suit up a little faster and be on our way?"

"Where's my gun?" Vee spoke up.

"I got it for you here, ma'am," said Johnny the Demon wrangler. He moved off to one side, returned proffering Jay in both hands.

"Did you try out that critter, too, Johnny?" Earl teased. "You stick your willy in that sweet little mouth?"

"Hell no! This thing ain't sexy like those purple things is." He snorted. "But yeah, I test-fired the thing. I thought maybe it wouldn't let me use it, but looks like it can't stop anybody who wants to trigger it...or trigger itself when it wants to, neither." He passed the short, blocky bone rifle into Vee's hands. "It's a lot of fun."

Vee looked down at the gun and saw its red eye roll to gaze up at her, too. She murmured to it, "Don't worry, Jay, I think you're sexy."

"Thank you, madam," the weapon whispered hoarsely.

"Sure you wouldn't want one of these instead?" Earl asked, showing her his own weapon, inspired by an earthly original. "M16A1, with a thirty round mag," he slapped it, "and a 40mm M203 grenade launcher under the barrel. Very sweet."

"Madam," Jay whispered again, "as a firearm myself, I have amassed some weapons information that has been introduced into the Mesh, and it has been cautioned that the M203 grenade launcher can have a bad firing pin that can cause misfires."

Vee had to smile. "Don't be jealous, Jay," she told him quietly, "I'm not going to trade you in."

"Oh, and here's this, too," Johnny said, handing over her pouch of spare magazines.

"Are we ready to march or *what?*" Fred asked.

"All set, Fred," Roper assured him, picking up a helmet for himself, "all set." Coming close to Earl and Johnny, Vee heard the security commander hiss in a less jovial tone, "Don't you dipshits embarrass me anymore in front of this guy, all right? Let's just do this."

Tim could barely meet Vee's eyes, and covered his head with his own helmet, its front decorated with a cross rendered in gold paint.

Johnny fetched two pouches apparently made of stitched human or Demonic skin, resembling her own, and hung them around the neck of both Demons so that the pouches rested between their folded wings. No doubt, Vee thought, the implements of their diabolic surgeries.

Then, Johnny took the chains of both Demons and gave them a bit of a yank to get the creatures moving. Watching them, Vee again respected the wounded one for bearing its pain so well. Though the Demons didn't regenerate like the Angels and Damned did, they still healed quickly, and she didn't doubt this was a recurring indignity. Should she pity them, though, when their fellows had spent innumerable years torturing *her*?

As the Demons were brought past Fred's Celestial warriors, the two pairs of manufactured organisms seemed to eyeball each other with wariness or restrained hostility, but it was hard for Vee to tell, the eyes of the mute Celestials being so flat and lifeless, and the Demons having no faces but for those golden eyes. She had to agree with Johnny on one thing: the naked Demons, as unearthly as they were, had an hypnotic beauty, particularly in their graceful, androgynous forms. More human-looking though they might be, she found the Celestials more unsettling.

They began their march, and their path took them onto an adjoining catwalk that passed through a threshold and out into the open city itself, which spread dizzily above and below them. A flurry of Essential Matter was falling from on high, like radioactive fallout, and Vee observed that citizens and shopkeepers were almost urgently sweeping it into piles and burning it, as if it were autumn leaves. As if destroying evidence.

18: *The Elevator*

The high catwalk finally led them through another threshold, and the sounds of the bustling city faded behind them. The party had become subdued as they threaded their way through a series of paths like narrow chasms in a mountain range of machinery hulking in the gloom. Occasionally, Roper would wave to white-garbed soldiers perched above. Eventually, they came to one of the colony's entrance points, demarcated by another series of those living severed heads hanging from long chains. She figured it must be the two Demons accompanying them that had capped the necks of the heads for their Angelic captors, to prevent the Damned from regenerating.

"I guess these people didn't merit forgiveness and conversion," she said.

Roper looked back at her. "I wouldn't convert a single one of them if I had my way, lady, but there are those that don't want to be converted anyway. These here might be hardcore Muslims or Buddhists or what have you. Or Satan worshipers."

"Satan," Vee heard Jay scoff.

She lifted him closer to her ear. "What?"

"They still believe in Satan even after all this time in Hades."

"There is no Satan?" Vee couldn't recall anything about this subject.

"No. Take it from a Demon; there never was. No Satan, no Lucifer, no ruler of Hell. Only the Creator. All is His creation – everything is from and of Him."

They slipped between the dangling, forlorn heads, and Vee glanced around herself as they continued on. "This isn't the way I came into your city."

Fred immediately came to a stop. "It isn't? Charles, which way are you taking us? I thought she went over this with you."

"She did, Fred, relax. I'm taking us to the freight elevator; we can take it down to Level 2 and retrace her path to the basement from there. A shortcut. It will save us time and make it easier, dragging these purple people eaters along with us."

"Mm," Fred grunted, sounding dubious.

"Don't worry, I been down in the basement a few times. You have too, as I recall. Weird that we never chanced upon the cells Rebecca and her dad were hidden in before. I remember not long after they disappeared, you took some of your Celestials down there searching for them and never found anything."

"That's right," said the red-haired man grimly, "I didn't." He gestured ahead of them. "Very well, Charles, lead on, if you're sure you know where we're going."

Roper did lead on, a little further, until they came to a blank iron wall guarded by some of his security force, including gun crews manning a pair of mounted .50 caliber machine guns that were trained on the barrier. Roper gave an order, and one of his men peered through

79

a slitted window in the wall until he seemed satisfied that all was well on the other side and gave a thumb's up to another man, who threw a large lever set into the floor. The wall split in the center, proving to be two sliding doors that parted with a loud squealing. Beyond was revealed a capacious elevator shaft, and as Vee watched a wide platform descended into view and then disappeared below. A minute later, an identical platform descended from above and vanished. This was repeated continuously, the platforms apparently spaced along a looping track; certainly, they had to come back up somewhere.

As yet another platform lowered, another lever in the floor was eased forward, slowing the platform's motion until it was brought level with the floor. "Okay," Roper instructed, starting forward, "all aboard! Stop us at Level 2, Jim."

"Gotcha, sir," said the soldier manning the levers.

Roper, Tim, Earl, Johnny and the two Demons, Fred and the two Celestials, and Vee all stepped onto the platform with its strong mesh floor, with plenty of room to spare. Jim at the controls got the nod from Roper, and the lever was thrown to allow the track to continue sending its chain of platforms down toward the lower levels.

"We have to be careful with the elevator," Roper told Vee, "because we aren't the only ones that use it, but not every floor has the mechanism we have to slow it down and stop it."

"It doesn't go straight down to the basement level?"

"It does, but there are unfriendlies in the vicinity at Level 1 and the basement. Better to go on foot from Level 2, like I say."

The men held their guns warily, so Vee did as well. The entrances to Levels 6 and 5 were sealed behind more iron doors, labeled with those levels' numbers, but 4 when it came level was open, stretching away into darkness upon darkness. They heard an uncanny howling, and Vee wasn't sure whether it was human or Demonic, a cry of pain or a call to fellow beings. She thought she saw movement back there in the unlit depths but couldn't be sure, and was relieved when the level and its echoing howls were lost above her.

Vee stood apart from the others, and with his helmet off Roper shifted closer to her. In a low voice masked by the elevator's loud humming, he said, "I just want you to know again, lady, how much I admired your father. We really need him back now more than ever, the way things are going. Fred's dad is getting senile, I think. He's letting that sinful Damned wife of his warp his mind, and dirty what Los Angeles stands for – the principles that sent us to fight in Hades in the first place."

"So you didn't take a Damned wife or lover, then?"

"No way. Never. I took a devout female soldier like yourself as my bride; an Angel. After all these years beside her, I've never given in to temptation, even with all these supposedly saved Damned women around me every day. We have no business claiming to save those who the Creator Himself condemned."

"But there weren't enough female soldiers to go around, were there? And homosexuality was out of the question."

"Prison sex? Yeah, of course."

"So what were the others supposed to do?"

"Be strong."

"Strong like you?"

The elevator jolted to a stop, startling Vee into gripping the double handles of her Demonic weapon more tightly.

"We're here," Roper announced, rescued from their debate.

19: The Well Of Flame

The walls and high ceiling here were webbed with thin gas pipes, which at irregular intervals gave vent to jetting blue flame. Glass globes had been fitted over the nozzles, to diffuse the flame glow as a subaqueous bluish light. The air was filled with a muted hissing, as though all those overlapping pipes might be masses of snakes slithering across the walls.

Ahead of the party, large crates were heaped into small mountains, all of them apparently long emptied of their contents. Some were metal, but most were made from ancient wood, bleached and rotting, constructed at a time when Hades in its possible infinity had still contained innumerable vast jungles and forests. There were signs that people had used some of these crates for habitation, though apparently not for some time.

Front and center, however, what commanded the emerging party's attention were three great hatches set into the floor. The hatches to left and right were closed and apparently sealed, though the hatch in the center was fully open on its massive hinges. The air rippled with heat above it, and a louder and more centralized sound like roaring air issued from it, drowning out the surrounding hissing as they started forward.

Vee flinched and looked back sharply when she heard the elevator resume movement behind her, as up on floor 7 Jim shifted one of his levers again. The platform sank into its cavernous shaft out of sight.

Looking forward again, Vee took note of the idle cranes, chains, and pulleys poised high over the trio of hatches, and there were also several large, ribbed flexible tubes like monstrous segmented worms that she figured could be directed this way or that in order to funnel matter down into the three openings in the floor. Were they incinerators, then, for disposal? Disposal of what? In a factory complex designed to churn out Demons, she wasn't sure she wanted to know.

"I've never seen that cover open before," Fred said, frowning as they drew closer to the hatches. To continue on their way, they had to pass between them.

"I haven't come down here often," Roper said, sounding apprehensive, "but I've never seen it open, either."

Earl and Tim had quickly moved ahead of the others, circling around to the far side of the opening, like the crater of a miniature volcano. Johnny hung back with his leashed Demons, while Fred, Roper, and Vee approached the pit on the near side. The Celestials lingered a little behind Fred, turning their heads slowly this way and that to remain attentive to their surroundings.

"It's like looking up the ass of a rocket ship," Roper remarked, and indeed it was. Vee didn't lean too far over the rim – none of them did, for fear of that rippling heat – but it was plain that fire roared down in the circular shaft, its radiance as intense as the heat.

"Sir!" Earl called from the other side. "You'd better have a look at this."

Roper made his way to join Earl and Tim, with Fred and Vee following. The Celestials remained on the opposite side, still vigilant.

Earl bent down and rose with what looked like a white bed sheet in his hand. It was a robe such as many of the Angels wore, heavily stained with dried, brown blood.

Roper took the robe from him, eying it grimly.

"What is that there?" Fred asked. He stepped closer to the raised collar that was the rim of the pit, and knelt down to retrieve an object from the floor. He held it out in his palm for Roper to examine.

The security commander came beside him, and took the object from his hand. It was a small gold crucifix on a thin gold chain. As Roper studied it, the chain slithered through his fingers and the necklace dropped between his feet. "Oops." Fred looked down to where the crucifix had fallen, and that was when Roper threw the bloody robe over Fred's head and upper body. With the man thus blinded and disoriented, Roper then shoved him mightily with both hands on his chest.

Vee's breath caught in her throat as she saw Fred topple backwards over the rim of the pit, and plummet screaming into it.

"Yee-ha!" Earl roared, crouching down a little to brace himself as he fired a grenade from the launcher under the barrel of his M16.

The Celestials were just bringing their own weapons to bear, ready to strafe Roper, when the grenade exploded against one of them directly. The faintly luminous entity was decimated, and its partner was near enough to be thrown down, too. Before the being could regain its feet, Tim and Johnny hammered it with gunfire, Tim with a long automatic burst from his assault rifle and Johnny with a flurry of shots from a handgun. The Celestial let out a horrible cry, the only sound Vee had heard from any of them, something like the high-pitched scream of a hawk, before its much-torn body went still beside the pulped mass that had been its comrade.

Vee had crouched low, too, and brought her own gun up for action, though she flicked its blunt barrel from Earl and Tim to Johnny in confusion, not sure what might happen next, barely sure of what had happened already. The thunderclap of the grenade's detonation made it feel like her ears had been boxed.

"Quick, Tim, the hatch!" Roper shouted. As Tim and Earl darted toward the hinged portion of the open cover, Roper swung toward Vee and held up both his hands. "Whoa, Rebecca, be cool, now...nobody's going to hurt you. This was done for your benefit, believe me."

"My benefit?" she said, pointing Jay at him.

"Easy now." Roper reached down, picked up the necklace he had purposely dropped, and looped it around his own neck with a smile. "I'm glad some Damned didn't come along and find this – I would have missed it."

"You planted it here. And the robe. So whose blood?"

"A little visit to the slaughterhouse, for that."

Vee had missed what Tim – a mechanic, she recalled – had done, but the hatch started into motion, rising and then descending slowly over the circular pit.

"Wait, the Celestials. Them, too," Roper said. "They can't regenerate, but let's clean up the evidence anyway."

Earl hurried to the one he had blown apart, and laughed, "I'm not gonna scoop up every damn bit of him, so this'll have to do." He dragged the ragged remains of the being by one arm, the other missing, as was everything below its ribs. He then slung the slack, tattered mannikin over the rim. Tim paused the cover from falling while Earl retrieved the other body, which was more intact but left a wide, long swath of blood across the floor as he dragged it to the incinerator – or cremator, in this case. The second Celestial was heaved over the side, and then Tim restarted the hatch's descent. It thudded into place, and there was the clunk of a lock clamping down.

"Do you know why we did this, Rebecca?" Roper asked her. "Why it was done for you – and your father?"

"I think I do," she said, lowering her bone gun gradually but keeping both fists on it. "In Johnston's office I saw a computer identical to the one outside the cell I was held in. I could tell my jailers used to have two computers, but somebody had taken one. And I told you I found a few Demon skeletons. One of them had its head split open – I'm guessing by a Celestial's sword."

"Bright girl, bright girl." Roper smiled. "So you were already getting the picture. I don't know if Fred meant to do the rest of us any harm today, to prevent your Dad from being freed – do him harm, too, or maybe move him to a new location. Maybe he only wanted to keep an eye on the proceedings, but I didn't want to take any chances."

"Fred and his Celestials put me and my father there in the first place, didn't they? Because my father and Johnston were at odds over how L.A. should be run."

"That early on, Johnston wasn't too radical," Roper said, "but I think your dad saw it coming, and he wanted to run L.A. his way, sure. I don't think Johnston went so far as to partner up with the Demons that held you. I do think, though, that he set you up somehow. Then later, either right away or after some time had passed, to ensure that your dad wouldn't be freed, he had Fred go looking for where the Demons had taken him, and Fred and his goons killed them."

"Aside from my father the other cells are empty, but I thought you said there was a team of soldiers with us."

"Maybe the Demons took them to another facility, or Johnston paid them off in advance and they relocated to another level." Roper gestured to the central hatch. "Or maybe they ended up in the furnace."

"Is Fred dead, then?"

"'Freddie's dead,'" Earl began to sing inside his helmet, nudging Tim, "'that's what I said!'"

"We can't be killed, you know that. But with him trapped down there, his soul can't regenerate. That's why we have to keep a lid on it, though – if so much as an ash floated out of there, he could regrow. That's why I had to make sure not to leave a drop of his blood up here, either."

"And what are you going to do now, go back to L.A. and tell Johnston what you did?"

"Hell no. For now, the story will be that we got ambushed by Demons, who dragged Fred off we don't know where. But before we go back to L.A., we're going to continue on and free your dad. He can decide what he wants to do – try to overthrow Johnston altogether, or just talk some sense into him and rein him in. But either way, that crazy man has got to be stopped and I know your dad will feel the same. With Fred out of the way it will be easier; I'll assume command of his Celestial troops myself."

"So you knew it was Johnston behind this all along?"

"Well, some of us suspected it a long time, but we couldn't prove it and we couldn't find you two. But when you came and found us, and told us where to find your dad, well...I knew it was time to act at last. So let's do this, lady. Let's go free your dad, and make L.A. what he intended it to be, and you can resume your role right there by his side."

Tim spoke up, "Sorry we didn't let you know what we were up to, Rebecca, but we didn't want to make you nervous or something, where you're still trying to remember your past and all."

"Thanks for your consideration, Tim. Not knowing your plan sure made it easier seeing you guys murder Fred and those Celestials."

Roper said, "We did *not* murder Fred...he's just, sort of a prisoner right now. Like he did to *you*, remember? He can always be released in the future. Lady, come on, we're on the same side here, don't forget."

"Rebecca," Tim said, stepping toward her, his eyes looking earnest in the goggles of his helmet, "I want you and me to start over again. If you'll come back to me, I swear I'll give up both Danielle and Miranda and make myself clean again, like Charles."

"Give up your harem? Wow. Hey, and then when my daddy is king of L.A., and I'm his princess, you can be the prince, huh?"

"Geez, Rebecca, how can you say that? I never stopped loving you, and once upon a time you loved me, too. If you could before, you can again, if you'll only give it a chance."

"Tim, you're an absolute stranger to me. I'm a stranger to myself."

"You're a stranger to me, too, these days," Roper said, "but I know you need more time. Let's continue this conversation later, people; I want to get to Pastor Phelps as soon as we can. Right?" Replacing his own helmet, he started around the curve of the closed pit toward Vee, and gestured for Earl and Tim to come along, too.

Vee glanced over at Johnny, beside the Demons. He had returned his pistol to its holster. Good. She turned back to Roper, quickly lifted Jay to eye level so she could sight along the shallow channel grooved into his upper surface, and started spraying bone bullets.

She had learned from her first encounter with Roper and his men to take into account the ballistic vests they wore, so she went for Roper's groin and upper legs. His thighs riddled, blood spurting heavily from a torn femoral artery, Roper dropped backwards, clearing the way for her to shoot Tim and Earl next. She fired short bursts toward their legs, then as they fell switched to their heads, remembering how the sutured plates in Earl's helmet had come open when she'd killed him the first time. As the men went down, however, it appeared that both their helmets remained intact.

Vee spun and opened up on Johnny just as he had fumbled his pistol out of its holster again. The Demons flinched away from him, but then seemed to understand that Vee did not intend to shoot them, too. With Johnny howling, thrashing on the floor, Vee returned her attention to the other three men, striding quickly toward where they lay screaming and squirming in their own leaking blood.

Roper tried to sit up and bring his assault rifle into play, but Vee kicked it aside, extended Jay and shot him through his neck where it was exposed beneath the edge of his helmet. She then moved on to Earl, and kicked him under the chin to dislodge his helmet. He looked up at her with one wide eye, the other already a raw empty socket from a bullet that had shattered a goggle lens. She discharged Jay into his upturned face, so that when he flopped onto his back his countenance looked more like a mass of pastrami.

Tim had pulled off his own helmet, maybe to let her see his once familiar face, and tears of pain streamed from his eyes. "No, Rebecca, please, don't do this! I love –"

"Nothing personal, Tim," she assured him, as she sent a dozen rounds into his face. He went limp, too. It would take a while for him and the others to regenerate, by which time she hoped to be far from here.

She collected the assault rifles from the men and dropped them into an open crate. Their pistols went in next, though she kept one of these – a 9mm M9 Beretta – and slipped some extra magazines for it into her pouch. She also found a pair of M67 hand grenades on Earl, spherical and green like some deadly fruit, and decided to take these despite reservations about using them. She just hoped her former self's instincts would stand her in good stead if need be.

Confident now that she wouldn't be shot in the back, she walked over to where Johnny lay writhing.

"*Ahh!*" he wailed. "You shot my balls off, you bitch!" He was cupping his groin with both hands. "I'll kill you! I'll kill you!"

"Been there, done that, you stupid Demon-fornicating fuck."

The winged Demons stood motionless, having chanced no attempt to flee despite the fact that Johnny had let go of their chains. Stooping down, with one hand Vee removed the Demon wrangler's helmet. He spat a wad of blood in her face. She pressed the muzzle of the Beretta under his chin and a chunk of skull hinged with skin flipped open at the top of his head, like a miniature version of the incinerator hatches.

Vee patted him down, in a zippered pocket in one leg of his pants discovered a key ring. She took this, and the Ka-Bar combat knife he had used to open up the wounded Demon, buckling its sheath to a strap on the outside of her right leg.

Vee faced the Demons, keys in hand. She jingled them meaningfully, and then moved in uncomfortably close in order to unlock their collars. They held still for her, golden eyes unblinking and unfathomable, as she tried several keys with trembling hands before finding the right one. She unlatched their collars, dropped them to the ground, and then selected another key as the entities held their wrists out in front of them.

As she unlocked the manacles around their wrists, she spoke to them. "This doesn't mean we're friends. Your kind tortured me in ways I don't want to ever remember. But I don't want you freeing my father. Understand? I want you to go as far away from these people as you can. But I'm sure you want that, too."

Now freed, the tall Demons regarded her enigmatically for only a moment more before they turned and sprang away toward the maze of stacked crates, ever silent, surprising Vee by dropping down on all fours and bounding with the grace of big cats. She supposed she could have simply killed them, to prevent them from being recaptured and used to liberate her father. Was it sympathy after all, and was it wise to allow such weakness in such a hostile world? She hoped the creatures wouldn't make her regret her actions later.

"Rebecca," a coarsened, wet voice blurted behind her.

Vee saw that Roper had gotten his own helmet off, and propped himself up on one elbow while he clamped the side of his neck to control the bleeding. His white uniform was almost entirely soaked crimson from his multiple wounds, his face blanched but quivering with the strain of self control.

"Are you fucking crazy? Why did you do this?"

"I'm sorry, Charles," she told him. "I won't stop you from looking for my father and freeing him, but I won't be a party to it, either."

"But *why?*"

"I'm not who I was," was all she'd say. She started moving toward the labyrinth of boxes, in the direction the Demons had taken.

"Lady," Roper rasped again. She looked back at him, and he said, "You keep this up and pretty soon you won't have a friend in Hell."

Vee patted Jay's polished bone form. "I got all the friends I need right here." Then she too sprang away and trotted off into the shadows.

20: The Pursuit

As Vee wove her way through the canyons of piled crates, she half expected the loosed Demons to spring out at her from around a corner and do what Demons were supposed to do. But then she remembered Jay – not that she could expect every Demon to be like Jay.

No Demons, but she did see a number of furtive figures – Damned, no doubt – peeking down at her from atop the castles of crates. So this warehouse area wasn't entirely untenanted after all. The further she jogged, however, anxious to put as much distance between herself and the Angels as she could before they were able to pursue her, if pursue her they intended, the more she saw signs that there had been some intense fighting here in the past. The crates began to show bullet holes, and then appeared blackened with soot. At last, she found that a great many boxes had caught fire and been reduced to an expanse of black cinders, punctuated here and there by scorched metal boxes and drums, ash billowing up under her tramping feet.

Now there appeared great conveyor belts – none of them operating – that slanted down from openings in the sky-high ceiling, and others that angled up from below, to connect with horizontal belts of steel rollers. A number of these conveyors passed straight through this level, from ceiling to floor, or vice versa, without even stopping here. Rusted hand trolleys waited to load or unload whatever materials had once been stored here.

A sound caused Vee to freeze, startled, and she looked back over her shoulder. At first, she thought the cry had come from the direction of the elevator, but when it came again – somewhat closer this time – she realized it originated from the level above. Something that was approaching one of the openings through which conveyors descended to this level.

The cry had been like the high-pitched scream of a hawk.

"Shit," Vee hissed.

"We'd better be going," Jay advised her.

"You think?" she said, and then she was bolting.

So Fred had sent more of his Celestials to tail the party at a distance. Had Roper's plan to use the elevator as a shortcut delayed their arrival? Had they followed the sounds of gunfire or the piercing cry of pain of their comrade, and were they now calling back to let it know they were coming?

Vee cursed the change in terrain, the charred rubble of wooden boxes offering her little in the way of shelter. She was out in the open here, the destruction spreading to all sides. Then, a chatter of automatic fire, and puffs of ash went up a little to her right in a string. She veered sharply to the left. Another distant rattle, but she couldn't tell how close the projectiles had been to her this time.

Ahead she saw a small cluster of blackened metal drums that might shield her, but she was reluctant to stop fleeing, reluctant to have to face her pursuers. The Celestials forced her hand, however, when bursts from two weapons at once stitched the floor to her left and nipped at her heels like an angry dog. She threw on a last spurt of speed, charged the barrels and vaulted up onto their lids, dropped down on the far side. An instant later, the loud metallic ping of bullets ricocheting off them, or punching right through. Vee tucked in her head to let the worst of the fusillade taper off, and then she popped up with Jay braced over the top of a barrel.

There – still small with distance but ominous, running straight toward her position with what seemed incredible swiftness: a pair of Celestials with automatic weapons in their hands. If they had been wearing robes like the two Roper's team had murdered, they had cast them off in the interest of speed and wore only white loincloths instead.

But not only that; a third Celestial with one of their long-bladed swords in hand had diverged to the right, toward the edge of the burned area, no doubt with the intention of circling around to cut her off from behind. And might there be others, too, that had already branched off to move in on her from multiple directions? She mustn't let them pin her down here.

She squeezed Jay's trigger, sent short streams of bullets toward one of the sprinting Celestials, then shifted and fired at the second figure. To her surprise, given the distance, this one went down hard, rolled like a fallen racehorse in the jagged cinders and ash, struggled to rise again. Its partner never even glanced back at it, and discharged its own weapon on the run. A bullet actually flicked Vee's hair. She sighted on the wounded Celestial and let fly a more prolonged blast, Jay shaking in her hands. The magazine ran empty with a small click, but by then the wounded Celestial had stopped its struggles. Vee ducked back down as bullets clanged against the drums, and rummaged in her pouch with nervous hands for a fresh magazine.

Another barrage of bullets, more sustained than any previously, and she knew that the oncoming Celestial was trying to keep her locked down to give the third (and others?) time to tighten the noose around her. She couldn't allow that. Rather than pop up again as might be expected, she threw herself onto her side and fired from around the curve of the farthest barrel. The Celestial was shockingly closer than she had judged, almost on top of her. But it was to her advantage, as she directed a chain of bullets straight into its bare, bony torso. It kept coming, as if heedless, until it actually crashed against her wall of barrels...and then slumped down into the ash, its eerie blue eyes still open, still glowing, unchanged in death.

Then Vee was up and running again, crossing the carbonized field of debris.

Not far ahead, another of those conveyor ramps angled up toward the ceiling. A decision had to be made. This storage area seemed to go on into infinity; a wall of seared but intact metal crates as big as a freighter's shipping containers was taking form at the far edge of the burnt tract, and who could tell how much more the warehouse extended beyond that? No, Vee decided on the ramp. Again, that instinct for ascension.

Vee hit the conveyor belt without losing momentum, her lungs filled with fire, the muscles in her thighs feeling torn fiber from fiber with her efforts. She found herself panting in gasps, "My body's not real...my body's not real..."

More gunfire; it marched up the incline beside her, outdistanced her a little. A fourth Celestial at least, then...and this one with a gun. On the broad ramp, she felt exposed, and wondered if this had been such a good idea, after all. It was still such a long distance to that opening in the ceiling.

Vee saw the Celestial with the sword coming in from the left, below and ahead of her. She fired as she ran, but missed, and the being was wise enough to swerve under the ramp itself where she couldn't see it for the moment. Gunfire clattered behind her, and this time a bullet struck her left shoulder blade, shattering it like a dinner plate. She cried out, pitched forward onto her front. Grimacing with agony, she rolled onto her back, so much pain coursing down her left arm that she could only hold Jay with her right.

A Celestial with a submachine gun was already racing up the ramp. Its gun shifted slightly and Vee seemed to gaze straight down its oncoming barrel. But she triggered her own gun, singlehanded, and a tight cluster of bone projectiles chiseled away an upper quarter of the Celestial's unnaturally beautiful head. The entity blundered sideways, and plunged over the side of the ramp to crash below.

Vee regained her feet with a long, shaky groan. She almost fell again immediately as she turned, but caught herself and resumed her ascent – though now only managing a drunken half-jog. Blood pulsed from her wound, inside and outside the second skin of her increasingly ventilated black uniform.

Her mind could barely form the question: where was the one with the sword? It had enough trouble just commanding one foot to continue on in front of the other.

She knew she couldn't be killed, but if she continued to accumulate lead like this she thought she'd soon be rattling when she walked, or be too heavy to walk at all.

She twisted to steal a fearful look back down the slope, even this movement excruciating. No, she couldn't be killed, but she sure didn't like pain. And she certainly didn't want to be secreted again in another hidden torture chamber for another millennium or two.

Still, no more Celestials behind her. Had the one armed with only a sword wised up and decided not to be a kamikaze?

Time seemed to stutter along like a scratched and damaged reel of film, missing frames of consciousness. In an almost somnambulistic trance, Vee glanced back to see the trail of blood drops she was leaving; it seemed to dwindle away forever like the dotted line of a desert highway. She faced forward again and lifted her eyes toward the ceiling, her mind sobering considerably when she realized the opening in the ceiling was not that much further, at last. Inspired, she picked up the pace of her jogging despite the thudding vibrations her footfalls sent up into her mending bone.

She was up, and through. The belt ended in a bed of those metal rollers, as did other conveyors that terminated around her, but this level – at least in this vicinity – bore an altogether different type of character. Its walls and floor were composed of a glossy black material like chitin, with the iridescent sheen of oil. The high vaulted ceiling was ribbed, looking like the interior of a cathedral as built within the belly of some fossilized leviathan. There were more of those metal freight cars standing about, rusting, and a deep channel recessed into the floor which contained rails like train tracks. Staggering ahead as she got her bearings, Vee followed the tracks with dazed eyes and saw they disappeared into the again organic-looking mouth of a tunnel.

In the opposite direction the tracks ended at the edge of another elevator shaft, this one even larger than the one that had carried Roper's team downward. Its chain of spaced platforms, however, was *rising* through the body of the Construct rather than descending.

Her attention was called back to the tunnel by odd noises: snuffling and snorting, and then a weird squeal like that of a pig. Vee could now see eyes gazing back at her from the tunnel's maw, shining red with reflected light.

It wasn't a difficult decision, choosing which way to go. Vee started toward the great, open elevator shaft, keeping mindful of those grunts and squeals and multiplying red eyes behind her.

She couldn't tell which of the other openings in the floor the white, phosphorescent figure leapt up from. Vee barely had time enough to turn her head and see the sword with its long straight blade cocked back for descent. She sprang forward, toward the elevator, but not quickly enough: the blade was swung in a whooshing arc, hacking halfway through her neck, scraping her cervical vertebrae.

Stunned, Vee clamped a hand over the wound, as much to keep her head from lolling off its base as to contain the blood that geysered between her fingers. She did not turn and try to fire Jay with her other hand; she thought only of that elevator, the rising platforms... and stumbled onward, legs weakening as her blood fled her body, consciousness threatening to flee along with it.

Vee crumpled, rolled languidly onto her back, Jay too heavy to raise in her fist. She expected to see the Celestial standing over her, drawing back its arm for another blow. A blow to finish the job, and then it could bag her head as a living trophy and take it back to Pastor Johnston to do with as he pleased.

What she saw, though, was the Celestial being dragged backward by four arms, the arms of two tall figures with skin the color of eggplant. One of the bat-winged beings had seized the wrist of the arm that wielded the sword, and the Heavenly warrior's other arm, as well. The second figure had grabbed a fistful of hair, jerked the Celestial's head back, and was drawing across its throat a bladed instrument like a scalpel.

Vee rolled over again, gathered her legs under her and pushed herself back to her feet, still pressing one hand to the side of her neck, her mouth hanging slack and drooling as if the muscles that controlled it had been severed. She lurched again toward the elevator, reached its edge and almost teetered over the brink while she waited for the next mesh-floored platform to rise. And here it came now, wide enough to carry a house. It came level with the edge of the shaft, and Vee all but threw herself onto it. Again, she fell onto her back, and felt herself being carried upward.

With the help of her clamped hand she was able to lift her head a little, just enough to see the two Demons pulling the Celestial toward the black tunnel, where those strange sounds rose to a slaughterhouse cacophony, hungry lurkers waiting for the butchers to finish their work. A few of these restless Demons stepped close enough to the mouth of the tunnel to be vaguely seen, appearing like bristly black boars walking on hind legs, their wrinkled tusked faces just human enough to be horrifying.

Vee saw the two torturers looking at her over the shoulders of their struggling victim. Two sets of golden eyes in faceless faces, unreadable, locked with her own.

Then the platform carried her up, up, until she could see them no longer. She heard a gurgling cry, like a hawk drowning in its own blood, and then those numerous pig voices in a rumbling, ravenous stampede.

Vee's head fell backward then, hitting the floor, coming half off, her blood dripping down through the mesh and raining far below.

"Madam?" she heard Jay say. "Madam?"

But then she heard no more.

21: The Bridge

A screeching sound brought Vee's dreams to a jarring halt. The dreams, already vague and scattered to begin with, receded behind the barrier of fog from which they had stolen. She opened her eyes.

Her head rested on her bent elbow, and her body lay on its side on strong metal mesh. Raising her head, she saw Jay lying a little away from her, but the gun was face down, on its left side, so that his eye must be staring through the mesh into the blackness below. Why not an eye on both sides of his body, she wondered groggily; wouldn't that be more useful for keeping enemies in view? Not to mention his inability to see straight *ahead* of him. *Great design,* she thought; *not so much Colt as Dolt.* Had he heard her rouse? His organs of sight and speech were obvious, but come to think of it, how the heck did the thing *hear?*

She sat up further, stretched as she looked around her, and remembered with a start that she hadn't laid down for a long nap no matter how refreshed she felt. She was in an elevator, and it had come to a jolting stop. She put a hand to her neck, but the awful wound had entirely healed, though further exploration found her hair caked hard with dried blood. "God, I need to wash my hair," she muttered. How long had she been out?

"Madam?" Jay said against the mesh.

She got to her feet and picked the bone gun up, turned it over so they could see each other. "Who stopped this thing?" she whispered.

"I don't know; it could have been anyone on any of the levels who wants to make use of one of the platforms. Or perhaps the mechanism has jammed on its own."

"What floor are we on?" she asked, looking out at the chamber the platform had come level with. "Shit," she then said, when she saw a floor-to-ceiling number 79 stenciled in white on the wall. "I've been thinking about Level 42."

"Why Level 42?"

"Johnston told me about a group called the Enmeshed. I thought I'd like to have a look at them."

"Ah, the Enmeshed, yes!" The normally laconic gun sounded almost excited. "We can disembark here, then, and search for a way to descend again to that level."

"Yeah, I know – you're anxious to get back into the Mesh, huh? Whatever happened to your curiosity about experiencing the tangible world again, face-to-face?"

"That was before all this shooting."

Vee snorted. "Wasn't that what you were made for?"

"I am aware of the Enmeshed, of course, from my own long submersion in the Mesh. They spend most of their time there, but you would also spend some of your time awake on guard duty. I should think it would be the best of both worlds for you. As I have said, you may find that being in the Mesh is the closest thing to dreaming."

"It sounds like the closest thing to being dead. It's hiding. Maybe in the end it will be the best place I can find to settle, but I'm not ready for that yet."

"You just said you were interested in them."

"Interested. But I'm interested in seeing more than them, too. We've already passed 42, so we continue up. Don't worry, Jay, I haven't forgotten what I promised you, but we have all the time in the underworld, right?"

She thought the Demon actually sighed, but in a patient voice he said, "Well, if you seek to explore aimlessly, we can do that, but if you want to observe another major colony in the levels above, then I might suggest Freetown to you. I'm aware of them, too, from their Mesh presence, though they don't dwell within it as the Enmeshed do."

"Freetown?" To Vee that didn't sound encouraging, despite the name. The only Freetown she knew of was from her mortal existence, one of the things she remembered about the world at large while the details of her own life remained walled up alive, held hostage by her own subconscious. Freetown had been the capital of Sierra Leone, established by freed African slaves. She had recollections of news stories about the descendants of these freed slaves maiming and killing each other with their ubiquitous machetes.

"Freetown is a settlement of Damned and several races of persecuted humanoid Demons, but it would seem there is a minority of Angels that dwell there also."

This sounded a lot more encouraging, but then Los Angeles had Damned, Demons, and Angels commingled, too. Vee's interest was piqued enough for her to want to investigate, but she needed to remain cautious. Hope for the best but expect the worst. "What level are they on?"

"Level 128."

"All right, then, we'll give it a look. We only have 49 levels to go to reach it." Vee looked straight up the vertical black tunnel of the elevator shaft. "We could wait some more to see if this thing starts moving again...but, hm, I'm not crazy about being at someone else's mercy. If this is being done on purpose, say by Charles' men, they might trap us between floors or something to ambush us."

"We're quite some distance removed from Los Angeles by now," Jay reminded her.

"Still...why don't we get off here and go on foot? Like I said, we're in no hurry, right? This being eternity and all."

Vee stepped off the platform, and into another channel through which rails like train tracks had been laid. But the tunnel before them was not like that in which she had glimpsed the boar people, this one being well lit by metal-shaded globes overhead. In addition, its metal walls, crisscrossed by riveted iron beams and struts, bore tall arched windows on either side. Their thick panes, maybe something like Lucite or clear plastic, had discolored to a dark amber color, no doubt from the molten lava that had cooled to solid volcanic rock against them.

They had only taken a few steps forward when Jay remarked, "Ahh, I know where this is, now. This was a bridge connecting the building we are leaving to the Research and Development Tower. The R&D Tower was the tallest single structure in Tartarus – two hundred stories."

"Well, we know the Construct has at least two hundred levels, then."

"I was created in this building, in Organic Weapons Systems. The technicians would trap Damned souls inside similar weapons, too – usually they had been pacifists in life, rendered into weapons so they could suffer from knowing the harm they were inflicting on their brethren. This is the kind of device I believe you first took me for. But I had no prior existence, as I've said, and the Damned weapons had no Mesh access." There was a hint of pride in this latter information.

"That's good, then," Vee said as they crossed what once would have been an elevated, enclosed bridge between titan skyscrapers. "Maybe I can find some more ammo for you, because I'm running low."

"Well, if this is the 79th floor that would have been within the area devoted to the design of infernal animals."

"Oh yeah? Such as?" Vee asked as she stepped over and around what looked like discarded office furniture thrown onto the tracks: chairs, a file cabinet, a metal desk that had been flattened by a passing train or some other such conveyance.

"Anything from creatures the size of earthly elephants, to hunt and attack the Damned – though many such beasts, of course, ended up being used by the Damned as a food source – to blood-drinking insects."

"Ah, right, and those crab things that were nibbling on my father."

"In fact, if memory serves, on Level 79 in particular they developed infernal microorganisms to afflict the Damned with illness."

They had crossed over to the Research and Development Tower now, and the tracks ended at a closed metal shutter again labeled with the number 79. So, their path in this direction was blocked. However, to their right a series of stairs were set into the side of the deep rail channel, leading up to a train platform and a metal door set into the wall. Vee mounted the steps, went to the door and pulled on its latch. It opened with a rusty creak.

"What's this, then?" Vee whispered, peeking tentatively into a corridor beyond.

"These are..."

22: *The Laboratories*

After so many chambers built to Brobdingnagian scale, the corridor that stretched off before them seemed cramped, confined, poorly defensible. Despite how high up in the Construct it was, the hallway had the feel of a passageway in a bunker, its plaster ceiling arched, its walls built of cinder blocks, and all of it painted an institutional green, no doubt providing a soothing environment for the development of new infernal diseases. But the paint on the walls was blistered, and that on the ceiling even more so, hanging down in dense tatters like a canopy of leaves. Set into either wall were more metal doors, heavily corroded, some standing open and others off their hinges. The floor of the corridor was littered with more office furniture and other debris, moldering papers and shreds of the fallen ceiling paint. Widely spaced bulbs lit the corridor, and Vee could see where it intersected with others further ahead.

As she started forward through the layer of rubble and rubbish, she tried to picture what kind of Demon might work in these research labs and offices. Surely nothing as primitive as those boar people, but it couldn't be anything too human – not after the turn of events Jay had described, when the Creator had mandated the elimination of all humanoid Demons because of the sympathy many of them had developed for the plight and rebellion of the Damned. Maybe, she decided, something like those globe-headed administrative beings she had seen in the memories Jay had culled from the Mesh, from that mortal man named Adam.

She peeked into one of the laboratories, deemed it safe, ventured fully inside. This lab, and she was sure the rest, had been ransacked. Computers had been shot up, their screens bullet-riddled, and other apparently torn out of the walls and carried away. Banks of gauges and meters were similarly smashed. In a corner, papers were spread so thickly that Vee suspected they had been used at one time as a bed. There was only one monitor screen still active, larger and maybe made of sturdier stuff, set into a wall. It showed a blizzard of static, but occasionally the snow would clear enough to reveal a black field against which scrolled red text written in Latin.

"There are Mesh ports here," Jay pointed out. "Would you like me to dive in and have a look around, to see if I can access enough of a former blueprint to get us more efficiently to Level 128? If the printer is still working, I can print you out a hard copy map that might be useful even if it is dated."

Vee gave a dry laugh. "If I let you in, I'm afraid you won't come back out again."

"Madam," Jay chided, "if you disconnect me, I have no choice but to reemerge."

"So you say."

"If you'd rather I didn't, then...but I thought it might be of help to you."

Vee found it amusing that she didn't want to hurt the feelings of a Demonic gun. "Okay, whatever, let your little dolphin have a look, then. Where are these ports?"

Jay indicated a socket set below the frame of the large, active monitor on the wall, and Vee pinched the end of his retractable interface cable, drew it out of his body and plugged it into the port. She then swept aside some broken beakers on a work station below the screen and laid the gun down.

Within moments, a huge closeup of Jay's mouth filled the screen – with its full, almost-feminine lips – though it was veiled behind that sizzling static. "I'm in," he said from a speaker, but despite the size of the image his voice was faint, ghostly with remoteness. "I will see what I can find."

"I'll be here."

His mouth faded, leaving only the static though the scrolling Latin text was gone. Vee poked around the room for a few minutes, and then, restless, returned to the hallway, wandered to another open laboratory and ventured inside.

This one was in much the same shape as the last, though there was a unit mounted against a wall that she recognized as an emergency eyewash station. She went to it, bent over it, stepped on a pedal and was rather surprised to see two bubbling jets of water rise above its basin. Vee tasted a little of it, found it rusty but acceptable, and drank ravenously. Finally she straightened, feeling lightheaded and nauseous from having filled her belly so much and so quickly after having trained it to ignore its yearning for sustenance. When the nausea had mostly passed, she bent down over the sink again, but this time to wash her face, which felt like one big scab of dried blood, and her gore-encrusted hair. She wrung this out again and again, until the water she squeezed out of it was clear at last. Slinging her wet hair back from her forehead, she then turned to explore her surroundings further.

A file cabinet lay on its side, papers disgorged from its open drawers.

She knelt down to examine some of them. More Latin, but also text or formulae in characters she didn't recognize as either Arabic or Devanagari, though it resembled these somewhat. As she dropped them to the cluttered floor, a slight breeze against her face caused her to lift her eyes and take note of a ventilation grille behind the cabinet, close to the floor. Stringy, grass-like vegetation had pushed through the slots – vegetation of a leeched white color. Something indigenous that had found its way into the air circulation system, now old and dead, or...a product of Essential Matter?

Vee moved the cabinet a little, stepped over it and hunkered down closer to the grille. Using the edge of her stolen combat knife, she managed to unscrew the grille's four corners, and then pry it out of the wall. The weedy vegetation grown through the slots was torn free, but there was a lot more of it back in there. Not enough to clog the opening, but the growth looked dense along the floor of the shaft. And all of it lacking pigment. Yes, Essential Matter that had blown through the ventilation system, and in accumulating had taken root somehow.

Vee rose, returned the big knife to its sheath, and gasped when she saw a huge eye with a blood red iris staring at her from a computer screen that had silently come to life, despite the bullet hole in its screen. "Shit, Jay!" she cried. "Are you trying to give me a heart attack?"

"Sorry, madam, but you startled me, as well. I didn't expect to find you in here, but it's fortunate that I did. I've found something I think you should be aware of."

"What is it?"

"I'll show you."

23: The Plague Of Locusts

Replacing Jay's eye on the screen was a kind of large, circular pool, more of a gigantic cauldron, Vee decided, its rim raised up a little above a floor of metal mesh, while the bulk of the cauldron's body was below this raised floor. Spaced along the circumference of the pool were maybe thirty or more of the Demons she had seen in the memories of the man named Adam, with their white, grasshopper-like bodies and small bone horns on their heads. They carried long iron pikes, and her first impression was that they were stirring the steaming, yellowish broth that filled the vat. Well, some were stirring, to break up sludge that formed on the surface, but most were jabbing, as if trying to spear fish. Vee furrowed her brow and leaned in closer to the screen.

She started when something like a flayed, horribly maimed seal threw itself out of the cauldron onto the mesh floor, its gelatinous body steaming. Two of the insect Demons speared it simultaneously, and levered their pikes to topple the blob-like form back into the broth. The thing thrashed as it sank – or melted – away.

A thick, quivering scum accumulated around the edge of the pool, though there were also floating islands of this. The pikes broke up the scum near the rim, but the islands were beyond reach, and occasionally the beginnings of living forms would rise up from these mounds, flop and writhe, before tumbling down into the liquid again or being reabsorbed into the general mass.

Vee continued to watch, as through a doorway two more Demons arrived dragging a slight young man between them. He was naked, his head hanging limp, all resistance beaten out of him. He barely seemed to notice as they manhandled him to the edge of the pool, and shoved him over the edge.

His body sank, steam rose up and briefly a flailing arm before it slipped back under.

Acid, Vee realized with horror. And those flopping little desperate attempts at life – they were the souls of the Damned, trying to regenerate, but being prevented by the ring of Demons that guarded the acid bath.

"Fuck *me*," Vee breathed. "So whose memory is this we're seeing?"

Jay's voice from the speaker replied, "This is not a memory; it is a security camera view of events transpiring now, two floors above us."

Vee hissed something that wouldn't even become a word.

Jay went on, "This tub was once probably used to dispose of expired or faulty matter. Later, I'm certain it was used during the campaign to liquidate all the humanoid Demons, beginning with the ones in the process of being grown in this city. Even the humanoid staff of

Tartarus, themselves. But now, it would appear these drones are trying to diminish the ranks of the Damned, either out of revenge or simply because the Damned in their numbers – and being immortal where they are not – pose a continuing threat to them. It could be, too, that they are merely operating on mindless programming."

"It's horrible...it's just too horrible. Please tell me these Damned aren't formed enough to have nerve endings that can feel pain."

"I couldn't say. But their souls are surely in distress."

Vee looked up at the shedding scales of the blistered ceiling. This grand nightmare, only two floors above her head?

"I've got to try to do something," she said, mostly to herself.

"Do something? Do what?" Jay almost sounded shocked, and exasperated. "Do you see how many of these drones there are? It's a hive of them."

"I'm immortal – they're not."

"Don't let it go to your head. They'll throw you in that acid, too, and you'll be an immortal smear on its surface. Don't be foolish, madam. Do you think you can save every beleaguered soul in Hades?"

"How many people are in that soup already? Thousands, maybe? They could've been in there for *centuries* – and those monsters are hunting down and adding more all the time. It has to stop."

"Very well; someday you can lead an army back here to rescue them. But for now..."

"What is it, Jay? Are you afraid of getting killed yourself, or are you afraid I'm going to kill your Demon buddies? I thought you said you have no politics."

"I do not. But that also means I do not subscribe to your politics. I have acquired a rough blueprint we can follow toward the upper levels – Level 128, and Freetown. I suggest we stick to that plan."

Vee glared at the screen again. The bullet hole was positioned over the center of the acid bath like the heart of a whirlpool. A vortex that sucked her in.

"All I need for you to do right now is help me find my way two levels up," she said in a flat voice.

"I am sorry, then. I will not print out the blueprints. I will not share

104

that information. I can not take part in these actions, because they are in no one's best interest. Not the Damned, because you can't possibly do anything for them, not my own, and yes, not these Demons' either. And certainly not in your own best interest. You want me to help you? I will help you find Freetown."

"For fuck's sake," Vee cursed. "I'd like to think you're worried about me, but right now I don't know about you, Jay. You've gotten pretty cocky since I first met you. You were afraid of me then, but you saw me help those two purple Demons back there and now you think I'm soft. Or else it's you who's soft. A cowardly, pacifist gun."

"I am only being logical where you are being impulsive."

"Maybe I liked you better when you were afraid."

"You may like me or dislike me as you please," the Demon said cooly.

"Nobody likes a disobedient gun."

"If a gun is all I am, then you may pull my trigger all you want and I can't stop you, but I don't have to talk with you any longer."

Vee spun away from the screen. "Okay, so don't help me, then. But I'm coming to get you now – and I'll find my own damn way up there."

She strode to the open doorway of the laboratory, stepped out into the corridor, and stopped short only several feet away from a strange white figure, shorter than herself. It whirled in her direction, the pink globes of its eyes luminous. Up close, she saw that the exoskeleton of the locust Demons had a rough, spackled texture, looking oddly more like plaster than glossy chitin.

In one of its four upper limbs, the creature carried a kind of metal truncheon, that it swung at Vee's head viciously, though the creature itself – without any features below those huge eyes – made not a sound.

Vee ducked under the swing. Jay was in the other room, and the Beretta was inside the stitched-skin pouch slung over her shoulder, but the Ka-Bar combat knife was in its sheath on the outside of her leg. Still in a crouch, Vee drew the knife and lunged forward with it, punched the long blade into the creature's thorax. One of the multiple arms seized her hair in its pincers, and another clawed at her cheek, raking her skin deeply, but she pulled the knife out, drove it in again, and again, snarling as she did so. The Demon tried to bring its iron club down on her head, but she blocked its arm with her forearm, stabbed the knife in one last time and then the two of them fell away from each other. Vee dropped back onto her rear, her hands braced behind her, while the mute entity crashed onto its back, kicking crazily with all six limbs until they gradually stilled, gnarled in the air like the fingers of a giant skeletal hand. The pink glow of its eyes faded away, leaving its orbs dark as dead light bulbs.

Vee got up, bent over the thing to retrieve her knife from its mid-section, saw how the overlapping wounds she had inflicted had torn the creature open. Its interior was like the paper layers of a wasp's nest, no viscera – or much of anything, really – inside, though she had obviously inflicted enough damage somehow to kill the insect golem.

Lest the Demon be too soon discovered, Vee sheathed the knife and then took hold of its legs, dragged its scarecrow-light body into the laboratory in which she had left Jay. She then turned to see his Cyclops eye watching her actions from the static-shot screen.

"We had best be going quickly," his distant-sounding voice advised. Was his tone a touch chilly?

"Why?"

His eye was replaced by a security camera shot of a cluttered corridor, two patrolling drone Demons advancing along it, both of them carrying those black submachine guns she had witnessed in the recorded memories Jay had unreeled for her. Jay's voice said, "This is a corridor that adjoins the one directly outside. The drones are headed in this direction. If you move quickly, we can return to the elevator and hope that it's resumed working."

"And if it hasn't?" Vee asked, and then she held her breath, as one of the drones stopped abruptly in the corridor and turned its face up toward the camera that was obviously set close to the ceiling.

The image flicked back to Jay's eye. "Stupid of me," he said. "It noticed that the camera had become active. Really, we need to go."

"Right," Vee said, but she had another idea. She disconnected Jay from the Mesh and let his interface cable snap back into his gun's body.

Then, she darted back into the corridor, but instead of heading toward the bridge that crossed over to what had once been a neighboring building, she plunged into the other laboratory she had investigated. She dropped down to the floor, dragged the fallen file cabinet closer to the ventilation shaft she had uncovered, and then crawled into the shaft itself, through the thick, dry bed of weeds that grew up from its floor. She reached out awkwardly and pulled the file cabinet a bit nearer to the opening, to hide it from a casual observer, and then faced forward again to scurry deeper into the shaft's cramped darkness, its cool breeze stirring up the musty smell of the colorless vegetation she crushed under her palms and knees.

24: The Shafts

She crawled in utter darkness, wincing at the crunching/rustling sound her progress made but there was no avoiding it. Soon she became aware of occasional slithering motions across the tops of her hands that did not seem to be merely tickling stalks of the vegetation. In her head flashed images of the huge red millipedes she had recalled nibbling on Damned imprisoned as flagstones, but Vee had the intuition that these were instead something generated from the Essential Matter, simple creatures like those barnacle-things she had seen, except mobile. She shuddered, but despite her revulsion hoped she wasn't squishing any of the creatures, in case they were indeed something born of the Creator's essence.

The only light that entered the shaft, far-spaced and feeble, came from other ventilation grilles that looked into illuminated rooms. More labs and offices, stripped and trashed, a few even with bright urban-style graffiti on the walls like the "tagging" of youth gangs.

Then the shaft came to a dead end, which Vee discovered by bumping her forehead into a metal wall. She cursed under her breath, thinking she might have to backtrack (and move backwards to achieve this) until a subtle breeze made her realize that a vertical shaft opened above her head. She was able to stand and stretch her back, and stare upwards into the shaft, dimly lit by the light of more grilles. There was no ladder affixed to any of the sides, and the grilles were too widely spaced to use for handholds.

Fortunately the shaft opening was low enough that she was able to climb up into it by bracing her hands and feet against the sides. To gain better purchase, she had removed her tall, heavy boots and crammed them partway into her pouch, or her "pocketbook from Hell," as she now thought of it. Once into the shaft, she braced her back against one side and bare feet against the other, and began pushing herself laboriously upward, this enterprise causing her to grimace and curse more to herself. But again, fortune was on her side that she didn't have to climb up this chimney-like branch of the ventilation system very long before encountering the opening to another horizontal section. She maneuvered into it gratefully, further grateful to find that its floor was devoid of any vegetative growth, cool bare metal alone under her palms.

Progressing forward again, she was able to slide her lower body across the smooth metal plates rather than crawl, and found this caused the plates to creak less under her weight. Again, some of the grilles spaced along either side permitted some degree of light into the shaft. Behind the grates, more of the same: research units emptied or turned upside-down by looters, salvagers, or in the heat of ancient battles.

But one grille she paused to glance through made her recoil sharply, before leaning closer again more stealthily so as to gaze into the room beyond...a room that was neither trashed nor unoccupied.

A figure in a white lab smock sat in a chair in front of a handsome computer with a translucent amber-like casing through which one could view the machine's brass mechanisms, black rubber hoses, and the orange-glowing embers of its circuitry. The figure's form was entirely anthropomorphic, at least appeared so in its smock and the white dress shirt and dark pants it wore underneath, except for the jarring effect of its head. From its white collar sprouted a bouquet of squirming tendrils, black and glistening, as if some kind of sea anemone had been grafted onto a man's neck. But Vee saw that the hands were in keeping with the head: numerous boneless tendrils spread across the computer's brass keys.

More unsettling yet was that another of these beings occupied the room, apparently at rest, though at first she had thought it was dead or the victim of some torture. This figure hung upside-down, bat-like, from a pipe running across the ceiling, the tentacles of its feet coiled around it. Weirdly, its arms were flat against its sides, as if to keep its lab smock from turning inside-out, but the Medusa-like tentacles of the head hung straight down, motionless in sleep, and had swollen perhaps with blood to twice the thickness of those of the seated figure.

Vee heard the plate under her knees buckle a little, and drew back from the grate as a single tendril of the seated figure swiveled in her direction like a periscope. She held her breath, didn't dare move even to withdraw further. After several moments, however, the worm-like appendage relaxed its rigidity and returned to its normal undulations, along with its neighbors.

Vee inched away slowly, slowly, then returned to her sliding advance. Well, now she knew, anyway, that the simple drone Demons were not the masters of this territory, that somehow some of the Research and Development Tower's scientists still survived, still maintained equipment, maybe even continued in their diabolic experimentations.

Further on, the shaft ended in a T, merging with a crosswise shaft. It was like a fork in the road. From the right-hand branch came a cool, pleasant breeze. From the left issued a stink like ammonia that made Vee's eyes sting. Acid fumes, she realized.

"The vat is to the left," Jay told her softly.

Vee had already deduced this, but nevertheless said, "Thank you, Jay."

And though she hadn't been sure she still wanted to find the acid bath – had only been intent on not being found by the Demons' patrols – she took the left-hand branch.

25: The Kitchen Sink

When Vee peered out through the grate, cupping a hand over her nose and mouth against the eye-watering fumes, she realized she was still one level below the rim of the acid bath. The high ceiling of this level was the mesh floor of the one above, with which the lip of the circular cauldron was level. The main body of the vat itself, however, was suspended below this platform. A system of pipes ran down from its belly into the floor, and Vee had the impression of being a mouse inside a cabinet below the kitchen sink. There was even a U bend in the trunk-like central pipe, though she imagined it wasn't to prevent the rising of sewer gas, as with a kitchen sink. Smaller pipes intersected with this major pipe, besides, and she couldn't make sense of any of it. She spied huge valves, and at the base of the central pipe, a control panel of some kind with arrays of lights and pressure gauges. The floor under the huge basin was a quilt of mismatched metal plates, obviously patches to repair damage from slops and spills of the acid from above.

On the high mesh platform, Vee could vaguely see the drone Demons as they silently went about their business, guarding the edge of the unmaking pool and breaking up, with their iron pikes, the primordial ooze that ceaselessly struggled to coalesce and resume the forms of humans.

She took further stock of her surroundings. On this level, beyond the drainage (and replenishment?) pipes, a huge window ran along a nearby wall, but it looked only upon the solidified lava that was flush against it. A ladder was bolted into the same wall, leading up to the mesh platform, but she noted that halfway up there was a small metal hatch set into the wall beside it. Access to a utilities shaft, perhaps?

Vee tested the vent by pressing against it with both palms, but it was screwed into its frame. There was room enough for her to maneuver her body around, and once she had slipped her boots back on, she planted her feet against the grille and pushed. It didn't give. After a few moments of reluctance, she bunched her legs then shot them out, pounding her heels against the grille – one, two, three, four times. She winced with each crash she made. Finally, the screws wrenched free of their sockets and the grille was dislodged. It fell onto the floor outside with a tinny clatter.

Vee peeked out again, up at the platform, but couldn't tell if any of the entities above had taken notice of the sounds far below. She slipped from the shaft, retrieved the grille and pushed it back into its frame as best she could.

She straightened, turned, dashed across the open floor and reached the cluster of plumbing. The fumes were stronger than ever, burning her throat despite her covering hand, her eyes streaming. She leaned close to the control panel, trying to make sense of its switches and knobs.

Jay whispered to her. "If you open a valve, the acid might well drain away somewhere, but then the Damned within it could end up worse off than they are now. They might end up in some other tank from which they will never have a chance to escape."

He had a point. A number of horrible scenarios flashed through her mind. She envisioned a great clot of sludge becoming mired in a narrow stretch of pipeline somewhere, the Damned souls as they sought to regenerate compressed against the confines of the pipe and each other's bodies, reforming just enough to feel pain.

Vee wagged her head at the instrument panel. "Don't they have label guns in Hell?"

"I can't figure it out, either," Jay told her discouragingly. "I tell you, we should go now. We can only make things worse for them... and for us."

"Please let me think," she said.

Vee looked up at the mesh ceiling again, the shadowy indications of the insect Demons. She flashed another scenario: her climbing the ladder to the platform, throwing a grenade or two, then mowing down the remaining drones in a wide crescent of gunfire before they got their bearings. Yet even if she could take out the thirty or so drones surrounding the pool, there were surely many more on this level and maybe the neighboring floors as well.

But her thoughts lingered on the grenades. Two of them in her handbag from Hell...

"Vee!" Jay hissed. "Behind you!"

Vee whirled, saw that someone had entered the large chamber: a tall figure in a long white lab coat and black trousers, and an incongruous mass of writhing black tentacles in place of a head. At first, she feared her clamor had attracted attention after all, but then noticed the scientist carried a clipboard.

She ducked down behind the base of the control panel, but to her dismay the Demon was coming in her direction. Its shoes clicked importantly across the concrete floor, and then upon the layers of overlapping metal plates.

The scientist leaned over the control panel and put a hand of tendrils out to the knobs, and as Vee popped up to its right it wheeled toward her in alarm. She doubted it could cry out, but a Demon of its station surely needed to be able to communicate and she wouldn't put telepathy past it, so she struck as quickly as she could – swinging her combat knife down in an overhead arc directly into the hollow of the jugular notch, above the clavicle. Or, where she would have expected a clavicle to be. Instead, the momentum of her strike carried the blade further, carving downward with no bones to resist or impede it. She split the front of the being open, and it fell back away from her with arms pinwheeling. As it struck the floor, it came apart. It was as if a nest of hundreds of snakes, twined all around each other, had been stuffed into a scarecrow sack of human clothing, and now spilled free. The headless, snake-like forms slithered frantically in all directions, some coming at her either blindly or with mischief in mind. She stomped a number of them and they thrashed wildly in death, while the rest spread out and disappeared into the shadows.

"We'd better be quick," Vee said. She fished a grenade out of her pouch, and quickly surveyed the system of pipes. After jumping up onto the control panel itself, she wedged the grenade between the spokes of a horizontal valve positioned at the area where the thick central pipe broke into its U bend. Then she asked Jay, "You said you know about weapons. How much time do I have once I pull the pin?"

"The M67 grenade has a fuse of 4 point 2 seconds."

"That long, huh?"

"It has a blast radius of 45 feet, but it can throw shrapnel 700 feet."

"It gets better all the time."

A clatter of running feet. Across the room, from the same doorway the scientist had emerged from, came three drone soldiers carrying submachine guns. Even from here, Vee could see the foremost drone's white body was swarming with black snake-like creatures: some of those that had made up the scientist's body.

Vee expected the drones to open fire, but it occurred to her that they were afraid to rupture the pipes. This gave her the seconds she needed to hook her finger in the grenade's pin while she steadied it with her left. When the pin came out, the grenade's safety lever flew off. She let go of the grenade, leaving it there on the valve, jumped down from her perch and bolted toward the ladder fastened to the wall, sprinting for all she was worth.

As she left the shelter of the pipes, the drones let loose with their submachine guns. Bullets whined off the concrete floor, but before the Demons could correct their aim the grenade detonated with an ear-clapping boom.

Vee didn't look back, but drew her head into her shoulders in anticipation of shrapnel whistling into her back. None found her, however, and she launched herself into the air, caught hold of the ladder and began climbing madly.

Vee was well up the rungs when she allowed herself a look behind and below her. What she saw was more dramatic than what she had expected or hoped for, and mesmerized her.

The pipe had burst at a welded join in the U, and acid was gushing from the tear in the metal as the vast basin above emptied, splashing the metal plates below and spreading rapidly outward in every direction. Once past the plates, the acid ate into the concrete floor itself, making it look like Styrofoam being melted by fire. The waves of acid chased the drones as they tried to flee, but their legs began to dissolve right under them and they went down, their bodies disintegrating altogether as they were swept along. The acid slapped up against the nearby walls, making Vee advance a few rungs higher. Where it lapped the walls, the concrete there became deeply pocked as it was eaten into, also. She saw with amazement that the glass of the giant window, too, was rapidly liquefying, looking like a great melting sheet of ice. Before the rising fumes became too much to bear, forcing Vee upward toward the small metal hatch, she saw that even the volcanic rock outside the window, outside the Construct, was being eaten into by the acid that splashed up against it from the force of the cascade.

She hoped that as the acid continued to spread across this level, thinned and eventually evaporated, it would leave behind the human traces it carried in places where they could reconstitute fully. At any rate, she had given those prisoners as much of a chance as she could, and even without Jay prompting her, knew that she could do no more. Especially with the frantic running she heard on the platform above her, the frenzied activity as the drones up there scrambled to investigate the damage that was draining the tank of acid.

Vee climbed the last rungs to the hatch positioned halfway to the ceiling, and almost said a prayer under her breath as she put her hand to its latch, fearing it would be locked. But the hatch opened easily, and she ducked into a low-ceilinged narrow passageway between formal levels, so long it trailed away into darkness. Walls, floor, and ceiling had been formed from sheets of brass but were now crusted a vivid aqua color with verdigris, maybe brought about by long proximity to the acid. Vee plunged forward down this weirdly beautiful tunnel, onward and away.

26: The Unborn

By no means did Vee make the journey upward in a straight line. The Construct – formerly a Demonic megacity – however towering its greatest structures, was wider than it was tall. When Vee couldn't find a more direct route to a higher level, she was often obliged to cover a great deal of ground laterally before finally discovering a viable means of ascent. Thus, she crisscrossed back and forth between the many former buildings of Tartarus, sometimes merely connected by bridge-like walkways, other times the buildings expanded so that they lay flank to flank with each other, or with their separating walls removed altogether. She occasionally encountered single rooms so immense that their far walls lay beyond the extent of her vision, misted with distance, rooms that themselves might contain a small town.

On the 83rd level, Vee encountered a building that she had never

114

been inside before, and which seemed to lie on what would have been the furthermost border of the city. She entered it through a tube-like corridor of black metal, lit by fluorescents, which finally gave ingress into a large round chamber. But it wasn't a mere chamber; Vee stood on a circular mesh platform, and leaned over its railing to gaze below. A circular shaft, burrowing its way downward in a straight shot, a well into darkness. She tipped her head back to look upwards and saw a mirrored effect there, realized she was in the center of a great circular building, inside its hollow core. A metal spiral staircase twined around the inner surface. It wasn't this that gripped Vee's attention, however, but the building's inner surface itself. Apparently, an unbroken tube of thick glass. And beyond the glass?

She stepped up to a section of the curving glass, and furrowed her brow in confusion. Water or some other fluid, certainly, was trapped between the outer and inner walls of this cylindrical tower, and lights spaced along the framework of the spiral staircase cast glaring illumination across the glass. But Vee cupped her hands around her eyes, and pressed her forehead against the cool surface to peer into the murky interior.

It seemed to be a gigantic aquarium, full of weightless organisms, drifting slowly throughout. Countless thousands of organisms. But when she realized what these creatures were, she gasped, and thought that the tower was less an aquarium than it was a titanic specimen bottle.

The constellations of suspended organisms were human embryos and fetuses, of every stage of development; everything from tadpole-like forms to full term babies. They were not connected by umbilical cords, but floated freely in their greenish amniotic solution.

"Jesus," she breathed, wanting to pull away but unable to. "Jesus Christ, Jay, what are these? Tell me they're Demons being grown, human-type Demons..."

"No," he told her. Tucked through the straps of her pouch, he too gazed into the great aquarium. "These are the children of the Damned, who were never born. The Creator felt pity for them, since they never had the opportunity to be baptized, but being the children of sinners or those who themselves were not baptized, they could not be delivered into Paradise. And so, they were confined in these Limbo Towers, spread throughout Hades. Again, it was deemed unfair for pregnant Damned women to carry them eternally – unfair to the children, not the mothers, given the violent hazards and punishments of those mothers in Hades."

"No...you've got to be kidding me. No, Jay, this is too terrible... this is just too terrible!"

"I understand your concern for them, but before you begin thinking about using another grenade to liberate them, madam, you should consider their situation. These creatures will never grow any older than they are, will never grow to adulthood. Where else are they to go? Are they to flop and flounder on the ground like suffocating fish? Here they float through eternity in absolute ignorance and innocence. Could human beings ever attain anything closer to bliss? This is an eternal womb they never need to leave. It's rather like being in the Mesh, I suppose, but they dream of nothing, forever. They're the lucky ones."

"*Lucky?*"

"I'm not trying to justify their condition...only reassure you in your anxiety."

"Reassure me? *Reassure me?*" Vee sobbed these words, realized that tears had filled her eyes. She thumped the heels of her fists against the glass in weak, helpless blows. "Fuck, Jay! Fuck this! Fuck all of this! What kind of sick monster would create something like this and still consider Himself the Father of humankind?"

"A conflicted being, madam. So tormented that He ended His own existence. A being rather like you, I might think."

Vee stepped back from the wall at last, and shifted the gun so they could look at each other directly. "What do you mean, like me?" she demanded.

"You both lost your sense of yourselves. You both grew disgusted with yourselves. You both set about destroying who you were. The Creator, through his self-immolation. And you...through your forgetting. Except that you have been reborn as a new being, in a sense.

Whereas He will never do so. Or so it would seem."

"Maybe I am the Creator, huh?" Vee snapped sarcastically. "Maybe that's who I really am, huh?"

"If in a way He dwelt within each human being, then I suppose in that sense and to that degree, you are."

"Now isn't the time to fuck with me, Jay."

"I'm not doing that, madam. Again, I am only trying to comfort you, while engaging in a stimulating conversation."

"Fuck you."

"I'll try to be helpful in another manner, then," Jay said, coolly unfazed. "We can obviously proceed upward from here."

Vee glanced up again, then moved to the spiral staircase and started to ascend. Around and around the interior of the cylinder, and eventually she saw a huge number 84 deeply etched into the glass itself. She climbed further, at Level 85 came to another platform and connecting corridor that obviously bored its way straight through the aquarium from outside. Resting a moment, she couldn't resist another look inside the tank. A full term baby floated disconcertingly close to her face, though she was sure the glass must actually be over a foot thick.

She asked Jay, "What about the unborn in Heaven, then?"

"Well, there is a choice given. If the mother would prefer it, she can keep her child inside her body forever, so as to retain her maternal bond, but later if she changes her mind she can do what most mothers choose, which is to have their child externalized. But again, since the child can mature no further, its soul remains at the stage of life it had advanced to at the time of its death. Thus, these mothers keep their child in an individual tank, in much the same state these creatures are in, rather like a pet they can talk to, even handle if they care to remove it from its tank for a time."

"Fuck, man," Vee said, her tears drying on her face, replaced with seething disgust, "I think maybe that's even worse than this. Keeping your baby like a pet lizard."

She was about to withdraw from the glass again when she saw the baby by her face open its mouth several times, like a fish. Like it was trying to say something to her. She flinched back in horror. Almost broke into sobs again.

Level 86, engraved into the glass. 87. Another platform. And then, at Level 88, the staircase abruptly ended, though the cylinder continued upward. No more lights spaced up there, though, the cylinder's uppermost level now uncertain. Was the ceiling not far above, or did the tower go on for many levels more? Was this the end of the staircase as designed, or had it been cut away by some group above, to prevent others from entering their territory by this means?

Vee descended again to the platform for Level 87, and entered the corridor there, leaving the heart of the tubular glass Limbo Tower – and hoping never to have to enter it again.

27: The Power Outsource

At Level 90, Vee came upon another large community, this one consisting of the Damned, but at their border the security forces were polite with her and she took the chance of trusting them with her weapons, curious to find out more about them. And also, it appeared she would need to pass through their district if she meant to continue her ascent of the Construct.

The colonists of this city, dubbed Naraka, were almost entirely of Indian descent, most of them having died in the Big Bang, and committed to Hades for being Hindus. When Vee explained she was an Angel her hosts seemed a little dubious about her, and she felt like apologizing to them for their unfair damnation, but they treated her no less politely, and gave her a tour of their domain.

The point at which Vee had entered Naraka had once been a barracks structure for the Damned laborers forced to work in Tartarus. It had a biotic feel, as if the whole former building had been a single growth of glossy gray bone, translucent where it was thinnest. The countless original chambers on this entire floor had been further subdivided by the colonists, though some of these spaces remained immense. Vee's guide, a soft-spoken man named Harvinder, who had explained he was a lead tech and technical instructor, guided her into the largest of the colony's chambers, and her mouth opened in awe as she took it in.

The gray bone walls, from the floor up to the soaring ceiling, were honeycombed with rows of organic-looking recesses, hundreds of tiny apartments more like shelves where the laborers had once rested. Now, each hollow had become a work cubicle, housing a desk and computer. These devices, Harvinder announced proudly, were the colonists' own design, constructed from materials and circuitry that had once served others purposes, linked into servers adapted from Demonic computer systems. Men and women typed diligently, their combined tapping creating an incredible chattering noise like that of the giant insects one might imagine swarming through this hive. Harvinder had to raise his soft voice above the din. Many of the workers wore headphones against it, and to communicate with others she saw that some spoke into microphones. Other workers, though, sat over their keyboards with their hands motionless and eyes vacant, as if dazed, or even slumped back in their chairs as if dozing. A cable ran from the computer terminal of each of these curiously inactive people and plugged into a hole in their right temple. Vee had already noted that Harvinder, and indeed every colonist she had seen, right down to the children, had one of these input jacks grafted into their right temple. The jacked-in workers she saw now, she knew, were interfaced directly with the Mesh.

"What is it you do, here, all of you?" Vee asked, still feeling wonderment at the immensity of the operation. "I mean, I always figured telemarketers were from Hell, but..."

Harvinder smiled. "Basically, it is through us that the Construct continues to function. Many of the people who live in it never realize this, so it is largely a thankless task, but one that must be done. We see to it that the electricity is maintained, the lights, the ventilation systems, the climate controls – indeed, the Mesh itself would not be possible but through our support and maintenance. Nothing would run at all, or at least not for long, and only in isolated sectors."

"Wow. Like you said, I had no idea. Doesn't anyone at all pay you, or trade with you, or something?"

"Well, it is not done entirely for the sake of altruism...mostly we do it to maintain these systems and comforts for our own sakes, but we feel that as long as we're doing it we might as well benefit others, too. But if an enemy were ever to threaten us, we could then shut down the systems in their region, unless they used their own systems to block us. I doubt any other colony in the Construct could challenge us in that way, though – no one else has anything nearly as sophisticated as our network."

"Not even the Enmeshed?"

"No, I would say not even them," Harvinder boasted. He might be quiet and polite, but he was exceedingly proud of his people. "It is because of our benefits to all, and our ability to shut down the life support and power facilities on other levels, that Naraka is almost never threatened by hostile individuals...and never by hostile colonies."

"Wow. That's pretty impressive, Harry." Harvinder had told her he preferred this nickname. He seemed a bit flirty toward her, in his own shy way.

They strolled closer to one of the walls of cubicles, and some of the workers looked down at Vee to smile or nod. They seemed a pleasant and mellow people, and she felt self conscious about her bullet-riddled and torn body suit and unkempt hair.

"You should stay with us," Harvinder told her. "There are a small number of non-Indians here. You would be comfortable."

"It looks comfortable enough. But I've already got it in my head to see Freetown. Do you know about them?"

"Oh yes. We interact with them through the Mesh – they're a friendly colony. But we never go up to visit them in person, because of the Mujahideen, only a few floors above us. And the Freetowners try to keep away from the Mujahideen, as well."

"Who are they?"

Harvinder told her. And then advised her, "So that's why I wouldn't try to reach Freetown, if I were you."

"There's got to be a way for a single person to sneak past them."

"I really don't think it's a good idea," Harvinder reiterated. "They leave us alone, too, but we don't push them. They can't be reasoned with."

"I appreciate the warning. And I will stay here for a while, at least, if you'll have me. Because there's something I want from you, Harry."

"Oh?" he said, smiling with nervous anticipation.

She tapped his right temple with her finger. "I want you to hook me up."

28: The Mesh

Harvinder took Vee to his own, more private and much less noisy office for her first immersion into the Mesh. In its heavy brass casing, thoroughly stained green with verdigris, his computer looked like it could survive a drop off a roof, though it sprouted cables and tubes gurgling fluid like a terminal patient on life support – a Frankenstein monster resembling something cobbled together by high school students in metal shop, or maybe in art class. However suspect its appearance, though, it responded quickly to his deft keystrokes. He sat Vee in his work chair, pulled another chair up beside her. She resisted a smile as he plugged the computer's interface cable into the fresh orifice, like a tiny bullet hole, in her temple, wondering if he found the procedure erotic. She felt no discomfort.

"What am I supposed to do first, in there?"

"I've made an avatar for you, scanned from your own body," he told her. "Try to move about as if you were using your physical body. Explore your environment, but remember that you can also control your environment. It may start out as little more than a void until you call into that space whatever information it is you seek. In order to better focus that information, try to envision some physical medium upon which to project it. A TV screen, a blackboard, the wall of a room familiar to you, or what have you. The Mesh is a very fluid medium, not as structured or predictable as our old Internet, which can make it frustrating and difficult but also very free and exciting in other ways. Don't worry – I will stay right here beside you, and pull you out if I see you're having difficulty."

"Difficulty?"

"Not to worry. I only mean confusion, nervousness, agitation.

I will be monitoring your experience out here, on the screen, seeing through your avatar's eyes. I want to let you get a feel for it yourself, so I won't go with you to hold your hand, and I won't speak to you inside the Mesh unless I absolutely need to guide or prompt or reassure you."

"Um, okay. Whatever. I guess I'll see when I get there."

"Do you have any idea what you might like to start out looking for? Some bit of information you'd like to research, that might have been stored in there by someone from Naraka or Freetown, or by the Enmeshed?"

"Well, hm. Actually, Jay...that is, my gun...showed me some memories he found recorded and stored inside the Mesh, from a Damned man named Adam. Maybe I could see if I can retrieve those same memories on my own, if I concentrate on them."

"Okay, that sounds like a good exercise. Are you ready, then?"

Vee settled back in the chair, gripped its armrests and closed her eyes – maybe a little too tightly, because she heard Harvinder snort in amusement. Then she heard him touch a single key.

And she was in.

If a total absence of everything could be thought of as being "in" anything. Maybe, outside of everything. She stood in a blackness more absolute than closing one's eyes, than having no eyes at all. It was not merely quiet; it was as though a "mute" button prevented even the possibility of sound. And as to having a physical sense of a body, well, maybe...a ghost of physicality. At least, she vaguely felt like she was standing on a surface, not floating in space, so that was something. She willed her avatar to move, willed it to raise its right arm, and maybe it did...maybe...but there were no air molecules to be stirred, to resist the movement, and without seeing her astral limb she couldn't be sure she had succeeded. The same when she ordered her body to turn around and face in another direction. Perhaps it had, but in this environment she couldn't really say.

If in Hades she was already a facsimile of her mortal self, now she was a facsimile of a facsimile, like copies that degrade in quality with each recopying. Was her soul now attenuated to the point where it might just cease to be altogether?

122

A teasing foretaste of panic fluttered through her. She was reminded of being entombed in her cement sarcophagus, utterly helpless, unable to move her body, let alone escape. What if the man who waited and watched outside couldn't pull her back, and she could never get out of this place? What if she were still encased in her stone coffin, had never actually been freed, and all of this was just a dream – just madness?

She willed herself to look up, though she expected up to be no different from down, from the void that surrounded her. She was wrong. Her avatar opened its mouth, and would have gasped in surprise if there had been any air to draw into her lungs, if lungs she had.

Dense constellations of stars filled the high heavens, stars that gleamed and glittered red against the blackness, like millions of tiny rubies dusted across black velvet. A universe of nothing but dying red giants. Myriad stars were moving quickly, as in time lapse photography of a night sky, though some moved in this direction and others in that direction, while others remained stationary. Some so far they were little more than a sparkling dot, while others floated by like glowing hot air balloons. There were those that moved languidly, others that streaked by like meteors. Some met and flashed in silent collisions, or else met and merged into one new star that drifted or shot off in a whole new direction.

Information, she thought. The information that had been introduced into, stored in the Mesh. Moving along pre-programmed orbits, or pushed and pulled, summoned or sent, by the minds of those who were interfaced with the Mesh at this time. The busy, insect-like workers of Naraka. The dreaming Enmeshed. People in who knew how many other colonies, or individual loners like herself.

Was she supposed to swim up there, then, and enter into those currents of information? What next?

Well that was up to her, wasn't it? Had she forgotten about the exercise she herself had chosen for her first venture?

A man named Adam. Waiting for the stomping boots of the bombs to advance on his frail shelter, and to reach his sister, his mother and brother, helplessly removed from him...

Mother. Brother. For the first time in a long while she remembered that she had a mother and brother of her own. In Los Angeles, Tim had told Vee that her mother hadn't accompanied her husband on his holy crusade into Hades, had remained in Paradise – but what of her brother? Maybe her brother had been too young to participate in the crusade, or even disinclined. Vee hoped disinclined. She hoped he was like she was now.

But thoughts of her own family were muddying her focus, and she was afraid she might end up conjuring some unwanted memory of her own instead of recalling the one Jay had screened for her. So she locked down on the name Adam again, concentrated on his fragmented memories. Adam, returning from his studio apartment to the house the bank wanted to foreclose on, hungry for their money even as doomsday loomed. The house where he kept the dog, a beautiful white Akita with a racoon-like mask, because he couldn't have her in his apartment, didn't know what he was to do with her. Adam walking his dog around a shopping center that had never taken off because of the crippled economy, having rented only a handful of its shop space. And then, Adam and so many, many others flushed through the gates of Hell. Prodded along by the drone Demons. But finally, pushed too far after what they had endured already as mortals. Rebelling. Adam leading others away in a new direction. Away toward the city that would ultimately become the Construct.

A sound reached her ears, the first she had perceived here; a distant noise like sawing. It grew, increased rapidly as it neared her. It became the roar of a train, but even as she registered this comparison the train was there beside her, hurtling past, and she rocked back from it. It was a luminous red like the distant streams of information, and looked as much like a ribbed snake skeleton as a train. Were those blurred human figures standing inside it? She had a flash of white faces peering out at her through a framework that glowed like red hot metal. Was it going to stop? Was she supposed to board it, so it could take her to the memory she was seeking to summon?

But the skeletal train never stopped, kept flickering by, until it receded and was gone.

Without any better idea, she started walking in the direction the train had taken, and she believed she was actually experiencing a sense of movement this time. Yes, yes, surely...one foot placed in front of the other, connecting with a solid if unseen floor, conveying her forward.

At last, ahead, the barest suggestion of light. She kept on toward it, increasing her stride, and as the dim light grew so did she begin to hear her own footfalls, muffled at first but finally coming clear.

The light was a mist, but through it she began to discern shapes: the hulking black suggestions of buildings, low and angular, arrayed around her at a remove. She kept on heading toward the nearest of these silhouetted structures. The haze was slowly dissipating, or else she was leaving it behind as she neared the buildings. Details finally started to become available to her avatar's sense of vision.

Brick walls – the bricks new, barely worn. Glass doors. A brick walkway, lined with young trees spaced between mock antique lamp posts, bordering a parking lot that still faded off into the mist. Walking at a more casual, exploratory pace along the brick sidewalk, Vee understood where she had arrived. The shopping plaza where Adam would walk his dog. She had not only downloaded his memory from the information currents, apparently, but entered *into* it.

The plaza was laid out like a little village square, the shops facing inward toward the empty expanse of the parking lot. Not only that, but with their bogus bricked up windows and other clever features, a number of establishments had been designed to look like old mills or factory buildings that had been converted into these shops and markets. Just as the factory buildings of Tartarus had been converted into the miniature universe called the Construct.

Vee approached the long front window of a supermarket, one of the mall's anchor stores, but she couldn't see inside even when she cupped her hands around her eyes close to the glass. Only blackness beyond; the void again. (She had thought she might see others like herself inside, shopping for glowing red information neatly stored on the supermarket's shelves.) The automatic door, when she approached it, wouldn't open. Everything here only a facade then, like a movie set?

She was beginning to turn away from the supermarket's door when a voice behind her said, "You're trespassing here. What do you want?"

She spun around the rest of the way, absurdly expecting to see a security guard or policeman there. What she saw instead was a youngish man with a dog on a leash – a beautiful white Akita with a black, racoon-like mask.

29: The Avatars

The dog looked friendlier than the man, its tongue hanging out and small eyes beaming, and Vee smiled at it. Not that she didn't find the man easy on the eyes; he put her in mind of the actor Kevin Bacon. Or was this avatar taken from that actor or another model, and not the man's actual form? She had viewed his memories through his eyes, and hadn't had the opportunity to see his reflection in a mirror or glass clearly.

"Are you Adam?" she asked.

"Was. People have been calling me *Adamn* for a long time now."

"Ah...right. I heard someone call you that in your memory."

"Heard who? What memory?" he asked warily, maintaining his distance, holding back the dog either to protect Vee – though it didn't seem at all inclined toward attack – or to protect the dog from her.

"Sorry...look, I'm Vee."

"Vee?" She saw his eyes run down and up her avatar's body in its ripped rubber casing distrustfully, though she hoped he found her attractive enough to hear her out.

"Yeah. I was a prisoner of the Demons from the early days of the Construct – almost two thousand years, and I just got free. I found a gun, a sentient Demonic gun that can access the Mesh, and it used your memories to fill me in a little on what had happened, because I was suffering from amnesia. I've gradually remembered the mortal world in full detail, but I don't really remember my own life at all, and –"

"Okay, wait, hold on." Adamn scrunched his face. "How did this sentient gun find my memory recording?"

"I don't know – just Mesh surfing, I guess. Did you record it yourself, or did the Demons pull it out of you, or...?"

"No, I recorded it myself. An experiment of mine. Not the cheeriest stuff I could dredge out of my brain, but they were the last memories before I died and the first since I came here, so I guess they were the most vivid. The easiest stuff for me to get my hands around."

"Why record it at all?"

"Why record anything? Why write books? It's to remind me who I was, and for other people to remember the life they had before. It's part of a project I'm involved in. We never really forget anything, right? Everybody has a photographic memory...it's just that we disregard what isn't immediately important to us. So what we're trying to do is extract the memories of movies we've seen, music we love, books we've read...call them out and record them so others can play them back and enjoy them, too. So they'll never be forgotten. All we've got left of our civilization is in our minds."

"Your dog." She nodded at it. "He's just a memory, too, huh? Not a soul like us?"

"It's a she. And no, you're right...she's not really here." That didn't stop Adamn from bending down to ruffle the fur between the burly animal's shoulders. "She's just a construct I generated. But I really worked on her until I got her just right. It took me centuries to refine her."

"You did a good job. And you made this, too, right?" She gestured at the mall village around them.

"Right. My dog needs a place to do her virtual pee, doesn't she?"

"It's like the holodeck on *Star Trek*, huh?" Vee said.

Finally the man smiled. She liked it – crinkly and unexpected after his leeriness. "You say you don't remember your own life, but you remember *Star Trek*?"

"Yeah. I guess that says a lot about our culture, huh? Or a lot about my life."

Adamn turned away from her, gave the dog's leash a tug to get her moving. Obviously, he was growing less wary of Vee – and obviously, inviting her to fall into step beside him. She did so.

He asked, "Where are you now?"

"In the city Naraka. They just adapted me for the Mesh, so this is my first time inside it."

He glanced over at her, impressed. "Really? Well, you're doing good for a first-timer."

"Thanks. So where are you at now...really?"

The man seemed to regard her for a moment before answering, a little of his wariness returning. "I'm in a city called Freetown."

"*Freetown?* Really? That's where I'm headed."

"You're headed to Freetown? Why?"

"Why? My gun told me about it...it sounds like a good place to settle. Isn't it? From what I understand, you've welcomed all kinds of people there. Damned, Demons, Angels..."

"I'm not saying we haven't, but if you're in Naraka on the 90th floor and you want to get to us on the 128th, you're going to have to get past the Mujahideen."

"I know – they've told me about them."

"It used to be a lot easier for people to get to us, but not anymore, if you're coming from below. They've really locked down their floors and it's a real problem. Every now and then they launch attacks on us, too, so we're always having to watch our borders."

"Well, I guess I'll just have to be extra careful getting past them, huh?"

Adamn looked over at her again, his avatar's face intense with thought, but she couldn't gauge what those thoughts might be. Suspicion? Concern? He looked like he wanted to say more but was restraining himself. Vee had the intuition that he knew a way past these Mujahideen, but was reluctant to share it until he felt her out some more. Was he always this untrusting, or was he just so disconcerted by her intrusion into his private little thinking place?

They had reached the far end of the plaza, and turned to cut across the parking lot toward the opposite line of stores. Out in the center of the lot, though, like an island in an asphalt lake, was a bank with a drive-through window. Vee nodded at it. "Can we stop there for a sec? I've got to hit the ATM."

Adamn snorted. "No need – I'll lend you a few bucks."

"Good. Where can a girl get a coffee around here?"

The dog stopped abruptly in its tracks, and growled. Vee looked down and saw it bunching its muzzle.

"Hey, what's the matter?" Adamn snapped at her, giving her leash a little jerk.

Vee lifted her gaze toward where the computer construct was looking, and hissed, *"Christ."*

Standing in the empty parking lot not too distant from them was an apparition in human form, but made of shimmering static. Again, she thought absurdly of the TV show *Star Trek*, of someone having difficulty being teleported. But then, a few horizontal bands passed through the image and it cleared. Became a life-sized figure standing there in a white robe with its cowl pushed off. An older man, tall and lean, with white hair in a crewcut and deep-set eyes that Vee could see were a startling blue even from here. It was from the eyes that she recognized him. Not so much because she remembered her father from life, but because his eyes resembled her own.

Her father began speaking, though those eyes of his stared away from her and Adamn, off into the mist. Speaking with the resonance of an evangelist.

"I call out to you, who were saved in life. I call out to you, who through our Lord had found the way to Heaven. I call out to you, my blessed brothers and sisters, who proved your commitment to your faith...who followed me and others like me into Hell itself, so that we could squash the unholy devils, squash the sinful Damned, who dared to rise up against Him. I call out to you, who are isolated, alone or in groups, to go forth and find your way to us. Find your way to the City of Angels, on Level 7. We must combine all our forces. We must become strong once more. Because the battles are not yet won! No, the battles are still not finished! We can never grow complacent again! I am freed from my captors, freed from the devils, and I will make them suffer for their crimes and rid this place of them! Together, we can demonstrate to our Father that we have not forsaken our holy task! And when we have fulfilled it, we will be delivered, my brothers and sisters! Returned to the Paradise we came from!"

"Oh my God," Vee breathed.

"Yeah, I know," Adamn snarled. "These assholes in L.A. have been hacking into our systems with this bullshit for a few days now. We keep blocking them, and they keep finding ways around it. But this is the first time they've gotten into my programs. Fuck!"

The specter went on, its voice becoming louder, more impassioned. "I know there are some of you in other cities. You have become frightened, or misguided, and dwell at the side of our enemies. You must turn away from them, brothers and sisters, and remember who you are! You need be afraid no longer! You must return to the bosom of your true family, and redeem yourselves! Stand by *my* side, and together we will avenge ourselves! We have become prisoners of the Tower of Babel itself, but Babylon will fall again! *'Yes, march against Babylon, the land of rebels, a land that I will judge! Pursue, kill, and completely destroy them, as I have commanded you...'*"

"I've got to get back," Adamn told her. "I've got to get this crap out of my program before it does some damage."

" '*...Let the battle cry be heard in the land, a shout of great destruction.'*"

"Insane," Adamn said, wagging his head.

Yes, Vee thought. *He is.*

So, Roper and his team had been able to find her father on their own, based on the information she'd given them, and release him. Return him to Los Angeles. Had Pastor Phelps overthrown Pastor Johnston, then, as Roper had envisioned? She was certain Roper would have told Phelps how Johnston had set him and his daughter up to be ambushed. And what more might Roper have told his leader?

The preacher continued, and even Adamn hadn't yet torn himself away from listening to his rant.

"How true am I to my own convictions, brothers and sisters? How devout is my own faith? The Lord told us, *'He that loveth father or mother more than me, is not worthy of me.'* And children, too...yes, children, too! For I will tell you that even my own daughter, my daughter Rebecca, has succumbed to evil and betrayed me! She left me in monstrous torture, abandoned me to my suffering, while she herself escaped the Demon prison in which we long were held. In the company of her Demonic familiar, she went on to the City of Angels, and lied to the commander of security, telling him she would lead him to rescue me – but instead, attacked the commander and his men viciously so that I might never be found. She did away somehow with the son of my friend, the Pastor Jacob Johnston, perhaps even now in the clutches of the Demons she allied herself with in return for her own freedom..."

"You bastard," Vee muttered. She was speaking more about Roper than her father. Apparently, Phelps hadn't had enough muscle to overthrow Johnston after all, if he was still referring to his former partner as a friend, and so Roper had lied and blamed Vee for Fred Johnston's disappearance. She imagined, though, that Johnston too had had to back off a little, and allow Phelps to resume his place at his side, rather than go against Phelps' supporters and bring about a civil war in their colony. Both former generals resuming their uneasy alliance. So much for the reforms Johnston had envisioned for the City of Angels.

Like the televangelist he'd once been, Pastor Phelps told his Mesh audience, "I urge those of you who would prove your loyalty, as I have, to seek out and capture my daughter Rebecca and return her to me, so that I might mete out the punishment she has earned for her sinful betrayal. I will not rest until I have found her and she has paid for her infidelity. I will not rest until the indignities I and my men have suffered have been avenged, and the son of Pastor Johnston returned to him. I shall go forth myself, with a team of my soldiers, and...and..."

The avatar seemed confused, its eyes flicking madly, and then suddenly the figure was turning, pointing a finger directly at Vee's avatar, its uncanny blue eyes locked on her own. "You!" the phantasm bellowed. *"You!"*

Vee stepped backward, and Adamn turned to her. "He sees you!"

"Rebecca!" the evangelist shouted, starting toward her with determined strides, still pointing.

Adamn's dog was barking, straining at her leash like Cerberus itself, so that he had to hold on with both fists. Through gritted teeth he asked, "Vee, what's going on?"

"He's my father," she said in a hollow voice.

"What? *Him? Pastor Phelps is your father?"*

"Yes."

131

"You didn't tell me. You said your name was Vee."

"I didn't have time! I..."

The wraith was nearly upon them. Adamn let go of the dog's leash – purposely. The 100-pound dog leapt at the evangelist, snarling, and when it connected with him the figure again became a static-filled silhouette before blinking out of existence altogether. The dog stood over the spot where it had vanished, sniffing at the ground.

Adamn turned back to Vee, his eyes full of wariness again. But Vee saw them widen in surprise, a moment before she felt herself blink out of existence.

When she opened her eyes, she saw Harvinder leaning over her, in his right hand the cable he had just unplugged from her temple.

"I'm sorry," he told her, "but I saw what was happening on the monitor. You seemed distressed."

"Distressed." Vee sat up straight in his chair, and touched the center of her head gingerly with her fingertips. "You might say that, Harry."

30: The Products Of Faith

Four entire levels – 97, 98, 99,100 – had been settled by those who called themselves the Mujahideen. Even if Harvinder hadn't told her so in advance, their extremist beliefs would have been evident to Vee right away. Here, her worst expectations of a netherworld were made manifest, and then some. Throughout the colony, the air was a ceaseless cacophony of zealous chants, and the screams of Damned prisoners of other religions being beheaded over and over again, though their bodies were never used as meat, apparently not being "permissible"... of thieves having their hands strapped to boards, and their fingers then chopped off with swords...of young girls having their clitorises ritually excised (though of course they grew back anyway)...of underage brides being beaten and raped by their middle-aged husbands.

Acid that Vee suspected was of the same type used by the drone Demons in their unmaking pool was sprayed on women's faces for the slightest infraction (for ease, men often carried acid squirt guns in holsters) and the women regrew their melted flesh until the next offense. In a ritual of manhood (though they would never grow to be men), twelve-year-old boys were given trussed up Demons both humanoid and inhuman to behead, and not being as adept as the adults, hacked sloppily at stubborn neck bones while the Demons' cries were reduced to the abattoir sounds of squeals, wheezes, and grunts from riven windpipes.

More than a little distressed at finding themselves Damned, these extremists had assumed their women were somehow to blame for their disfavored state, and so every woman on a rotating basis was processed through an automated beheading factory adapted from existing Demonic machinery, in what was essentially mass produced honor killings. By their reckoning of time, the rotating schedule worked out to be monthly, corresponding with the abhorred menstrual cycles of their women's former lives. This ongoing sacrifice might not make their exploded deity take notice and deliver the Mujahideen, but it apparently helped them vent their inexhaustible hatred a tad.

Vee spent many tense days stealing her way through this region, the most threatening she had encountered, darting quickly here, inching slowly there, often lying in wait for hours until the coast was clear to gain a bit more progress. She tried sticking to air ducts and little-used catwalks, the less patrolled passageways, but finally on floor 100 arrived at a point where she saw little chance of continuing unobserved. If Adamn had known a safer, easier way through this turf but hadn't shared it, then she was going to have some words with him when she reached Freetown. *If* she reached Freetown.

She decided the best way to proceed now was openly, but concealed under a burqa, and cursed herself for not thinking of fashioning one for herself back in Naraka. Consequently, she came close to killing a lone woman in a long black burqa whom she watched from a hiding spot. After all, wouldn't the woman regenerate anyway? And why have qualms when this woman might very well turn Vee over to the men if she spotted her? But Vee couldn't bring herself to do it, couldn't be a hypocrite when the suffering she had seen inflicted on women in this colony filled her with more rage and sickness than anything she had felt since reviving from her catatonia.

As luck would have it, she was later able to steal a burqa from a laundry basket instead. This one was a beautiful blue color, patterned in the style of the Afghan *chadri*, with a mesh covering the hole for her eyes. All the better, since her eyes were blue – but then again, the colonists included everything from white-skinned Chechens to dark-skinned Somalis to Asian-eyed Indonesians, all brought together in a brotherhood of faith that had endured from primitive times into the modern world Vee had known, and from that time until now, unchanged in many ways. Though of course, just as with Christianity, Vee was aware that by no means did that faith always manifest in such an extreme form. Still, the Mujahideen's approach to their faith almost made her wish she'd never left the colony of Los Angeles. Almost.

The burqa's loose folds helped her cloak Jay as well, the gun pointed downward, as she navigated through a network of hallways and interconnected chambers both small and immense, trying to keep in mind pathways and landmarks Jay had told her to look out for when they'd been alone, based upon the blueprints he had gleaned from the Research and Development computer system. She mingled with crowds, but was never accosted, never challenged...until she was alone in a certain corridor, not far from the point where she hoped to ascend to Level 101.

Here, a patrolling soldier with a slung assault rifle called to her from behind. She pretended not to hear him, but he spoke again in Arabic in a tone that was both threatening and seductive at the same time. He hastened to catch up with her, reached out and took her arm to jerk her around to face him.

She did face him, bringing the Ka-Bar knife out from within her robes in the same movement and burying its blade in the side of his neck. Then, just as she had witnessed from the experts here in the colony, she drew the blade around the front of the man's throat, until blood gushed out of his gaping neck in huge flopping sheets as if poured from a bucket. She spun the man around and sawed at him from behind, pulling back on his hair as he made vomit-like gargling sounds of protest. She let him drop then, barely squirming and half decapitated, enough damage to keep him from regenerating too soon.

Now, though, her hands and burqa deeply stained, she again sought out an air duct or such in a panic of being discovered. She just might have to shoot her way to the staircase leading to Level 101, fight every patrol that stood in her way. Fight all the Mujahideen, in their great numbers, even if – unlike the drones – they were immortal. And behead the Demon-decapitating twelve-year-olds, too, if they came along with the rest. Behead those larval monsters gladly. If she'd had a nuclear weapon in her pocketbook from Hell, she'd have used that, too, just as terrorists in the mortal world had brought about the Big Bang with their suitcase bombs.

But there was an air duct, and there was no further opposition. By the time the man she'd half beheaded could relate what had happened, Vee had left the Mujahideen behind – but her relief was tempered with despair at the victims she had left behind with them, beyond her powers of salvation. It had been demonstrated to Vee that not all the Damned had been consigned to Hades unjustly; that some of the Damned would be evil by any standard, except their own standards, which were warped in ways that only religion could accomplish.

31: The Road To Freetown

Like the floors immediately below the region of the Mujahideen, several floors immediately above it were largely unoccupied. Vee could certainly understand it, though she felt it was a mistake, only giving the Mujahideen more room to expand in the future. As she continued further up, though, she encountered other settlements large and small, the equivalent of cities and tribal villages, though nothing quite of the scale or ambition of Los Angeles or Naraka. She briefly stayed in a town mostly inhabited by Africans, and these mostly Ghanaians, who proved friendly (even overly friendly, as nearly every man in the colony seemed to fancy her for a wife), but she fled desperately from another area – labyrinthine and all but lightless – prowled by packs of baboon-like Demons with bat wings and spiral scars branded across their bodies, repeatedly firing Jay behind her to break up their loping, pursuing charge.

Level after level was gained, sometimes swiftly, other times arduously. Level 110...115...120...

There were times when she felt Freetown would forever be beyond her reach. Another intervening floor, and another, and there would always be one more. But at last, with her snug uniform so tattered that she'd lost one sleeve at the shoulder, and most of one hip lay bare – with all but maybe one more burst of Jay's ammunition remaining – the time came when Vee found herself emerging from yet another, vertical ventilation shaft onto the level that towering, red-stenciled numbers labeled 128.

32: The Guardians

But it seemed a dead end. The room she found herself in was not all that spacious, taller than it was wide, and there were no doors or any other features besides the stenciled numbers. That is, aside from scorch marks on the floor and the walls, which looked to be made out of some thick amber-colored plastic, or resin. Vee moved close to the wall upon which the numbers appeared, but couldn't see through the translucent material, it apparently being too dark on the other side. Still, the scorch marks hinted at fire – or explosions. Had hostile forces, like the Mujahideen, tried blasting their way into the confines of Freetown here? If they had indeed tried entering through here, then that must mean they had a reason to believe they could.

Even as Vee thought this, the entire wall on her right started to slide upward with a subdued sound. Two entities were gradually revealed, at the mouth of a metal-walled hallway, and Vee had not seen their like before in Hades. They appeared to be automatons; bulky, tall, intimidating – all the more so in that their multiple insect-like limbs included several that terminated in automatic weapons. The robot on the left was chiefly made of a black material like chitin, though chrome-bright joints, pistons, and gears showed through gaps in its glossy exoskeleton. Its broad flat face, ringed in long horns, put her in mind of the skull of a prehistoric Styracosaurus. The exoskeleton of the machine being on the right was instead fashioned, or grown, from ivory-hued bone, fissured with sutures. Its joints and undercarriage were of brass, its wide flat face like a shovel blade. Their bodies were configured somewhat differently, their only identical feature being a single large eye, set in a deep socket, in the middle of their otherwise blank faces – these eyes with a blood red iris, like Jay's.

Recognizing this kinship, Jay spoke up, "They're Demonic sentience housed in mechanical bodies, like me. The final line of Demons produced in Tartarus – the most removed from human or even organic form."

"I can see that. And I hope you can convince them we're friends."

"I don't know if these two can speak."

"I can speak," said a voice behind Vee. Though she wouldn't have wanted to startle the mechanical Demons into action with any sudden movement, she couldn't help but wheel around with Jay leveled. She was too reminded of how she had been snuck up upon from behind when engaging the guardians of Los Angeles.

And as in L.A., the men who had sneaked up the same ventilation shaft that she had were human soldiers, attired in black with camouflage patterns in shades of gray. Two of the men wore full-head black helmets, but their leader – the speaker – wore a black beret. He was attractive, if severe, with dark hair, a dark goatee, and intense dark eyes. The handles of the soldiers' black semi-automatic pistols and black assault rifles appeared to be made from the same gray translucent bone that comprised the computer center in Naraka. Handsome weapons, like the man who addressed Vee, but with his steely menace, too.

"Easy, there," the man warned her, his own rifle pointed at her. "Take it slow."

"You, too," she said, trying to sound as calm as he.

"You're Rebecca Phelps, correct?"

"I'm Vee."

"Okay, Vee, as you wish."

"So Adamn told you I was coming. And you've been waiting out here for me all this time?"

"No, just them." He nodded toward the formidable mechanical Demons, behind her. "But we saw you approaching on our security cameras. I'll take you inside now, if you want, but you're going to have to turn over your weapons."

"Standard routine."

"Right." The man kept his own gun pointed toward her, but not as rigidly – a more polite form of threat – while one of his men went to take Jay from her, her sheathed knife, and her pouch.

"And you are?" Vee asked the leader.

"I'm Michael Palladino, security chief of Freetown."

Great – another Roper? At least he wasn't likely to be as religious a security commander. Vee said, "Let me guess...in life you were killed in some war or other. Vietnam?"

"I served in the Gulf War, but no, actually, I died in a house fire. I'm willing to tell you more...along the way."

"Are you bringing me to see your leader?"

"Sort of. Freetown is governed by an elected board of officials, but there's a man we go to for advice and consultation. We asked him to be our leader, but he never wanted that. He's still important to us, though – the father of the revolution, I guess you'd say."

"Okay, well," Vee spread her right arm, "lead on."

Michael gave the mechanical Demons a look, and they parted to let the group enter into the metal-shielded hallway. The ambery plastic door slid down again behind them, and the Demons remained to guard it.

The party of four passed through several more doors, these all metal and each one guarded by two human soldiers, who saluted Michael when they saw him coming. Along the way, since Michael had offered, Vee asked him more about himself, hoping to win his trust.

"My family died in the fire with me, and my wife and I became Angels – like you, Rebecca – but my son Mark was Damned, because my ex-wife never let me baptize him. So my wife and I came to Hades to find him."

"But you got trapped here before you could take him to Heaven with you?"

He looked over at her. "We weren't allowed to take him with us. They wouldn't let a Damned person into Heaven...even an innocent child." The bitterness is his voice was palpable. "So my wife and I chose to remain in Hades with him."

"Wow. You must really love him." Vee envied having such a father.

"So do his foster parents, Roger and Davina. They're a Damned couple who took Mark in and protected him, like their own son, until I came to find him. So we ended up living together, all of us, like a big happy family. A big happy family in Hell. We were in a city called Apollyon, but when the Conflict escalated the city was razed by Demons, and we fled all the way here, to Tartarus. But at least we were able to stay together."

"That's admirable."

"And what about yourself?"

"I'm sure Adamn told you people. I was held prisoner by some Demons for so long that I lost my memory. My father was a prisoner with me."

"Yes. Pastor Karl Phelps. We've been seeing his messages since he showed up back in Los Angeles. He's calling for your head, it looks like."

"His followers have turned him against me. Plus, he lost his mind when he was a prisoner."

"Hm. So you say. But it could also be a very elaborate scheme between the two of you, to make us trust you and take you in."

"What?" Vee stopped where she was. "Are you joking? What am I, a suicide bomber infiltrating your city?" She held out her arms. "Go ahead and frisk me, Mr. Palladino."

One of his men raised his hand. "I'll do it, sir."

"Can it, Leonard." Michael tipped his chin toward the door ahead of them. "Come on, let's go, okay? I'm sorry. I'll keep the speculations to myself."

"No, please, let's get them out in the open."

"I said I was sorry. Let's go."

Begrudgingly, Vee allowed herself to be led onward, through one last door, and then they emerged into Freetown.

33: *The City Of Colors*

Like Los Angeles, Freetown had expanded from its original level into the one above:129. Whereas the entire upper floor had been removed in L.A., however, in Freetown only portions of it had been cleared here and there, with an abundance of ramps, staircases, ladders, and even escalators communicating between the two levels. The dwellings and places of business looked much the same as those in that other city – boxes built from salvaged materials, or machinery adapted for habitation – but with the striking difference that the buildings here were painted in a multitude of hues. Pastel shades like aqua, pink, and yellow abounded, but there were plenty of crayon-bright shades of red, blue, purple, and so on. Vee didn't know where they had come by these pigments, but it definitely made for a pleasing effect. Almost like a town of toy blocks, assembled by gleeful giant children.

There was an even more significant difference between L.A. and Freetown, however, and that was the citizenry that massed in these haphazard streets. They were a mix of Damned (and, apparently, Angels) and Demons of numerous humanoid races. Among these were a class of Demon with an African appearance, but devoid of any hair or even eyebrows, with raven-like wings, and a race of Caucasian Demons with skin as white as paper and wings like those of a dragon. Seeing this latter type of Demon gave Vee a shiver of recognition, stirred repressed memories of the Demons who had imprisoned and tortured her, so very long ago.

She was surprised that these Demons as often as not were naked (she was hardly offended, however, as every one of them had a beautiful physique), though some of the bat-winged Demons wore uniforms much like her own. Which caused Vee to turn to Michael and ask, "Do you think I could get a change of clothes and maybe a shower before I meet this important person of yours?"

The security commander sighed. "He's waiting for us right now."

"Please. I mean, look at me."

"I'll have something arranged. *After* your appointment. I'm sure he won't care how you look."

Vee didn't press the issue further, and Michael took her directly to a rather nondescript, three story structure, its heavy walls of riveted metal slabs made less formidable-looking by having been painted lime green. Two more guards posted by its front door saluted Michael and allowed him and the others entrance.

Vee looked around her, at a large open office subdivided into work cubicles, each housing a sturdy computer with a white enamel casing, looking like a toilet turned on its side. Several of the people seated before them were wired into the Mesh. Over an intercom system played a lovely, gently melancholy song that Vee recognized, though not by name or by artist. *"Music?"* she said. It sounded a bit faded and tinny, but it was the first music she'd heard in Hades.

"Yeah," said Michael. "I love that one. *Here's Where the Story Ends* by the Sundays." He gestured around him. "This is what we call the print shop. That's Roger over there – the guy who cared for my son in Hades before I was able to find him." Michael nodded at a pleasant-faced man in his late twenties, who had been reading text off a terminal. Roger gave a little wave back. "Roger worked at a print shop in Apollyon, until the city was ruined. The Damned made books for themselves there. So we started making books here, too. But paper was scarce, so we decided to use the Mesh instead."

"Adamn told me about that. That he's helped find ways to draw books and movies and music out of people's heads."

"Well, movies are easier to dig out than books, and music is easier than movies."

Vee could believe that. As her memory of the mortal world had slowly filled in, she had sometimes found songs running through her mind, as exact as recordings. (One of these had been *Heroes*, by David Bowie. Jay's revelation that his avatar was a dolphin had caused her to recall specifically the lines, *"I, I wish you could swim... Like the dolphins, like dolphins can swim."*) But remembering a book word for word?

"Books are tough to recapture from memories," Michael said, as if reading her mind, "but we still liked that idea. So what they do here in the print shop is have people with writing skills rewrite their favorite books, directly into the Mesh for anyone to access on their own computer, or in our library's computers. This guy over here is Frank Lyre, one of our best writers, right Frank?"

A man seated in a nearby cubicle swiveled around to smile up at Vee. She found him good-looking, rather reminding her of the actor William Hurt. His amicable reaction to her suggested that, despite her bedraggled appearance, he wasn't displeased with her looks, either. He said, "Uh, well, I just want to point out that I prefer to write original books, myself. But right now I'm editing a re-imagining of *Gone With the Wind* that one of our citizens has written." Lyre indicated the screen of his computer. "I never read the original, but I imagine it didn't have this many typos...or sex scenes...but who am I to judge? I'm cleaning up the typos and letting the sex stay."

"Can't wait for the movie," Vee told him.

"If you like that, you should read *The Godfather*. I rewrote that one myself. I didn't take any liberties like having Sonny survive his ambush or anything, but I did cut out that whole 'Lucy with her big box' subplot."

"It's funny...it reminds me of a movie. *Fahrenheit 451*. Everyone remembered one book."

"Ha, right," Lyre said. "That was a book first, and it just happens to be another of the ones I've done. I'm no Ray Bradbury, but I do my best. I hate to admit it, being a writer, but it does help me remember a book if I've seen the movie, too."

A figure stirred at the back of the office area, differentiating itself from the shadows, and Vee switched her gaze there. Returning her stare was a tall, almost androgynous female Demon of the dark-skinned African type, her finely formed hairless head gleaming with reflected light, her features glowering but intensely beautiful. She was without clothes, onyx rings pierced through her black nipples, four claw-like keloids above each breast, her black wings folded behind her. Why was she glaring at Vee with such seething menace?

"Come on upstairs," Michael said, taking Vee lightly by the arm. "There's another writer I want you to meet."

142

34: The Author

At each landing were stationed two more heavily armed and helmeted guards – the only sign that someone of great importance to this city made his offices on the top floor of their "print shop" building.

Michael knocked, and rather than call for them to enter, seated imperiously behind a desk, the man himself opened the door to admit them. Michael, Vee, and the two soldiers entered. Over the intercom, softly, played *Everyday I Write the Book* by Elvis Costello.

"Sit down," said their host. Michael and Vee took chairs that had been set out for them. The two soldiers remained standing in front of the door, holding their assault rifles.

Vee watched the man go to a chair in front of his own ceramic-coated computer, take a seat and turn to face them. If the writer downstairs, Frank Lyre, evoked William Hurt, this man made Vee think of a young John Hurt; a little haggard, a little haunted. It wasn't that he looked physically old – he must have only been in his thirties when he died – but his soul seemed worn far beyond those years. Made old by the burden of immortality. He had bristly short hair, wore a simple brown t-shirt and baggy tan trousers, and sandals.

Vee squirmed a little under his gaze, and even though only a second or two had passed broke the tension by saying, "So...you're a writer?"

"Yes. You've never heard of me? Dan Alighieri?"

"Um...it sounds familiar..." Vee wasn't lying. Where had she heard that name? The odd unease she was feeling was making her thought processes stutter.

"Those are some of my books, behind you," Alighieri said.

Vee half-turned, and Michael passed her three perfect-bound volumes he'd picked up from a table. She read the titles. *Letters From Hades*, *Beautiful Hell*, and *Voices From Hades*.

"Ah, I didn't write *Beautiful Hell*," the author pointed out. "That was a friend of mine, Frank Lyre, writing about his own experiences in Hades."

"Right...I met him downstairs."

"*Voices From Hades* is a collection of stories based on the experiences of a number of Damned, Angels, and Demons I interviewed or was told about. One of the stories concerns Michael, here, and his efforts to locate his son."

Vee nodded. "He told me about that."

"*Letters From Hades*, though...that's my own story. Based on a journal I kept for a while when I first came to Hades." He seemed to lean forward just a bit in his chair. "Sure you've never heard of it?"

Was this some kind of trick question? Dan Alighieri...Dan Alighieri...

"Wait...yeah, okay. My gun told me about you."

"Your *gun?*"

"She has a Demonic gun," Michael explained. "Sentient, Mesh access. It's been confiscated."

"Ahh. So, Rebecca Phelps, what did your gun tell you about me?"

She didn't correct the author about her name. "Um...let me think. He said you rescued a Demon woman, who was captured by Damned rebels..."

"She had been captured, yes, and nailed to a tree. Left to die when I found her."

"You freed her. And that caused a big commotion. It sort of broke the camel's back, or something – stirred up more rebellion. Because... because you fell in love."

"Very good, Rebecca. And do you by any chance remember her name? My Demon lover's name?"

"Uh...no, I don't. Sorry."

"You're sure of that?"

Vee was getting tired of this line of questioning, said a little more firmly, "No, I don't know her name. Why are you asking me this?"

"Her name was Chara. Chara, Rebecca Phelps. And I loved her. And more surprisingly, perhaps, given what she was, she loved me. She was the love of my afterlife." He gave a bitter little smile at his own pun. "And the reason I'm asking you this is because – since you claim to have forgotten so much – you killed her, Rebecca Phelps. Rebecca the 'Demon Hunter.' You murdered my Chara."

"What?" Vee looked over at Michael, partly to see if he might confirm this, partly because she expected a trap to be sprung on her at that moment. Michael was watching her grimly, his assault rifle lying across his knees. Its position looked casual, but it was pointed in her direction, and his hand rested on it lightly. It was Adamn who had set the trap, though. He'd found out who she was. Told them she was coming. And they had been waiting.

Vee looked back to the author, found she was trembling – either from fear of her captors, or from how this information might further define the person she was. "You'd better fill me in, Mr. Alighieri, because I swear to you I don't know what you're talking about."

"Really, Rebecca?"

"I'm telling you!"

"Okay, Rebecca, I'll play along for now. You do know your father is the Pastor Karl Phelps? And that he led an army of Angels into Hades to help fight the uprising of Damned and Demons?"

"Yes, yes...I've found that out. But I was a prisoner of the Demons, and I've forgotten –"

"Yes, Rebecca, I'm familiar with all that from Adamn. Anyway, you accompanied your father. You were quite fearsome – the 'Demon Hunter,' they called you. Your father and most of his troops became trapped inside the Construct with the rest of us, when the deluge came full force. You entrenched yourselves on the 7th level, but that wasn't enough for you, apparently. You ventured out from that base on raiding parties, to continue your attacks on Damned and Demons both. It was in one of these raids that your party encountered Chara, who was on her own mission with some other Demons – in the Construct's basement, trying to convince a group of Demons of her own race to come back with her to Freetown. Your team engaged the Demons. You were defeated, and taken prisoner in the basement outpost – as you've related – but not before Chara was killed in the exchange. By *you*, Rebecca Phelps. That was quite a coup for you, Chara being seen as the catalyst for rebellion, and all."

For a long moment Vee couldn't say anything. And that was because she couldn't deny it. Wouldn't try. She knew it had to be true. When her voice returned, all she could do was restate her ignorance of what had occurred. "I promise you, Mr. Alighieri, I swear to you on whatever's left of my soul to swear on, that I don't remember doing that. If it's true..."

"*If?*" Now she saw that Alighieri was trembling, too.

"Okay, look, I don't doubt that it's true. But I don't *remember* it, okay? I don't remember! And more importantly...more importantly, I'm *sorry*. I'm truly, sincerely sorry."

"You're...sorry," the author said in a dry, dead tone.

"Yes." Vee sat up straight in her chair. Firm in her testimony, as if she were on trial – both innocent and guilty at the same time. "I'm sorry, Mr. Alighieri. I'm not the person I was. I can't imagine myself doing that."

"I see you've been in a scuffle or two along your way here to Freetown." Alighieri indicated her ripped uniform. "You haven't killed a few more Demons in more recent times?"

"Okay...yes, I have. And some Celestials. And some Angels, too – some of my father's men, except they don't stay dead. Of course I've had to kill people to get here. And you've never killed anybody since you came to Hades, Mr. Alighieri? In the rebellion you started? In the Great Conflict?"

Now it was the author's turn to say nothing for a long moment.

Vee went on, "So you were aware I was taken prisoner down in the basement. Did you order it?"

"It was the Demons' choice. I was simply informed about Chara. I never sent anyone down there for revenge. But I never sent anyone down there to free you, either."

"I'm not saying I blame you," Vee muttered. "I understand your anger."

"Thanks. Thanks for being so understanding."

She swallowed, feeling defiant and contrite at once. "What are you planning to do with me? Return me to my prison, maybe?"

"What would you suggest I do?"

"I suggest...well, I would hope that you could – forgive me."

"Forgiveness," he said. "There is always that. Or...isn't."

"Look, why don't you talk to my gun? It won't lie to protect me... it's a Demon itself, isn't it?"

"You may have lied to it, too."

"Oh for...what about my father, in the Mesh? Hasn't Adamn told you about that? Why would my father be calling for my capture? And please don't tell me you think that's just some plot my father and I came up with to trick you into trusting me."

"Yes, your father in the Mesh." The author leaned back in his chair now. "I've seen his messages about you, Rebecca. Since his return, he's been a real nuisance in our systems. Not that the fine folks in Los Angeles haven't irritated us before. Once in a while they get into our library system and delete our books, or substitute the Bible for every title, but luckily we have them backed up so we just restore them and put up new firewalls. They have some good hackers on their side – maybe even Demons they force to work for them – but we've got our own people working on crashing their access to the Mesh altogether."

"So if you've seen my father in the Mesh do you believe me or don't you?"

Alighieri sighed, and seeming not have heard the question, asked, "Did you see the beautiful Demon downstairs? I'm sure she was keeping an eye on you."

"I saw her."

"She's my wife, Olisha. She respects me, protects me, she's considerate and helpful and...accommodating. I just don't know if she loves me. And to be honest, I'm not so sure I love her. I mean, I care for her. She's the only wife I've ever taken in Hades. Frank downstairs has had six wives since coming to the Construct."

"Seven, I think," Michael cut in.

"Maybe you're right. He's tried them all – Damned, Angels, Demons. And loved every one of them. It's not that those marriages ended in hatred, necessarily. It's just that over time, love wanes. I don't want that to happen with Chara, Rebecca. I want my love for her to be truly immortal. And so I suppose I've resisted falling in love again."

"It's nice that you honor her like that. But maybe not so fair to Olisha."

Alighieri's eyes seem to spark. "Fair? Are you going to teach me about *fair*, Rebecca?"

"I'm sorry." She dropped her gaze in repentance. "I guess I really don't know what's fair or just. I don't even know if I should be forgiven."

Alighieri stared at her hard for a moment longer, but couldn't seem to sustain the effort or the emotion. He lowered his own eyes to his knotted hands, in an aspect almost like prayer. "It was always my intention to forgive you, Rebecca. Adamn believed you, but he wanted to let me know who you were. And I believe your father's messages are genuine."

Vee lifted her eyes to him again. "So why did you question me like this?"

"I just wanted you to know what you'd done. It isn't right that you should forget it."

After a few beats, Vee nodded and said, "Fair enough. And I'll tell you again, whether you care to believe it or not...I am deeply sorry about it."

"Sorry. Yes," Alighieri said. "Michael, why don't you let Miss Phelps get cleaned up a bit. If she cares to stay with us, get her settled somewhere until she can decide what she wants to do here. What she might want to do for work." He faced his guest again. "We all contribute something of ourselves here, Rebecca. We take care of each other. But I have it easy. All I do is write."

"I suspect you do more than that." She rose from her chair, and said, "Thanks for the act of faith."

"Everyone we've let into Freetown has been an act of faith."

Michael opened the door for Vee, but at the threshold she turned back and said, "I can promise you...Rebecca Phelps is dead."

"I hope so," said Alighieri.

"And if means anything – I killed *her*, too."

35: *The Escort*

The tiny apartment Vee had been temporarily assigned was in a section of the 128th floor that had once been a level in one of Tartarus' mecha-organic buildings, every surface here a glossy black like obsidian but compounded of dense, unfathomable detail: printed circuit boards, pipes (that occasionally gurgled disconcertingly), cables (or were they veins?), teased out entrails and large organs (one of which pulsed regularly like a rubber bladder), together oddly suggestive of the mechanical, the insect, and the reptilian all at once. Even the shelf that served as her bed, which seemed to grow out of the wall, was of this glistening material, but at least it was uniformly smooth on its upper surface and she had been given a thin mattress to place atop it, and blankets.

She had also been given new clothing, something in keeping with the uniform she had acquired from the skeletonized Demon in the basement. This uniform was also a one-piece suit of Lycra-like material, even thinner and more flexible than the other, without the first uniform's padded elbows and knees and ribbed chest, making her look as if she'd simply been dipped in black paint. The back was open like the first, to make room for the Demon's wings she didn't possess.

Before leaving the "print shop," Frank Lyre had handed Vee a package of well-worn books to borrow. They were the same titles Alighieri had shown her: *Letters From Hades*, *Beautiful Hell*, and *Voices From Hades*. He had tapped the cover of *Beautiful Hell* and said, "I wrote this one, but read *Letters* first. Consider it orientation material on pre-revolution Hell. And there are some hot sex scenes in my book, too." He'd winked at her, and Vee had chuckled, relieved at having been dismissed from Alighieri's office as a citizen of Freetown.

She was in her little cubicle, seated on her sleeping bench and several journal entries into Alighieri's *Letters From Hades*, when there came a knock on the wall outside her doorway, which was covered only by hanging strips of black rubber. She parted these with her hands, and was startled to see the figure that stood beyond her threshold. It was one of those robot-like Demons, perhaps the same one she had seen on guard duty when entering Freetown, with its shovel-like face of bone and the single red eye in its center. Not to mention, the limbs that ended in automatic weapons. Before, Jay had questioned whether these entities could speak, but now a clear if uninflected voice came from somewhere on the large automaton's body. "Come with me, please. Someone is waiting for you."

149

"Who?" She couldn't help but feel a little wary. Had they had second thoughts about her? "Palladino? Alighieri?"

"You know him as Adamn. He has volunteered to help you become orientated in Freetown – to show you around, assist you in finding work and a permanent dwelling, and so forth."

"Ah. So Adamn volunteered, did he?" Vee snorted. "Okay, I guess it's about time I met my virtual friend Adamn in the flesh...so to speak." Vee placed the book aside. "Let's go."

They ended up traveling quite far together – it felt like they crossed the entire length of the city-building – but she supposed the time spent in such endeavors meant little when one was immortal. (What must a work period be like? Could "working overtime" amount to an extra decade in the office?) At least, this way she got to see more of Freetown, its characteristics varying according to the many former buildings of Tartarus – fused together to form the unified Construct – they passed through. They cut through an interior farmland, where edible infernal plant forms were cultivated in abundance, their growth accelerated by solutions and processes once used in the production of new Demons. There were markets where these food stuffs were sold (though, with relief, she saw no meat for sale in Freetown), alongside clothing and numerous other articles, often ingeniously fashioned from unlikely materials. She looked forward to spending more time exploring such markets in the future – not to mention the sight of the rows of vegetables awakening suppressed hunger deep in her guts.

Finally they arrived at what turned out to be one of the buildings that had defined the border of Tartarus – the terminus of the Construct. There was a great open chamber here like the inside of an airplane hangar, and it was filled with activity; machinery being assembled or disassembled, computer terminals being manned, by both humans and a variety of Demons – many of the automatonic variety, like her escort, in a diversity of forms. Thick power cables crisscrossed the floor and sparks showered from arc welders.

From this confusion a man emerged, and strode toward Vee and the machine Demon. He was lanky, dressed in an oil-stained, short-sleeved top and baggy trousers, rather like green hospital scrubs. She recognized his face from his virtual hideaway – the desolate shopping plaza – if not from his memories. *Yeah*, she thought, confirming her earlier impression of him, *a nicely aging Kevin Bacon*. Late thirties, early forties?

Adamn gave a crinkly, pleasant smile. "Hello, Vee."

"Hello yourself," she said, making her own face look stern. "So you let them know I was coming, huh?"

He stopped before her. "Hey...I had to, didn't I? But here you are, right? You obviously passed muster."

"Lucky for me. So, you want to make it up to me by being my guide or whatever?"

"Or whatever. You know, we can't just set you adrift in town without holding your hand a while."

"You mean you can't set me adrift without having someone keep an eye on me a while."

"Hey." Adamn grinned and threw up his hands. "Come on...if you're not so on guard, I don't have to be on guard, either."

"So what are you doing in here?" She gestured around.

"Oh, we have all kinds of projects going on here."

"I mean you specifically. You told me you were involved with memory recording."

"That's one of the projects I've been involved in, yeah. Are you interested in restoring your own memories? You told me you'd forgotten almost everything. I think I could help you, you know."

"Help me how?" she asked warily.

"There's a machine that belonged to the Demons – they used it for torture, but I've helped adapt it to more positive uses."

"What are you, some kind of mad scientist? I didn't get that impression from your memories."

"When you saw me I was a machine adjuster on the graveyard shift for a pharmaceutical manufacturer. I was divorced, losing my house...I was even going to have to give away my dog or else put her down. In Hell, it's funny – and it's not just me who feels this way – but it's like I've been forged again. Everything got burned away, and I had to start over, but I became better than I ever was alive. I feel like I do valuable things here. I feel like part of a community, which I never really felt before. In life I was basically a loner, uncomfortable with other people. I guess two thousand years have helped me hone my people skills." He shrugged. "Hone everything."

"That is pretty ironic. In Hell, they're supposed to break you, not remake you."

"Well, it's like I say about this machine. It was intended to punish, but we've made it into a tool. So do you wanna see it or not?"

"Okay, sure, show me."

He motioned for her to join him, and as they began crossing the huge open space Vee glanced back to see the robot escort wasn't accompanying them. She said, "There's a lot of these machine Demons here. I'd have thought they'd be the last Demons to align themselves with humans."

"That was the idea when they were designed, but interestingly enough the opposite has been the case. A lot of them resent that their souls – well, Demons don't have souls, so I'll say minds – are confined in a mechanical form. They could sympathize with the imprisonment of the Damned, in a way. After all, didn't you arrive here with a Demonic gun as a sidekick?"

"Yes. And speaking of which, when can I have my sidekick back?"

"Only our security people can carry firearms, but if you ever choose to leave us of course they'll give him back." They passed another automatonic entity, and when Adamn nodded to it the robot nodded its own head, a riveted brass globe like a deep sea diver's helmet, in return. "They do have one interesting advantage, we've found, which is you can transfer their sentience from one Demonic machine to another, and you can even store their mind for a time until you can find it a new vehicle."

"Store it? On like a flash drive or something?"

He snickered. "No. In the Mesh."

"You're really a cybergeek, huh? You should be with the Enmeshed, not the Freetowners. My gun seems to think what they've got is the closest thing to a Heaven that can be achieved these days."

"I'm not ready for a virtual Heaven, yet." Adamn smiled anew as they continued their comfortable, unhurried pace. "But I did have a virtual girlfriend in Naraka."

"The Indian cybergeeks? Really?"

"I've been married a couple times in Hades, but she was the woman I cared for most. And our virtual sex blew away any real sex I've ever had, even as a mortal. And yet, we never once met face-to-face."

"Huh."

"You know that shopping plaza where you met me? A building of condo units is one of its anchors, and I have a virtual apartment in there. My girlfriend and I used to spend whole days in there at a time."

"Romantic," Vee said drily. "But you don't shack up anymore?"

"No...afraid not. I caught her avatar with another guy's avatar – one of the Enmeshed, and in my own apartment." He wagged his head, smiling, but she saw a vestige of pain behind it. "Just like my wife all over again. But that's life. And death, too. So how about you? You have any significant others here in Hades – besides the gun?"

"I have an ex-fiancé, in Los Angeles. But the last time I saw him, I blew his face off."

Adamn looked over at her steely profile. "Why am I not surprised?" he said.

36: The Mechanics Of Life And Death

They reached the far wall of the projects hall, and a pair of sliding doors. Set into the wall beside them was a small control panel from which Adamn pulled a retractable Mesh jack, which he plugged into his port. It appeared to Vee that in his brief communion with the Mesh, his identity was being verified. The doors opened, he unplugged the jack, and Vee followed him across the threshold. The doors clanged shut again behind them.

On the other side stood two fierce-looking female warriors in the uniform of Palladino's security forces, but these uniforms were much modified to accommodate their physical state. Owing to the fact that they were Damned and thus indestructible, both women – in addition to being heavily tattooed – were extensively pierced with spikes and shards and strips of metal, as if filled with exploded shrapnel, wed into and *through* their bodies in ways that would be impossible, if not lethal, for a mortal. The guards were both jacked into the Mesh with long black rubber cords, but looked very alert in the here-and-now, challenging Vee with their scrutiny. Tough as she was, she avoided their eyes, which were themselves like cutting bits of shrapnel, as Adamn led her past them.

"Environmental control for Freetown," he explained, as they now threaded their way through crevasses between house-sized machines, banks of gauges with quivering needles, walls of valves and knobs and orange glowing lights. "Alighieri would probably be pissed if he knew I'd brought you here – this would be a prime target for terrorists – but he did make you a free citizen and all, so..."

Vee read little plaques and labels identifying the functions of various machines and processes as they passed them. *Differential Pressure. Cooling Air Suction. Heat Zones 1 and 2. Cool Zones 1 and 2. Recirculated Water Pressure. Manifold Controller. Vacuum Pump Connection. Filter Station Tank 12 Control Panel. Fan Interlock. Manual Valve. Bleeder Valve. Environmental Monitoring Station Viable and Particle Counter.* It all sounded pretty important, if incomprehensible, to Vee and she could see why this area would be protected, and Alighieri protective of it. This time it was she who nodded to a robot Demon, this one checking the readings on one of the control panels, and it nodded back to her politely. There was a deep pulsing thrum in the air that Vee could feel vibrating through the chambers of her body. It sounded to her as if an endless train were running below the floor she stood upon.

"So has any terrorist ever tried to get in here?"

"We don't advertise the location of our environmental control center, but recently a Mujahideen did get into another part of Freetown through a pretty clever method. See, we've made sure any ventilation shafts or utility passages or whatever that might give access to our city are too small to negotiate, or at least are barred or solidly grated, but this guy cut one of his own fingers off and pushed it through the bars of a grate. Normally his finger would grow back in no time, but he had buddies with him who quickly dissolved his body with acid. So

154

the finger, on the other side of the grate, regenerated into our terrorist friend. But Michael Palladino's people caught him before he could do any damage, luckily."

"What did Palladino do with him?"

"Well..." Adamn stopped to face her. "Michael has his own invention he's worked on in the projects hall. It's a kind of gun, that he was hoping to make small enough for a man to carry, though the prototype is the size of a howitzer. Its purpose is to destroy a human soul. I mean, not just disintegrate a body that will regrow later one way or another, but totally make a soul cease to be. To...I don't know...just punch it right out of existence."

"Is that possible?"

"Apparently. They tried it out – on that Mujahideen terrorist they captured. But who knows...maybe a soul can never be destroyed, and the gun actually sent his spirit to another plane of existence. Maybe it sent him back to Earth to be reborn into a new body, either after the Big Bang or maybe even before it. But whatever happened to him, it made him disappear, and he's never returned *here*, at least."

"Oh wow. Oh Adamn...I don't know about that one. I mean, I have no love for the Mujahideen, believe me, but my concern would be about them or even my father's people getting their hands on such a thing and posing a threat to everybody in the Construct. *Everybody.*"

"I agree, and fortunately so does Alighieri, and while he tries not to wear that leadership hat, he definitely made his voice heard about this. I hope Alighieri has Michael dismantle it entirely one of these days. This is our second chance. It was things like that gun that brought about the Big Bang. No, we're all immortal, so we have plenty of time to try to change things in other ways."

"Do you *really* think some people will ever change? Even given all of eternity?"

Adamn remained quiet by way of response.

37: *The Black Cathedral*

They stepped out from the maze of machines into a clear area, and found themselves facing the opening to an elevator shaft larger than any Vee had encountered yet. There was another, more striking difference as well, but before Adamn addressed this he explained, "We are now officially at the outermost boundary of the Construct, and that elevator shaft does not officially exist. It used to be a major ventilation and utility shaft. Well, it does still serve those functions, but we've also adapted it into an elevator system." They stepped in closer, while other people and Demons moved or worked about them. "We didn't want to use any existing elevators for this, for the sake of security. This only stops at a few floors of our choosing, and the doors there are camouflaged. As far as we know, no one outside our colony is aware of it, or at least has wanted to cut through any adjoining wall to get at it. We've done a good job with it keeping its movement quiet – it rides nice and smooth." Said with the pride of someone who had had a hand in that fact. "We've sealed off access to the shaft through even the smallest vent or grate on all the other floors except those it stops at, and there are cameras inside the shaft, too."

"Okay, but what the hell is that thing inside it?" Vee asked – the obvious question. "It looks like a...church."

A structure rested on the elevator platform, which appeared to have rails set into it that the structure could be moved along. The structure itself was in the form of a smallish, narrow-bodied cathedral, with an array of spires and steeples as serrated and threatening as knife blades or arrowheads, most of them either bent or badly gouged or else broken off in whole or part. Its body seemed welded together from innumerable bits of machinery, like junkyard salvage forced into a whole and then all of it painted black, though now greatly splotched with corrosion. Steam gusted from various grates and orifices, and Vee thought it looked like an ancient steam locomotive wed with one of the weird Art Nouveau cathedrals designed by Antoni Gaudi. Set into its flanks were arched windows of red stained glass, with a circular red glass window over the double front doors. Inscribed into these iron doors were the words: THE SPECTRAL DRAMA THOU THYSELF HAST MADE! – GOETHE.

"They called it the Black Cathedral," Adamn said, "and like I

156

told you, it was intended as a place of punishment – a mobile torture chamber. The thing would move along tracks laid into the streets of Demonic cities, stop here or there for a while, and Damned would be randomly rounded up and taken inside. But the torture wasn't physical. The subjects would be hooked up to a system that forced them to relive their saddest or most horrible memories. That's what I was telling you – that we adapted its technology to help us with memory extraction put to more benevolent uses, and to perfect our interface with the Mesh."

"But why do you keep it in the elevator?" Vee asked, watching as a robot Demon welded a metal patch to the side of the iron building amid a shower of sparks. Power cables ran out from the ajar front doors, down the iron front steps, to where they connected up with an apparent diagnostic cart on wheels, a human worker bent over its monitors and keyboards.

"Like I said, it's mobile. It's a vehicle. And aside from all the stuff we've learned from its groovy computer, it's become the most important tool in my own pet project, in another way. Again, though, with a lot of adaptation."

"And that project is?"

"Come on." Adamn led her directly onto the spacious elevator platform itself, and Vee followed him around to the back of the iron building. Here, the corrosion was much worse, the mechanical body heavily patched and reinforced. But drawing Vee's attention more were the various drilling apparatuses affixed to the back of the Black Cathedral. There was one very large boring auger, plus a variety of smaller drills on boom arms, looking like robotic insect limbs. Adamn pointed and said, "These nozzles here shoot a powerful acid that can actually melt the volcanic rock outside. Adding them has really advanced the project a lot. Though the back-splash from the acid does do a lot of damage to the building itself, as you can see, so we have to keep up with repairs."

Vee had herself witnessed how the acid used by the drone Demons could dissolve the pumice-like stone that entombed the Construct. "Why are you melting that? What are you drilling for?"

Adamn appeared to take in a deep breath, and when he spoke it was as if to a soul newly delivered into Hades rather than one trapped there for two thousand years, because that was what she essentially was. "In the past, before the Big Bang, Demonic administrators scanned the mind of each and every Damned that came into Hades, and based on what they learned from them they sent them off to different parts of Hades – a lot of times by train systems – to keep them away from any family and friends, since being with them might lessen their misery. But the amount of new souls after the Big Bang was so great that they didn't have time to take these kinds of measures. After the Big Bang, if people died in proximity to each other, chances were they would enter Hades through the same portals, and would skip the...whatever you'd call it...orientation period the Damned would go through in the past. When I came into Hades, there were people who came in with me from the same town I lived in. Because of this, I'm pretty confident that my mother and brother and sister, who also died in the Big Bang, can't be all that far from the portal I came through, which was close by to Tartarus. My mother was staying with my brother and I'll bet anything they remained together when they came through. Given the scale of Hades, in the past I might never find them in an eternity of searching, but I think they can't be unreasonably far from the Construct."

"You mean, out there fossilized in the rock, Adamn?" Vee said, not sarcastically but with sympathy for what she took to be a surprising amount of idealism – or naivete – after two millennia in Hell.

"Maybe, but as bad as the deluge was, it was still gradual, and I bet most of the Damned found at least some kind of shelter before they could be caught out in the open like that. Not that we haven't dug out scattered individuals from the rock when we burrow along, like you say, but there are who knows how many cities out there – either constructed by the Damned or the Demons or both – and smaller settlements like villages, and individual houses and shelters, and caverns even. Maybe no other city was ever able to seal itself off into one big unit the way we did with the Construct, but you could have two people in a little Damned-built stone cottage here, ten people in a cave there, people hiding in apartments in a big city, cut off from the people in other buildings but still protected from the Pompeii treatment."

"But without life support systems like ours, they might be starving for air...suffocating in agony for century after century on the floors of these apartments."

Adamn didn't look too pleased by this picture, when his own family factored into the discussion, but surely he had thought of it before himself. "Maybe. Or maybe they went into a catatonic state – shut down, like you did. That's the way most of the individual people we've dug out have been. But we've had contact with people in one city called Oblivion through their own version of the Mesh, and some spotty radio messages from a farther city, too. There are people out there who are *conscious*...but conscious or unconscious, we can go to them. It will take time, but time is what we have, if nothing else. Time enough to dig out every last soul in Hades, if I have my way."

"There will be billions...and billions. Too many to take back to the Construct."

"We'll make the Construct bigger. But we'll free other cities from the rock. I'll dig out all of Hades if I need to."

"But it's your mother and sister and brother you're really thinking of."

Adamn's face was grimly resolved. "I won't give up on them. I'll get to them and bring them here if it takes forever. Like I say, the Black Cathedral was designed to give us suffering. I take great satisfaction in using it to relieve suffering. We're taking back our damnation, Vee."

"But how are you doing it? How does the Black Cathedral get outside to dig?"

"Like I said, trains used to link up the far corners of Hades, and a lot of these tracks were underground, like subways. That was how the Black Cathedral would travel from city to city. Not all that many decades ago one of our exploration teams found it below the Construct in a sub-basement garage. This vent shaft goes all the way down there, so we made our humongous elevator and rerouted the cathedral's tracks so we could bring the thing up here to be repaired and retrofitted, and protected when not in use. But down there, we've excavated some of the old subway tunnels it would use. These were either purposely filled in by the Demons during the Great Conflict, to keep enemy forces from sneaking into Tartarus from below, or else they were caved in by the pressure of the lava and volcanic rock. But we've been digging them out more and more, laying down new tracks when we have to." Adamn reached out a hand and pressed it to the metal of the Black Cathedral, as if fondly touching the hide of some loyal beast of burden. "We're close to reaching the city Oblivion now, and who knows how many people there. New friends, and new enemies too I suspect, but that's always the way. We've already liberated a few small towns entirely, every soul that was in them. Many of them were in comas like I describe, but some who hadn't shut down had adapted to being without breath and coped with it pretty well – blocked out the sensation. We're very resilient creatures, Vee. You ought to know that."

"I'd say you're pretty resilient. Two thousand years hasn't broken you." She said it with true admiration, and not a little bit of wonder. "You're a rebel without a pause."

"I told you, I feel reincarnated. Reborn."

"Me too, I guess, but I think what I really want is to feel *redeemed*."

"Redeemed?" He was studying her face. "Let me help you. I can take you in here –" he nodded at the Black Cathedral "– and help you get back the memories you've lost."

Vee looked up at the closest of the blood-red stained glass windows, its panes held in a metal web of strange geometric patterns like formulae from a sorcerer's grimoire. "That's not what I want, Wizard of Oz. I don't want to go back to Kansas."

"Well this here ain't no Emerald City, Dorothy."

Vee's mouth raised at one corner. "Ha. If I'm Dorothy, I guess my gun is Toto." She stepped away from the Black Cathedral, and her expression became serious again. "No, I don't want to remember, Adamn. I don't want to dig up the past. That's one thing I'll kindly ask you to leave buried forever."

38: The Swimmers

She was floating in a sparkling, scarlet sea.

Far above her, as she swept her arms and pedaled her legs to keep from sinking below the surface, the night sky was sprinkled with winking red stars, some of them like shooting stars zipping this way or that. In one section of sky, the stars were so dense they formed a luminous curtain like a crimson aurora.

Vee looked down at the ocean she was buoyed in, its lava-like glow rippling over her naked chest and shoulders. She could not see far below the surface, but the water seemed a living thing made up of countless tiny red organisms. Rather than producing a feeling of wetness, they were a subtle electric fizzing sensation against the bare flesh of her avatar.

She was in Freetown's library, surfing the Mesh. Well, almost surfing; in the distance she had seen a man riding a great wave of information on a board, and crying out, *"Whoo-ee!"* though the area she bobbed in was thankfully more tranquil. Rather than seeking out a particular book to read, however, she was trying to better acquaint herself with navigation through the Mesh, if she wanted to work closely with Adamn on his projects – particularly, join the crew of the drilling and rescue crew he supervised. For this was the vocation she had chosen to pursue as a citizen contributing to the good of Freetown.

Beyond the water's horizon, a city of glittering red towers soared against the starfield, with what looked like huge red dirigibles and small darting red helicopters moving between those neon skyscrapers of information. Many of them were still just skeleton frameworks and scaffolding, but the citizens of Freetown – and the Enmeshed, and those of Naraka, and even of L.A. and other colonies she hadn't encountered – made this world larger every day. She wanted to go ashore and explore. But she also wanted to submerge and explore the ocean's depths, to see what treasures lay at its bottom, to better observe what appeared vaguely like schools of fish swarming around her legs down there. All in good time. There was so much time, as Adamn said. She was a novice, still learning the basics of swimming.

She cupped some of the water in her hand, let it trickle between her fingers, and watching it closely this way realized the particles it consisted of were actually numbers; computer code, each unit in itself nearly microscopic.

A huge fish, maybe even a whale, was passing below her beyond the edge of gloom, and she couldn't help but feel uneasy at its size. Yet the pale, ghostly leviathan – or was it a submarine, filled with more experienced explorers than herself? – soon passed from sight, maybe sounding deeper, and she relaxed, let the waves cradle her up and down in gentle swells.

Then, her right foot was seized at the ankle. She gasped. She hadn't seen this fish rising. Was it a shark? It gave a great yank, and Vee almost went under, splashing her arms wildly, nearly in a panic not to be drowned. Her slapping hands sent up sprays of phosphorescent droplets, like water falling past a strobe light. Like beads of blood flying from an ocean of blood.

The creature that had hold of her leg gave another, stronger tug, and this time Vee's head was pulled below the surface, her eyes wide with terror. She looked below to see what had hold of her, at the same time that she kicked at it with her free leg.

The thing that stared up at her had a familiar visage, its own eyes ballooned with hate. It was not a shark, despite its menacingly bared teeth, but a man. It was the unclothed, swimming avatar of Pastor Karl Phelps.

His gritted teeth parted, and a stream of glassy red bubbles carried distorted, burbling words to her ears.

"So here you are, you traitorous whore! I've found you! Here in Babylon with the rest of the sinners!"

Could he drown her? It felt that way. Maybe not snuff out her spirit, but perhaps disorient it, so that it became lost down here in the deep currents of the Mesh for the rest of eternity?

She kicked out at his face, but the medium she was submerged in diluted the strength of her attempts and he batted at her limbs with his free hand. As she looked down at him, clamping her mouth shut for fear of her lungs filing with tiny red numbers beyond counting, she

162

saw a white shape streaking toward the both of them like a torpedo. Vee's dread was doubled, as she feared this time it would be a shark, for it looked like something of that kind. But to her surprise, this white streak drove itself into her father's side. A great column of bubbles was disgorged from his mouth at the impact, and he let go of Vee's ankle. As Vee churned her arms to propel herself back to the surface, she watched the white form turning sharply to come back toward Phelps a second time.

Absurdly, for a moment Vee thought it was Adamn's dog, the white Akita that had lunged at her father in the virtual shopping plaza. But no, its shark-like form belied that. And now, as the creature drove its long snout into the small of Phelps' back, Vee realized what it actually was she was seeing. An albino dolphin, with eyes that were not only pink but a vivid red.

Jay, she thought. Wherever he had been stored away or taken for study, he had been connected to the Mesh.

Vee didn't linger to witness the avatar's further attacks on her father's avatar. Taking advantage of Jay's intervention, Vee swam upward to the surface, and not only to the surface of the ocean, but broke free of the Mesh itself – and found herself in her library chair, lustily gasping for air.

39: The Restless

"You don't have to do this," Michael Palladino told her, as he handed Vee her pocketbook from Hell. She peeked inside, saw her sheathed knife, her M9 Beretta and spare magazines, and a single remaining M67 grenade.

"I don't want to lead my father here and make trouble for you people," she said, slipping into the straps of her skin pouch to wear it like a backpack.

"From what we glean from the Mesh, he's taken a seat beside Pastor Johnston but hasn't replaced him. I don't think he's going to lead a whole army up here to wage holy war against us, just so he can get to you. Whatever his own agenda is, Rebecca, the Construct isn't like it was back in the Great Conflict." Next he handed her Jay, and Vee resisted grinning at the gun as its single eye rolled to gaze up at her face. "The war settled what? We just ended up with new combinations of enemies and comrades, like after *any* war. It wasn't really this big ultimate finale, this war to end all wars, to end everything bad and begin everything good. So – except for some hardcore fanatics like the Mujahideen – for all this time since, most people have been *weary* of war. Even L.A. for the most part, I'd say. We've all had enough war, a long time ago. The Great Conflict shell-shocked most of us into accepting its spoils. We had to concentrate on other things, like making this city a unit and keeping it hospitable. Sure, there'll always be little skirmishes, but nobody really has the ambition to march into a full scale battle again. And win what? A couple more floors of this place? What's there to win when Heaven and Earth might no longer exist, for all we know? What's there to win when we're all already dead?"

"Your point being?" Vee said, after having extracted Jay's last remaining magazine to check its bone bullets and then clicking it back into place.

"My point is, even if your father can manage to rally a small group of his most loyal followers to come up here to find you, he doesn't stand a chance of attacking our city. We can handle him. You don't have to run away like this."

Vee smiled at the security chief. "Are you sure you're not trying to discourage me because you suspect I'm going to rendezvous with him, now that my spy mission here is complete?"

Michael didn't look amused by this accusation. "I'm showing you real concern here. If you don't want my concern, so be it."

"I'm sorry. Forget I said that. Anyway, Mr. Palladino, it isn't just that I'm afraid to lead my father to Freetown." She glanced over at Adamn, who also stood in the room she'd been given to stay in, as she continued. "I haven't seen all of the Construct yet. I haven't been to the top. There's so much here that I still haven't explored."

"You think you're going to find better than Freetown?" Michael asked with surly defensiveness.

"Probably not, but I didn't say I was looking for better. I'm pretty sure I'd like to come back here later, if you'll have me. Once I've...I don't know...satisfied my wanderlust, my need to see and learn more. This restlessness or whatever it is I feel. Look, forgive me for saying this, but you guys in your little colonies all seem a little *too* settled in to me. I mean, I know you're afraid to venture out and end up tangling with other clans, but I think most of it has to do with you being too comfortable, settling for too little. I guess because I still feel like a newcomer, I've got a different mindset from most of you – except for a minority, it seems, like Adamn here. I still think we should try to find out what *more* there might be beyond these walls. If the Creator is gone and the old order of things has fallen, maybe we might even be able to escape."

"Escape what?" Michael asked.

"Hell."

He snorted. "Escape to where?"

"Heaven...Earth...if they exist."

"Even if they do, you think it's just a matter of *walking* there?"

"I don't know what to think. I won't know how much to expect until I know more. But you see what I mean? No disrespect to you or the rest of Freetown, Mr. Palladino, but it's like you don't even want to wonder."

"I think what's really making you itchy is that you're still confused about yourself," Michael told her. "Are you running toward self-discovery, Rebecca, or running *from* yourself?"

As if to derail the tension before a real argument could develop, Adamn cut in, "Well, as for seeing the top floors of the Construct, you can forget that idea. Believe it or not, we have actually done some exploring in our time, and we know that the top thirty or so floors of the Construct are mostly collapsed – crushed under the weight of all the solidified lava resting on the roof, we figure."

"Totally flattened?"

"Well, no...I mean, you can still work your way through a lot of the rubble, maybe, but at the risk of getting crushed yourself and maybe trapped for a real long time. I don't know that there's a lot to gain from it, except for being able to say you saw it."

"Maybe that's what I need to be able to do, then. But my mind and every nerve and cell in this phony body of mine keeps telling me to go up. Until I can't go up any more."

Michael sighed and held up empty palms. "Hey, we aren't going to stop you. But after you get that nice new outfit of yours all torn up again, feel free to come back here where it isn't really so bad, as far as Hell goes, and I promise I won't say I told you so."

Vee turned to face Adamn. "It'd be nice to have somebody to explore with me, you know. Aside from a talking gun."

"Ha!" He grinned broadly and shifted from one foot to the other, plainly flattered at her suggestion. "Me? Oh, Vee, come on...I'd be too scared for that. I'm not much of a fighter, and outside Freetown you're always going to need to fight."

"I'll cover your ass. Me and my 'gat,' here."

"Oh no, no." He shook his head, looking sad now. "I have my work, you know. My digging project and all."

"I know, and it's important – of course. But you couldn't put it aside just for a short while?"

"I'd like to, Vee, really...but..."

"I understand." She touched his arm. "Forget it. I'll be back. And I'll help you with your project then, like I said I would."

Adamn visibly brightened with sudden inspiration. "Maybe there's something I can do to speed you along, if it's getting to the top of the Construct you're so obsessed with. A little shortcut, unless your plan was to explore each and every damn level."

"That might be my long-term goal, but there are a lot of floors I missed below this one, too, by riding in elevators and all."

"Well that's what I had in mind. The elevator we move the Black Cathedral on only stops at a couple of floors, like I told you, this being one of them and of course there's the sub-basement, but we also have a door disguised on the 175th level. That'll take you right into the ruined section, only twenty-five or so levels short of the top floor, if the top floor is even accessible at all. The 175th level had some machinery one of the robo-Demons knew about, that we cannibalized to complete the Black Cathedral's makeover to a super drill."

Vee shrugged. "Okay, that's cool – I'll bum a ride, then. There's always eternity to explore the floors I'll be skipping. But maybe getting to the top quick will satisfy this urge or intuition of mine. For now, at least."

Adamn turned to the security chief. "Think we can clear that, Michael?"

"I think so, as long as some of my people go along with you. Let me talk to the board about it. I've got nothing against it myself."

Adamn looked back to Vee and said, "I'll go that far with you, then. Sound okay?"

"I guess it'll have to do."

40: The Ascent

There was a cramped control room, or "cockpit" as Adamn called it, at the far end of the Black Cathedral from where they entered – the "back" of the cathedral actually being its front when it was moving along its tracks. An abundance of levers were set into the walls and steam valves were prevalent as well, while a large glass tank of green fluid gurgled above a circular, flaming gas burner. Vee settled into a seat beside Adamn, watched him flip some toggles on a console in front of him. Before them was a large view screen which outside the cathedral appeared like one of its red stained glass windows. Through it, Vee watched the back of the elevator as it jolted into motion, and began its stealthy, silent ascent.

"The cathedral won't be leaving the elevator – we're just going to drop you off, I'm afraid," Adamn told her.

"So what are you doing here at the controls now?"

"I'm the one operating the elevator. We can control it remotely from the cathedral itself. Not to mention, from here I can open our disguised door for you on the 175th floor."

"Ahh."

Aboard with them were two of the mechanical Demons – one of them the same creature that had escorted Vee to meet Adamn in person for the first time – plus four of Michael's security people, including those two female guards with the alarmingly pierced bodies and alarming eyes, and even Dan Alighieri's wife, the severely beautiful dark-skinned Demon Olisha. Maybe Alighieri was suspicious of Vee's intentions, and wanted Olisha along to keep an eye on her. Or was it possible he was feeling supportive of her quest? Had she roused the man a little, reawakened his sense of curiosity with her own?

The numbers of the floors they passed were painted on the back wall of the elevator shaft – by Adamn's people, he told her, for their own reference – and Vee watched them in a partial hypnotic state as they sank below her, wondering what kinds of lone scavengers, or bands of nomads, or mini-civilizations lay on these levels they bypassed so easily. As they proceeded past the 134th level, even inside the Black Cathedral they heard the rhythmic pounding of some kind of machinery on the other side of the wall. And as they rose past the 148th level, they heard a wild chorus of high-pitched screaming that couldn't, she hoped, be human.

Briefly she dozed, then opened her eyes and sat up in her chair with a start. Outside the view-screen the number 162 lowered into view. The elevator moved slowly, but so smoothly that it felt like it was standing still and the Construct sinking into the earth around them.

"Not long now," Adamn said, noticing she was awake.

Vee pulled Jay into her lap, and spoke to him in the soft voice of a confidant. "So you still can't tell me anything about what we might expect up here?"

"As I told you when we first met, madam," the Demonic weapon replied patiently, its pink lips moving in their socket of bone, "the Construct has continued to evolve during the time that you were imprisoned, and I was immersed in the Mesh. I can only with accuracy tell you about various buildings of Tartarus, and the states they were in before they became the Construct. It is news to me, even, that the top floors have partially caved in as our hosts have told us."

"Well, we'll just have to find out the hard way, then." She patted his bone flank. "Hey, I wanted to thank you for helping me out there, when my father attacked me in the Mesh."

"You needn't bother. It might not be for me to say this, but I really don't care for the man, anyway."

168

Vee smiled. "No offense taken, believe me."

At last, the number 170 appeared, and Vee saw cracks in the back wall, dark glistening streams of water trickling down the surface from some rupture still above them. "This is it," Adamn announced, swiveling toward her in his chair. "We're into the ruined sections now. Actually, the elevator can't go any higher than the 175th floor; we capped the shaft with a few strong layers of metal mesh and crossbeams to catch any heavy debris that might drop into it, while still keeping the shaft open for ventilation purposes. But I'm sure it's bent and blocked and inaccessible, anyway, for the top ten levels at least."

"But is there still a service ladder up there?" she asked. Though not within their present view, she had seen metal rungs affixed to another wall of the shaft when they had mounted the steps of the Black Cathedral.

"Um, yeah, but how far it goes beyond the ceiling we made, I couldn't say."

"Did you seal the doors to any of the levels above this point?"

"No, we didn't."

"Okay, good to know. Maybe another shortcut," she explained.

"Good. Take all the shortcuts you can. The faster you'll come back to Freetown." He looked away, busied himself with peering at some gauges set into his console, obviously trying to appear casual despite his words. Vee smiled at his averted profile. Actually, he did make her want to return to Freetown all the sooner.

41: The Last Stop

The elevator came to a halt, with a shudder, at the 175th floor. "Now watch this," Adamn said, throwing a lever beside his seat. Vee felt the building begin to turn on an axis, to swivel around clockwise. She had noticed previously that the cathedral rested on a circular section of mesh apart from the rest of the elevator's tight mesh floor, but hadn't thought about it consciously. Now she knew this was how the structure reoriented itself, so that when it emerged from the elevator onto its rails the "back" of the cathedral, with its array of drilling equipment, would be to the fore.

But Adamn's intention now was to monitor the door to the 175th floor through his view screen, and watch over Vee as she disembarked here.

The rotation completed, Adamn waited for the security people to leave the cathedral first and take their positions, guns held ready. A set of high intensity lamps retrofitted onto the cathedral above the drilling apparatuses shone on the door like spotlights.

"All set," Adamn told Vee. "Guess this is it." He looked up at her. For a few moments, she didn't move away, and their eyes didn't stray.

At last, Vee smiled and said, "See you again, Adamn. Thanks."

She left the cockpit, moved to the front doors of the Black Cathedral and descended its steps, walked around the side of the building to where the four security people waited, two to either side of the door to the 175th level. She saw the guards look past her a second before she heard footsteps thumping across the floor's metal web. Turning, she saw Adamn jogging toward her.

"Fuck it," he said, stopping beside her. "I guess I can take a little break from my drilling, huh?" He addressed the security personnel. "I don't suppose anyone would be willing to part with a gun?"

One of the scary women came forward and handed over her own assault rifle, with its smoky buttstock and overabundance of bewildering detail on its mean black body. She added some spare magazines that Adamn slipped into pockets in the legs of his green scrubs pants. She said, "I'll let them know you went with her."

"Thanks."

"Who'll control the cathedral on the ride back?" Vee asked him, suppressing the grin she felt inside.

"Gort." When he saw her lack of recognition, he explained, "One of the robots. It knows what to do. Now, I hope you'll cover my ass like you promised." He held up the assault rifle. "You know this is just for show."

"I'll take care of you, little boy, no worries. So, are you ready to do this?"

"Guess so." Adamn turned, and waved at the stained glass window that was the cockpit's view screen. He called out, "Open the door, Gort!"

Vee saw that Olisha, Alighieri's wife, had debarked also and stood off to one side watching the proceedings ominously. Her goddess-like figure was nude but for a leather belt from which hung a long, straight-bladed sword in a scabbard. Vee nodded at the Demon but she didn't respond, so Vee looked forward again as the door to the 175th floor slowly began to crank upwards.

"Let's do this fast, people," the scary female guard advised in a tense voice, having pulled a pistol to replace her donated rifle. "Open and shut, quick-quick."

The door was halfway up when Vee heard someone call out, "Wait!" behind her. Looking back, she was surprised to see it was Olisha – the first time she had heard the dark-skinned Demon speak. Olisha's head was cocked, her features more intense than ever, and Vee realized she was hearing something the rest of them couldn't yet detect. But gradually, the sound became audible to the others. It was a distant but mounting discordance of many individual sounds, each one of them profoundly unsettling. There was something like the wailing of an infant, mixed with the snarling of feral dogs, mixed with the ranting gibberish of a madman, mixed with cackling laughter and shrieks of agony. Growing closer, closer, as the door continued up and up. Beyond its threshold, the cathedral's spotlights were the only illumination in evidence on floor 175.

Then, before anyone could suggest abandoning this endeavor, the door was all the way up and the first wretched figures emerged from between shadowy machines, bounding wildly into the spotlights' glare. Some sprinted on human-like legs, while others loped along on all fours like dogs. One creature hurled itself across the floor by slapping down rubbery pseudopods like the flippers of a seal.

The guards framing the door had begun firing, letting loose automatic bursts and pistol shots. A creature hit the floor and rolled almost to Vee's feet, twitching horribly in its death spasms. It had raw pink/red flesh and a face like a clenched fist. Another being – dead on its feet but propelled onward by manic momentum, ripped through by a full magazine before it went down – possessed a knobby head with a face of gnarled little tendrils, like a celery root. No two of these things were alike.

THE FALL OF HADES

"What are they?" Vee shouted to Adamn over the painful racket of gunfire. Pointing Jay at a figure bolting toward her, she reluctantly emptied the last of the Demonic gun's bone bullets. The weird humanoid figure, stark white but covered in glossy red nodules like embedded beads and globes of glass, never made it through the broad doorway.

"Mutants!" Adamn shouted back, trying to fire his new weapon but finding the safety was on. Later, when this chaos was behind them, he would further explain that these disparate entities were either the rejects of former Demonic production, somehow escaped and still surviving after all this time, or else automated processes up here continued to churn out product, albeit defective. Unless these mutant Demons manufactured more of their own kind, themselves.

Vee couldn't tell if it was hunger, or territorial instinct, or sheer madness that accounted for the ferocious intensity of the mutant Demons' charging attack. A few of the creatures were too swift, or else there were just too many of them, and made it through the line of fire – but then Olisha would leap forward and cut them down with wide, powerful swings of her sword.

"I'm out!" Vee cried, setting Jay on the floor beside her with the intention of digging inside her pouch for her Beretta, or maybe even her remaining grenade. Before she could withdraw either, Adamn pushed his new assault rifle into her arms.

"Here!" he said, then turned and raced back toward the cathedral. Vee glanced after him in confusion. He'd said he was no fighter, but he wasn't cowardly enough to retreat from a fight without her, was he?

In looking back at the Black Cathedral, she saw that the other of the two robots had emerged to lend its support, those limbs that ended in weapons emitting strobe flashes of hot gas and shaking with a metallic jangling chatter, spent shells cascading. Even still, two Demons had leapt onto its body – one looking like an orangutan turned inside-out, the other like a decomposing gargoyle. They were trying to tear at and actually bite into the robot, and in their frenzy might have eventually succeeded, but the robot reached back with a claw hand and seized the orangutan, swung it down onto the floor with great force three or four times until the creature went limp. Vee dislodged the other mutant from the robot's back with a couple of careful, short bursts from the rifle Adamn had abandoned as quickly as he'd acquired it, using the gun's scope so as not to hit the machine Demon itself.

Then, a voice boomed from the cathedral. "Fall back! Fall back! I'm hitting the hoses!"

It was Adamn's amplified voice, and by the time Vee guessed what he meant by hoses, the nozzles that aided the drilling operations were already sending jets of acid over their heads – straight through the open door to the 175th floor. The nozzle arms panned left and right, following concentrations of the oncoming mutants, sometimes even jerking suddenly to spray one charging Demon in particular.

If the mutants' cacophony of war cries had been terrible, their screams of pain were doubly so. Some were already half dissolved before they fell. One creature, lacking arms and tightly bound in filthy bandages that bared only one red eye and a lipless mouth of gnashing teeth, came hurtling straight at Vee shrieking like a woman on fire. She smashed it in the face with her rifle butt to save on ammo, and stepped back quickly as it rolled on the floor still shrieking until the acid that had spattered it had eaten into its throat. Its rolling and screams ended at the same time.

Either the acid killed the rest of the mutants back amongst the machinery, or the survivors had sense enough at least to turn and flee from its sweeping, far-reaching arcs. Of the mutants that had already emerged, the fighters picked off the ones that hadn't been sprayed or finished off those that had been sprayed but hadn't yet succumbed. Vee saw the robot step on the skull of a Demon with a head like a mummified jackal, flattening it, apparently trying to conserve ammo, too. Olisha chopped and slashed at a number of the wounded or dying, at one point stopping to look up at Vee with another of her grim, impenetrable stares.

Cupping a hand over her nose and mouth, her eyes tearing from the acid fumes, Vee slung the assault rifle over her shoulder with her free hand and then retrieved Jay. When she rose, she saw Adamn striding toward her. He had found a pouch of his own inside, and held up a flashlight to show her, though Vee already had one attached to the body of the assault rifle.

"Looks dark in there," he explained.

She raised her brows. "You're still going with me, after that?"

She saw him look over her shoulder at the gaping blackness leerily, his face blanched, and knew it was the last thing he wanted to do, but that he wasn't willing to back down in front of her. Wasn't willing to let her go in there, and onward, alone.

"Let's just do it before I change my mind," he told her. "And before those things come back."

42: The Wastelands

It was a long, tense, furtive undertaking weaving their way through the machines that dominated the 175th floor. Early on, they held their breath against the stink of the acid fumes that formed an acrid mist, swirling in their flashlight beams, and the stench of the freakish bodies strewn around them. A few of these still gave jerks, twitches, and inhuman groans, despite the steaming and bubbling of their liquefying forms.

Further in, the bodies, fumes, and bullet holes punched into the machinery were left behind. It became oppressively, heavily quiet. Vee would have preferred to hear at least a few distant cries, just to know the deformed Demons weren't crouching behind this next rank of machines.

Further in, also, evidence of the damage Adamn had informed her of started to become evident. Sections of ceilings had collapsed, girders and partially fallen walls blocking doorways, forcing them to double back and find alternative routes more than once. They located one staircase leading up to floor 176, but it was totally choked with rubble and impassable.

Several times they almost ran into one of the defective Demons; once, they hunkered down behind a machine with their flashlights doused while something passed on the other side, wheezing and apparently dragging one hard, unusable limb. Finally, however, they found a stairwell of red brick – wide as a courtyard – that was only partly obstructed by heaped debris from a tumbled portion of wall. Iron steps like fire escapes wound around and around the shaft, and they were able to bypass floors 176, 177, 178, 179. Narrow windows were spaced irregularly in the brick walls; oddly, some had bars or metal shutters, while others simply had curtains veiling them – some of the latter with glass broken but others with their cloudy panes still intact. In her rifle's stark flashlight beam, Vee caught a glimpse of a ghastly white face peering at them from behind a torn shade, but instead of crying out the creature, whatever it was, withdrew in terror.

The stairwell terminated at the 180th level, and here they ventured forth in search of a means of accessing the next floor...and the next.

This level, though, appeared to be entirely caved in by its collapsed ceilings and heavy machinery from the floor above. The only way Vee and Adamn could navigate through it was, at best, hunched almost double, but more often on hands and knees or even crawling on their bellies. Vee wormed her way first, dragging herself by her elbows, sweeping the dark jumble ahead of them with the assault rifle's flashlight, while Adamn came behind, carrying his own flashlight and with Jay jutting out of the supply pouch he had taken from the Black Cathedral. None of them, including the gun, dared even whisper, so shaken were they still by the confrontation back on the 175th floor.

Now, through a gap in the wreckage to her right Vee could see a ladder bolted into the wall, set back in a recess that seemed to have been protected from collapsed debris, and so she changed direction, squeezing like a spelunker under a low slab of concrete with sharp twisted lengths of rebar fringing its edges. She was halfway under this slab, with barely enough room to raise her chin from the floor, when a loud hiss blasted her cheek with rank steaming breath, and she swung the gun – scraping it against concrete – to illuminate a horrible face only a few feet from her own. The thing had a head like an eyeless horse skull grafted onto a limbless grub-like body that she could almost believe had evolved over time to facilitate the movement of such creatures through these ruined areas. The body was wriggling hideously, like a man bound in a straightjacket, as the creature fought to reach her, its jaws yawning wide like those of a python.

Vee fired the assault rifle directly into its mouth, down its gullet, and for a few moments the thing's thrashings became even more frenzied, though it had stopped advancing. Then, it went still, and through the ringing in her ears Vee heard Adamn call up to her, "What the hell was that?"

"Another freak. Come on, there's a ladder ahead – let's get to it before his friends get here."

She reached the metal ladder, pulled herself to her feet inside its niche. Looking up, she saw light bleeding into the shaft high above. She began to climb, and Adamn was soon following behind her. When they were quite a way up – having already bypassed a door labeled 181 – they heard a few wild, warbling calls from the level below them, so they quickened their ascent.

Nothing came in pursuit of them, though, and they were left alone with their own enclosed, laboring breaths.

43: *The Divine Golem*

The light cast into the ladder's shaft was deceptive, farther away than Vee would have judged. They climbed past stenciled metal hatches that gave into levels 182, 183, 184, 185. They tried none of these doors to see if they would open, or what might lie behind them. A few of the ladder's rungs almost pulled out of the wall under their weight, and Adamn slipped precariously once but caught himself before he could plummet.

For whatever architectural reasons the ladder didn't go all the way to floor 200 (likely, because this former building of Tartarus had possessed only 186 floors), the shaft came to an end at the door to the 186th level. The hatch lay open, too, blackened and twisted and hanging on only one of its hinges; hence the light that had entered the ladder's shaft.

There had been a serious fire on this floor. An inferno. They could walk upright – at least in this part of the level – but amongst scorched machinery, charred floors and walls. In a series of large lab-type rooms, desks and work counters were badly buckled from the heat, glass beakers and test tubes half melted as if made of ice that had frozen again. Some computers, resting on the tables or set into walls, had had their screens shattered or melted, as well...though, miraculously, a number of screens still flickered with a snow of pixels or vague, distorted images they couldn't interpret. Vee swore she saw a man's face peeking out at her from behind a shroud of static, but she did a double take and by the time she looked back the indistinct face had receded.

In the next lab room, they came to a startled stop when a clutter of debris resting alongside one carbonized wall abruptly reached out a clawed arm, which clutched at the floor and dragged itself a few inches forward. A blackened head like a huge metal flower lifted, turned in their direction, but the robot Demon's single eye had been burst by fire, leaving only an empty socket. Still, the crippled thing seemed to be aware of their presence. They stole into the room guardedly, Vee training her weapon on the creature as they crept past it. One of its limbs was tipped with a gun, and might it still fire despite the damage the Demonic contraption had endured?

Yet the mechanical Demon only pivoted its head slowly to follow their progress, while continuing its own, putting out that feeble claw again to drag its ruined body a little further. Vee was tempted to shoot the thing, not to eliminate a threat but to put it out of its misery. But she didn't, and they reached the opposite doorway unharmed and left the creature behind them.

There was another such creature in the next room, however. This one sat on the floor with its back against a wall, into which were set rows of computer monitors and control panels. Some of the screens, and buttons on the control panels, still glowed despite the ravages of flame. The explorers had been alerted in advance that something was active in here by a continuous, rapid rattling sound, and they now understood what it was. This machine Demon was jacked into a port in one of the instrument panels. Its red eye stared into space as if entranced, while its seated body jerked continuously with violent spasms. Vee wondered if electrical current were flowing into the convulsing robot, and asked Jay if he thought that might be the case. Poking up out of Adamn's pouch, the Demonic gun replied, "No – its system is reacting to whatever it's experiencing via its interface."

"It's in the Mesh?"

"This archival technology predates the Mesh, but it did form the foundation for it. It could be that this being has found a back way into the Mesh through its interface. I can't tell from out here."

"Well I'm not hooking you up to find out...it isn't important."

"I hadn't asked you," the Demon replied stiffly.

"I know you, you Mesh junky." Vee smiled, and gestured for Adamn to resume moving.

Onward through a few more rooms, these without any robot Demons and with no functioning equipment. When their progress was blocked by a closed hatch, Vee opened it warily for fear of attack. What she hadn't anticipated was an attack on her olfactory sense. Quickly, she clapped a hand over her nose and mouth.

"Jesus," Adamn whispered behind his own hand, "what is that stink? It smells like a storage room for roadkill."

With no great enthusiasm, they stepped through the threshold into a chamber that was radically larger than the series of labs, with a ceiling that defined the limits of Level 186 and made them angle their heads back to look up at it. The ceiling, crossed with girders, was buckled and bowed and had actually given way in some places; machinery from above had fallen to the floor below, or hung suspended from thick tangles of cable.

The right side of the chamber was lined with metal warehouse-style shelving, still packed with steel drums and piles of cinders that must have once been wooden crates. A robot Demon that was configured like a forklift, no doubt utilized to access these high shelves, stood immobile beside them, its head hanging. It looked like it had been sprayed with bullets in addition to having been swept with fire.

The left side of the room had shelves, too, but these supported rows of glass cylinders like those Vee had encountered early on, several of which had contained the tick-like Demons with their surgical forelimbs. These dozens of glass tubes were all empty, however, even of the greenish amniotic solution of those other breeding cylinders, maybe having been stocked here until needed.

At a wide break about midpoint in these left-hand shelves stood two mammoth cylindrical glass tanks that reached from the floor almost to the ceiling itself. Both tanks were filled with what Vee first took to be a milky white fluid, until she realized it was some sort of solid matter. The tank on the left was intact, but the one on the right had sustained damage from a dislodged girder, its fallen end resting against the tank's ruined cover. Great cracks ran down the sides of the tank, but up until now it had held together.

A thin film of Essential Matter covered the floor around the base of the tanks, a stark white contrast to the surrounding black charring. Thin, drooping white stalks had grown up from this patch. Vee noticed more of the weeds growing from the upper surface of that half fallen girder, as well. The Essential Matter must have drifted down through the rift in the ceiling, from the floor above.

"What's in the bottles, Jay?" she asked as she and Adamn reluctantly started walking down the wide center pathway between the flanking metal shelves, still shielding their lower faces. The stench was intensifying, and now Vee understood why. The smell came from whatever was in that second, compromised tank. Either that was its natural odor, or exposure to the air had caused the matter to spoil. Or decompose.

"It's raw material for the formation of Demons," Jay explained, Adamn having positioned the gun for a better view of the tanks as they approached them. "Blank, undifferentiated cells waiting for their programming, as it were."

"It's like dough," Adamn told her. "Or clay."

The tanks were just ahead of them now, but the stink was too great for them to want to move in for a close inspection; their destination was the doorway at the far end of the chamber. But Vee glanced again at the tanks curiously as they drew level with them. This near, the twin cylinders towered even more imposingly.

And then Vee noticed something, a kind of *shift* within the damaged tank, and said, "Hey..." a moment before the terrible howling began.

She flinched back so violently from the giant cylinder that she crashed against Adamn and sent him stumbling, as well – as a huge mouth big enough to swallow both of them opened in the side of the white, rubbery matter contained within. The mouth worked against the glass barrier as if to chew its way through, though it presented no teeth within its dark maw. Yet it was another mouth, above the first, that had begun the howling, and a few moments later several more mouths yawned open and added their own shuddering roars and ululating wails to the deafening assault. Vee and Adamn went from covering their noses and mouths to clapping their hands over their ears, as they backed further and further away from the base of the cracked container.

Vee thought she even saw a white, rudimentary attempt at a giant eye form in the side of the great amorphous mass of cells before the orb lost its form. Mouths would close without leaving a trace, and new mouths open elsewhere to resume their raging, disharmonious chorus.

But when they had backed across the room, almost to the opposite shelving, the cries gradually died down to merely – if it could be called merely – deep moans and sob-like sounds. The mouths opened and closed, flattened against the glass, but less frantically. Vee and Adamn slowly lowered their hands from their ears, and Vee took up her assault rifle but kept its barrel pointed down so as not to alarm the substance within the cylinder again.

"What the fuck?" Adamn hissed, looking as though he might vomit from fear.

Vee again regarded the girder resting against the lid of the container, the weedy growths that had sprouted along its length. "It's the Essential Matter," she said, nodding at her own intuition. "It trickled down into the jar from above. It rooted in that stuff. Jay, you said this protoplasm or whatever it is was waiting to be programmed. Well, I think it has been programmed with something, accidentally."

Another long, bass deep moan made the floor vibrate beneath their soles.

"Whatever it is, I just hope that bottle can hold it," Adamn said.

"We'd best get moving, Vee, before it gets stirred up again and breaks out of there."

But Vee was mesmerized, as she watched a new mouth stretch wide and let loose another short, forlorn bleat. It sounded like the lonesome call of the last dinosaur.

She said, "It's like the Creator, isn't it, Jay? The way you described Him to me...the way He was before He blew Himself to bits. Confused. Tormented. Enraged at everything – all the war, the chaos. Enraged at Himself."

"Are you suggesting we're seeing the accidental rebirth of the Creator?" Jay said, from Adamn's pouch.

"Maybe that's what I'm saying. Or at least, an aspect of Him could have been seeded in there. It's richer soil than anything the Essential Matter has encountered. It's primordial soup."

"Madam," Jay said, seeming wary, "I fear your buried self may be surfacing."

Vee tore her gaze from the bottled golem to look back at the Demonic gun's solitary red eye. "What do you mean?"

"You're hoping for His return. You loved Him once. You want to love Him again."

"I'm not loving anything. I'm only suggesting a possibility."

"Perhaps you're being too imaginative."

"So what if I am? And so what if I was to be hopeful? Those are human qualities. But maybe you can't relate to that, Mr. Spock."

"Human," Jay said. "Yes. Forgive me, then, for not being more human."

Vee drew in a long, calming breath. "I'm sorry, Jay."

"No need. How can you hurt my feelings? I'm not human. But if you ask me, the best thing we could do – if we had the time, and the ability – would be to kill that thing in there. *Especially* if it's the Creator. It seems to me, we might all of us be better off for it. Humans and nonhumans alike."

"*Why?*"

"We've been more free since He's been gone."

"Seems to me things haven't been any freer or any better...just the cards got shuffled, is all."

Vee wanted to say that killing this entity wasn't for them to decide, even if they did have the means. She wanted to say that such an act could be the greatest crime of all eternity, an act that in some way might bring down upon the head of every being in existence a doom from which this time there would be no phoenix-like rebirth. But she knew Jay might also be right. She knew that she knew too little to say more, so she didn't.

"Let's *go*," Adamn urged them both.

"All right," Vee said. "Let's go." She motioned with her gun toward the far doorway, and they resumed walking toward it. But she threw looks back at the cylinder, saw how only one or two mouths would gape open now, as their groans and laments became fewer and more subdued. She again believed she saw an eye blink into and out of existence, and then the white matter went inert. Returned to its troubled slumber.

They had reached the door, which stood open, and since Vee had lingered a second or two for a final glance back at the quieted golem, it was Adamn who started across the threshold first.

But Charles Roper, security commander of Los Angeles, stepped into view on the other side of the doorway, leveled a craftily improvised flamethrower weapon, and blasted Adamn point-blank with billows of holy, purging flame.

44: The Hunting Party

Adamn was a fireball on legs, a running and screaming comet trailing a tail of flame, black smoke, and glowing flakes of ash like bits of burning paper. He dashed off at an angle, and Vee thought he had the intention, if he was capable of forming any intention beyond sheer flight, of hiding amongst the right-hand shelves and their heaps of cinder. (In his present condition, perhaps he thought to blend in.) Roper didn't try hosing him again with the flamethrower, maybe because he was out of range, but Earl – the former Vietnam tunnel rat – stepped through the doorway firing an M16. Vee recognized the man from the words REBORN TO KILL painted across his white helmet. Adamn flopped to the floor before he could reach the start of the shelves, rolled over a few times, then curled into a ball, no longer able to form screams. Vee saw Jay skitter across the floor away from him. Flames lapped along the bone body of the Demonic gun, too.

Before Vee could think of racing to Adamn's side, however, or could even choose between discharging her own assault rifle at Earl, in the doorway, or Roper, who was darting off toward the left-hand shelves, she was whipping around to confront gunfire that came at her from behind – the doorway by which she and her party had entered the vast chamber. She dove to the floor, rolled on her shoulder, came up firing back at her attacker as she sped toward the right-hand shelves herself, meaning to work her way over to where Adamn and Jay lay burning. She caught a glimpse of Johnny, the Demon-raping Demon wrangler, the Confederate flag painted on his helmet visible even from here. Also equipped with an M16, he withdrew from the doorway to avoid her stitching line of bullets.

Vee threw herself behind a row of drums, which rattled loudly as slugs punched into them. She popped up and fired at Roper, as he sprang behind a line of glass tubes. These shattered, some falling into exploding shards, but she was soon crouching low again as both Earl and Johnny – on opposite ends of the room – nailed the drums in a crossfire. The barrels sang like a church bell assaulted with a jackhammer.

The barrage tapered off – were they loading fresh magazines? – and Vee took the opportunity to rush to a position nearer to Adamn. Too late, Earl resumed shooting, as she ducked behind a stack of metal crates. Peeking between two of them, she saw that at least the flames had died out across Adamn's roasted, motionless body.

Again the fusillade ceased, but this time a voice replaced it. A familiar voice, calling out from the doorway where Johnny had positioned himself.

"Rebecca!" cried Pastor Karl Phelps. "It's your father!"

"No shit!" she shouted back.

"I just want to talk to you!"

"Really?" Hunched down, she shifted to another bit of cover –

183

some machinery that had dropped through the ceiling – closer to Adamn. "Is that what you've been doing?"

"Well, do I have your attention now?"

She moved again, scurrying behind a jagged mound of charred wood. Buying time, she called back, "I'm listening!"

"I'm willing to show you the mercy, pity, and compassion you did not show me when you left me as a prisoner in that devils' den. Come back to Los Angeles with us, my poor confused child. Let your father help you remember your love for me. Your devotion to me, that you've forgotten. And your love and devotion for our Lord."

"You want me to believe you won't hurt me or lock me up somewhere?" On hands and knees, Vee crawled behind a long, low wall of rubble. They could probably guess, by tracking her voice, that she was on the move, but talking with them was her only way of stalling, of holding back a renewed attack. She wondered if maybe her father were being sincere – whether he truly hoped to bring her back to L.A. unharmed, and give her another chance at making a home there. But from what she had learned of her father, at least in the state he was in now after all his years as a prisoner, she thought it much more likely that he was baiting her. He was a relentless avenging Angel. But then, she thought, what was she?

"It's no trick, lady!" Roper yelled from somewhere behind the cylinders. "Just cool down and think about this! Think about why your father came all this way to find you!"

"Look at me, Rebecca!" From the far doorway, Pastor Phelps walked into the open, holding out his empty arms beatifically as if waiting to be bodily delivered back to Heaven. "I have faith in you! Can you show some faith in me?"

She was close to Adamn now, but he lay out there in the open, smoking, looking like the victims of nuclear holocaust with whom he had entered Hades. Already beginning to regenerate, he was moving his legs slowly, no doubt painfully. "Keep coming!" she cried to her father. "Maybe I'll believe you if you can talk to me face-to-face like a real father, instead of having your lackeys fill me full of lead first!"

"Here I am, child!" He was indeed still coming. "Now where are you?"

"All of you!" Vee barked. "If this isn't a trap, prove it to me! All of you come out here!"

"Ease up, lady, will ya?" Roper hollered back.

"No, she's right," said Phelps. "Come out here, men. Earl, Johnny. All of us will prove to Rebecca that we only mean to take her back to our bosom!"

"Yeah," Vee murmured under her breath, watching her father proceed further and further down the central pathway. "That's it... keep coming."

"Come on, boys!" Phelps encouraged the others. "Yes, that's it! Lower your guns, let's go now!"

Earl and Johnny reluctantly obeyed, stepping out from their cover and dropping the barrels of their M16s. They started toward Phelps from either side of the chamber. And after a few more seconds, Roper too emerged from behind the glass cylinders and moved toward Phelps, his flamethrower slung low.

"Closer," Vee whispered. "Closer..."

She saw an eye open in the side of the blob trapped inside its titanic genie's bottle.

Her father was still advancing, as his three soldiers converged on him. They moved at a quicker pace than he, no doubt wanting to protect him as he made himself more vulnerable. The pastor was almost opposite the enormous twin cylinders now. "Come out, Rebecca...please!"

She stood up slowly into view, to coax them all just a little bit further and a little more close together. "Here I am!" she cried.

"My daughter," her father said, near enough for Vee to see the trained, camera-ready smile on the televangelist's face.

And behind him, another mouth parted and spread. A mouth like a garage door rising open. The gears in Vee's heart jammed to a stop in that second, before the howling began anew.

45: The Wrath

The three soldiers snapped around with their guns poised, and started

185

dancing backward, Roper placing himself in front of Phelps and nudging him into retreat.

"What the fuck is that?" Earl shouted, his voice all but drowned out by the dissonant caterwauling.

Of course, Vee chose this as her moment to break cover. She sprang over the low wall of rubble, reached Adamn's side and squatted down beside him. She began to slip her free arm under his shoulders. He turned his head a little, but his eyelids were seared shut and so she bent close to what was left of his ear and said, "I used to think you look like Kevin Bacon, but now you just look like bacon."

She wasn't sure if he'd heard her. She began to hoist him up, found it difficult without laying the gun down. As she turned to do so, she saw a figure step into view from around one of the far-spaced riveted metal columns that supported the high ceiling. The man wore a white uniform, and a white bone helmet with a cross painted on it in gold paint.

"Tim," Vee breathed.

Her former fiancé carried a craftily improvised weapon that could spray acid from a tank attached to its underbelly—she could tell from the acid's familiar caustic odor—and he leveled this gun at Vee's face.

"Hey!" cried a hoarse voice just behind Tim. He half turned toward the exclamation, startled. It bought Vee the single second she needed. She swept up the assault rifle she had just been about to lay down, and triggered it with one hand. A sustained release that sent the gun shuddering upward with its recoil, until its mag ran empty.

The bullets pounded up Tim's body like bombs dropped across an enemy landscape. They didn't pierce his ballistic vest, but one bullet did catch him in the neck below the edge of his helmet, and he fell to writhe on his back, clutching his gurgling throat.

Vee looked back toward her father and the men who had meant to divert her while her unsuspected fiancé snuck up on her from behind, and saw them glancing at her in turn as they pulled back from the formless, bottled monster. They had heard her gunfire over its thundering and screeching.

She dropped the empty assault rifle, plunged her hand into her pouch and drew out a heavy ball, like a metal apple. Letting go of Adamn, she pulled her last grenade's pin, stood up as Earl and Johnny began firing at her, and hurled the M67 with all her might before throwing herself down again, covering Adamn's body with her own.

Raising her head, she saw the grenade go past the men. Hit the floor. Skitter almost to the very base of the giant, cracked tank before it detonated. Just as she had hoped would happen.

Vee cringed as the explosion's shockwave clapped her ears and passed as a vibration through the floor and Adamn's body into her own. A thin cloud of smoke hung in the air following it, revealing Phelps and his three holy warriors, all of them fallen to the floor like tenpins except for Johnny, who was staggering and lifting off his helmet. Maybe he was screaming beneath the monster's screams, because the goggles of his helmet had been shattered and blood streamed from both eye sockets.

There came a loud crack, loud enough to be heard over the blob's roars, like a rifle shot. Another followed, with a distinct crackling sound trailing off in its wake. This time Vee saw a crack zigzag up the side of the glass cylinder, from its base to about midpoint.

Suddenly it seemed all of the golem's mouths were positioned one above the other along this one especially long crack, opening and closing against it from the inside. Exerting pressure.

The men hadn't been close enough to the explosion to be badly injured, and Roper was helping an unsteady Pastor Phelps to his feet when the compromised cylinder finally gave way under its internal pressure, and split open like an egg. Glass fragments went flying. A long dagger of glass embedded itself in the back of Earl's neck as the stunned Vietnam vet was still rising, but it didn't matter much, because a moment later the golem was surging out of the ruptured tank and Earl was crushed under its bulk. Absorbed *into* its bulk.

There was a released foulness so prodigious that Vee held her breath, and held back a retch. It was like another shockwave rolling over her.

No longer contained, compacted inside its glass sarcophagus, the golem seemed to grow in size, to spread out its oozing mass in all directions. But it was also definitely moving *forward*, toward Phelps, Roper, and Johnny. Its unstable, uneven edges rippled across the floor like pseudopods and slapped for purchase like flippers that formed and unformed. All the while, mouths—dozens now, and as many eyes—flashed open and shut across its mountainous body in agitation. Glass shards poked up out of it, maybe adding to its furor, but the disturbances across its body were dislodging them so that they fell away to the floor or else were swallowed up by the flurry of temporary mouths.

Roper was pulling Phelps along with him, fleeing awkwardly, but Johnny seemed unaware that the behemoth towered behind him, and was still staggering with his hands clamped over his punctured eyes when an especially wide mouth stretched open. With a lurch forward, like an avalanche of bloodless flesh, the golem closed its maw around the Demon wrangler and gulped him out of sight.

Vee had risen from Adamn, onto hands and knees and ready to push herself to her feet, and saw that his eyes had cracked open as his body fought to reconstitute, his mouth moving and maybe speaking but she couldn't hear. "Wait a minute," she told him, maybe unheard by him as well, and then with one eye on the progress of the golem she was bolting toward where she saw Jay lying on the floor.

She took a detour first, however, veering toward Tim as he struggled to sit up and reach for his dropped acid gun. Vee swept up the gun, sent Tim's helmet flying from his head with one savage kick, and thrust the weapon's nozzle into his gaping mouth. She pulled the trigger, and Tim flopped onto his back again as bloody foam bubbled up from the deflating basketball of his head. "Sorry, honey," she told him.

Having slung the acid gun across her back, Vee turned again toward the Demonic gun and knelt down beside it. At first she couldn't bring herself to touch Jay, as if afraid to be burnt. The sentient weapon's once ivory form was now black, rough in texture and still smoking. His eye was rolled up white in its socket, though he must have been able to see only minutes ago; she knew it was he who had called out, "Hey!" to distract Tim before he could use the acid gun on her.

In their circular hollow, Jay's lips were moving soundlessly, too.

They were cracked, flaking, and she could see that even his teeth were black behind them.

"No," Vee said. "Oh no…come on, Jay. Come on." Finally she picked him up—he wasn't too hot to the touch—then she was racing back to where Adamn lay. She saw him reaching up with one arm as if groping in the air for her.

She also saw that Roper was slowing the advance of the golem with short blasts from his flamethrower, as he half dragged Phelps toward the doorway in which he'd appeared before frying Adamn. The immense amorphous body would crisp like marshmallow where the flames lapped it, but the flesh would fold in on itself to swallow the damage and douse the flickering embers, presenting fresh cells as it remade the ruined ones. The thing's eyes seemed larger, the mouths wider, the roars louder as Roper stoked its fury. And yet somehow above the noise, Vee could hear her father's voice, trained as it was to shout out to audiences both physical and virtual.

Pastor Karl Phelps was bellowing, "Thou preparest a table before me in the presence of mine enemies thou anointest my head with oil my cup runneth over surely goodness and mercy shall follow me all the days of my life and I will dwell in the house of the Lord for ever amen amen amen amen amen fuck fuck nooo Satan! Lucifer! Beelzebub! Adversary!"

Vee ducked her head under Adamn's arm, and in straightening lifted him to his feet. He let out a sob of pain in response. "Move, move, come on!" she ordered him. "Move your legs with me!"

Shuffling along beside her, supported by her, Adamn croaked close to her ear, "Not this way." She was moving in the opposite direction from the one Roper and Phelps were taking—toward the door through which they had entered this area. It was farther away, and a step backwards in their quest.

"I promised him," Vee said. "I promised him."

She forced Adamn along at a loping pace, almost lifting him off his feet with every other stride, and when she had removed herself sufficiently from the commotion behind her she paused long enough to look back. It was just in time to see Roper's flamethrower run out of fuel. In time to see her father babbling incoherently—she realized he was speaking in tongues. In time to see the two men engulfed, and lost within the raging mass as it rolled over them.

Vee didn't look back again. Lest the monster turn its myriad eyes her way, and come in pursuit of her next, she forged ahead at a desperate pace, one arm around Adamn and carrying Jay with her free hand. The golem continued to howl, but she didn't know if it was at her or at something else. If it howled at its own condition, or at the human condition…at the past, present, or the future. She left it to its laments as she plunged at last through the far doorway.

46: The Heroes

Vee closed the doorway's hatch behind her; it latched but didn't lock. The horrible cries, and horrible stink, were deadened. She hoped the blob wouldn't force the hatch open with pressure, then squeeze its body through into the rooms—the rest of the Construct—beyond. She hoped that when her father and his men had met their maker, so to speak, they had been so thoroughly digested inside the mobile sea of cells that they could never again reform their own bodies. But she also hoped, in that event, that they did not in any way program the cells as the Essential Matter had. Bring their own brand of corruption to its simple, pure rage. People had always made God in their own image figuratively, but Vee thought that men making their own maker literally might be the most frightening thing imaginable.

They retraced their way through several empty rooms until they had returned to the chamber in which a mecha-Demon sat on the floor with its back against a wall of control panels and computer monitors, still convulsing and rattling as when they'd encountered it before. Vee let Adamn slip down to the floor in a similar position, his back also propped against the wall, then rushed to where a rubber-sheathed cable from the automaton was plugged into a jack. She tugged it free and the cord snapped back inside the Demon's mechanical frame. It slumped forward into its own lap like a marionette with its strings snipped, going still after who could say how long.

Vee rested Jay on the floor, saw that his eye was still rolled up white but his lips were no longer moving. "Please," she whispered. "Please not yet." She took hold of the end of his own retractable cord, pulled out its length and inserted the tip into the wall jack.

The monitor directly above this instrument panel held a faint glow, showed gray static with occasional black bands crackling through it. When she plugged the gun into the jack there was a burst of loud hissing and the picture rolled several times like a badly tuned TV channel. But then, a return to the softly fizzing, dimly glowing field of gray static, a sandstorm safely locked outside a thick window.

"I'm sorry, Jay," Vee said, looking down at him again. "I'm sorry I ever pulled you out of there." She fought back tears as she rested her fingertips against the blackened bone.

A few feet away, Adamn had managed to stand up on his own. He was slowly healing, but still a scorched effigy of himself. He tore away the last rags of his clothing and dropped them to the floor, a cicada molting its old shell. Vee went to him, helped support him again. As she did so, she saw Adamn looking past her, over her shoulder. "Vee," he rasped.

"What?" She turned to look back at Jay lying on the floor below the wall and the sizzling monitor.

A red glow emanated from the screen, the static having gone from gray to crimson. Vee left Adamn leaning his back against the wall so that she could draw closer to the monitor again.

There was a barely distinct object moving beyond that red sea of static. Actually, moving *through* the red sea of static. It had a sinuous, fluid motion, and it was white. A white dolphin, swimming away into the static, receding from sight.

Vee smiled, and this time allowed the tears to come. The picture rolled again, and the gray static returned, but she knew that Jay had made it into the Heaven of own choosing. Once more remembering that song by David Bowie, she whispered, *"We can beat them, For ever and ever."*

47: The Keyhole

They searched through the more demolished areas of Level 186, and eventually found another means of continuing their ascent of the Construct. As he recovered, Adamn's physical discomfort turned to a sense of discomfort at his state of undress, and Vee teased him about it. Once, when he was clambering up a ladder ahead of her from the 192nd to the 193rd floor, she reached up and pinched a buttock, telling him he was climbing too slowly.

Everything above the 194th level appeared to be completely squashed flat, so that they no longer ascended by climbing stairs or ladders but by crawling up through the rubble like ants through impromptu tunnels, squeezing into any claustrophobic passage they could find, not knowing even that they had passed from the remains of one floor to the next unless they chanced upon a broken slab stenciled with the number 195, a fragment of wall reading 196. They ventured into crevasses and crannies so tight, or amongst heaped moraine so precariously balanced, that they wouldn't have attempted it had they not been immortal. Repeatedly they had to retrace their path and find another avenue when they encountered an impassable dead end, sometimes after what must have been hours of progress. Several times, after much strenuous and frustrating effort, they nearly gave up trying to access the next level altogether, almost relented and turned back toward Freetown, until they would find at last just enough of an upwards slanting gap in the debris to worm their way through.

At what could have been the compacted ruins of either the 197th or the 198th floor, a hand thrust out of the wreckage close by Vee, its fingertips brushing her cheek. She flinched back, brought up the 9mm pistol she had been carrying in one fist while she crawled, and saw a face sandwiched at an angle between two slabs, the mouth squashed so that the person's words were badly slurred.

"Get me out of here...please...please...been here so long... please..."

"Adamn," Vee said helplessly.

He moved up beside her to look. "We can't dig him out ourselves...

but maybe if we could ever get the robots up here. Even then, we're talking a whole lot of work."

"I'm sorry," Vee told the face lodged in the shadows. "We'll be back later on. We'll come back for you in the future."

"No you won't!" the Damned man wailed after them, his hand grasping at the air as they resumed their squirming passage. "No you won't! You won't!"

"Adamn," Vee groaned.

"I know," he said. "I know."

Up through a vertical channel, like a chimney, and finally into a space open enough for them to stand in. What they did, however, was lie beside each other on their backs, smeared with concrete dust and blood, panting from their exertions like exhausted lovers. "I'm so thirsty," Vee moaned.

"Please don't even say that," Adamn said.

"What's that?" Vee sat up, frowning at the ceiling. She regained her feet, reached up and poked a finger at a tiny breach in the little cavern's ceiling. With her nail, she dug out some pebbles, and light gleamed in the opening she had widened. "Adamn," she said in an urgent whisper, "I think it's sunlight."

"Sunlight?" He got to his feet as well. "Vee, come on, that's crazy. Even if this is the top of the Construct, there wouldn't be any sun out there. This was Hades. The sky was a ceiling of lava."

"Lava that all fell in the deluge. Until there wasn't any more ceiling."

"But a sun…come on now. It must be a lighted room…another level, still."

"Boost me up," she said.

"Okay, wait, hang on." He shoved a block of masonry over for her to stand on. Stepping onto it, Vee found her head almost touching the ceiling, and she probed some more at the gleaming hole, worrying at it with the muzzle and front sight of her handgun. Watching her, Adamn asked, "What is it?"

Vee stood on tiptoes, tilted her head back awkwardly in an attempt to bring her eye right up to the hole. "Oh my God. Oh my God, Adamn."

"What? What?"

"Look." She stepped down from the block and they switched places.

Soon enough, it was Adamn who was exclaiming, "Oh my God. Oh man…that can't be!"

"We've got to get your robots up here, for sure," Vee told him. "All your digging crew."

"Yes…God yes, absolutely! We should go back for them right away!"

They discussed what they saw out there, took more turns peeking at it, and Adamn speculated on how he might direct excavation efforts up here without the use of his burrowing Black Cathedral.

Once again peering out the hole at what lay beyond, Vee said, "I don't want to wait for all that, Adamn."

"What do you mean? You want to go back and see if we can find another way up here? A bigger hole, maybe?"

"No. I had another idea." She turned her face toward him. "Remember that terrorist you told me about, who tried to sneak his way into Freetown?"

Realization dawned on Adamn's face, mixed with a look of horror at the implications. But the horror lessened, and he had to wag his head in wonderment, as Vee jumped down from the block and started unzipping the front of her jumpsuit. "What are you doing?"

"I don't want to ruin my clothes, do I?" she explained. "I want them waiting out here for me when I come back."

"Maybe this isn't such a bad idea, after all," he said, looking her long straight body up and down as she stepped out of her garment like a snake shedding its skin.

But his expression became more horrified again, as he saw Vee fetch her combat knife, kneel down in front of the stone block as if before a miniature sacrificial altar, and spread her left hand flat upon it. She looked up at him. "Are you ready?"

"Ready to…?"

"You know what I'm talking about. Come on, are you ready?"

He braced his bare feet, in both hands holding the acid gun they had brought with them. "I don't know if I can do this."

"Don't be squeamish; you should be used to the mechanics of Hell by now. Anyway, it's going to be a lot worse for me than it will be for you."

"In one way, it will."

Vee poised the knife's blade over her pinkie finger, seemed to pause to collect her breath or her will, and then bore her weight down on it and started sawing. Adamn grimaced, winced as he heard the metal rasping against bone, then the crunch as it made its way through the joint.

"Ow...ow...oh shit...fuck," Vee was chanting through gritted teeth. When the blade scraped against stone, she rapidly stood up with the severed digit clutched in her hand, blood in ribbons wound around her pale arm. She mounted the block once more, standing in a little puddle of her own blood, and pushed the finger into the hole in the ceiling. Through the hole. It dropped, unheard, somewhere on the other side. Then, she looked down at Adamn, her face tensed with pain and anticipation, and hissed, "Do it!"

"Vee..."

"*Do it!*" she snarled.

Adamn brought up the acid gun and pulled its trigger. He sprayed her white, naked body up and down, as if using a garden hose to clean a statue atop its pedestal.

She screamed. How she screamed. She toppled off her pedestal to the floor, and he stepped around the block to spray her some more. What was left of her tried to crawl away, despite her orders. Soon enough, though, the pathetic mewling thing that had once been her body could do nothing but curl in on itself like a fetus. A fetus in a reverse conception, being unborn, waiting to disappear.

48: The Fruit Restored

A voice called to her. Was it the voice of her own mind? She opened her eyes.

Above her, a sky not so much overcast as cloaked in steamy white clouds that diffused the light of the sun—if there was a sun behind them. The sky's uniform white glow made translucent-looking silhouettes of the intervening canopy of foliage spread over her. Notched fronds like those of palm and banana trees. Closer to her face, ferns crowded about her. She felt their feathery touch all across her body, and realized she was lying on her back on the ground. She propped herself up enough to see that she was nude, and that her body was white, pristine. She sat up further and looked around her groggily.

The air was heavy with humidity. The surrounding abundant vegetation was tropical, even prehistoric in aspect. And all of it lacked pigmentation. All of it, absolutely white.

The scaled or ribbed trunks of trees, whiter than birch bark, swept up from the undergrowth like the half-buried bones of extinct monsters, that had somehow sprouted lush new life. Cycads abounded, with their explosive bunches of leaves, stout trunks and evergreen-like cones; all of it pure white. The jungle was like a photographic negative or a weird infrared photograph. The effect was almost wintry, as if every leaf and blade and vine, every stalk and branch and trunk had been encrusted with snow, but the air was steaming with heat.

Pollen floated in the air around her, like dust motes. No, not pollen, she realized, and then her awareness came washing back whole. Drifting spores of Essential Matter.

A forest grown from Essential Matter, extending to the limits of her vision in every direction.

"Vee," came that voice again. It was not inside her head, though she couldn't see its owner. A man's voice. Adamn.

"I'm here," she croaked, the first words from her new throat. She had slept through her entire regeneration, as if the weariness of her former body had carried over to this new minting.

She stood, wavered only a second before she felt more firmly grounded.

"Thank God," she heard Adamn say. "I was worried something had gone wrong. Or you'd wake up without any memories again. What's it like up there?"

"Beautiful. Scary beautiful," she said. She looked behind her, down at the ground. It was uneven, rocky, being as it was a broken landscape of rubble, but a thick white moss covered most of the stone and appeared to form a fertile bed into which or through which the other vegetation had put down roots. "Where are you?" she asked.

"Here. To your right."

Vee turned some more and saw the blade of her knife flashing, where Adamn had thrust it up through the hole and moved it to catch the light. "Okay. Got you."

"How the heck are you going to get back down here again?"

"We'll figure it out. Right now I just want to explore a bit."

"Come on, Vee, don't you be getting yourself lost, now."

"If I get lost, I'll find my way back eventually. We have the time for that, don't we?"

"Yeah, but you're up there, while I'm stuck in this hole."

"You'll have your chance, I'm sure. We all will." She started away, stepping tentatively at first as she traversed the dips and rises made by heaped slabs. Hard surfaces and jagged edges were cushioned by the spongy moss, though fangs of shattered concrete and punji sticks of rebar did jut up from it in places.

She waded through ferns, pushed between drooping branches and dangling loops of twisted vine. Something like Spanish moss hung from tree boughs in ragged curtains like masses of cobwebs. If Adamn were to call out to her now, she was already too far away to hear him.

The stands of trees thinned out and she found herself at the edge of a sizable clearing, a sea of shoulder-high elephant grass that stirred in waves in a languid, hot breeze. On the other side, though, the dense trees resumed, their masses of leaves like earthbound clouds, limiting the extent of her view. Did this forest cover only the top of the Construct, or the surrounding deep bed of solidified lava as well? Did it blanket, had it transformed, *all* of creation?

Vee learned that not all that swam in the air around her was Essential Matter. She found herself brushing away a curious winged insect that hummed away too swiftly for her to get a good look at it. And even as it fled, a movement amongst the trees across the clearing drew her attention. She held her breath, as if the barest sound might give her away, as the long neck of a brontosaurus-like creature reared up into view. The wavering flexible horns atop its featureless head told Vee it wasn't a dinosaur, however, but something like a gigantic albino slug.

She had the intuition that the creature would be harmless, but nevertheless she turned back into the jungle to follow another direction.

Deeper she went, surely lost, but not afraid. Instead, what occupied her mind was a tug of war of desires. On the one hand, she was desperate for them to share this discovery with the people of Freetown as soon as they could. On the other hand was an equally desperate impulse to hide this revelation from the rest of the Construct for as long as it could be concealed. This was a world unto itself, here, with life that had been evolving and flourishing for some time. It didn't need them. Did she dare to think it could ever be for them?

When after much random exploration she had begun to feel tired, her bare feet sore and skin flushed with heat, and guilty for leaving Adamn alone this long, she decided to work her way back to her point of entry. She hadn't had anything, like her knife, with which to mark a trail, but even if she had she wouldn't have wanted to defile the bark of a single tree in this virgin world.

It was during her efforts to return to Adamn that she chanced upon the fruit.

She spotted it from a distance even through the branches, the fronds and creepers, because the fruit was a vivid red amidst all this whiteness. Like a beacon, it drew her.

Vee approached the base of the otherwise undistinguished tree from which the fruit hung. She saw no others depending from its branches. Were there any others at all in this jungle? If not, how had she managed to stumble upon this single specimen, unless it had somehow called to her, attracted her in a way she wasn't conscious of?

The fruit, she saw, was large—big as her fist—but irregular in shape. Her brow furrowed as she stared up at it. Were those raised, squiggly markings on its skin...veins?

Vee understood, then, that the fruit had grown in the form of a blood-red human heart.

The heart-shaped fruit was just above her head. She could pluck it if she wanted, and she reached up to at least touch it to see if it were actually hard inside, or as soft and pulpy as it looked. To see if those veins were really pulsing, as they appeared.

But before her fingertips made contact, Vee stayed her hand. Slowly, she lowered her arm.

At that moment, the warrior Vee thought she might very well want to ensure that no one ever touched this fruit, even if she had to stand here, gun in hand, and defend it from every last soul and Demon and Angel in Hades, unto eternity.

Whether or not that would be possible, or even necessary, one thing she knew for sure.

She herself would not touch it. No...this time, she would not touch it.

THE LOST FAMILY

"Please be careful not to dislodge me, madam," Jay said, riding across the woman's back. "If I fall from this distance I'll surely break."

Vee paused in her climb to glance downward, into the shaft through which she ascended. They had entered the vertical service shaft through an access hatch on Level 119, but the shaft ran deeper than that. Maybe all the way to the basement?

"Even if you didn't break, Jay, sorry but I don't think I'd go down there after you."

"Understood," Jay said drily. "All the more reason for caution, if you will."

The Angel named Vee had heard there was a settlement called Freetown on the 128th floor of the Construct. A large colony where the Damned lived cooperatively alongside Angels, and even Demons – though not all races of Demon, surely, for she had just barely escaped a pack of small, skull-faced Demons several levels below her present position.

She had learned of Freetown from Jay, her only companion in her exploration of the Construct. Only recently had she awakened from centuries as a catatonic prisoner of war, many levels below in the bowels of the Construct, without any memory of her past either as a mortal woman or, after her death, as an Angel. Nor did she remember the infernal war she herself had apparently participated in – the Armageddon that had left the last remaining Damned, Angels, and Demons sheltering inside the impossibly vast structure called the Construct, with the shattered remnants of Hades outside its walls buried under solidified lava.

In this utterly alien world, Jay had served as a most useful guide; the Virgil to her Dante. But to add to that he also shot bullets, being a mecha-organic rifle grown from bone, with a single eye and a pair of lips set into his side, and the sentience of a Demon. To top off his usefulness, he could jack into the Mesh. And it was through the Mesh that Jay himself had learned of Freetown. For Vee, who couldn't recall anyplace from life or afterlife that might have felt like home, it sounded as good a destination as any.

Vee had gained the many floors of her ascent by any number of means – from crawling up through ventilation ducts to riding freight lifts, from metal spiral staircases to opulent marble staircases. Presently she ascended to Level 120 by shimmying up a thick bundle of cables that ran through a concrete shaft. Corroded rungs were set into the side of the shaft, but after one had pulled out of the wall in her hand she had decided the cables were safer. Also set into one wall was a series of lights, about every third light still providing illumination. The Construct's technology had been added to over the centuries, but many systems had never run down even without repair or modification after nearly two thousand years. That said a lot about Demonic technology – but then again, it was only an illusory corporeality anyway, like Vee's own body.

Illusory or not, by the time she reached the top of the shaft and passed through the soaring heights of Level 119 into Level 120, Vee was gulping make-believe air and sweating make-believe perspiration inside the form-fitting second skin of her rubbery black jumpsuit. Her shortish, reddish hair was plastered in spikes across her forehead.

She poked her head up through the opening warily at first, poking up the blunt muzzle of the bone gun with her, but she saw no one about. For all the many Damned, Demons, and Angels who made their home inside the Construct, they were so dispersed and the Construct so unthinkably immense that anywhere you went within it seemed desolate. Sometimes Vee felt that she and the gun were the only beings in the entire structure. Sometimes she wished they were.

There had been a metal plate in the floor covering this opening at one time, but it had been unfastened and set aside before her. She was grateful; though she had a few simple tools in the pouch slung over her back, it would have been awkward if not impossible clinging to the rope of cables and unfastening the cover herself. Plus, if those skull-faced Demons had continued tracking her and were to follow her up the shaft, it would have been all the more unpleasant trying to get that cover off.

She pulled herself out of the hole and to her feet, turning this way and that alertly. However peaceful Freetown might truly prove to be she couldn't as yet say, but she had not only encountered hostile Demons since awakening from her coma, but hostile tribes of Damned and Angels as well.

She was in a room so long and wide that three of its walls were lost in the murk. The nearer fourth wall was composed entirely of huge windows that had once let in the glow of Hell's churning red sky. Now, outside the windows was only solid volcanic stone flush right up against the panes.

A forest of riveted metal support columns lay around her in all directions, and the ceiling – low in this particular room, not reflecting the true ceiling of Level 120 – was similarly crisscrossed with support beams. But other than that, and puddles on the floor where water had leaked through the ceiling here and there, the room appeared absolutely empty. It had the look of a construction project that had never been finished. She was surprised one of the larger, more ambitious tribes hadn't staked out this open territory in order to build a community.

She had opened her mouth to express this thought to Jay – and to ask if he had any idea what direction they should take from here to find a means of continuing their ascent – when she caught her breath.

She smelled the Demon before she saw it. It was a scent of incense, burnt into the entity's flesh. Up close she knew the scent would be choking. She didn't want to get close enough to experience that.

A moment later and she could hear its approach, too, but by then she had already ducked behind the nearest support girder, wide enough to mask her long lean body. Peeking around its edge, she stared into the dark haze of the distance where the lights were too far-spaced or feeble to illuminate. A pair of white eyes beamed from the shadows, followed gradually by a hulking dark shape that began to form from the gloom.

Jay had told her that when the more human-like races of Demons had begun sympathizing with the rebellious Damned, Hell's response had been to mass produce less anthropomorphic Demons. This was one of them. It was a bulky thing, so wide it barely passed through the spaces between the metal pillars. It looked like a great soft body partly hatched from a hard chitin exoskeleton; a horrible synthesis of obese human and predatory insect. It was sepia in color, though its scorpion's forelimbs shaded to black.

Its glowing white eyes slowly turned this way, then that, sweeping the girder forest. Was it patrolling its territory? Hunting? Or merely pacing this vast room in a mindless state to pass the hours of eternity, like a sleepwalker, just as she herself had lapsed into catatonia in the Construct's dungeon? It didn't matter; whatever motivated the creature, it was a being she didn't care to encounter – certainly not one of the Demon races she expected to find living in Freetown.

Could she cross the room column to column, waiting for its head to swivel in another direction each time she needed to advance? But how wide was this room; how long before she found a doorway? After her arduous climb, she didn't want to backtrack to the shaft and descend, then have to seek out another means of gaining this level. She might run into those little skull-headed Demons again; out of the frying pan and into the fire. Anyway, if this Demon were to look into the shaft while she was descending, though it was far too large to follow her inside it might still find something heavy to drop down on her, or even snip the cables free with its pincers.

No, she would take her chances crossing the room, advancing toward the creature as it advanced toward her until they'd passed each other. Its bulk and slowness were to her advantage. When she saw the

Demon turn its burning eyes away from her, she darted to the next closest girder. That incense scent was stronger. She only hoped the Demon couldn't sniff her out, too.

Vee had advanced a half dozen girders and was growing more optimistic about stealing past the Demon without it becoming the wiser, when she heard Jay whisper, "Madam! Behind you!"

Pressed close to her present shelter, Vee looked over her shoulder. Through the metal tree trunks she caught a glimpse of eyes like very distant headlights, moving slowly at an angle from left to right. Another wandering Demon, her back exposed to it. She was lucky Jay had spotted it; with him, she had three eyes.

The one in front of her was shambling nearer. How much sooner before the one behind noticed her? And how many more Demons might be patrolling this great room? A dozen? A hundred? This could well be why the space hadn't been claimed by would-be colonists.

Vee glanced around the floor, looking for a plate covering another shaft entrance. Unless one were hidden by one of the scattered pools, there didn't appear to be any. Scattered pools...from leaks in the ceiling. Vee cast her eyes to the ceiling. A system of open latticed joists. Yes! She could crawl along the lower portion of the beams, above the heads of the Demons until she found a safe spot to return to the floor...a spot with an exit from this chamber.

The rivets in the girder were large, distended, and she planted one foot on the lowest of them to boost herself up. She needed both hands free to take hold of the girder's rusting, flaking edges, so she had quickly secured Jay through the straps of her pouch, across her back, just as when she'd climbed the rope made of power cables.

Vee made it to the top of the column and immediately pressed herself flat across one of the iron beams, a surface just broad enough to conceal her. The Demon that had been ahead of her began to pass directly below her. It stopped suddenly, swiveled its head, appeared to be sniffing at the air or listening. Vee held her breath – not that her body actually needed to breathe in any case.

Finally, as if reluctant to give up the scent, the Demon gave a deep, irritable grunt and continued on. Answering grunts came rumbling from three or four other directions. Vee congratulated herself on taking this approach instead of the former.

Not that it was easy inching along on her belly, the beam's surface interrupted in the center by the angled latticework that connected upper and lower portions, crowding her movements. And she did her best not to let the bone gun scrape noisily against the metal. It would be a slow, stealthy process. She was still learning patience, having to accustom herself all over again to the notion that the immortal didn't need to hurry.

She soon came to one of the spots where water had leaked through the ceiling, maybe from a fractured pipe somewhere above. Here, the concrete of the ceiling went from water-stained to actually fallen away, chunks like miniature islands scattered in the puddle below. When Vee was under the irregular hole, she lifted her head and tried to peer into its depths. Her thoughts were rolling. If she pulled herself up inside there, would the going be easier? Or would the risk of falling through another weak spot be too great? Maybe she'd be able to keep to straight lines where the ceiling joists lay beneath her.

She waited until none of the Demons – and she saw three of them now from her vantage point – were facing her way, then rose and pulled herself up through the opening, expecting its ragged edges to give way under her weight at any second. She made it up without even an untoward sound, however, and positioned herself over where she knew the joist would be. Then, she looked about her.

She was in a narrow crawl space through which a large water pipe ran (and it was indeed rusted through at the point just above the hole in the concrete), plus some thinner conduits and power cables fastened along the space's confining walls. She could almost rise to a crouch but remained on hands and knees. Just a little light bled in through the hole, and through a few more far-spaced gaps ahead and behind her. Anyway, all she had to do was move in a straight line now. She was very satisfied – except which direction to follow? She decided just to keep heading in the direction she had already been taking, and started crawling forward on hands and knees.

Gradually a light source shone up ahead like a beacon, and it became brighter the closer she drew to it – this time not the weak glow up through a collapsed section of concrete. This light came from the left-hand wall: a solitary fluorescent tube affixed there. Directly opposite the light, a panel was set into the right-hand wall. An access hatch for the crawl space, no doubt. Vee went into wary mode again, but was also hopeful that this would deliver her into an area where she could walk upright, maybe find a secure shelter in which to rest. Already being dead, she couldn't die, but she could feel fatigue.

This access panel was no typical metal hatch, she found when she came up on it. It was a sheet of thick translucent plastic, more a window than anything. Its surface was rippled and frosted to admit light but it couldn't be seen through. Vee glanced from the plastic pane to the fluorescent tube, back to the window again. Was this some primitive means of security – a stranger's silhouette showing in the window, while the stranger himself couldn't see a thing? But Vee had faced more threatening situations since coming out of her long mental hibernation, and her curiosity was too strong for her to bypass the window and keep moving. So, laying Jay down just beside her knee, she tested to see if the window might open. It was not hinged, but neither was it fixed in place; she was able to push the panel out on the other side yet maintain hold of it so it wouldn't drop noisily.

She tensed up, expecting a burst of gunfire perhaps. It didn't come.

She found herself looking into a small room with a closed door. In fact, it was a bathroom, and directly below the window rested a toilet.

A toilet? The Damned (and Angels like herself, who had invaded Hell to battle the rebel armies of the Damned) didn't need to eat, but one still felt the craving and enjoyed the process. Fortunately there were various kinds of edibles to be found or produced. But no one in the netherworld needed to void waste. True, some Demons shat, only so that they might rub this shit on restrained prisoners, or collect it in great vats in which to submerge their victims. A toilet for a particular race of Demons, then?

Vee leaned her body in and as quietly as possible rested the plastic window panel on the closed toilet lid. Then she eased one leg through the window, onto the toilet tank until she could squeeze the rest of her through. A bit tight, but she was slim enough. When she had her feet under her, on the tiled bathroom floor, she drew Jay down, then pressed the windowpane back in place.

She heard no sound behind the closed door. It was wood, apparently, but then there had once been forests and jungles aplenty in the vastness of Hades. It was not the door that filled her with a sense of confusion bordering on wonder...

There was also a shower stall enclosed by a plastic curtain. The pipe that fed it ran across the ceiling and disappeared through a little hole in the wall, obviously patched into the water system that passed through the crawl space outside. But when Vee opened the toilet, she found its bowl was empty. So was its tank when she lifted its cover off. Further, the insides of the lid and the tank itself were of a terracotta color, whereas the outsides were glazed white. So the toilet was a sham, then, fashioned out of hardened clay or some other pliable material.

Clean white-painted walls. Towel racks bearing crude towels. A sink, with a mirror over it. Vee winced at her reflection. She hoped she might make use of the shower herself, if this place proved abandoned. She tried the single faucet on the sink. Cold water came forth, a little tinged with rust. She didn't doubt the simple drains for the sink and shower contributed to the puddles on the floor of the barren factory floor below.

Now, Vee turned to the door. Reached for the knob with her left hand, Jay tucked against her right side with her finger on his trigger.

Opening the door slowly, cautiously, she found herself in a dark little hallway. At its end, warm light and a funny fizzing sound. Static.

There were three other doors in the hallway. Vee closed the bathroom door behind her, and just as cautiously as before cracked open the door directly opposite.

Dark inside, but just enough light fell into the room for Vee to make out a wide, comfortable-looking bed. A chest of drawers. On the walls, a few apparently original paintings and drawings in wooden or metal frames. Vee suddenly felt like Dorothy delivered from a crazy world back to prosaic Kansas. Under her breath she muttered, "Jay, we're not in Oz anymore."

"Madam?" he whispered.

She ignored him, closed the bedroom's door and opened a third wooden door. When she saw what lay inside, she leveled Jay at the bed with both hands and stiffened in a firing stance.

A human woman lay in the bed, covered by a rough blanket, eyes closed. This bedroom was much like the other, except that a single muted bulb glowed from atop the chest of drawers. Vee crept closer to the woman, closer, until she stood directly over her pointing Jay at her head. But the woman's face remained unmoving, even peaceful. She was elderly. Vee looked up at the walls. In this room the walls were decorated with needlepoint projects. One of these read: HOME SWEET HOME.

Vee wagged her head. Not Kansas, then, but the Twilight Zone.

She left the room, shut the door, opened the last of the hallway's four doors but only looked in from the threshold. A much smaller bed, and scattered crude toys.

Vee eased the door shut, turned at last to gaze down the hallway toward the source of that warm light and sizzling static. Four beds… only one occupied…

She stole down the hallway, listening for more sounds beyond that irritating screen of static. At its end, she slid her back along the wall and gingerly peeked one eye around its edge into the room beyond.

It was, of course, a living room. A Black woman perhaps in her thirties (before she became an immortal, at least) sat on a makeshift sofa with a drawing pad on her knees and a stick of charcoal in one hand. A white man sat in an armchair, gazing at a TV. And sitting cross-legged on a woven rug in front of the TV was an Asian boy of maybe seven. The TV wasn't a TV, however, but a computer terminal showing only churning pixilated snow on its monitor. None of the three people appeared jacked into the Mesh. Vee wondered if the TV were only another prop, then.

None of the three people stirred in the slightest. She couldn't see the faces of the man or child, but the woman's eyes were open and unblinking. Her drawing hand didn't move. They might as well have been mannequins in a department store's showroom.

Vee stepped fully into the room but remained leery of a trap, an ambush, Jay still at the ready. She neared the man in the chair enough that she could see his open, glazed eyes, the snow from the monitor reflected in them.

"Hello?" she said to him. "Excuse me?"

No response. She resisted the impulse to reach out and shake him a little. Instead, she leaned close to the woman. "Hey," Vee said. "Can you hear me?" The woman remained frozen, the tip of the charcoal stick touching the paper unwaveringly. Vee cocked her head for a better look; it was a pleasing drawing of a cottage in a snowy forest, wood smoke rising from its chimney.

Finally she hunched down beside the little boy, and in a softer tone said, "Hey, guy, can you hear me in there? Kid?"

The boy didn't turn his head nor even blink, perhaps enraptured by images that played only in his head. Vee straightened.

So, they had shut down, then – just as she had once done. But she had apparently been tortured, and finally encased in a cement sarcophagus…left alone and forgotten for centuries until that cement prison had eroded away. She had turned her consciousness off to escape her pain, her loneliness. The only escape that was possible to her.

She looked around again at the great effort that had gone into making this little apartment secreted between the bottom and top of Level 120, like an extra hidden level. All these meticulous details, crafted over time. Why go through all that only to sit down and go into a vegetative state for the remainder of eternity?

On the far side of the room was a doorway leading into a kitchen. Vee crossed the living room to enter it and look around. As in the bathroom, there was a single frosted window. Now she realized the reason for the fluorescent tube situated outside. It gave the illusion of sunlight shining into the room.

A small table and four chairs made of mismatched but white-painted wood. A working stove, tapped into a gas line. A mock refrigerator, not cold inside. If the fridge and the cabinets had ever contained food, the mixed little family had long ago exhausted it all.

A mixed family was right. Black mom, white dad, Asian son, and dear old grandma turned in early for the night, sleeping in her room. Hell had been too vast, limitless in fact, for families to find each other and be reunited, and some members had gone to Paradise while others – more often than not no great sinners but simply not having satisfied the strict qualifications to escape damnation – had been consigned to Hades. And so, new families had formed and taken in Damned children, showing more compassion than their Creator ever had. Vee was glad that, overwhelmed with pain and madness at the breakdown of His system, the Creator had obliterated Himself and was no more. Jay had told her all about that.

And to think she herself had once been one of the blessed. Despite the frustrations it had brought, she was thankful she had forgotten herself.

Vee sighed, returned to the living room and once again looked from immobile figure to figure. "Fuck it," she said to Jay, "I'm taking a shower."

Jay leaned against the toilet close at hand, keeping an eye on the door while Vee showered. The door had no lock on the inside, so first she had removed the windowpane in case she needed to make a fast escape, but when she'd heard the distant grunt of a passing Demon below she had set it in place again lest it hear her, too. Let the Demon believe the water dribbling down from the ceiling was another fracture in the ancient plumbing.

After donning her jumpsuit again she returned to the living room to contemplate its museum-like tableau. Idly she approached the large screen of the computer monitor, knelt down and looked over its keyboard. In her hands, Jay said, "I could try jacking into the Mesh from this port," he offered.

"No…I was just thinking it would be great to watch an old movie right about now," Vee said, straightening up. "Watch a two thousand-year-old rerun or something." She studied the glassy-eyed family once again. "Maybe they created all this so it would be a psychologically comfortable environment to shut themselves down in. So they'd feel safer doing it." She picked up a sculpture from a wall shelf, apparently fashioned from the same material the toilet was. "Makes me think of the tombs of the pharaohs, with all the comforts of life entombed with them. I have to say, though –" she set the sculpture down again "– it really is on the cozy side. Coziest spot I've come across in Hades."

She went to sit down beside the woman on the sofa, tempted to take her sketch pad from her and page through it, but she was afraid that might rouse her. Vee realized she was no longer afraid the woman or the others might become hostile; it was more a matter of conscientiousness.

She leaned her head against the backrest, Jay across her thighs, and said, "I'm so tired. When was the last time I slept in a real bed? I can't even remember. I could fall asleep right here and now."

"If you like, you could lie down in one of the bedrooms. I'll keep an eye on the door for you."

"Jay, you're the best Demonic gun a girl ever had."

๑ა

"Madam!"

In her dreams she was not an Angel warrior who had named herself Vee, but a child named Rebecca, waking in her bed on a Saturday morning. The window by her bed was open, letting in a warm-cool breeze and the sound of some extra-diligent neighbor already mowing his lawn. Smell of new-cut grass. Bird song. And a bone gun with one red eye calling to her...

"Madam!"

If Jay could have triggered himself maybe he would have, but he wasn't pointing at the old woman anyway. She, however, was aiming a semi-automatic pistol inches from Vee's face.

"Who are you?" the elderly woman demanded in a voice shaking more from fear than from age.

"Goldilocks," Vee said, staring up at her.

"Don't try to be smart!"

"Please, relax. Clearly I'm like you."

"It doesn't matter what you are, Damned like us or an Angel – this is our house! You're not a part of our family!"

"I thought you were in a trance like the others."

"I was only sleeping."

"Do you take turns watching over the rest?"

"No." The woman's frown deepened. "I can't go to sleep the way they did. I've tried, but I can't. You might think I'd be the easiest one to do it, but no. Maybe it's the opposite – because I lived longer. More to let go of."

"So you watch over your…family."

"Yes, just me. Which brings me to my question again – who are you, and how did you find us in here?"

"Purely by accident. My name is Vee. I swear I mean you no harm."

"No harm? With that infernal gun of yours?"

"He's the most pacifistic gun you'd ever want to meet."

The old woman backed off a few steps but kept the handgun trained on Vee's face. Though she gripped it in both hands, the weapon trembled in the air. "You have to leave now."

Vee sat up slowly, keeping her arms spread so her empty hands remained visible. She wasn't afraid of being killed, since her immortal soul could never be destroyed – and she would regenerate even the most severe damage to her mock body – but that didn't mean she couldn't feel pain. Pain was always something to avoid.

"Okay, okay, sorry I intruded," she said. "I can see this is a very private place." She realized something now, as she thought of returning to the crawl space through the bathroom window. She had seen no doors leading outside from this apartment. It was not meant to be readily entered, or departed from.

As if considering the same line of thought, the old woman asked, "How did you get in here?"

"Bathroom window. I was hiding from some Demons – you're lucky they're too big to explore up here. All I want to do is make my way to the 128th floor. Have you or the others ever heard of Freetown?" Vee stood beside the bed now.

"I'll take that for the moment." The old one switched her gun to one hand and dragged Jay against her leg. "No, I haven't. We're fine here."

"So how long have the others been out of it?"

"Have you seen any clocks or calendars in Hell?" the woman snapped. But then she said, "I've been alone a long time. I mean – awake alone a long time. I'm not alone. I feel comfort that my family is around me. They may not be fully conscious but part of them takes comfort, too, in all of us being together."

Vee slowly lowered her arms to her sides. The elderly woman didn't protest. She said, "So they didn't start out with the intention of going to sleep like this?"

"No. We made this place to escape all the horror, and we lived here for a long time as a family. But the three of them found themselves falling asleep for longer and longer times. They knew what was happening. So one night we all sat and discussed it, and decided to give in to it. We were all right with the decision. We weren't escaping each other. We wouldn't be interacting anymore, but we'd all be here, close together."

"Except they could do it. And you couldn't."

"Yes."

"You must get lonely, even with them beside you. I'll bet you still talk to them, even if they don't answer you back."

"I want you to go now."

"Do you really? Isn't it better to have someone to talk to?"

"Not if it's you!"

"Do you ever miss your real family?"

The old woman's angry voice quavered. "Did you come here to torment me? You're an Angel, aren't you? I can always tell. You hypocrite Angels are more sadistic than the Demons!"

Vee felt guilty for prodding her. "I'm sorry, I'm not trying to hurt you. I guess I just want to understand you. I was unconscious like your family for a very long time, myself. But I'm not sure escaping is the answer. Maybe we should be changing things instead. Maybe we need to remember the life we left behind, and hurt ourselves with the memories so we won't accept how things are."

"If we didn't remember how things were we would never have built this place, would we? Or made a family for ourselves. We did change things – but we four couldn't change the whole of the afterlife, could we? So we changed this much of it." She gestured around her with the pistol.

"Yes, I know. And I admire you for it. Really. I envy you that you have a family you love."

"You don't have any family anymore? I thought Angels were allowed to reunite with their families."

"I have a father. I don't have any clear memories of him from before I was imprisoned by Demons during the Conflict. I've learned he was an evangelist in life, and nowadays he's leader of a community of Angels here in the Construct. They're pretty hardcore, like the Conflict never ended. He feels I've rejected him and betrayed the cause. So he'd like to hunt me down and capture me to – I don't know – brainwash me back into who I was. Or just torture me for not being like him anymore." Vee gave a bitter smirk. "So no, as far as I'm concerned I don't have any family."

The elderly woman nodded. Now it was her turn to say, "I'm sorry." Consciously or not, she had lowered the handgun. She sighed, looked down at the sentient gun. Jay's lone eye with its red iris gazed up at her with curiosity. The old woman lifted her head again and said, "I'm Judy. You can stay here and rest awhile, if you want. I don't have food anymore – my son Andrew used to sneak out for it, but with him asleep now…"

"That's okay. Thanks anyway, Judy."

"Well, maybe…maybe you wanna go back to sleep for a while? It's all right. You just really surprised me, is all."

"I understand." Vee glanced behind her at the bed. "I guess I would like that, if you're sure it's okay."

"You said your name is – Vee?"

"Yes."

"It's okay, Vee."

215

Vee followed sounds from the kitchen, a little groggy from her nap. She didn't want Jay to feel excluded but she didn't carry the bone gun with her, to better put Judy at ease. The old woman looked up at Vee and smiled pleasantly. Vee was relieved to find she hadn't lapsed back into suspicion. Judy had already arranged two dishes made from that glazed clay, some crude utensils snipped from sheet metal, and was in the process of setting down a platter upon which rested two misshapen, tendrilled white roots with something of the appearance of ginseng. One of the former species of infernal plant life that had been successfully cultivated inside the Construct. Vee cocked an eyebrow.

"I know I told you I was all out of food," Judy explained. "Sorry about that. I had a few of these stashed away. I was saving them for my grandson if he ever woke up. He likes them. They're not as bad as they look."

"That's very kind," Vee said, taking a seat. Her stomach rumbled at the very concept of food, no matter how unappealing it might look.

"It's best eaten raw, not cooked," Judy said, taking her own seat. "I don't know why, but it sort of breaks down into a terrible stringy mush."

"Raw is fine."

Judy plunked a root onto Vee's plate. Cutting into her own, eyes downcast, she said, "My grandson liked to help me prepare food. I remember my daughter used to love to help me cook when she was small."

Daughter…small. Vee knew the woman was talking about her mortal life now. Did she always drift into these memories, or had Vee's words stirred them up from the silt of her mind?

Judy looked up to meet Vee's gaze and said, "Do you know why I was sent to Hades instead of Paradise? I'm Jewish. I never killed anyone, never robbed anyone. But I'm not a Christian."

"It wasn't fair, the whole system…I know."

"And so where is my daughter now? My grandchildren? Where did my husband go when he died before me? Are their souls out there, outside the Construct, fossilized in that rock but *aware* for eternity? Or somewhere here in the Construct and we just haven't found each other?"

"I understand," Vee said inadequately. Again she felt guilty for being an Angel.

"Maybe it's better if they are in the rock," Judy reflected. "Just so long as they've gone to sleep, like my family here has done."

Vee chewed a piece of the crunchy root. "Mm," she grunted, smiling around her mouthful. "You're right, it isn't bad. Could use a little salt, but..."

She succeeded in pulling Judy back to the here and now. The elderly woman smiled in return.

A sound came from beyond the kitchen, small and unidentifiable. The look Vee and Judy exchanged altered in character, and they had already begun turning toward the doorway to the living room when a diminutive figure appeared there. The figure was as tall as Judy's foster grandson would have been, had he awakened and come to join them at the table to partake of the roots he enjoyed. But it was not the little Asian boy.

The Demon was unclothed, with a withered little body like a mummified monkey come to life. The black claws curling from its fingers resembled an eagle's talons. The head, disproportionately large for its gnome-like body, was a hairless skull barely covered in skin, but with a tapir-like snout hanging down in front of its bared grin of jet black teeth. Deep in hollow sockets, its tiny eyes glowed entirely white, like those of the much larger Demons patrolling the factory floor below the apartment.

The snout snuffled noisily. It had used its sense of smell to track her, no doubt. The lipless grin seemed to stretch wider, if that were possible. And then – with movements that looked like speeded-up film – the creature was launching itself at Vee.

But Vee had risen, too, and swung her arm at the oncoming Demon. In her fist, the knife she had been using to cut into her root. She cried out as the Demon's wildly flailing claws sliced deeply into her left forearm through the material of her jumpsuit, and dug channels along her jaw as they sought her neck. Vee sought the neck as well, and found it. She plunged her knife all the way to the handle in the center of the Demon's throat. It backed away with the same uncanny speed,

217

the knife still protruding from it, crashed its back against the mock fridge. A burst of black blood snorted out from its snout.

"Judy," Vee cried, "go get me my gun!"

Judy scurried from the room, babbling and sobbing to herself, while the Demon gurgled and collected itself to spring at Vee again. "You stupid fuck," she snarled, picking up the chair she'd been sitting in and cocking it back over her shoulder, "you know you can't kill me. You know I can kill you. So why do you do it?"

It was true. While an Angel or a Damned person, both formerly human, could not be killed, a Demon had no immortal soul. Though natives of the afterlife, Demons were essentially mortal.

The pigmy Demon lowered its bony head as if it might charge her and drive it into her guts like a battering ram. It slashed at the air furiously, its arms a blur, but foul inky blood was running over its lower teeth and down its jaw.

"Nature of the beast, huh?" Vee barked at it. "Well come on! Come on and see the nature of this beast!"

Maybe the Demon felt it was dying and had nothing left to lose. It sprang. Vee swung the chair. And a stream of automatic fire rattled from the doorway to the living room. Vee cried out and let go of the chair as several bullets crashed into it mid-swing. But the bullets struck the Demon, too, in the side of its oversized skull. Its head shattered like an earthen pot and something looking like a fist-sized cauliflower soaked in oil thudded off the refrigerator.

Vee turned to see Judy standing in the doorway, holding Jay in both hands. "You almost blew my hands off, but thanks."

"You're cut!" Judy whined, badly shaken.

Vee took Jay from her. "Angels heal faster than Damned, don't worry. You better go get your pistol."

"Why?"

"That little bastard followed me up here from Level 117. He was small enough to take the same path as me." Vee glanced past Judy warily toward the living room. "And he wasn't alone. There were a half dozen of those things on my trail."

"Oh...my," Judy said.

"Fuck me," Vee hissed, wagging her head. "I'm so sorry I led them here."

❧

Vee was standing on the toilet lid, peeking out through the hole where the Demon had removed the windowpane just as she had, when Judy joined her with retrieved pistol in hand. Vee said, "Even hearing gunfire, none of your family has woken up?"

"You think they've never heard gunfire before? But," Judy admitted, "not from inside our apartment. I've never had to really defend it before – you're the first one who's found us."

"That's me, always stirring things up. Look, I've got this window covered. You go watch the one in the kitchen. Maybe we'll get lucky and it was just the one –"

Something breaking in another room…a sudden commotion. "The kitchen!" Judy blurted.

"Okay, you stay here!" Vee said, hopping down from her perch and tearing from the room.

She plunged down the hallway, turned into the living room, saw a new figure added to the still life there: a Demon standing beside the sofa, head cocked to one side curiously as it took in the unruffled scene, as if absorbing an unexpected display of taxidermy. It started to whirl around when it heard Vee and she stitched it with bullets made from bone – but even as she did so, another of the Demons flashed into the threshold of the kitchen, spotted her, and came hurtling at her maniacally. Flung itself into the air, talons spread. As the first Demon crumpled, Vee swung Jay toward the second. She strafed the Demon in midair and sidestepped it as the body struck the floor and rolled past her. It thrashed a few moments violently, then abruptly went still as if an "off" switch had been thrown.

Vee saw that the mother had slumped onto her side on the sofa. The drawing pad was still on her lap, but it now bore a composition in her own blood. Vee cursed inside; a stray bullet had spiked the woman in the right temple. Blood was soaking into the sofa's cushions.

Gunshots from the bathroom. Judy was screaming in panic – or pain. "Shit," Vee said, and as she started that way she saw Judy blunder into the hallway, still on her feet somehow and bouncing from wall to wall, one of the miniature Demons riding on her piggyback.

Vee ran to meet them, raised Jay over her shoulder and when she came within range lashed out – the butt of the bone gun striking the Demon's skull. It dropped onto its back and Judy dropped onto her front, tattered and bleeding as if a whole flock of eagles had been at her. As the dazed Demon lifted its head, Vee blew its whole skull into shards.

Judy could barely raise her head from the floor, her hair matted with blood. Vee crouched by her and took hold of her under the arms, but Judy made an anguished sound of protest and Vee let go of her again. Still squatting beside her, she cooed to the old woman, "Hang in there…it will pass. It will pass…"

More sounds of entry from the bathroom, and Vee rose from her crouch already firing. The bathroom's door frame splintered but the Demon that appeared there was so inhumanly fast that it shot straight at her unharmed, as if it had lunged through a gap in the stream of bullets. It got one of its talons into her left eye socket, puncturing the orb and hooking into the bone. Vee couldn't help but scream and fall to her back with the Demon atop her. Couldn't help but let go of Jay when another pair of hands jerked him out of her grasp. It was a second Demon that had snatched Jay from her and flung the bone gun aside, and now this creature joined the first in bending over her, both slashing madly with their clawed hands. It felt to Vee as if twice their number at least were working at her body in a frenzy, and she was too overwhelmed to fend them off. Her blood splattered both of the walls that composed the hallway.

Then, the chatter of automatic fire. With a kind of *oomph* sound expelled from its drooping proboscis, one of the Demons was blasted off her body. The second Demon lifted its head toward the source of the gunfire, obliging the shooter nicely. The next discharge uncapped its skull as if cracking the top off a soft-boiled egg. The creature fell away from Vee and she lay there on her back with her rubbery jumpsuit shredded, one sleeve torn off and a hip laid bare. The hip itself was sliced to the bone. Her own blood ran down the back of her throat, her one good eye staring at the ceiling through a wet mask. Slowly, as if drugged, Vee turned her head on the floor toward the source of the gunfire, curious as the Demon had been.

The family's father – Andrew, she remembered Judy had called him – stood there holding his own assault rifle. Unlike Jay, it was fully made of metal, without sentience or any other ability than the power to kill Demons.

Andrew stepped around Vee to kneel beside Judy and help her into a sitting position. Though she was clearly still in great pain, the eternally elderly woman was mending rapidly. Judy sobbed and clutched at Andrew. He held her to him, and close to her ear said, "Shh. Shh."

Vee didn't dare try to sit up just yet, for fear of blacking out. All she could do at the moment was lie there and wait for the worst of the pain to pass. Wait for her ruined eye to reform, her full vision to return.

Andrew looked over at her and asked, "Who are you?"

Judy lifted her head from his shoulder and explained, "She's my friend."

When she was strong enough to do so, Vee staggered into the kitchen and sat down in one of the chairs at the little table. Already seated there was the family's mother, her surrogate son standing beside her. The mother's hair was wet from having the blood washed out of it. The small entry hole in her temple was gone and the larger exit wound almost healed. Fortunately the stray projectile had passed entirely through her head so she wouldn't have a bullet trapped in her skull.

"I didn't want to sit in there and get any more blood on the upholstery," Vee croaked, hooking her thumb back toward the living room.

"Me, too," said the attractive Black woman.

Andrew came into the kitchen leading Judy by the elbow, helped lower her into a third chair. He looked at Vee dubiously. "You sure no more of those things will follow you here?"

"Don't worry, I'll be on my way in a couple minutes."

"Oh Vee, maybe you should stay here with us," Judy said, wincing with concern.

"Thank you, Judy. That's kind of you. But I've got my mind set on finding that place called Freetown. Anyway, you've got enough of a nice little family here as it is."

Judy turned to look up at Andrew, holding one of his hands. She reached over to take the mother's hand, too. "Please," Judy pleaded, looking from one to the other. "Please...don't leave me alone again. I was alone for so long."

The mother rose from her chair to wrap her arms around the old woman. "I'm sorry, Judy, I'm so sorry. We didn't know. We didn't know you were still awake."

Andrew moved closer to join them in their embrace, and said, "Don't worry, mom. I guess we've slept long enough."

Vee rose from her chair, still not entirely regenerated but ready to return to the bathroom and hoist herself back into the crawl space. She didn't want to be the guest that stayed too long after the party. She said, "Well...sorry about the mess."

Andrew straightened up. "Ah, don't worry – it'll give me something to do. Maybe we'll remodel." He looked at Judy again and in a thoughtful tone said, "If you hadn't come, we might never have known our mom was alone like that."

"I didn't want to try to wake you," Judy said, suppressing a sob. Now her grandson hugged her along with the mother. "I didn't want to be selfish."

Vee stepped toward the doorway, but leaned in its threshold and said, "Maybe you guys will consider coming to Freetown yourself sometime. It might be worth the effort, if it's as civilized as it seems, anyway."

"I don't know...maybe," Andrew said, but he didn't sound convinced. Vee couldn't blame him. Maybe if the apartment had been a little bigger – and maybe if she hadn't been of such a restless spirit –

she might have wanted to stay here insulated from the horrors outside, herself.

"You can always come back and visit anytime," Judy said hopefully. She smiled, and added, "Visit your new Aunt Judy."

"Thanks. Thanks, Aunt Judy."

Knowing that she would likely never see them again, Vee took a mental snapshot of the family grouped around the table. If she had no memories of a family of her own, at least she would have this. Then she turned away, to fetch her bone gun and return to Hell.

BELOVED
SUCCUBUS

Before the Creator at the peak of His madness had self-destruct-ed – which thereby caused the suspended sky of molten lava to rain down upon all the limitless regions of Hades, burying them under solidified volcanic rock – Demons had been manufactured in great numbers in factory-cities like Tartarus. The Demonic breeds had been more numerous even than those of terrestrial creatures like insects, that the Creator had so enjoyed designing for millions of years by mortal reckoning, before He ultimately became overwhelmed at being the Father of so many hungering, striving, suffering lives...too many of whom were too primitive to be aware of His role in their existence, or doubted His own existence even if they were intelligent enough to contemplate Him. These doubting creatures, of course, be-ing His favorite but most frustrating offspring: the humans. The prog-eny that had driven Him most to despair...when He wasn't despairing at Himself.

Many were the breeds of Demons who bore a resemblance – sometimes profound, or perhaps only in general outline – to that of the human beings, who when their mortal existence came to an end were designated as either Angels or Damned...depending on their fealty to the Creator during their lives. The immortal souls of Angels were rewarded with an afterlife in Paradise, where their every need – even of the carnal variety – would be met by beautiful but mute human-like beings called Celestials. These Celestials, like the Demons (though less varied in form), were essentially golems: manufactured beings, and thus they possessed no immortal soul. Whereas the seemingly organic body of an Angel or Damned could not be permanently destroyed, and would thus eventually regenerate no matter how much damage was inflicted on it, this was not the case with Celestials and Demons. Though they were hardy and could live indefinitely, barring violence, both types of manufactured being could be killed.

Those humans Damned to Hades would be overseen, and tormented, by these countless varieties of Demons, and the tortures they inflicted were equally diverse in nature. After all, even if a torment is great, the tormented might well become accustomed to it in time, so it was essential that a soul be exposed to as many different types of torture as possible over the span of eternity. Therefore, often Demons were specifically designed to inflict these varying methods of punishment. And not always was the punishment merely of a physical nature, inflicted on the immortal soul's mock-corporeal body.

There were a number of Demonic types that the Damned took to labeling Succubi (since Demonic races did not have official designations). Some of these Succubus breeds sexually assaulted the Damned, mutilating them in the process, to bring about a combination of pain and humiliation. But then there were those Succubi for whom the suffering they inflicted was purely of a psychological nature...unless one took into consideration the biological imperative to pair with – to *mate* with – another being, and thereby continue the species. In life, this had been a difficult impulse to repress, and the source of great turmoil...and loneliness...and emptiness. So too was the yearning for the flesh exploited in Hades, even where flesh was in truth illusory.

The Creator, that consummate artist – the conductor of evolution's grand symphony – had known this all too well, and had designed certain races of Demons accordingly. For there was no Satan to oversee such tasks. There had only ever been the Creator, and all His works. All His children, burdened with the freedoms of choice He had gifted

226

them.

But the Demons had possessed the gift of freedom, as well. An oversight on His part, perhaps; maybe an unforeseen byproduct. Because, while the Creator had loved *creating* His colorful Demons, the question was: had He ever truly loved *them*?

When after many millennia the Damned had finally begun to revolt against their state of eternal punishment, it came to pass that more and more of the anthropomorphic races of Demons began to sympathize with them. In their freedom, these Demons chose to fight alongside the Damned against armies of Celestials sent from Paradise to quell the uprising.

And so, new and less human-like breeds of Demons were rushed into development. Those who would be less likely to sympathize with, and side with, the Damned. Even those human-like Demons that had remained loyal to the Creator and continued on in their designated roles were slated for destruction and replacement, just to be on the safe side.

And yet, this replacement project had only escalated the great war in Hades, which in turn had exacerbated the Creator's growing madness...

Until He had *exploded*, and ceased to exist as a sentience – as the prime sentience – and the lava had come down in its torrents to bury the majesty of all His former infernal works.

But even buried under the cooling volcanic rock, fossilized within it, the Damned lived on...as did, unfortunately, those Angelic soldiers who had volunteered to descend into Hades to fight alongside the Celestial forces. But the more vulnerable Celestials and Demons who had been trapped outside during the deluge had been snuffed out under the fallen sea of magma. That they were not trapped for eternity, still conscious like the immortals, was perhaps a mercy.

However, many were the Damned, Demons, and even Angels and Celestials who had had time to take cover inside some of the larger of Hades' infernal cities...such as that grandest of factory-cities, Tartarus. And over the millennia since the suicide of the Creator and the time of the deluge, the many varied races sheltering in Tartarus had expanded upon that industrial city, connecting up its massive towers until they eventually formed one immense conglomerate structure they dubbed the Construct. These races claimed different floors or sections of the two-hundred-story Construct...and in some of the communities that were established, Damned and Demons even lived together cooperatively.

Though in other sections of the monstrous, buried Construct, certain races aggressively kept to themselves. Whether out of long-held resentments, or stubborn adherence to their former roles...or for other reasons of their own.

Such was the case with a particular race of the Succubus type of Demon, that the Damned in former times had come to nickname the Beloved.

-1-

Vee's destination was the Construct's 128th floor, where she had heard a community that called itself Freetown had been established. She had learned of it from Jay – her talking gun. Jay in turn was aware of Freetown through the Mesh: a system used by the former Demonic technicians and engineers within Tartarus to exchange and record information. Jay was able to jack directly into the Mesh, being that he was a Demonic intelligence housed in the form of an assault rifle-type weapon fashioned from a bone-like raw material. On one side of the sentient weapon's body was a single eye with a red iris, housed in a skull-like socket. Framed within another socket nearby was a pair of lips, by which the Demon was able to communicate with Vee. Upon discovering him she had disconnected Jay from the monitor station into which he had been jacked for many a lost year, in a forgotten control room near the chamber in which she herself had been imprisoned in a block of stone for nearly two thousand years, before that stone had finally crumbled away and released her.

They had been an unlikely duo ever since, though perhaps Jay (as she had dubbed him, rather than use his serial number J611821) might have been less willing to assist her had she not been one of the Angels

– who in pre-war times all Demons had been subservient to. Vee had accompanied her father, in life a famous televangelist, into Hades to help lead an army of Angels in engaging the Damned rebels. However, during the years upon terrestrial years in which she had been encased in her stone sarcophagus (trapped there by Demons sympathetic with the Damned), she had lost all memory of her life both as a mortal and as an Angel. Had lost the memory even of her own name. Now she was only Vee, reborn and renamed by herself...and in all of the Construct with its many microcosmic communities, sometimes friendly but too often threatening, she felt that Freetown sounded like the most promising destination in which to settle and begin a new life – or rather, a post-Creator afterlife. There, Jay had informed her, Damned and Demons and even a number of Angels apparently eked out a comfortable existence – relatively speaking.

But the majority of the Construct was either abandoned or in decay, and some of the levels Vee had passed through in the amalgamated body of the Construct had been difficult and even dangerous to navigate. Though she could not be killed, there was always the threat of being trapped for a century or two under collapsing rubble...or by another vengeful band of Damned, Demons, or fellow Angels. In her travels since being freed from her prison, and especially being a former Angel herself – if she could even think of herself as that – she had made every type of enemy.

By now her rubbery black, body-hugging outfit was torn and bullet-riddled, missing a long sleeve entirely and exposing one pale hip. Despite this, beneath the uniform she had stolen from a Demon's corpse her unerringly regenerated skin was young and unmarked. She was tall and lean, with shoulder-length red hair that could use another wash if she could only find herself a sink or burst pipe somewhere. She wouldn't mind having a drink of water, either, despite the fact that immortal souls required no sustenance – no matter how urgently their sham bodies made them crave it.

For Damned and Angel alike, being thirsty was another fake biological imperative...like the desire for sex.

They were finally approaching Level 124. So close, now, to finding out what this Freetown was really all about. Whether it was a place where she could truly stay, or if she would be disappointed, or even chased out, and have to continue her climb up, and up – but toward what?

In search of a means of reaching 124, Vee realized they were passing from one tower of the former city of Tartarus into another, simply because of all the horizontal traveling she was undertaking. She had climbed into a metal conduit like a large sewer pipe, that instead of conducting water housed thick, clamped bundles of power cables that appeared to be sheathed in rubber. Other, smaller cables were stapled into the sides of the power conduit. Thankfully it was all but clear of debris, though crawling on hands and knees atop the bundled cables was awkward for Vee, especially given the pipe's considerable length. At least the cables prevented her from having to crawl directly upon the conduit's heavily rusted interior. To make things easier, she had secured the bone gun across her back through the straps of the pouch she wore, which was made from stitched patches of skin no doubt taken from the Damned: her "pocketbook from Hell," as she called it.

Outside this extensive metal tube, which once must have crossed through open air from one tower to another, Vee knew there was only solid rock...rock that had completely filled Hades, right up to where its former sky of lava had hung overhead. But beyond *that?*

"This can't be the only way up into 124," Vee panted as she crawled.

"It may be only one of numerous ways, madam," replied Jay, from behind her. "But on the other hand, we may not be able to reach Level 124 by this means at all. In the next structure, we may well find that we can only descend to lower levels."

Vee stopped crawling, turning her head a little. "Hold up...you told me your blueprints said we could get up there this way. And now you say you're not sure?"

"Madam," Jay seemed to sigh, though the voice of the Demonic intelligence had an unmodulated, almost robotic quality, "as I have told you, the blueprints I was able to access for you in the Mesh are incomplete, in that this city has been greatly modified during the long period in which both you and I were dormant. Much has changed since the time of Tartarus – this is the *Construct* now. In addition to that, as I have also pointed out in the past, large areas of the Construct have been damaged over time from a variety of causes...whether through natural decay, or from the crushing pressure of the stone outside, or the accidental explosion of equipment or volatile chemicals, or..."

"Yeah, yeah, okay," Vee said, starting to crawl forward again through the near-utter darkness of the power conduit. There was, though, pale light filtering into it from either end.

"...or even from communities that may have purposely blown up sections or otherwise caused damage to seal their territory off from potential bands of raiders..."

"I get it, I get it. Okay, then...if we find ourselves at a dead end over there, then we turn around and come back and look for another way up. It's just that I thought you sounded sure, is all."

"Nothing is sure anymore, madam."

"Thanks for the philosophy."

For all Vee knew they had crossed over into this other tower before, at a lower level, via a pedestrian bridge or such...or it might even be the building that contained the dungeon-like basement she had started out in. She couldn't keep track of the haphazard path she had taken in her long ascent. How could she, when even Jay – who had been created here – was often too uncertain about it himself?

Up ahead, Vee saw sparks spitting from one of the thinner cables bracketed into the conduit's curved wall. There was a smell like burning plastic. She hoped a fire wouldn't start and spread, in case they needed to come back this way. She squinted her eyes and averted her face as she crawled past the sizzling spray of sparks.

What held her attention more, though, was that the dim bluish light at the end of the tunnel was growing closer...within reach. In addition to the increasing illumination came a deep humming sound that Vee realized her bones had been aware of before her ears registered it.

At the end of the power conduit, the various bundles of cables thick and thin made a turn from the horizontal to the vertical, leaving the conduit's mouth to rise up the wall the tunnel ended in. Bracketed in place against this wall, the cables rose up for a good distance until they eventually branched out in a chaos of directions, slung crazily overhead like powerlines in a mortal city of old like Ho Chi Minh City – that is, before the nuclear Armageddon that had destroyed that city and every other around the globe, and sent the last of humanity to either Paradise or Hades in one massive immigration of souls.

The branching powerlines connected up with various hulking machines that loomed out of the dimness of this large chamber...with some cables entering the mouths of other power conduits positioned around the room to continue on their journey. Dotted with blue lights – either steady or blinking – that indicated it was still functioning, this hulking automated machinery was the source of the bone-vibrating hum, in particular one vast block-like structure in the center of the chamber.

And here, Vee locked onto two things immediately. One was a metal ladder, painted yellow, that rose up the flank of the central machine structure, until both machine and ladder were all but lost in shadow high overhead. And the other thing Vee had immediately noticed was a human man, standing at the foot of this ladder with his arms upraised, outstretched, as if he waited to catch the body of someone soon to fall from those rungs affixed to the side of the enormous thrumming block.

Either because of the deep hum, or because he was so fixated on whatever he was staring up at, the man didn't hear Vee as she slipped around the bundles of cables to lower herself from the conduit's mouth to the floor. Once her boots met its solid surface of tarnished metal plates, she reached behind her to draw the bone gun out from under her pouch's straps. She crept toward the man stealthily...and now it wasn't so much the man himself who intrigued her, but a kind of garment he was wearing.

Vee had never seen a garment so beautiful in all her afterlife.

-2-

Luckily, when the man had shot Vee he'd blown the top of her head

232

off completely, from the eyes up. This way, when her head fully regenerated there were no bullets trapped inside her skull to irritate her later. She sat up on the floor and felt the shape of her head, satisfied to find the regeneration complete, but groaning from the last dregs of pain brought about by the process...and with disgust at herself for having dropped her guard and allowed this to happen.

It was all because of that stupid garment the man was wearing around his shoulders like a shawl.

It was an irregular patch of material, almost enough to cover his back, apparently tied in front loosely with two crude sleeves – worn like a sweater one might remove when the air outside grew too warm. Despite the thing's roughly-cut outline, the garment itself was of exquisite color and design...exquisite beyond words. It had a sheen rather like silk, or satin, but strangely not entirely like those things. The background field was obsidian black, but all across this was a vivid red pattern, as if embroidered with crimson thread – though it was not embroidery. And *was* it a pattern? It almost seemed like there were interlinked repeating shapes, but Vee couldn't be sure. Whatever those shapes were – whether meant to be flowers, or schools of jellyfish, or even a kind of complex calligraphy or hieroglyphics – they mesmerized Vee in her effort to decipher them. And still she crept closer to the man...

...until finally he heard a metal plate creak under her boot, and whirled to face her, wild-eyed. As he turned, he revealed himself to be not an Angel like herself, but a Damned man, likely in his forties when he'd died. She could tell he was one of the Damned by the raised brand on his forehead – the one scar a Damned could never heal away. In his case, the branded letter was an M, indicating that in life he had been a murderer.

Vee took her hand off Jay's curved magazine, which served as a forward handle, and pointed the blocky gun of sutured bone toward the ceiling in her other hand to indicate she meant this man no harm. "Don't be afraid," she said.

"*Be not afraid*, huh?" the man babbled, backing away from her. He reached up both his hands to grasp the loosely knotted sleeves of his shawl protectively. "Stay away from me!"

Vee slowly continued to advance on him. "I'm not going to hurt you," she insisted gently.

"Madam," Jay said, "this ladder is no doubt a straight shot to the 124th level. You don't need to trouble with this man."

"Stay out of it, Jay," she told him.

"Keep back, Cherub!" the man cried. "You can't have her!" And with that, the Damned man spun around and bolted off toward a narrow alley between the body of the central machine and another. As he ran he continued to babble, "Go get your own!"

"Wait!" Vee shouted, starting after him. "I just want to...I just want to talk!"

"*Madam*," Jay said to no avail.

Vee saw the man take a corner at the end of the murky little alley. She charged right after him, and took the corner without hesitation. After all, the man had not had a weapon in his hands or strapped to his body, having only that gorgeous shawl and a standard black uniform of shirt and trousers like those all the Damned would be given upon their arrival in Hades – at which time they would also receive the brand that designated their greatest sin.

However, when Vee rounded that corner and arrived at a dead end – where this man had made a little shelter for himself, including a sheet of packing foam or such to use as a bed – she saw that he did possess a weapon, after all. It must have been leaning in a corner back here in his little metal cave, and he had snatched it up and turned it now toward her.

In the second before he fired, Vee saw that the weapon was a Demonic gun like Jay, except instead of being made from ivory-colored, lab-grown bone – as even some of the buildings in Tartarus had been – this gun was made from black, lab-grown chitin. The single eye set into one side of the chitin gun was an insect's black compound eye, and instead of human lips, in a second socket nearby were framed the complex mandibles of an insect. These moved rapidly, emitting a chittering sound that Vee doubted the Damned man could even understand.

Also in that second, before Vee's head was shattered by a stream of bullets from the sentient gun, and before she could even get out a cry of protest, Vee noticed an odd altar of sorts set against the far wall of the cave, behind the man. Atop an old metal toolbox he had scavenged rested a human – or human-like – skull, framed by two crude candles that he had perhaps made himself somehow, maybe even from the fat of some victim. The candles lit his little shelter intimately, casting flickering shadows across the skull, giving it a false semblance of life.

And then...the bullets, and darkness.

The man hadn't dragged her outside his shelter, and thank goodness her uniform however tattered hadn't been removed or unzipped, so he hadn't molested her half-decapitated body. Instead, when Vee sat up she saw that she lay beside that improvised foam bed. The toolbox was still there, but the two candles were gone...and so was the skull. The man had abandoned his shelter, and taken those apparently precious items with him.

"That skull," Vee muttered, rubbing at the temples of her own. "It can't have come from a Damned or Angel. They would have regenerated."

"Obviously," Jay said, fortunately lying on his eyeless and lipless side so he could see more than just the floor. She had dropped him beside her, and she was more than thankful that the fleeing Damned man hadn't taken the bone gun with him...only his own black chitin gun.

Vee brushed her hair out of her face. It was already as long as it had been before her head had been blown apart, though it would grow no longer than her shoulders, and on the bright side: because most of her upper head was freshly made, most of her hair was new and clean, no longer greasy and in need of washing. She pushed herself to her feet, then reached down to pick up Jay.

"I wonder why he abandoned this cozy little hiding place," she said.

"No doubt, he had no idea what to do with your body. I'm sure that he must be aware of other hiding spots in this vicinity."

"I guess he has a thing against Angels. Can't say I blame him. But still..."

"Yes?" said Jay.

"The way he was talking...it's strange. He said something like 'you can't have her'...and 'go get your own.' I think he was talking about that beautiful piece of cloth he was wearing." She looked down to meet Jay's cyclops gaze. "Didn't it seem like that?"

"Perhaps instead of that material, he was speaking about the skull."

"Maybe," Vee mused. "Maybe."

"In any case, I suggest we forget about him and ascend that ladder... if the next level is what you seek."

"You're right, Jay. I don't know what I was thinking, chasing that guy. I guess all I wanted to know was where he got that material from. Funny, isn't it? I must be losing my mind."

And so Vee found her way out of the narrow alley, and gazed up at that ladder rising into the darkness. She once again secured Jay behind her, through the straps of her skin pouch, took in a deep breath (despite immortal souls not actually needing air to fill their lungs), and reached out to the rungs to begin her climb.

-3-

As Vee climbed the metal ladder, its rungs vibrating from the massive machine it was bolted into, she spoke quietly with Jay.

"What if we can reach Level 128 in this building," she was saying, "but it turns out Freetown isn't there? Instead, it's on the 128th floor of some other building in old Tartarus? Maybe on the far side of the city?"

Though the majority of the many diverse towers that had composed the former infernal city were pressed directly against each other – as if to compose one continuous structure even before the later modifications of the Construct – some buildings stood a bit distance from each other and were connected by elevated walkways and trams. It was likely that numerous buildings here shared one interconnected 128th level...but also possible that the 128th level they sought might be in a building which stood somewhat apart. Jay's imperfect information, gleaned from the Mesh, was not sufficiently detailed in this regard. In the Construct, a path straight upward was by no means a guarantee.

"We may very well find that to be the case, sorry to say," the Demonic gun replied. "Though, I suspect we'll cross back into the main cluster of towers after another level or two."

"Well, we certainly have time enough to keep looking, if Freetown isn't in this building," Vee said...immortal being that she was.

Finally, the ladder ended at a metal catwalk, coated in the same yellow enamel paint, that clung to all four nearly-blank faces of the humming machine with its unknown purpose. Vee walked around to the other side of the machine, where there were two small gauges set into its surface: one lit green, one lit red. She leaned in to watch their needles waver. The green one's needle seemed to flick in sync with the machine's pulsing vibration. There were no other features, no controls.

"Any idea what this means?" Vee asked Jay, holding him close so he could see the gauges.

"I have no idea...but I can confirm that this tower is, as I thought, one of the four main power stations for the former city of Tartarus. Thankfully, still in operation."

"Automated...or maintained?"

"Perhaps both."

Here on the machine's far side, too, was a set of yellow-painted metal stairs that led up to a metal door, also in that chipped yellow paint, set into an angle of the ceiling. Across this door, in large red characters, was stenciled: 124.

"That was easy enough," Vee said. "Apart from the climb. Well, and having my brains blown out."

She mounted the stairs, pausing halfway to the door to peer into the depths below, but the floor of the 123rd level was all but lost in darkness aside for the constellation of blue indicator lights set into the various machines. That Damned man who had shot her had not reappeared. She continued on up the last of the steps, and holding Jay ready for trouble in her right fist, she reached out to the metal door's latch. She was able to slide the door to the left, it fortunately not being rusted in place or too warped to glide along its tracks. It made just the barest scraping sound and squeal. Yes, she thought: perhaps this power station was maintained in part, as Jay had said.

Vee looked into the chamber beyond, was greeted by no enemies lunging toward her. She stepped across the threshold, and slid the door back into place behind her. No boobytraps were set off, no improvised alarms were triggered. Perhaps the inhabitants of the power tower were in agreement about allowing for easy access between its levels? Or maybe no community had formed on these few floors? She didn't want to let down her guard about that.

Vee turned to take in the room, and here she saw that the great machine pierced through the floor from the level below, and culminated in an apparently flat surface above her, at about the height of a three-story building. She saw steam rising from up there, toward a row of huge, quietly spinning fans in the chamber's high ceiling. Sizable pipes ran from all four sides of the machine to connect with other machinery or to vanish through the chamber's walls...some of these conduits made of rigid metal, some looking like flexible plastic, and all of varied width.

"I believe this was a cooling tower," Jay said now. "Circulating coolant to various adjacent stations to prevent this power plant's fuel rods from overheating."

"Jeesh, that's all the Construct needs...to suffer a nuclear meltdown. Where would we all be then?"

"If there are people in this area keeping things running safely," said Jay, "we should all be grateful to them."

"I imagine the people of Naraka have a lot do with it," Vee said, referring to the friendly Damned community on Level 90 where she had stopped for a time. Those people remotely maintained much of the Construct's power and other environmental processes, not to mention the Mesh network, though they no doubt never ventured far, physically, from their safe enclave.

"Indeed."

"Let's go up and have a look," Vee said, starting toward another set of yellow-painted metal stairs, this one bolted into the side of the colossal machine. She started up.

"Shouldn't we be looking for a way to the 125th level?"

"It might be right up here...and why the big rush? You got somewhere to be?"

"The Mesh," the Demon replied.

Vee had promised Jay that when she settled safely somewhere within the Construct, and no longer had a pressing need for him, she would jack Jay into the Mesh again – the way she had found him – and once more set his consciousness free in that virtual universe he preferred to think of as his home.

"All good things to those who wait."

The stairs zigzagged up the side of the machine, pausing at two small platforms, but Vee finally reached the top. And indeed, here she was confronted with a large pool of sorts...which didn't descend all the way to the machine's base on the level below, but stopped short almost at the floor of this level. It was deep enough. Did this coolant consist of water, or some chemical, or a combination of the two? Its color was a deep, artificial green, almost as if it were filled with algae...but it was too clear and clean-looking for that. As she had spied from below, thin wisps of steam played across the pool's surface, drawn up toward the large exhaust fans. The air here was almost tropically humid.

Down there, centered in the pool, were tight rows of vertical cylinders, ten by twenty: two hundred cylinders in total. Above them was a bridge-like platform that spanned the top of the pool, and could be positioned along tracks by means of a control panel fixed to its railing. Attached to this movable platform was a crane, all of it painted that same industrial yellow, heavily flaked away from age and the moist air.

"That crane," Jay explained, "is for replacing the fuel rods in those tubes down there."

"Holy moly...those are fuel rods? Exposed like that, unprotected, where just anybody could come up here and mess with them? Some zealots hoping for Armageddon part two...or just some crazy guy like the one who shot me?"

"So it would seem."

"Wait!" Vee exclaimed, having spotted something moving in the tank's green coolant...a dark shape emerging from the shadows of a far corner. It was difficult to make out this moving thing's outlines, but it was *big*.

"Not so unprotected, after all," Jay observed.

The submerged creature – or amalgamation of creatures – had heard them speaking, even under the surface, perhaps due to its multiple sets of ears. Though it emerged into a better lighted area of the tank, it was still difficult for Vee to wrap her head around what exactly she was seeing. The thing was beginning to bellow and howl from numerous mouths, and there also came a scraping sound from the tines of a trident, gripped in the foremost pair of arms, as the points raked across the tank's floor as the creature surged forth.

Vee pointed Jay down at the creature, gripping the bone gun's two handles. "Don't make me do it!" she yelled at the thing.

"Madam...can we *go?*" Jay protested. "You're running low on ammunition, and that guardian has too many vital organs for you to kill all of it with what you have left!"

Vee could believe him. This Demon was actually composed of different Demons – she counted at least eight – whose bodies had been fused together either surgically or by some other means, forming one composite entity that Vee would think of from this moment on as the Horde. The only feature these individuals seemed to have in common (though she didn't know if they had started out this way) was that their flesh and fur, if they had it – and even the horns several of them bore on their heads – were a muddy red in color, though a few had wild black hair. All of them, also, had eyes that glowed white in their fearsome faces. Vee realized then, too, that no matter their differences, these were all obsolete types of Demons, deemed too human-like in general form. Only one of them, however, to Vee's mind, had a face that could have passed for human in the mortal world, aside from its coloring. One's head was more ghoulish, with only a pit for a nose, while another had three white-glowing eyes on either side of its dome-like head, and a fang-filled maw of a mouth. One's head was very much like a goat...but then Vee realized this "individual" was wearing, like a helmet, the decapitated head of a more bestial race of Demon. Another, she then noted, wore an oversized fleshless skull like that of a giraffe.

Were they, in defiance, trying to masquerade as less human in aspect... or were these trophies from enemies they'd defeated, or lost comrades they paid tribute to? Maybe former members of the Horde's body?

Besides the trident that one pair of arms gripped, another arm held a saber. The Horde propelled itself across the floor of the tank on a mix of legs: some humanoid, some satyr-like, one pair even insect-like, though the upper torso was like that of a muscular man. The entire creature was covered in decorative scars and tattoos, and the impression the whole of it gave was of a small army in a single body.

It used those mismatched legs in conjunction to launch itself off the tank's floor, and came paddling wildly toward the surface. It wasn't a creature designed for swimming, but it wasn't letting that stop it.

"Madam!" Jay said again. "I won't be able to reason with it!"

"Okay, let's go," Vee said, turning back toward the stairs that would return them to this level's floor. She figured – or at least hoped – the guardian wouldn't leave its tank to pursue them down there.

In turning, however, Vee spotted someone who had been watching them, crouched down behind the railing of that movable crane platform...and even with the Horde struggling awkwardly to reach the surface behind her, she stopped in her tracks to gawk at this person – who, having been discovered, rose to their feet as if to allow the whole of their body to be seen.

Vee had never seen a creature so beautiful in all her afterlife.

But then, she realized she had...though only *part* of one.

-4-

The Demon who stood upon the crane platform was definitely of human shape, if not coloration, though from here Vee couldn't tell if they had been created to resemble a female or a youthful male. Either way they were shortish in height, slender and exquisitely proportioned, and without any hair. Whereas the section of flayed skin the Damned murderer had worn like a shawl was black with a strange pattern of vivid red, this being's body had a base color of deep indigo blue with that same pattern, apparently – but in metallic silver – covering it from its feet to its perfectly-shaped bald head. The Demon was without any clothing.

"Hey!" Vee called to it involuntarily.

She could hear the Horde splashing to the surface at last, madly flailing its collection of limbs to tread water and move closer to the walkway around the top of the tank , where Vee stood. Still, Vee kept her eyes on the blue-and-silver Demon, as it climbed up onto the platform's rail nimbly, and then stood erect there for a moment, poised to leap...

"Wait!" Vee cried out.

But too late: the Demon gracefully dove into the tank of strangely green fluid, shooting down into its depths.

Vee jolted forward to watch it...so abruptly that she almost lost her balance and fell headfirst into the tank herself. As she caught herself, she watched the beautiful Demon's body undulate like a porpoise as it swam to the bottom of the tank...toward a square-shaped hole set into one wall near the floor.

The Horde caught hold of the edge of the tank, not far from where Vee stood. Now that it had a grip, more hands seized hold and the massive composite Demon began dragging itself out of the tank, rivulets of coolant running down its dark red flesh. With its heads out of the pool, the roars and inarticulate shouts it made were thunderous, echoing throughout the open cooling tower chamber. The saber and trident clanged and scraped against the tank's walkway as the Horde got the upper half of its body/bodies hoisted onto it.

"Madam!" Jay said. "I really must insist!"

Vee knew Jay was right, but she continued to watch a moment longer as the beautiful Demon disappeared into that opening at the bottom of the tank. Only then, when its feet were gone from sight, did Vee whirl away from the tank and rush toward the stairs bolted into the side of the great machine, which they now knew housed the fuel rods for this power tower.

Vee paused when she made it to the first of the staircase's two landings. Looking up, she saw the Horde's heads over the edge of the tank, their luminous eyes blazing down at her, still growling and barking. It cocked back the trident as if to throw it, but Vee doubted it truly meant to lose that weapon, intending only to drive her off. In fact, the creature seemed disinclined to exit the pool completely...leaving the fuel rods unprotected. Mostly confident the Horde wouldn't continue to pursue her, Vee continued on down the staircase...again to the floor of the 124th level.

The Horde kept watching Vee until she reached a doorway that led into another, adjacent room. She passed into this, then ducked around the edge of the doorway and waited a few minutes. In the meantime, she glanced around her at this smaller chamber's contents. In the room's murkiness stood more machines, discolored with encrustations of rust from the enclosed humidity, and a number of control stations bearing monitors that displayed indecipherable information: sometimes scrolling rows of numbers, sometimes strange glyphs like a secret code of dingbats. Finally, Vee chanced a peek around the corner and saw the Horde was no longer propped at the edge of the tank. It must have submerged again, thinking she'd fled the area.

To Jay, Vee whispered, "I want to go into the pool and see where that Demon went."

"What?" the Demon replied, somehow sounding shrilly incredulous despite his uninflected voice. "But why?"

"It might lead to the 125th level."

"With all respect, that is simply ridiculous! Even if that way did eventually take you to the 125th floor, there are absolutely other ways to get there than through a drainpipe!"

"I still want to have a look. I don't think it was simply going in there to hide. Escape, maybe...but not hide. Why not check it out?"

"You saw the animosity of that guardian. Even if it realizes you're an Angel, not one of the Damned, it won't spare you...and will most likely hate you all the more. Not to mention, and mean *me* harm, as well." Jay was actually one of the most advanced types of replacement Demons: a pure sentience housed in a mecha-organic body. As such, it was likely most obsolete races of Demon slated for destruction before the fall of Hades would resent him profoundly.

"We've gone up against plenty of angry Demons before," Vee

reminded him. "And we've gone through plenty of challenging environments. We can do this, Jay. You know I can't be drowned, even if I have to swim through a whole maze of drainpipes."

"But what of me?"

"Oh!" She looked down into his lone eye. "Can you be drowned?"

"No...but water or whatever that fluid is, getting into this gun housing, might damage it or its ammunition."

"Maybe I should hide you out here somewhere, until I'm back, then..."

"Please no, madam! If you insist on leaving me behind, then I ask you to connect me with one of these monitoring stations, in here, so I can return to the Mesh as you promised."

"Oh no," she chuckled, "you're not getting away from me that easy."

Vee thought it over for a minute. During that time, Jay spoke up again, sounding as if he felt he'd won the argument and reasonableness had prevailed. "Clearly, the best course of action is to explore the other rooms on this level to look for an easier means of –"

But before he could finish, Vee set the bone gun down on the floor, slung the skin pouch off her back, and began unzipping her tattered black uniform. She struggled to peel it off her sweaty body, and it felt strange doing so, as it had become like a second skin to her. She had nothing on beneath.

"What are you doing?" Jay asked.

"I'm going to wrap you up in my clothing, to keep the coolant out of you. I hope that's enough to do the trick. Just bear with me, Jay."

"No, madam, please!"

Ignoring his protests, the now nude Vee squatted down and rolled Jay into her shed uniform. She tucked him into the improvised rubbery sheath as snugly as she could, then stuffed him about halfway into her pocketbook from Hell. Into this, too, she crammed her boots, their tops folded over. She managed to snap the pouch's flap shut over the jutting, bundled bone gun, and secured the package further by using one of the pouch's two straps, wrapping it around the pouch and knotting it tightly to help hold Jay in place. Then, she slung the remaining strap over her neck and across her chest, and rose to her bare feet.

"If you don't make it to that drainpipe before the guardian reaches us..." Jay said.

"That there's the challenge, isn't it?"

"I still don't understand why you need to see where that Demon went, anyway," Jay complained.

More to herself than to her companion, Vee muttered, "I'm not sure I understand it, myself."

For the truth of the matter was that she was less interested in seeing where the beautiful Demon had disappeared to, than in seeing the Demon again itself.

-5-

At the top of the stairs, Vee poked her head up just enough to gaze below into the green pool, through its ghostly tendrils of steam. She couldn't see the Horde from this angle, and could only assume it had returned to that dark corner from which it had first appeared. There might even be a recess in the tank wall there that she couldn't see from here.

"Okay, then," she whispered, not expecting Jay to hear her, wrapped up and stowed in her skin pouch as he was. She said it more to steel her own nerves.

Then, she quickly climbed up onto the walkway, stood upright at its edge with the pouch's strap pressing between her breasts, and dove in as she had seen the indigo Demon do. Even as she plummeted through the air, she hoped that the coolant didn't consist of some strong chemical that would burn her eyes and skin. She might not sustain lasting damage from such, but pain was pain, even if the pain was only inflicted on faux flesh.

As her long body broke the surface, Vee found the coolant to be no more irritating than water, and warm but not uncomfortably so. The only uncomfortable thing was knowing the closeness of the Horde... and sure enough, immediately upon plunging below the surface she heard its gurgling, underwater howls again...and the dragging of the trident's prongs across the bottom of the tank as the creature came scrambling in her direction.

Vee felt the drag of the loaded pouch across her back as she pushed herself down toward that opening at the bottom of the tank, where she had been careful to note its position so no time would be wasted in locating it. There were other features down here, such as pipes affixed to the tank's walls, but she saw nothing of relevance. All that mattered was that hole...not even the creature scuttling across the floor of the tank and approaching from her left. Though, as she had said to Jay, there was no threat of drowning, the last thing she needed was to be slowed down by the involuntary *sensation* of drowning, so she held the deep breath she had taken before diving off the walkway. It wasn't far to that square opening now...and she could already feel the push of fluid from its mouth. So, excess fluid didn't drain out of the tank here; coolant flowed *into* the tank through it, but the current was minor. She imagined there was some overflow hole as in a sink, up at the waterline, that she hadn't taken note of.

Thank goodness the Horde kept up its animal-like noise as it came (sounding like a whole zoo full of enraged animals), so she could judge its distance from her without looking. Not that there was anywhere to go now to avoid it. She had seen no ladders or steps back up to the walkway down here. It was do or die...and die a thousand deaths. If the Horde caught her, it could tear her body to pieces...which would reconstitute, only for the Horde to dismember her again, and again, ad infinitum.

Closer, closer to the opening. Closer, closer came the Horde's cacophony.

Then, the hole was right in front of her, and Vee reached out a hand to grab onto its edge. Her air felt like it was ready to give out, and she had to force herself to remember that she needed no air; that the air she normally breathed in Hades was nothing but part of the whole elaborate trickery of a synthetic physical existence.

Just as she began pulling herself into the opening, elated that she had reached it and knowing it was too small to allow the Horde to follow, the creature thrust its trident out ahead of it. One of its barbed prongs lodged itself in her calf, and against her will Vee let out a cry that sent the last of her imagined breath bubbling out of her mouth.

She held onto the opening's frame with both hands, resisting as the Horde tried to haul her back with the trident. She looked over her shoulder, and through the swirling of her own blood she saw multiple sets of white eyes glaring with triumph. However, as the Horde gave its trident a savage tug, thinking to drag Vee back and into its clutches, all it succeeded in doing was ripping the trident's prong free of her flesh, leaving a nasty tear.

Abruptly released, Vee wasted no time. She was so intent on pulling herself through the opening that she even forgot about the lack of air in her lungs. In a moment, she was entirely inside the square-shaped narrow passage beyond. By the time the Horde crowded up against the wall, inserting the trident into the passage in the hopes of snaring her a second time, it was too late. Vee was now safely out of its reach.

The only question now was, what would she find on the other end of this little tunnel?

With the threat of the Horde behind her, thoughts returned of the beautiful blue Demon. Vee even imagined it was waiting for her somewhere ahead, just as intent on meeting her as she was on meeting it. She entertained the notion that the Demon had stood up and revealed itself to her on the crane platform so that Vee would take notice of it. Like a silent siren, it called to her. Somehow, called to her mind.

She had to admit it now – she was utterly beguiled. She wouldn't rest until she saw it again. All thoughts of reaching the 128th floor, and thus Freetown, had been shoved aside. She *must* see the blue Demon... must *talk* to it...

"Go get your own!" the Damned murderer had told her.

Still, despite her single-minded determination to push ahead and locate that Demon, Vee feared she was beginning to black out. Whether that was due to her losing her struggle against the sensation of drowning, or due to loss of blood from her deep leg wound, or simply an illusion brought about by the blackness of this narrow passage – the length of which was impossible to determine – she couldn't say. Likely a combination of all these things, plus the odd, disorienting state of mind she found herself in.

There was no turning back; that blue Demon had gone somewhere, and she would find where that was. But the blackness closed in more insidiously, her mind grew increasingly foggy, and she wanted to suck in great gulps of coolant to fill her lungs in lieu of air – anything just to feed them! But just as the blackness around her and the blackness of her mind were on the verge of becoming complete, a sudden pale light entered into the channel from above. A hatch had been opened. And through that opening in the ceiling of the passage, a slender arm reached down into the flowing coolant...its hand open, and waiting for her to clasp it. An arm of indigo flesh, seemingly embroidered with a lacy pattern of mysterious silver designs.

Vee reached for the offered hand, grabbed onto it. Then, with surprising strength for so slight a creature, the Demon drew Vee up through the hatch...and into air again.

Another figure lowered the hatch back in place, and sealed it with a large two-handed valve.

This room was quite unlike the other, more industrial chambers of the power tower Vee had seen thus far, though she had been to similar areas throughout the Construct in the past. It was of a mecha-organic character, such as the body of bone Jay's mind was housed in: fashioned from materials that looked more grown in place than manufactured and assembled. The walls of this room were of a glossy purplish-red material – like raw meat coated in varnish – and where the ribbed walls curved and met overhead a series of evenly-spaced, egg-like globes glowed dully, with something like a pinkish bioluminescence. Pipes ran along the walls here, but they pulsed like a giant's veins.

The indigo Demon stepped back from Vee, leaving her to roll over and cough out the green coolant convulsively. Naked, she lay back upon her bulky pouch helplessly. Meanwhile, not only the blue Demon but three others stood over her, looking down silently as if appraising her.

Though tears flowed from Vee's eyes from the strain of expelling the coolant from her lungs, she looked back at the four Demons with unabashed awe.

They wore no clothing, and so their bodies were plainly displayed. One of them had metallic gold flesh, covered in patterns of bright red. Another's base color was jade green, and its patterns were of metallic gold. The last, besides the blue Demon, had glossy jet-black flesh like the partial skin the murderer had worn, but instead of red this one's patterns were sapphire blue.

Otherwise, all four of them were as identical as clones. The exact same height and build and features. Their noses were somewhat flat, their lips voluptuously full, their eyes far-spaced and rather almond-shaped, though the eyeballs themselves corresponded with the base color of each: either entirely indigo, entirely gold, jade green, obsidian black. Up close, it still wasn't possible to tell if they were meant to look typically male or female. They were flat-chested, but though they had not been designed to breastfeed, since Demons did not give live birth, they did possess nipples. Though they had not grown in a womb, attached to a placenta, they each had a navel. Yet between their legs was only a smooth pubic mound, instead of male or female genitalia. These four were as sexless as a row of mannequins.

That notwithstanding, Vee was overcome with a tsunami wave of pure desire. Mutely, lying there on her back, she reached out her hands to the four Demons, grasping at air, and let out a horrible sob of longing.

"She's overwhelmed," said the gold Demon. "It's too much for her. You shouldn't have led her here, Aicha."

"I honestly didn't mean to," said the blue Demon. Their voices were soft...the softest, most beautiful voices ever to bless a human's ears, each word a heartbreaking song. "I was trying to get away from her."

"And now what do we do?" asked the jade Demon. They all had the exact same voice.

"You brought her here, whether you meant to tease her or not," said the gold Demon disgustedly...though even in disgust its voice was an unbearable gift. It turned away, gesturing for the others to follow it as it started toward an opening in one of the organic walls, that looked more like a huge orifice than a doorway. "You can deal with her. Put her in a room for now until we decide what to do with her."

"We should get her out of here right now, before she becomes even more intoxicated," the black Demon argued, pausing at the doorway.

The gold Demon stopped, too, and turned around to face the others, just short of passing into the corridor beyond – which was equally mecha-organic. "The way she is now, especially after having seen all four of us at once, if we throw her out she'll just find her way back to us. The only thing we could do then is move ourselves elsewhere...and I don't want to have to do that, do you? This shelter has been good for us."

"Then we must imprison her here, Leanan" said the jade Demon. "Maybe even put her to work for us. We've had slaves in the past."

"Oh yes, we have, haven't we? Like that madman who loved Xana so much that he killed her to eat her flesh! We should have imprisoned him from the start, but we were fools to think he could live among us."

"Right," said the black Demon. "Then, if it won't do any good throwing her out, we should imprison her here in such a way that she can't interact with us...or even see us."

"I'm an Angel," Vee sobbed, still clutching at them. "I'm not Damned...I'm an *Angel*..."

The Demon named Leanan looked back at Vee with those blank gold eyes of hers, seeming like a statue brought to life. "*And?* So you came to Hades to kill all the betrayed Demons, like us Succubi? And we should show you mercy for that? In case you didn't realize this, madam, with the Creator gone we no longer kiss the feet of Angels."

"I...I," Vee stammered, "I only mean..." But she didn't know what she meant. Had she really thought that her status as an Angel – or "former Angel," as she thought of it – would matter to these furtive Demons, and inspire them to treat her with respect as in days long gone?

"Put your unwanted pet in a room, Aicha," their leader repeated. "And you can take the first watch over her. In fact, you can take every watch over her...until, as I say, we decide where to put her."

"I will do that," Aicha said quietly, without any hint of resentment. The blue Demon hadn't taken its eyes off Vee all this time. "I promise you, Leanan."

-6-

"Get up," Aicha said, standing over Vee. This time the Demon didn't offer its hand, as if afraid its touch would only overwhelm Vee that much more. Its voice was firm, but not harsh; it was impossible for it to truly sound harsh. And for the first time, it dawned on Vee that not one of the four Demons, even confronted with a potential enemy, carried a weapon.

Succubi, their leader had called them.

"You would do well," Aicha went on, "not to look at me. It may be difficult, but it will only be more difficult if you do."

Vee did as the Demon suggested and looked away as she got to her feet. She thought she felt the Demon's solid-blue eyes on her bare body, or did she only hope that was the case? "Thank you for pulling me out of there," she croaked, her own voice raspy from coughing.

"I recognized you as an Angel," said Aicha, "and I suppose even after all these many years, it's still in my programming, so to speak, to afford you a measure of respect...as ill-advised as that might be. In any case, please hand over your bag."

"My...bag?" Vee fought against turning around to face the Demon. "Please, I'd rather not. My...I have a friend in there."

"A *friend?*"

"It's a Demonic gun. He's been my companion for a while now. I can't lose him."

"A gun? All the more reason for me to take your bag."

"Can you please let me keep him with me? Look, you can watch me unload the ammunition from him, and you can take my other weapons, but like I said...he's my friend. I call him Jay."

"Such nonsense," Aicha said. "I hardly think the others would approve of you keeping a gun, even unloaded."

"What harm could it do? And you heard your boss...she's leaving

251

me in your care. Isn't that decision up to you?"

"We'll see," said Aicha. "But for now, you must hand your bag over."

Vee hesitated, but then extended the skin pouch to the Demon. She thought she heard Jay's muffled voice protest inside. How much of what was going on was he aware of?

Aicha took the pouch, and said, "First, I need to put you somewhere secure for now, until Leanan decides where to put you permanently. Come with me." The Demon moved to the doorway through which the other three had disappeared, gesturing for Vee to follow. She did so, keeping her eyes on her own long bony feet as she walked. She fought against the urge to look at Aicha's small feet with their silvery lace of mysterious designs, instead.

They moved along another mecha-organic corridor, again with curved, ribbed walls and those pinkish globes inset above them. The air was dense with humidity. Grown across the floor unevenly, like an infestation, was a thick web of vivid red tissue, that squelched softly – unpleasantly – as Vee walked across it. She said, "We've left the power building, haven't we?"

"Yes," the Succubus said, glancing over its shoulder. "This building lies against Reactor Tower 2. Once, certain types of Demons were grown in this structure's nurseries, but no more."

"Is that drain in the cooling tank the only way in here?" Aicha stopped abruptly and turned. "Why do you ask? Do you hope to convey this information to your friends, so they might invade us?"

"No...no, I swear!" Vee said, unable to prevent herself from looking up into the Demon's night-blue eyes. "I'm only curious because I've been exploring the Construct since I regained my freedom. I've been trying to get up to the 128th floor, so I can see what Freetown is like. Have you heard of it?"

"We have."

"If you're afraid of people finding you in here and harming you, then why not join me in going to Freetown? I'm told there are old school Demons, like you, that coexist there with the Damned and even other Angels like me."

252

"That is why we can't go there," Aicha said. "Our presence would effect the human inhabitants too profoundly. We would bring about disorder, and find no rest ourselves. We are a race that can only safely coexist with those of the betrayed Demonic races."

"Like the Horde?"

"What is the Horde?"

"I'm sorry...that creature in the cooling tank."

"Ah yes, the Sentry."

"Did you put that thing together, or was it fused in some kind of accident?"

"When the orders came to replace the betrayed Demons with less human-type breeds, there were experiments to make use of some of the Demons that were currently being grown, instead of wasting their materials by destroying them. Some experimental Demons were created, such as our Sentry, that utilized those materials...but combined in such a way as to be less human. Also, the Sentry's minds – which are more or less linked together – were left undeveloped, so it would remain beast-like and less likely to sympathize with the Damned. However, these prototype Demons were not considered satisfactory – being too awkward in their movements, for one thing – so ultimately, other types of Demons were designed from scratch, many of them based on insect-like forms."

"Yeah, I've seen those kinds. The Creator sure did like insects."

"Yes. Insects were the most abundant type of animal in the mortal world. In any case, are you done interviewing me for now? We need to get you secured."

"I'm sorry." Vee couldn't tear her eyes away from the Demon's. In a faraway voice, she said, "Please, lead on."

Aicha turned away, but Vee stared at the back of the Demon's hairless head – elaborately covered in swirling silver designs like the veins in a globe of marble – as the Demon led her past what appeared to be sealed openings on either side of the flesh-like corridor. Rather than having doors, however, each opening was puckered tightly shut like a sphincter.

They came to the last of these sealed sphincters on the right, after which the corridor sloped up and opened into a larger, murky chamber beyond. Aicha whispered something that Vee couldn't decipher, and the orifice drew back its wrinkled, glistening flesh to permit entrance into a tiny womb of a space beyond. "In here," the Demon said.

Vee ducked through the orifice, then faced Aicha again, afraid the Demon would then seal her in the closet of a room without giving her pouch back. But as she watched, Aicha knelt down in the corridor and opened up her pocketbook from Hell. The Succubus set aside Vee's sheathed Ka-Bar knife, and then a handgun replicating an M9 Beretta, and some extra magazines for this. When the Succubus discovered a single M67 grenade, it held it up for Vee to see. "So you say you no longer fight alongside other Angel forces?"

"I don't! I only have those things for my own protection."

Aicha set down the grenade and opened the bundle that contained the bone gun. Jay's solitary eye with its red iris met Aicha's wary gaze. "This Angel claims she is your friend," the Succubus said.

"I am flattered," Jay replied, his pink lips moving in their bony hollow.

"She claims she did not come into our shelter with the intention of harming our group."

"She speaks truthfully," Jay replied. "I find this Angel to be a trustworthy individual. She means only to explore. Her curiosity drives her on. Ultimately, her intention is to investigate a community called Freetown on Level 128."

"That matches what she told me," Aicha said.

"Bless your heart, Jay," Vee said.

"I have no heart, madam."

The Succubus lifted Jay and examined the bone gun from various angles until it ascertained how to remove the magazine of bullets, which were also fashioned from bone. Then, the indigo Demon gathered the other weapons back into the pouch and slung it over its own shoulder. Standing, Aicha handed over the unloaded bone gun to a grateful Vee.

"Do not make me regret letting your Demon familiar remain with you."

"I appreciate it, Aicha. That is your name, right? It's beautiful.

Aicha..."

Aicha didn't respond to that, only handed Vee the shredded black uniform she had wrapped Jay in, and her pair of tall black boots. "Your garments."

Vee took these, too, and smiled at the Succubus. "Thank you," she said.

Again the Demon did not respond, keeping its own eyes averted from the Angel's. Aicha simply stepped back, whispered that secret word or phrase again, and the room's orifice reacted by tightly squeezing shut its membrane, cutting the two off from each other.

"Oh dear," Jay said. "What have you gotten us into now?"

-7-

"I should have realized the Demon you saw was a Succubus," Jay said. "From the obsessive way you reacted to it. But you see, no other Demon can suffer the Succubi's effects...only the Damned and Angels."

Vee couldn't guess the purpose of the small chamber Aicha had sealed her in. It had no sharp corners, floor merging smoothly into walls, walls into ceiling. One globe overhead gave off its wan pink light. Two organic pipes, almost thick enough to permit the passage of a body, emerged from the ceiling on either side of the globe, ran down the far wall about halfway, then bent and disappeared into collared ports in the wall. One pipe looked dark and diseased, covered as it was with clusters of tumors and crusted old ulcers. The other pipe, though, was translucent...showing a motionless dark shape wedged within. Vee didn't want to imagine what it was, or might have been had it continued on its passage through this living factory.

As she and Jay conversed she was zipping herself back into her body-conforming suit, which served as a testament to the harsh journey she had undertaken to get this high into the Construct. She asked, "Why would Angels feel so powerfully affected, too?"

"Because in former times, Angels often ventured into Hades as tourists...to hunt the Damned for sport, or to sexually exploit them, and to take Demon lovers as well. No Demon lover has such a potent

255

effect as a Succubus; they are designed to cast a spell, so to speak. Not magical, of course; there is no magic. Unless you consider that *all* of this is magic, in a sense."

"Okay, I see. However the effect works, it works a bit too well, I guess. But then, so why gift the Damned with such a…a rapturous sensation?"

"For the Damned, the longing for such a being is a form of torture, because they can never have what they desire. Their frustrated yearning is a profound psychological, rather than physical, suffering. There are numerous types of Succubi and Incubi…and many names by which the Damned have come to label them. Many are equipped with genitalia, for the enjoyment of visiting Angels. Or, with which those types of Demons might assault the Damned. In the case of these particular Succubi here, however…I don't think they were designed so much with Angels in mind, but as I say, to frustrate the Damned with a desire for coupling that can never take place."

"I see."

"Again, it's not something I myself can experience, but I imagine their presence is highly disconcerting for you."

"It's highly…something," Vee muttered.

"So now," Jay continued, "the problem is, how can we escape from them – before they imprison you in some way similar to what you suffered for two thousand years. And this time, it could be for longer than that."

"Escape," Vee echoed, sounding lost in thought. "I'm not sure…"

"Not sure of what, madam? Of course we must escape!"

"Maybe I can talk to them some more. They haven't treated me with violence…not yet…and they don't even have weapons, that I've seen. It seems like they rely solely on their power of seduction, or whatever, to protect themselves."

"We can't be sure of that, and their Sentry as they call it is certainly a kind of weapon in itself."

"Maybe between the two of us, we could convince them we don't pose a threat. That I'm not a psycho who plans on eating one of them, like that guy who shot me."

"I truly do not believe that either or both of us would be able to get them to trust us. Please tell me you aren't thinking of remaining here willingly, instead of continuing on to Freetown!"

But Vee said nothing...only continued looking thoughtful.

Where Jay lay on the net of red veins that crept across the floor and up one of the walls like out of control vines, he rolled his eye to follow Vee as she began pacing. "I can't believe you just handed over your weapons," he chided her. "You said it yourself – they are unarmed."

Stopping near the sealed orifice, Vee swung around to snap, "Would you rather that I had killed them? Your fellow Demons?"

Now it was Jay's turn to say nothing, at least for a few moments. Then he changed the subject somewhat. "Now that you're away from them, do you feel their effect lessening?"

Vee faced the orifice again, touched its tough membrane lightly with her fingertips. "I...don't know. I can still smell them, I think. It's a smell like musky incense. Maybe it's like...pheromones or something."

She returned to where she'd placed Jay and sat down on the disturbingly pliable bed of veins beside him, rubbing at her leg through her uniform, though the spot where she had been gashed by the Horde was already little more than a shallow crease. Her hair was still damp from the tank. Considering her present state, she said as if in realization, "I'm tired, Jay. I'd like to sleep. Maybe my mind will be clearer when I wake up."

"One can hope," Jay said.

She stretched out beside him, propping her head on one bent arm rather than rest it on those squelching veins or vines. "No matter what, these Succubi weren't designed for fighting. I'm sure they can be reasoned with. I'm sure of it."

"The question is," Jay said, "can *you* be reasoned with?"

Vee snorted, smiling wearily as she closed her eyes to let darkness gradually overtake her.

It seemed only a few minutes later, though it may have been hours by mortal reckoning, when the doorway retracted its membrane to admit two visitors. Jay whispered, "Madam," but she had already snapped awake and sat up on the bed of veins. Into the makeshift cell had come the apparent leader of the group, Leanan, and the black

Succubus with blue patterns, whose name was Qandisa. Again, neither carried weapons.

"Well" said Leanan, "it seems like you're making yourself comfortable. You and your familiar."

"You can see," Vee said, "I mean you no harm, like I told you. I willingly turned my weapons over to Aicha."

"Willingly?" Qandisa said. "You *think* it was willingly."

The gold Demon glanced around the room, as if satisfying itself there was nothing in here to use as a weapon. "This room may serve as your permanent dwelling, I think. No need to make you any less, nor any more, comfortable. Of course, you will not be permitted out of it, and we will not bring you food or drink – as you don't need such nourishment, in any case – but I think this is a merciful enough compromise. Especially considering how many of my type of being you and your fanatical friends have hunted down and killed over the centuries."

"If I ever participated in any acts like that against your kind," Vee said, "I swear to you that I have no memory of it...and if I did, I'm sure I'd now regret it deeply."

Leanan ignored Vee's sincere tone, and went on, "There were eighteen of us when we chanced upon this forgotten little corner of the Construct. But over time, strays like yourself discovered us. Damned, Angels, the next generation Demons. Fortunately, the Sentry and several other Demon companions protected us each time, but not until we had lost members of our group. Like Aicha, they ventured out from our shelter and made themselves vulnerable."

"Maybe after so many years they became bored...restless."

"They became *foolish*," Leanan said. "And now we are only four. Even our other protectors are gone...with only the Sentry remaining."

Vee realized she was staring up at Leanan, and then switching her gaze to Qandisa, and back again, with her mouth parted open. She realized her heart was pounding...and that she was trembling...and that she was becoming wet. Oh, this artful golem that housed her soul. She wanted to look away from them, but with the both of them standing over her it was too much. Maybe that was why they had come together:

to keep her properly subdued through their combined power.

"If you let me stay," Vee heard herself saying, in a tremulous voice, "I mean...to live among you, not just in this cell...I can protect you like the Sentry does."

"Oh, madam," Jay groaned.

The gold Demon chuckled, its voice honey-smooth despite the bitterness of its words. "We've tried that. It didn't work. We will never make ourselves vulnerable like that again. You want to be our companion, but we have companions enough in each other. We do not betray each other."

Leanan nodded to Qandisa, who stepped back out into the corridor. As the gold Demon turned to follow, Vee asked desperately, "But do you *love* each other?"

Leanan paused and looked back. "Is that what you propose to gift us with? Your love?"

Vee started to say something but caught herself, just barely. Partly out of embarrassment in front of Jay...and partly out of horror at herself.

Leanan said, "As I say, we have companionship in each other. That is a comfort, and comfort is enough. And here...in this room... is where you must now find your comfort. But is that precaution so terrible a punishment? No more fighting whatever enemies you have had to fight. Only rest from now on, and with your own companion beside you. Yes, I think that is a more than merciful resolution to this problem, madam Angel."

And with that, Leanan stepped into the corridor, muttered that odd word or phrase, and the orifice's membrane closed up.

-8-

They sat in silence for a while, perhaps tired of each other's voice. Vee had propped her back in a hollow between two of the wall's ribs, hugging her knees and staring into space...mainly trying to envision the patterns on the Succubi's skin, and wondering if she could decipher any of it from memory alone. These tattoo-like interlinked designs were so densely detailed that she couldn't tell whether or not the exact same pattern was represented on the skin of all four of them, or if it was individualized for each.

The door's tough membrane suddenly opened, and framed there was Aicha, with the jade Demon, whose name was Moura, standing behind the indigo Demon. The green-and-gold Demon craned its neck, trying to see into the cell past Aicha – who held a cup in one hand, made from a short section of pipe with one end capped. Aicha stepped into the little chamber and held the cup out to Vee, who sprang to her feet to accept it.

"Water," Aicha explained. "I see no harm in bringing you some, even if you don't require it."

"Thank you so much," Vee said, accepting the cup and gulping down its contents. Wherever it had come from, the warm water tasted clean enough. "Did Leanan say it was okay?"

"I didn't ask," Aicha said. "Leanan told me you were my responsibility, because I'm the cause for you discovering us." When Vee handed back the emptied cup, Aicha went on, "If you're hungry, we don't gather food, ourselves...but perhaps you'd want to eat that tissue that grows in this room spontaneously." Aicha pointed behind Vee, at the tangled mat of vein-like growths she'd been resting on. "Ken used to eat it."

"Who's Ken?"

"The Damned man Xana took in. The man who killed her, and then escaped with her body."

"And ate it."

"Yes. Leanan would have punished him for it, somehow...probably by giving him to the Sentry...but he got away before we could trap him."

"I ran into him on the 123rd floor. He keeps your friend's skull as a kind of idol. He shot me pretty good, and when I regenerated he'd gone...and taken the skull with him. But I'll bet he didn't go far. He likes to stay near the rest of you, seems to me."

"We know this, but we choose not to venture far from our shelter looking for him. No farther than the Sentry can protect us, anyway.

Self preservation comes before revenge. Xana was the first of us Ken met, accidentally, so it was Xana he bonded with. Perhaps Xana took pity on him, but it was their undoing. In any case, when he lived here among us for a time, Ken would eat that tissue there. I can't give you a knife to cut it, but you should be able to tear it up with your hands."

"Thanks, I guess. Maybe I'll give it a try, but I'd rather fight the urge."

"Perhaps it would have been better had I not put the thought in your mind."

"No...I appreciate that you're trying to help me." Vee took a step toward the Demon, started to reach out a hand to its shoulder – just to touch that perfect, rounded smoothness – but caught herself. "You're merciful. That surely wasn't part of your 'programming' as a Demon. You see? Demons can change...and so can Angels. That's why I'm hoping you'll come to trust me. I'm not like that Ken."

The jade Demon tried to follow Aicha into the room, its full lips lifting in a smile. "Her hair...it's quite lovely, isn't it?"

Aicha turned sharply and said, "Moura, stay outside. The presence of both of us will be too much for her." Then, Aicha uttered that quiet command that caused the doorway's membrane to seal shut again, cutting Moura off from entering. Vee briefly saw disappointment replace Moura's smile. To Vee, Aicha said, "Moura is too curious."

"Maybe you are, too," Vee teased. Then, she said. "When Leanan came to see me, she brought the black one with her..."

"Qandisa."

"But this one, Moura, is with you. Does that mean she's...your partner?" Listening to herself ask this, Vee was embarrassed, and hoped the irrational jealousy she felt wasn't revealed in her tone.

"If you mean my lover, we are not each other's lovers. None of us are. We are companions, equally...no more and no less."

"You don't form special bonds with any one individual, ever?"

"I told you, no."

Vee chanced a closer step, cocking her head to study the silver designs that flowed across Aicha's entire body, even upon the Demon's eyelids when they blinked. Only the solid indigo eyeballs were untouched, and the sensual lips, and the indigo teeth and tongue Vee had glimpsed within the mouth when Aicha spoke...and the small, hard nipples...

"Those patterns all over you," she said dreamily, her eyes snared in them...becoming lost in them, "I've been trying to understand what they mean."

"They mean whatever you want them to mean. And nothing."

"Are they like a code? Some kind of subliminal message...to influence a person's mind?"

"If you think that's what they are."

"A language only the soul can read," Vee mumbled, as if talking in her sleep. She stepped even closer. Reached out both hands to Aicha's head, like a phrenologist, to read its form with her fingertips.

"Stop," Aicha said, almost backing into the door's closed membrane.

Vee obeyed. As if jolted awake, she wrenched her eyes away, looking down at her boots, which she had donned along with her uniform. "I'm sorry," she managed to get out, gasping for air.

"It would no doubt be better for you if we wore garments," said Aicha, "but not much, and going without them is our way. You must always try not to look...and try not to think overmuch about these patterns on me, henceforth."

"I've bonded more with you than the others, haven't I?" Vee said. "Because I saw you first. Like that guy Ken and Xana."

"Yes."

"Even if I try not to look at you, I can still smell your smell, all of you...it's in the air here. And when you speak, all of you...your voices..."

"If Leanan wants to punish you," Aicha said, and Vee wanted to believe her voice sounded regretful, "it seems to me what you're experiencing is punishment enough."

"Please, Aicha," Vee whispered, daring to look up into the Demon's eyes again, her body shaking hard as if the room had turned frigid. "Can I touch you...just for one second? Can I touch your face?"

"No," Aicha said firmly. "Don't make me regret coming in here just now. Control yourself, if you ever want me to bring you water again." With that, the indigo Demon faced the door, uttered that command again, and the membrane opened. Vee caught a glimpse of Moura waiting outside in the corridor, before Aicha repeated the secret utterance and the membrane contracted. They were gone. Though their proximity was still felt, their immediate absence was jarring.

Vee slowly dropped to her knees, there in the center of the womb-like chamber. "Oh God," she said in a shuddery breath.

Then, she heard a voice whisper something behind her. And again. She turned toward it.

Where Jay leaned in the corner, having watched Aicha's visit quietly, he gazed toward the puckered-shut door and repeated the whispered word or phrase a third time.

"What are you doing?" Vee asked him.

"Trying to learn the key they use to open and close that door," he said. "If I can, we could escape here that easily."

Vee said nothing in response to this; only turned her head to stare at the sealed orifice. She neither encouraged Jay, nor told him to stop... as if placing matters into the hands of fate.

-9-

After a while, though, Vee paused from pacing her cell like a caged animal to snap at Jay, "Will you please stop saying that? It won't work for you!" But this was not to discourage him from trying to free them, so much as out of the sheer maddening repetition of it.

"I think it's a matter of inflection," Jay protested. "I believe I can do it."

"Enough for now, *please!*"

"In that case, then, can you bring me closer to those two big pipes in the wall?"

Vee glanced toward the pipes Jay mentioned: one darkened and diseased, the other translucent and with some shape lodged inside. "What about them?"

"I wonder if you could dislodge one of them from its socket, and crawl inside. They're tight but appear flexible. You might be able to crawl up one of them, or maybe down, to enter into another level away

263

from our captors."

"Or maybe I'll end up stuck in there for who knows how long, like that thing?" Vee said, stepping toward the translucent conduit and prodding it with her finger.

The small dark shape within convulsed, like a child bound in a straitjacket. Vee let out a cry and backed away, but after only several seconds the mysterious shape went still again.

"Did you see that?" she gasped.

"Not too well, from this angle, but it's obviously just a larval Demon...one that never completed forming."

"Well, that tube could be *filled* with unformed Demons...what makes you think I could get through it?"

"Don't you at least want to try, madam?"

"Will you give me time to *think?*" she snarled. Then, she crouched down abruptly, got her fingers hooked into the red webbing that grew across the floor, and wrenched at it. Some of the vine-like tendrils tore free, and encouraged by this, she pulled harder with both hands. She expected blood to spurt from the snapped ends, but there was only a little yellow fluid like plasma. "I'm so hungry," she said through gritted teeth. "So fucking hungry!"

Vee had ripped free a section of the web, and she brought it to her mouth, tore into it with her teeth. It was tough, chewy, like overcooked squid, but she managed to swallow a bite of it. Her face contorted at its taste, but she promptly went in for a second bite. As she chewed, she said, "I can imagine why that crazy Ken guy decided to eat that Demon Xana instead of this stuff."

"Perhaps you shouldn't give in to your hunger," Jay observed, watching her from his corner.

She glared at him, that yellowish fluid dribbling down her chin. "Why?"

"Madam, with all respect, you're being very much unlike yourself."

"And you know me so well, huh?"

"I believe I do."

"So now you're not just my gun, but my psychiatrist? What is it you're afraid of? That I'll try eating one of *them* next? Or maybe *you?*"

264

"I don't have much meat to offer, I'm afraid."

"There's that eye of yours. I bet that would go down like a nice slippery oyster. And those pretty lips of yours, so I don't have to listen to them nag me."

"You're not amusing me, madam."

Vee stood up and hurled the remaining handful of web against the wall, where it splatted before dropping to the floor. In a low voice, she said, "I'm sorry, Jay. I know you want out of here...into the Mesh, like I promised...but I know you're worried about me, too."

"Just please remember that, madam," Jay said. "Also, there's something I need to tell you, in case it hadn't already occurred to you."

"What's that?"

"The Demon Aicha took my magazine...but did not clear the round that was chambered from the last time you fired me. That means there is still one bullet left in me."

"What are you...what are you telling me?"

"I'm telling you what I just said. That there is one bullet still in me. One shot you could fire."

"Fire at...who?"

Just then the doorway's membrane widened open, and through it stepped Aicha. Startled, Vee whirled to face her, as if guilty from being caught at something. The Demon looked Vee up and down, saying, "I heard you cry out."

"Your hearing is good," Vee said, giving a tremulous smile. Self-consciously, she wiped the fluid from her chin with the remaining sleeve of her uniform.

"I wasn't far. So why did you yell?"

"I was startled by that." Vee pointed toward the shape silhouetted inside its fleshy tube. "It moved when I poked it."

"It can't harm you. It has no consciousness. There are many more like it in this factory. Insect beings that were being made at the time of the Creator's self-destruction. The processes here were abandoned."

"I understand. It was just a little unexpected, is all."

Aicha looks Vee up and down again, the touch of the Demon's gaze causing her to shiver. "Perhaps I can find you some garments that are more intact."

"Maybe I should just go without...like you."

"If you wish."

"Could you..." Vee's voice went husky. "...help me out of mine?" She reached to a zipper.

Aicha turned toward the still-open orifice. "Please...you're an Angel...don't degrade yourself."

Vee threw herself to all fours and choked, "Don't go!"

Just short of the opening, Aicha turned, and Vee crawled closer. Quaking all over, she bowed her head over the blue Demon's bare feet, the metallic patterns upon them seeming to swirl and churn with restlessness so directly before her eyes. In those designs, Vee seemed to see gigantic jellyfish with glittering silvery bells – bells that were themselves tattooed with even more designs, designs within designs – floating in a school against silver constellations of stars in a midnight-blue firmament. Vee lowered her face to these living patterns – afraid that at any moment Aicha would jerk back, out of reach – and gently touched her lips to the top of one foot.

The Demon glanced over its shoulder, out into the empty hallway.

With her lips so close to Aicha's foot that she was sure the Demon could feel her breath upon its skin, Vee whispered, "I know how lonely you must be, even with your companions. Hidden for hundreds of years from any other beings. How empty you must feel...how unfulfilled."

"I am a Demon. I'm not like you. We were made to live indefinitely, if not immortally, and to serve a single purpose without faltering."

"If that's the case," Vee said, lifting her head to look up at Aicha, "then why did so many, many Demons of the older races – like yours – end up siding with the Damned?"

"Because they were *betrayed*. We were to be eradicated, without regard to how we had loyally fulfilled our duties."

"Even so, the fact that they wouldn't just try to survive, but to fight back...and not alone, but beside the Damned..."

"What is it you're trying to say, madam Angel?" Aicha said. "What are you trying to *do?*"

"I want to love you," Vee said, tears brimming in her eyes. "And I

266

want you to love me, too."

"You are not in your right mind. I'm not trying to seduce you, but that is what's happening. At the same time that you, consciously, are hoping to seduce *me*. But don't you understand that can't happen?"

Vee let out a harsh sob, and lowered her forehead to Aicha's foot where she had kissed it. "Please...*please*..."

"You're an Angel," Aicha repeated. "This is beneath you. It makes me uncomfortable that I should be causing you to act this way... whether your people descended into Hades to wipe out my kind, or not."

"Then if you don't want to see me this way," Vee wept, "please help me. *Help* me!"

"Help you *how*?"

Vee rose up on her knees, and grasped Aicha by the waist. "If you can't love me, at least please...please *make* love to me."

"Do you not see how I'm made?" the Demon hissed, trying not to be heard outside this room. "I cannot!"

"Just let me love you," Vee sobbed. "If you can't return my love, just let me love *you*."

The Succubus glanced over its shoulder again, and whispered the utterance that caused the orifice to seal itself shut.

Vee edged closer on her knees, close enough that she could press her cheek against Aicha's belly, eyes shut in tortured bliss. This near, the being's deep musky scent was the most intoxicating of drugs. Vee turned her head and kissed the smooth abdomen...here...and here... and inside the mysterious peephole of its navel. Through all this, the Demon only looked down at the undying woman blankly, though there might have been pity in its face, with arms hanging passively at its sides.

Vee ran her tongue along the flatness of belly beneath the navel in long strokes, then suddenly ducked her head low, still holding onto Aicha's waist, and licked at the blank mound where sexual organs would have been in a mortal being. Their absence caused Vee to groan in frustration, and in a frantic reaction to this she rose to her feet to feed elsewhere. She wrapped her arms around Aicha, ran her hands up and down the curved smoothness of back with its central furrow. She kissed Aicha's chest, then took a nipple into her mouth and sucked at it, hard. She had all she could do to keep from *biting* it...afraid she might bite it off. She kissed her way higher, nuzzled her face in the crook of Aicha's throat.

"Madam," Jay pleaded, watching from the corner.

Vee tried to clamp her mouth over the Demon's, to suck at its plump bottom lip, to find its tongue with her own, but it turned its face away. Not with a brusque disgusted motion, but the rejection still caused Vee to let out a moan as if from pain.

"You shouldn't let her do this," Jay said to the Succubus.

"Quiet," Aicha told it. "We are only Demons, you and I."

Kissing Aicha's neck again, Vee had reached behind to cup a buttock, squeeze it in her hand. She ventured further, her fingers probing into the crease, but she didn't find the opening she sought.

"I want you inside me," Vee breathed in the Demon's ear.

"You can see that isn't possible."

"Your tongue...your fingers..."

"I'm sorry," Aicha said.

"Please...kiss me...put your hand on my breast..."

"I mustn't."

"God damn you!" Vee cried, and she took one of Aicha's hands and forced it between her own legs. The Succubus did not resist. Vee rubbed the hand there, across her own pubic mound, which – encased as it was in her uniform's second skin – seemed just as featureless as Aicha's own. While she did this, Vee clung tightly to Aicha's body with her other arm.

Vee jolted, as if an electric current had suddenly been sent through her body at the throwing of a switch. She let go of Aicha's hand, hugged the Demon's body hard against her own as if to force their two bodies into merging. Then, with that switch thrown again, the current left her and so did all her strength. Vee sank down the front of Aicha's body, to her knees again, clinging to the Demon's legs and then finally releasing them. She folded down upon herself, in something like an upright fetal position, her head hanging low, her red hair covering her face.

"Thank you," Vee wept almost inaudibly. "Thank you."

"You mustn't say anything about this in front of the others," Aicha said. Then, after a moment, the Succubus added, "If you want it to happen again."

Vee looked up in surprise, grinning even as tears wetted her cheeks. "*Again?* You mean —"

"Don't say anything more — please." Aicha faced the closed door, said the strange command, and stepped out into the hallway. The Demon and Vee held eye contact until Aicha spoke the command once more, and the membrane squeezed shut.

Immediately, as Vee sagged forward again — lacking the strength to regain her feet just yet — Jay began speaking. It wasn't to admonish her, though, for what had just taken place.

Instead, he resumed testing the phrase that might allow him, too, to command the door membrane to retract open.

-10-

With little else to do, Vee slept again...and again, she couldn't say for how long...but the sound of someone entering the cell caused her to sit up on her bed of crimson veins, with heart leaping. *Aicha...*

But she saw it was the jade Demon instead, Moura, and even now after having seen Aicha's silvery designs up close she couldn't tell if Moura's gold designs were the same. The Succubus held the improvised cup Aicha had brought before, and said, "Aicha asked me to bring you some water."

"Where are they?" Vee asked, getting to her feet. The sight of Moura made her insides crawl with hunger, despite or because of her different coloring from Aicha, but the fever Vee felt with this Demon was more manageable, and for that she was glad. She would not want to betray Aicha by lusting after any of the other three Demons equally. But what a strange thought for her to have, she recognized. As if Aicha would actually feel jealous.

She was concerned, though, that perhaps Aicha had sent Moura because the blue Succubus wanted to avoid her now after their

269

intimacy – despite having suggested such intimacy could be repeated. Maybe Aicha had had second thoughts, and preferred not to see her anymore...handing off the responsibility of monitoring their prisoner to this Succubus instead. The possibility caused Vee to feel something like encroaching panic.

Handing Vee the cup, Moura replied, "Aicha has clearing duty. We alternate, and all take our turns."

"Clearing?"

"The organic material of which this old factory is made continues to grow on its own. That growth there..." Moura gestured at the network of vines on the floor and up one wall "...will continue to spread, for instance, unless you eat enough of it. If it runs too rampant, we'll have to come in here and clear out the excess. In other areas, the growths are different and more pronounced. Unless we tend to it, the chambers we use for our own purposes might become swallowed up. Hence... clearing."

"I see." Vee felt a measure of relief at this explanation, though she hoped it wasn't only an excuse. "What do you all do when you aren't taking turns clearing?"

"We rest."

"Sleep? Or you mean, like, shut down?" She thought of a little family of Damned people she had met on Level 120, who had gone into a state like suspended animation until Vee had stumbled upon their hiding place and caused them to awaken from their long trance.

"Something like that. We go dormant."

"I guess that's something to do." Vee emptied the cup and offered it back to the Demon. "Thank you, Moura."

The Succubus smiled, and as it accepted the cup said, "As I said before, your hair is lovely. I haven't seen that color often, even in all the time I've existed."

Vee chuckled. "You'd have seen a lot more redheads, and blonds too, if humans had come with dyed hair when given their immortal bodies." She hesitated, and then managed to choke out a question. "Do you think Aicha likes it?"

"Likes it? Your hair?"

"Well I mean...likes *me*," Vee said.

"*Likes* you?" The Demon cocked its head, then smiled again...this time sadly. "Poor Angel." Then, it turned back to the open doorway, returned to the hallway, and the membrane closed after it.

Immediately, again Jay began practicing the whispered utterance.

Vee whipped toward him and cried, "Stop it! Just stop it!"

Jay stopped, and Vee was surprised when he said nothing. No arguing, no criticism, no avowals of concern. Was he giving up on her? Accepting his fate, too, as the other prisoner of this cell? He only stared, unblinking. That was even worse.

She closed her eyes, and said, "Look...I'll ask them to take you out of here, and find an interface so you can rejoin the Mesh."

"I doubt they would bother with that. It would be a risk for them to leave this hideout of theirs. You've heard them, madam. They're afraid to venture far from it, lest they encounter any Damned – or Angels – who would be affected by their presence."

"For all we know there might be a work station right here in the area they've claimed. I'll ask them, okay? I promise."

"You would prefer to be without me, then?"

"It isn't that! You know it isn't! I just don't want to force my decision on you any longer, if I can help it."

"Madam..." Jay began, with something like a heavy weariness.

Then, from somewhere distant – but not so distant that the sound didn't carry to them inside their cell – Vee heard a burst of automatic gunfire. Right on the tail of it came a scream of perhaps surprise, or pain, or both. Another short burst of gunfire...

Vee lunged at the contracted membrane, tried to dig her fingers into the tiny puckered hole at its center, but was unable to pry it open even a fraction. She then whirled around, darted to Jay and lifted him from where he leaned against one wall.

"Jay," she said breathlessly, "try it again! Try the command!"

"Bring me closer," he said.

Vee leapt back toward the membrane, holding the sentient gun out in front of her – as near as the Succubi stood whenever they spoke the command. "Do it!" she begged.

271

Jay uttered whatever word or sound the command consisted of, and instantly the membrane retracted. "Huh!" he said, pleased with himself. "All this time, I simply wasn't close enough."

Gripping the bone gun in both fists, Vee plunged through the doorway and into the hallway lined with curved ribs...without hesitation running in the direction of a third burst of gunfire.

-11-

Beyond the orifice of Vee's cell, the corridor immediately began sloping up like a ramp to the wide, arched entrance into a larger chamber. Vee bolted up this ramp, but had the presence of mind to pause at its top rather than blunder straight into the new area. Cautiously, she peered around the edge of the glistening bony doorframe.

There, off to the left, she saw a figure hunched over the body of the jade Demon. The empty cup that Moura had brought her only minutes earlier lay on the floor a short distance from the Demon's upturned hand.

From here, it appeared Moura had taken two concentrations of bullets: one through the torso, and one in the head. There was no blood, only ragged flesh as green inside as out, but without the metallic gold filigree. Moura's head was horribly shattered, like that of a classical Greek statue smashed with a sledgehammer. Was this what her own head had looked like, Vee thought, when exploded by that same sentient gun of black chitin?

The Damned man with the M for Murderer branded on his forehead – Ken, she remembered his name was – had set his gun down beside him, and with a knife in hand was carving into the flesh of Moura's left thigh, muttering to himself as he did so and wearing a cheek-splitting grin.

"Do you know how many times *I've* been carved?" he asked the defiled corpse. "Do you know how many times *I've* been eaten?"

The large gloomy chamber, lit only by a scattered few pink globes, was semicircular and domed, a nexus-point branching off into what were apparently four other hallways. And even as Vee decided to rush the Damned man, and – in order to conserve ammo – club him with the butt of her bone gun before he could pick up his own sentient gun again, she saw Aicha come running suddenly out of one of those four arched doorways. Running straight at the Damned man, with the long handle of some implement gripped in both fists. To Vee it resembled a scythe, with a gleaming crescent blade, and it might once have been used by other Demons as a weapon or torture instrument before this little group had put it to use clearing the ever-growing infestation of organic material.

Another type of Demon might have been screeching a war cry just then, but such a sound from these Succubi with their alluring tones seemed impossible. But even from here, Vee could see the rage in Aicha's gorgeous face. The scythe was cocked back for a powerful swoop.

Yet Ken was already grabbing the chitin gun and rising from his crouch, leaving his knife embedded in Moura's leg. There was no way Aicha would get to him in time to swing that scythe.

Vee jumped into view and Aicha caught sight of her, beyond the Damned man. Their eyes met for a split second, and then Vee raised the bone gun to fire the lone bullet it carried.

Ken noticed that Aicha had looked past him, at someone coming up from behind, and in alarm he jerked that way just enough that Vee's bone projectile struck him in the shoulder blade instead of dead center in the back as she had intended, in order to shatter his spine. He let out a whoop of pain, but he didn't go down.

"Hey!" Vee yelled, hoping to keep his attention away from Aicha. He wouldn't know that she had no more bullets in her own gun. "Remember me, fucker? You want some more of this, huh?" She charged at him then, holding Jay pointed toward him as if to let loose more gunfire. If the man shot her, that would be okay...as long as she distracted him long enough for Aicha to reach him, and strike. As long as he didn't fire on Aicha, instead, who could no more regenerate than Moura had.

Trapped between two charging enemies, and having suffered a traumatic wound – however temporary – the man named Ken decided to flee rather than fight. He took off running toward the leftmost and nearest doorway. Plunged through it, and kept on going.

Vee and Aicha met over the ruined carcass of the jade Demon. "This should have been me," the blue Succubus said, no tears flowing but its face twisted with suffering. Even wearing such an expression, Vee was transfixed by the Demon's beauty, and its pain pierced her, too. Aicha said, "I shouldn't have sent Moura in my place."

"Don't say that," Vee said. She nodded toward the wide doorway through which the man had fled. "What's down that way?"

"Aicha!" someone called from across the chamber, their voice echoing off the domed ceiling with its intersection of bony spokes. "Get away from her!"

Vee looked around and saw the other two Succubi running toward them: Leanan, with a sickle-like implement clutched in one fist, and Qandisa having taken up a long metal pike like a boat hook. Other of the tools they used in their clearing tasks. Vee realized they believed it was she who had fired the shots that had killed Moura...and yet they still came running at her, to avenge their companion, even if they would essentially be throwing their own lives away if the bone gun was truly loaded, as they believed. And if Vee was inclined to kill them, which she wasn't. Yet Aicha had told Vee that "self preservation comes before revenge"...and tried to insist that what these Demons felt for each other wasn't love. They were lying to themselves, she thought.

"It wasn't her," Aicha called to them as they came. "It was Ken! He found his way back into our home! Vee wounded him and he ran off that way!" She pointed.

Leanan and Qandisa reached them, and still glared at Vee warily though they lowered their weapons. "How did she get ammunition for her gun? From you?"

"I had one bullet left, in the chamber," Vee explained. "Now it's gone." With three of the impossibly beautiful Demons grouped so close to her, she tore her eyes away and looked back down at Moura...but horribly, despite its ghastly wounds, even *that* body nearly caused her to swoon with craving. That glossy thigh, even with a thick strip of meat carved out of it and the knife handle standing up from it...she still wanted to caress its

274

smoothness...to run her tongue along it. Vee scrunched her eyes shut.

"But why did you let her out?" Leanan demanded.

"I didn't!" Aicha protested.

"Didn't Moura remember to seal her cell?" Qandisa asked.

"I got out myself," Vee said, without elaborating...in case there might be a need to make use of Jay's trick again. She dared to open her eyes and face the gold Demon again. "Look, I'll go after him and handle this...I promise. But you need to give me my pouch back...my ammunition and other weapons, or I won't be able to get close enough to deal with him."

"He *loved* us," Qandisa said, confounded, gazing down at Moura's body. "Why would he simply want to kill us now?"

"Because he's insane," Vee said. "And hungry."

The gold Demon bounced its sickle weapon against its outer thigh for a moment, staring hard at Vee, until it finally said, "Get the Angel her weapons."

Qandisa looked up from Moura, alarmed. "Leanan..."

"If he's here in our home, we're in danger."

"We should all leave, then! Our safety's been compromised! We need to find another place!"

"If we leave and expose ourselves we could be in even greater danger," Leanan stated. "This is our place...*ours*. It's all we have. We must defend it."

"All right, then, I understand...but how can we trust the Angel?" Qandisa persisted.

"I never meant you any harm in the first place," Vee said. "But he does. I'm your best hope that he doesn't kill another of you. *All* of you. That Sentry of yours in the pool is no use to you in here. I'm all you've got."

Leanan nodded, and repeated to Qandisa, "Go get the Angel what she needs."

-12-

In the off-branching corridor – dimly-lit as it was, and with its floor of glistening red meat -- it wasn't easy to make out the trail of blood spatters the Damned man had left in his wake like strewn rose petals, but Vee had seen him go this way in any case. As opposed to the hallway that had contained her cell, this corridor was narrower, without any doorway orifices set in its sides – unless they'd been swallowed up over time – and followed a more randomly winding path. Somewhere beyond its curved walls a muffled throbbing, like a slumbering titan's heartbeat, grew louder and deeper. The living factory still lived.

Qandisa had brought her pocketbook from Hell quickly, from some room off one of the nexus-point's other hallways, and Vee had reloaded Jay with his magazine. In addition, she now had her combat knife sheathed on the outside of her right leg again, and inside the pouch strapped across her back were the handgun and the one grenade. She didn't think she'd be resorting to the latter.

She rounded a corner warily, and saw that here the corridor narrowed even more, so that she had to bend low to proceed. If this continued, she figured she might need to go on hands and knees like a tunnel rat. That she wouldn't relish, given that she had nothing like a flashlight or lantern. The pink globes that lit these hallways had been overgrown here, by thick translucent flesh, causing their buried glow to be weak. Vee assumed this corridor must once have been wider, like the one containing her cell, but its organic material had been growing on its own and the Succubi were allowing its progress – at least in this passage – without trimming it back. Perhaps this process of unchecked growth was what had helped cut off this section of the former factory in which they'd settled, helping to provide the Succubi the isolation they required.

Hunching low, Vee crept onward...until, around a radical bend just ahead in the flesh tunnel, she heard the man's voice, muttering and whimpering.

"You there," she said. "Don't make me hurt you again!"

"Go away!" the man shrieked, startled.

"You know I can't. Look...I'll take you out of here unharmed so long as you just don't resist."

"The Beloved seduced you, didn't they, Cherub?" he sobbed. "Now you're in their thrall!"

Vee ignored his accusations. She couldn't deny them. "How did you get in? Through the cooling tank?"

"I found another way! I had to dig through meat!" He laughed wildly through his tears. "I never learned to swim!"

"Why did you come in here? Why do you want to hurt them? I thought you loved them, too."

"I was watching...I saw you go into the tank. You wanted the Beloved all to yourself, didn't you? It isn't *fair!*"

"Now you've killed two of them...but do you feel any more fulfilled for that? What's the point? Leave them be!"

"Easy for you to say, but will *you* leave them be, Cherub?" And with that, the Damned murderer fired his chitin gun, straight through the flesh that formed the bend in the corridor.

Taken by surprise, Vee didn't have a chance to pull back. On the man's side, where the bullets penetrated the flesh they no doubt punched neat holes, but on this side of the bend they blew out ragged pits. Blood gushed free from one of the thick purple veins, now severed, that could be seen snaking through the translucent flesh, and blood spurted from Vee as well, where she had taken two chitin bullets in the left side of her abdomen. She was hurled against the wall, where soft meat had overgrown its supporting ribs, and she knew that there must be two ragged pits in her own back now.

As she slumped down the wall, though, she returned fire with Jay... one short automatic burst, straight through the bend as the Damned man had done. She might have squeezed off another burst, too, but she saw it wasn't necessary. Only a second after she'd fired, the man fell forward into view, landing on his front with the upper half of his body exposed. She had struck him in the head and neck, with one of his eyes shot out, leaving a messy hollow, and blood pulsing thickly from the neck wound.

"You fucker," Vee hissed through gritted teeth, trying to stand up against the pain but finding herself unable. She lay Jay aside, pulled her Ka-Bar knife from its sheath, and started dragging herself toward the man on her belly instead...jabbing the knife into the floor to help pull herself along. Tears streamed from the agony in her guts, but she held back from giving voice to the pain and kept on inching toward him.

Just a little further.

When Vee reached the man, both he with his remaining eye and the chitin gun with its single compound eye regarded her blankly. Was the man still conscious? If so, he watched helplessly as Vee grabbed the chitin gun from where it lay beside his hand and threw it behind her. Then, she raised up her arm and brought the combat knife down with all the strength she could muster...plunging the blade through the man's ear and into his head. She left it there, half buried.

Vee collapsed beside him, panting. Since her wounds, however painful, were less severe than his – and because Angels regenerated faster than the Damned, anyway – she figured she would be whole again long enough before him that she could tie him up somehow or otherwise secure him before he did any more damage. But what to do with him then?

She heard footsteps approaching behind her...someone had followed warily, waiting for the firefight to be over. *Aicha?* She lifted and turned her head, and saw it wasn't the indigo Demon but the gold Demon, Leanan, who still carried that sickle-like implement.

"I got him," Vee rasped.

And then she saw the gold Demon crouch down beside her, its statue-like face composed, emotionless, and cock back its arm with the sickle held high.

"Wait!" Vee cried, trying to push herself up. "Don't!"

But Leanan brought the crescent blade down with great force, severing Vee's head from her neck almost completely. She lifted Vee's head a little higher with a fistful of red hair, and all it took was one more chop to finish the job.

-13-

They had brought her back to her cell.

Not just her, but the Damned man, Ken. Their heads lay on the bed of red veins, and both of them were conscious now but mute. She met the man's roving, frightened gaze. He hadn't yet regrown the eye she'd blasted out, but the caved-in socket was beginning to fill with

278

the start of it. Both of them had stopped bleeding from where they'd been severed, and a small mass she saw growing from the base of Ken's head – looking like the rough beginnings of an embryo's body, with its head buried in his neck stump – she knew would be growing from her own neck, as well, though no doubt further developed in her case. She tried to flex whatever she might have for budding limbs, but couldn't feel any sensations there as yet.

Looking elsewhere, she saw Aicha kneeling beside her decapitated body, unzipping her black uniform, tugging it free of the long motionless limbs. She had once asked Aicha to undress her, and now she was doing so. Insanely, watching Aicha do this aroused her feverishly, but that lifeless body was certainly not sharing her excitement. It would rot now, quickly, with its replacement to be regenerated from this smaller but more vital part of her.

Near her body, like an unwanted lover, lay that of Ken...already stripped of its clothing. Qandisa stood over the two corpses, watching Aicha work, gripping the softly-chittering chitin gun by its two handles. It belonged to the Succubi, now.

But Jay? Vee rolled her eyes again, saw Leanan kneeling down, too, and helping sort Vee's belongings. Jay leaned against a wall, with the pocketbook from Hell beside him along with Vee's boots, plus the sheathed knife. They had pulled it out of Ken's skull.

So they were going to take their belongings, no doubt even Jay, and leave the two of them in here together as cell mates...she and Ken. She had misjudged them. This was her reward for saving the last of them from the obsessed murderer. A punishment, really, for having unintentionally inspired Ken to return to his former captors.

Vee looked toward Aicha again, working her jaw, trying to speak to the Demon...but of course she couldn't emit sound, let alone words of entreaty, with a ruined larynx and her lungs in that shell over there. Could not plead for mercy. Even still, despite her desperation, her gaze couldn't help but trace the curve of Aicha's back as the Demon finally pulled her uniform free of her pallid body. Couldn't help but stare at the bottom that faced toward her, with the silver designs that adorned its bisected halves. She wanted to lose herself in those designs again:

the celestial jellyfish floating amongst the constellations. To float with them, into dreams and madness, and never return.

Aicha folded the uniform and handed it to Leanan, who then began packing all Vee's things, including the pocketbook from Hell, into a larger tool bag of human leather they had found somewhere. Last to go, jammed in halfway, was Jay...whose eye pivoted to meet Vee's gaze. Though he could speak if he chose to, with whatever mechanical larynx he possessed, he said nothing. So, now the Succubi had two sentient guns, and her handgun and grenade too, to defend themselves with against any further trespassers who might come here in the eternity that lay ahead.

Leanan rose, turned to the room's back wall, and reached out to the collar into which one of those two thick pipes was socketed: the diseased one, covered in tumors and sores, not the translucent one in which the larval Demon was wedged. She watched Leanan turn the collar several times, counterclockwise, having to exert a bit of effort, until finally the end of the pipe came free from the wall with a hiss and a puff of reddish gas that quickly dissipated.

Aicha met Vee's eyes for a second but looked away, and reached out for Ken's head. His lips were working soundlessly, too, as if mouthing some prayer frantically over and over as Aicha lifted him and stood. Then, she approached the black opening where Leanan had freed the end of the pipe from its socket.

Oh please no, Vee thought. What they had planned for them was worse, even, than leaving them in this room together to regenerate as cell mates, she and the Damned man.

Vee saw the man's eyes flash frantically toward her one last time as Aicha inserted his head into the opening – and then let go of it. The head dropped away into darkness...wherever that pipe led to. Some lonely dead end, no doubt, where it would lie until its body finished regrowing, only to find itself trapped.

Vee knew she would be next. So...she and Ken would be cell mates, after all, but not in here. Not among the Beloved, as he had called them.

Aicha stepped back from the lightless opening and watched as

Leanan repositioned the end of the pipe and tightened its collar again. Then, looking down at the two headless, naked bodies laid out side by side, the gold Demon said, "Qandisa and I will feed these to the Sentry. Why let them go to waste?"

"Be careful when you go out there," Aicha said.

"It's you who need to be careful," Leanan replied. "Are you sure you want to do this? The risk is great."

"I doubt I'll encounter anyone else, the way I'm going," Aicha said.

And with that, both the indigo Demon and gold Demon turned to look toward Vee's watching head. Leanan said to Aicha, "We'll seal up this chamber...let the growths in here go unchecked, until they fill it solid. Ken will not find his way back up here...and we will never again bring into this room neither prisoner nor pet."

Aicha went to Vee, lifted her head in her hands, and carried her over to the leather tool bag. She was the last item to be stuffed into it, pushed down into its dark interior. Even with the fear she felt – though it had lightened somewhat into uncertainty, when Leanan sealed the pipe – she found herself intoxicated by the smell of Aicha's hands, and the feel of them upon her cheeks.

Inside the tool bag, she couldn't see what was happening, but she felt the bag being lifted and apparently slung over someone's shoulder. Aicha's. And then, she bobbed along in this darkness to the rhythm of Aicha's steps, as if carried inside Aicha's body like the Demon's own child. This near to the Succubus, Vee lost her fear completely and experienced only contentment. She felt she could remain in this state forever, with Aicha walking endlessly without any real destination. However, Vee knew they must be headed *somewhere*...

In their shared darkness, Jay didn't try speaking with her, perhaps because he knew she couldn't answer.

After a long period of walking – during which the tool bag sometimes bumped against walls that must be very narrow, almost sealed up with flesh – they seemed to cross over into another building, because Vee heard a metal door squeal and scrape open on long-rusted hinges. Aicha paused, no doubt waiting to see if the noise drew attention, but then continued on.

Then, they came to a place where Aicha began climbing. Even in the bag Vee could hear the Demon's hands and feet finding purchase on the metal rungs of a ladder, bolted into some wall. Up and up. The hum of a large industrial fan came and went.

Vee found she could just barely jerk the flipper-like starts of her nascent limbs, but she still had quite a way to go. Anyway, there was nowhere she wanted to escape to. Run away from *Aicha?* It was unthinkable.

Aicha must have come to the top of the ladder, because now she was walking again...and soon, from the ring of metal steps, ascending a staircase. Again, the protest of another heavy metal door being dragged open. Again, a hesitation, as Aicha waited to listen for trouble.

The bag was set down, opened, and weak grayish light greeted Vee's upturned eyes. Aicha's face came into view overhead, looking in. The Demon reached into the bag and once more lifted Vee's head. She was set to one side, and could tell from their immediate surroundings – a room with cinderblock walls – that they had indeed crossed from the living factory into another former building of the city Tartarus, now simply another region of the great Construct. So the Succubi had more than one way into and out of their secret home, after all.

And, after all those ladder rungs and the staircase besides, there was no doubt in Vee's mind that they had ascended to the 125th level.

Vee watched as Aicha reached into the bag again and removed Jay, laying him down on the floor beside her head. Then, the Succubus pulled out the boots and set them down...and her uniform, now with even more bullet holes. The stitched pouch of human skin. Lastly, Aicha placed Vee's sheathed knife like a paperweight upon the folded uniform.

Before rising to its feet – to leave, and descend again to the 124th floor – the Demon reached for Vee's head again, lifted it, and brought it near to its face. Those entirely midnight-blue eyes stared directly into hers, and it said, "You mustn't follow me back down. But, I think here you're far enough away that you won't want to. It's I who will miss you...not you who will miss me." And then, before placing Vee on the floor again, Aicha kissed her once, lightly, on the lips. "Goodbye, my

Angel," the Demon whispered.

Vee watched, unable to cry out or even to sob, but with tears streaming from her eyes, as Aicha walked toward the metal door through which they had come, and without looking back hauled the door back into place.

She lay there, not being able to observe the progress of the fresh body growing from the stump of her neck, but eventually she could feel her burgeoning limbs...move them. She didn't try to crawl prematurely, supporting an oversized head on a toddler's body, but just lay there... patiently, quietly, until the process was finished, and she once again possessed her long, lean body with its bloodlessly white, illusory flesh.

And while her body had been growing, something else had been changing, too. It was a feeling of *receding*. As if she were being emptied of something, a poison draining out of her. By the time she finally sat up, stood, stretched her creaking new limbs and reached for her clothing, she knew she would not be following the Beloved back down to its hidden nest on Level 124.

At last, watching her pull on her boots and then strap the combat knife to her leg, Jay spoke up in a tentative sort of way. "Madam..."

"Please don't talk to me about it, Jay," she said without looking at him. The tears had dried on her face, but her voice broke a little when she continued, "I'm sorry, but please...don't ever talk to me about it."

"I only wanted to ask you, madam," the sentient gun said. "Where to now?"

"Up, of course," Vee said, bending down to pick him up last. "To Freetown."